Lord Bainbridge

Lord Bainbridge

A NOVEL OF THE SINKING OF THE TITANIC

DAVID VINCENT

Library of Congress Control Number: 2008900238
ISBN: Hardcover   978-1-4363-1562-3
                   Softcover   978-1-4363-1561-6

To order additional copies of this book, contact:
Xlibris Corporation
1-888-795-4274
www.Xlibris.com
Orders@Xlibris.com
42908

To Cheryl,
It was so much
fun working with
you, Best wishes
David Vincent

TO THE MEMORY OF DJ

Author's Note

Although this is a work of fiction, it is based on an actual event and therefore, a number of characters in the book are based on real people. The rest of the characters are entirely fictitious and are not meant to resemble anyone who actually sailed on the *Titanic* or anyone else, known or unknown to the author. All details pertaining to the *Titanic* itself, its sinking, and the subsequent rescue of her survivors are portrayed as accurately as possible to fit the confines of the story being told.

Chapter I

Sunday, April 14, 1912

Leaning on the starboard rail of the boat deck, the ship's topmost deck open to both sea and sky, Lord Jeremy Bainbridge stared out at the ocean intently as if he were keeping watch for something, or someone. Taking his cigarette case from the inside pocket of his black dinner jacket, he opened it, carefully selected a cigarette, and lit it. He held the cigarette before his eyes for a long moment, studying it with great concentration. Flicking the ashes, he watched as the red embers started to fall the seventy feet to the water below only to be swept away by the morning breeze before they ever reached their destination. Close by, just off his left shoulder, there loomed the canvas-covered hulk of one of the ship's lifeboats lashed to the side of the deck like some giant sea catch.

In the predawn darkness, the breeze became stronger, ruffling the front of Lord Bainbridge's silk shirt, twirling the ends of the white silk scarf he wore around his neck, and pushing his short brown hair back from his forehead. His young face, caught in the lone field of light that still emanated from the raised roof over the first-class lounge behind him although the room below had been empty for hours, frowned in thought.

At twenty-four, Lord Bainbridge would never have been considered a strikingly handsome young man. But with his deep blue eyes and easy natural smile, he had an attractiveness that drew people to him. One acquaintance said he had the look of a person whom you knew you could talk to and whom you knew would listen intently to what you had to say.

Finally, Lord Bainbridge turned to the young man at his side. "One of the ship's officers told me we should be in the ice fields some time today," he informed his companion.

Tom Kennedy, still looking slightly uncomfortable in his unaccustomed suit of evening clothes, nodded and took a moment to digest this news. "Might that not prove dangerous?" he asked.

Lord Bainbridge shrugged his shoulders. "The chap didn't seem overly concerned."

"Probably didn't want to frighten you," Tom concluded with a teasing smile. "You ever seen ice before?"

"No," Lord Bainbridge answered, "this is my first time on the Atlantic."
"Mine too," Tom acknowledged.

"Are you cold?" Lord Bainbridge asked, his own voice trembling, but whether it was from the temperature or the emotions he was feeling, he wasn't sure.

"Nah," Tom assured him. "I've been a lot colder than this."

Lord Bainbridge turned toward him, offering him a cigarette from his case that Tom took readily and with a polite thank-you. As he held the match for him over cupped hands, Lord Bainbridge caught a mischievous wink in Tom's eye as he glanced up at him for a second before his cigarette caught. Lord Bainbridge smiled to himself as he sensed once again that underneath Tom's good manners, there was a bit of the rascal. He leaned back on the rail and took a fresh appraisal of this young man who had so recently come into his life.

In his early twenties, Tom Kennedy was small in stature, between five six and five seven. He had a tight compact body, which Lord Bainbridge knew from intimate firsthand knowledge to be well muscled and developed like a young bantam prizefighter's. His broad open face with its snub nose might have easily been referred to by some as a typical Irish face. His black hair was a mass of curls and, there always seemed to be a few of them tumbling impishly down over his forehead while his skin was as white as alabaster, with neither a blemish nor a freckle to mar its surface. Where one would have expected his laughing eyes to have been green, or at least blue, they fooled everyone with their rich and deep brown color. But the outstanding feature of Tom's face was indisputably his mouth, in particular, his thick sensual lips that came to full beauty when they burst into a broad grin, which they did frequently. This grin, Lord Bainbridge had concluded at almost the first moment of their meeting, could quite easily break one's heart.

That meeting, which had taken place scarcely more than thirty hours ago, had hardly been one that would have been sanctioned by what was then known as polite society. In fact, their coming together would have been considered in the minds of most people a perversity. But to understand this, one had to first understand, or at least try to understand, the nature of the man who had initiated the encounter, Lord Jeremy Bainbridge.

Lord Bainbridge had always known in which direction his sexual preference lay. And he accepted that knowledge easily and without a struggle. Not for him was the hand-wringing and bemoaning for a normal life that so many others went through when they first realized their true calling. Of course given the tenor of the times, it was not surprising that so many protested their own natures when it came to the love that dare not speak its name. Buggery, as it was more often called, had, until 1861, been punishable by death in England. Now, it was merely penal servitude, often at hard labor, which was one's reward for loving one's fellow man—a fate poor Oscar Wilde had suffered only a few years previous, emerging from prison a broken and wasted shell of his former brilliant self. But still this forbidden love flourished, and a sort of underground community sprung up, complete with secret signals, code words, and hidden private clubs with no signs on their entrances. Lord Bainbridge, having suffered no personal or public persecution in his years of practice as a sodomite save for one minor incident of which we will hear later, took much delight in being a member of this clandestine fraternity. To him, it was a great adventure to have another life one indulged in behind closed doors, away from one's everyday companions. He had known since he was thirteen that he did and always would prefer the company of men in the bedchamber as well as the parlor, and he calmly surrendered to his predestined fate. The doors that opened before him were ones he walked through quite willingly, and the rooms into which they led him were ones he took up residence in with quiet contentment even though they were rooms the rest of the world couldn't bring themselves to even mention. Lord Bainbridge was that most fortunate of life's individuals, one whose expectations were matched equally by his existence.

Lord Bainbridge's existence, or more exactly his position in life, was one of privilege. He had had the good sense to be born in a time when class mattered and the equal good sense to be born into a family of the upper class. Had he had the bad luck, at least for him, to have been born into a family dwelling far lower down the social scale, then the timing of his birth would have been far less fortuitous. Of equal importance was the fact that the Bainbridge family, at the moment of Jeremy's arrival, was a family of substantial means. For to be of the upper class and yet have no money was considered the worst fate that could befall one of good family. One of Lord Bainbridge's many maiden aunts—of which at times he was quite convinced there were at least fifty of them, so frequent were their comings and goings from Bellington House, the London residence of the Bainbridge family since Elizabethan times—often expressed her opinion that the poor were much better off than they or anyone else realized. "They have no knowledge of a better life, so they are free from longing for things they can never have," the elderly spinster theorized. To her, the real unfortunates were "those poor dears of the upper class who indeed knew what they were missing but had not the means to secure it."

The Bainbridge family fortune came from inheritance rather than endeavor and was therefore looked upon by some with disdain, especially by those who had recently made their own fortunes through pluck and hard work. Old money, the Bainbridge wealth was called and, by inference, unearned money. Of course there was a time, generations ago, when the Bainbridge fortune, on which the family now so comfortably rested, had been earned by dint of hard labor. But this had occurred so many years ago that, even in the family archives, there was no mention of what precise type of manual labor had been employed or by which exact member of the family. In any event, enough of what had once been earned through industrious toil still remained to guarantee the present holders of the Bainbridge name a comfortable living.

"More champagne?" Lord Bainbridge asked, breaking the silence that had fallen down between them for a few moments. He stooped to retrieve the bottle and two glasses, which he had set carefully against the rail at his feet—booty he had secured from the smoking room, which they had visited after dinner.

Tom shook his head. "No, I've had plenty, thank you. My head's already spinning. Can't think straight as it is."

"Sometimes it's better not to think straight," Lord Bainbridge said, pouring himself a half glass with a steady hand, which betrayed not a hint of the turmoil he was feeling inside.

"My father told me I should always keep a clear head about me, especially in America," Tom stated.

"I never knew my father," Lord Bainbridge returned rather flatly as he now found the champagne to be.

Tom was instantly sympathetic, "I'm sorry."

Lord Bainbridge gazed out to sea. "I think about him often, wondering what he was like."

"It would have perhaps been easier for you to have had a father around when you were growing up," Tom ventured.

"A strong male authority figure you mean?" Lord Bainbridge asked. Tom nodded. "I've found more than enough of those to make up for any lack of parental guidance," Lord Bainbridge answered. He noticed at once how Tom turned away as if embarrassed. "I'm sorry," he apologized quickly. "I didn't mean to be crude."

"I find it difficult to talk about that in public," Tom said.

Lord Bainbridge kept his tone light. "So if at this moment I crushed you in my arms and kissed you madly as I damn well want to do, I take it you would not appreciate it?"

Tom smiled but would not look back at him. "I would probably throw you over the side of the ship," he replied.

"Ah yes"—Lord Bainbridge nodded—"that of course would be the proper response."

Now Tom did turn back to him, and his face was, in spite of its youth, troubled. "What we do and say in private is one thing, but out here in the world it's different," he explained. He struggled with a thought. "In the world, we must keep it different."

Two young ship's officers, muffled in their greatcoats against the morning chill, walked past them, probably heading to the bridge for a change of watch. The two crewmen cast them quick unimportant glances, but looks that nevertheless were of disapproval. Their condemnation, no matter how slight, was something Tom did not miss, and as if in response to it, he moved a little away from the man beside him at the rail.

"They don't approve of us," Lord Bainbridge informed him, "because they see us as a couple of rich toffs in fancy evening clothes, guzzling champagne at this rather inappropriate hour of the night or, rather, morning. That's all they saw, trust me."

Tom relaxed and shook his head. "Me a toff? Hardly!"

"Do I sense that you have a prejudice against the upper class?" Lord Bainbridge asked. "Should I take that personally?"

For just an instant, a crack opened in Tom's reserve, and all the fear and caution he had just displayed vanished if only for a moment. "I don't have a prejudice against you," he answered, once again displaying that incredible grin that Lord Bainbridge was convinced could easily get them both into a whole lot of trouble.

"There's hope for you yet," he told the young Irishman, his words so soft they were almost a whisper but words that resounded much louder deep inside his own soul, and words that meant, at least to him, so much more than their simple construction would reveal to a casual listener.

Having found the champagne no longer to his liking, Lord Bainbridge tossed the bottle and the glasses over the rail.

"I think there's a law against throwing things off the deck of a ship," Tom suggested.

Lord Bainbridge raised a quizzical eyebrow. "Really? But just moments ago you were quite ready to give me the heave over the side."

Tom nodded. "People yes, things no."

"So," Lord Bainbridge began in a humorous tone, "let it be resolved then that only people shall be thrown from the deck of this ship. Agreed?"

"Agreed!" Tom laughed, and as if by mutual consent, they moved closer together, leaning on the deck rail beside one another, close but not touching.

Behind them, the first light of dawn, a thin sliver of gray daring to pierce the eastern seam of night, broke through the darkness, announcing the arrival of the new day.

"We should be in New York by Wednesday morning," Lord Bainbridge said. "Your sister will be meeting you there?"

"Yes," Tom answered, "and my brother-in-law too." He struggled to pump some enthusiasm into his voice. "He has a job all lined up for me."

"What kind of job?"

"In a factory that makes ladies' shirtwaists," Tom answered. "My brother-in-law's a foreman there. I'll be taking care of the machines, fixing 'em. I'm good that way with my hands."

"Last night," Lord Bainbridge reminded him, "you told me you wanted to be an artist."

Tom was silent a moment before he answered. "Last night I was telling you my dream. This other, the factory, is my life." He looked into his companion's face. "We can't always have what we want, you know," he said.

"How intensely sad life would be if that was really true," Lord Bainbridge remarked.

"There'll be someone else waiting for me in New York as well," Tom added quickly. And before Lord Bainbridge could ask the obvious he pushed on. "A girl my sister has lined up for me to marry."

"A job in a factory and a girl both lined up, I don't know which I find the more depressing," Lord Bainbridge returned with scorn he only felt on the surface.

"I don't even know her name," Tom continued. "My sister sent me her photograph, but she forgot to tell me her name. I have the photograph down in my cabin. I'll bring it up some time if you'd like to see it," he suggested like a young boy eager to win over a new playmate with the promise of an exciting new toy.

"Why would I want to see it?" Lord Bainbridge asked rather petulantly.

Tom nodded, suddenly very subdued. "No, of course you wouldn't want to see it. She looks to be a very pretty little thing," he added as if that fact in itself soothed over the whole situation and made everything all right again.

"Well, thank God she's not ugly!" Lord Bainbridge shot back sarcastically.

If I only knew her name, Tom mused to himself, where he had momentarily retreated to escape the little storm his words had blown up.

"Sorry," Lord Bainbridge hurriedly apologized. "I was being a bit of a beast."

"It's all right," Tom assured him. "It's just all rather complicated in my head. I keep tossing it back and forth." He looked away, far out to sea. "I'm not sure what I want."

"It can be a very difficult decision for some," Lord Bainbridge said gently. And then he said no more, content to gaze at the young man beside him and remember the first time he had set eyes on him.

As he emerged from the glass-enclosed promenade on A deck, an innovation designed to provide first-class passengers with protection from sea spray should the weather on the voyage suddenly turn nasty, Lord Bainbridge walked out onto the open deck and took the sun full in his eyes. For a moment, he was completely blinded. The sun was setting swiftly into the western sky ahead of them, setting into the land for which he was bound and for which he had such high hopes. And as his sight returned and the last golden rays of the day began to dip like molten lava into the ocean, he wondered if he would find, as he had so often heard, that the streets of America were paved with gold. Of course he didn't think the streets were literally made of gold as unfortunately many others did. Rather, Lord Bainbridge was hoping he might find gold of another kind, the kind of gold he had searched desperately for, sometimes nightly, in the private clubs and secluded parks. The kind of gold he had not been able to find in England, the kind of gold found in a smile.

Drawing to the rail, he gazed down at the decks below him. Beneath his own was the second-class promenade filled with everyday people, husbands and wives, children in tow, all taking the air in an ordinary civilized but completely, as far as Lord Bainbridge was concerned, boring manner. As his eyes traveled down the decks below him, he dwelled on the fact that, like the real world, life on board this ship was divided by class—first class, his own secure niche, second class, the ordinary, third class, the poor. His own class was of course important to him, and so was the third actually, for it was there he found the type of young men he desired. But what of the second class, the middle class? Lord Bainbridge had to admit that they meant little to him. They were just there. He knew few if any who belonged to that segment of society. Certainly, he was not attracted to the young men of that group—clerks and schoolteachers mostly, hardly the champions of anyone's erotic dreams. Most assuredly not his! His preference was for lovers of the working class—the soldiers, gamekeepers, and tram conductors. To him, as to many men of privilege, these types of men were seen as symbols of virility. "The men of the lower classes are never self-conscious, and therefore, they will do whatever they have to to survive. This makes them vulnerable as well as virile," someone had once said to him. And this was a combination Lord Bainbridge found irresistible. No, definitely not for him were the pallid, lifeless members of the middle class. Unlike their brothers of the lower class, Lord Bainbridge found them to be colorless and nondescript like inferior copies of rare masterworks someone had knocked off to rake in a few quick coins. And there was one other reason why the men of the middle class held such little charm for him. Most of them seemed to be infested with respectability, and to Lord Bainbridge, there was nothing quite so boring as respectability. He much preferred a young man who had a bit of the hooligan, the trickster, in him. He had even, on occasion, consorted with thieves and other petty criminals. But whatever their calling, or lack of calling as it were, he had never found them dull. And the men of the middle class, as far as Lord Bainbridge was concerned, were so dull they merited not even a casual glance.

So as he leaned on the deck rail, Lord Bainbridge's eyes quickly passed by the second-class promenade below him and on down to the third-class recreation area toward the bow of the ship. Here, a number of young men had come up from their cabins far below deck and started a rowdy game of football to the cheers of those standing around watching them, including some from Lord Bainbridge's own deck. Their football was a makeshift affair, appearing to be made out of cloth and leather, and it didn't always go where it was supposed to when it was kicked, but this only seemed to be adding to their fun.

"Oh, I say, well played there, lad!" an elderly gentleman in a fur coat and a derby, standing close to Lord Bainbridge, called out to one of the players down below.

The player turned and looked up in the direction of the call. He grinned and tipped his cap in appreciation to the elderly gentleman, and then instead of immediately returning to the game that his mates had already restarted, he swung his eyes over and rather boldly planted them on Lord Bainbridge. He let his eyes linger on him for a long moment, long enough for Lord Bainbridge to get a good look at his face that, in spite of the distance between them, he was able to ascertain had a boyish look of snub-nosed perfection. Unfortunately, the next moment, the young man paid for his inattentiveness to the game when the ball smacked him square in the head, and he tumbled in a heap to the deck. He sat there for a long moment as if he were stunned. The game came to a sudden stop as people on all three decks fell silent and strained their eyes toward the fallen player as if fearing he might be seriously injured.

Lord Bainbridge would have gladly rushed down and given him medical aid had he any such knowledge.

But not to fear. The young man bounced back to his feet, swept up his cap, which had been knocked from his head by the force of the blow, and offered those on the decks above him, in particular Lord Bainbridge, a most marvelous grin, which was at least partially one of embarrassment. Then he returned to the game with a vengeance, greeted by a rousing cheer from all decks.

"You didn't care for the Italian?"

He had been so mesmerized by the scene bellow, Lord Bainbridge actually jumped at the voice by his side. "How long have you been standing there?" he asked, quickly recovering himself.

"Long enough," Alfred Watkins answered. His gray eyes narrowed in that way they did when he was concentrating on something as he was now on the spirited game continuing below. "Which one is it this time?" he asked.

Lord Bainbridge paused for a long moment, turning things over in his mind and still watching the young man below but thinking perhaps this one time he would let it go, this one time he would decline the invitation. But the little tussle with his own nature lasted only a few moments, and he quickly surrendered as he had known he would even as he had been valiantly fighting the good fight.

"The one in the cap who has the ball now," he observed.

"A little short, isn't he?" Alfred observed. It was in Alfred's nature, Lord Bainbridge had come to realize during their years together, to be critical. Alfred Watkins had this passionate need to point out the obvious as if by doing so, he somehow reinforced his own superiority or at least his powers of observation.

"Not in the least," Lord Bainbridge returned rather sharply.

"Shall I go down and speak to him then?" Alfred inquired, leaning on the rail, his body twisted around so that he was now staring at Lord Bainbridge rather than down below at the young man who was the object of their discussion. His lips were twisted into a smile, a smile that was smugly sure of the answer to his question even before he asked it.

Staring back at him, Lord Bainbridge realized that there were moments when Alfred could truly irritate him. And yet, he had to acknowledge that there was a deep bond of affection between them, for their history went back more than four years. They had been lovers once and now; though Alfred was officially designated as his manservant, his valet, in the coarser light of reality, he could also be called his procurer. He was at various times disdainful and devious, but he remained devoted to Lord Bainbridge. He had certainly all his life been one out for his own, and the devotion and loyalty he gave to Lord Bainbridge was given in part because it served him as equally well as it did his master. Never let it be said that Alfred Watkins failed to know a good thing, especially when he had it in the palm of his hand. He was quick to question and criticize, and though he often overstepped the bounds between master and servant, he knew just how far to step and when to retreat.

Looking at him now as the football game below came to an exciting conclusion, Lord Bainbridge had to once again remind himself that the two of them were the same age, within a month of each other, and yet Alfred had always seemed to him to be much older. This, Lord Bainbridge had always reasoned, must be because Alfred had been on his own since the age of thirteen and had undoubtedly known more than a few hard knocks in his early years. Adversity can age one faster than years, was Lord Bainbridge's rather pat conclusion.

The face that continued to smile back at him however certainly bore no traces of premature aging. It was as youthful as his own. Except there was a certain degree of toughness in Alfred's features. You could see it around the corners of his full lips, especially when he smiled, and in his wide nostrils that he flared at the slightest provocation. His gray eyes too had a hard look to them, and he had a habit of hooding them with his thick brows when he was looking at someone, almost as if he feared if that person got a good look at his eyes, they might obtain some great power over him or they might, in the least, see into his soul. He wore his dark blond hair longish and tousled, and it was startingly set off by thick darker sideburns and eyelashes that were darker still.

"Well, do I go down and speak to this one?" Alfred asked again, the impatience he was feeling obvious. Lord Bainbridge nodded, swallowing hard, his lips pressed tightly together. "What time shall I tell him?"

"Tonight at ten," Lord Bainbridge answered, looking away at something.

"Right you are," Alfred returned, and he was off on his mission.

Lord Bainbridge watched him make his way down to the lower deck, passing through gates meant to keep the various classes from mingling. But then he knew gates or doors or barriers of any kind were never an obstacle to Alfred. He saw him approach the young man who, the game having come to an end, was about to leave the deck. Observing them as they stood together sharing a few words, Lord Bainbridge could not help but notice the difference in height between them, and he could see Alfred was right—this one was quite short. Alfred was, like himself, of average height with a muscular if in no way overdeveloped body. Also, Lord Bainbridge could not help but notice that Alfred was standing on the third-class deck with a distinct attitude of superiority among people he obviously considered his inferiors. This pose of his was certainly enhanced by the clothes he wore: an expensive wool suit and topcoat, fancy gloves of fine Italian leather, and, on his head, a smart bowler hat with a turned-down brim. It was part of the agreement between them that Alfred would always have the best of clothes, and he took great pride in them and in his appearance in them. Lord Bainbridge smiled to himself; Alfred was more of a snob really than most of the passengers on this ship who held first-class tickets.

His brief conversation with Alfred over, the young man turned once again and looked up at Lord Bainbridge. And once again, he offered him what Lord Bainbridge could only describe as a magnificent grin. Then the young man bounded away, disappearing through an open door as if he were on some urgent errand.

A few moments later, Alfred returned to Lord Bainbridge's side. "It's all set, ten tonight. This one at least speaks English, he's Irish," he added. "At least you won't have to struggle to try and understand him like with the Italian."

"His English was fine," Lord Bainbridge declared, knowing Alfred's disdain for the lower classes was only surpassed by his dislike for foreigners.

"You can wipe that smirk off your face," he told his servant, annoyed by the smile on Alfred's face.

"It's not a smirk, sir," Alfred returned.

He would sometimes address him as sir in public, but more often than not, he would call him by his Christian name. This was something Lord Bainbridge did not object to; in fact, it had been his idea. It seemed to be rather ridiculous to be called sir by someone you had been to bed with.

"What is it then?" he asked with patience he wasn't feeling at the moment.

"A smile of satisfaction that you will be having an enjoyable evening tonight," Alfred answered.

Lord Bainbridge gave him a look, and then turning away from him, he directed his steps back toward his stateroom. Alfred trailed obediently after him, still smiling.

Lord Bainbridge's stateroom was located on B deck, starboard side. Included with the stateroom itself were a wardrobe room for his trunks, a private bath and lavatory, and an adjoining inside cabin for his manservant. Although it was quite luxurious—with such amenities as hot and cold running water, an electric call button that could summon a steward at a moment's notice, a fireplace with an electric heater in its hearth, so welcome on those cold North Atlantic nights, and a bedstead four feet wide—it was not considered the most lavish of the first-class accommodations that the ship provided. These were the two deluxe parlor suites, also on B deck, one on either side of the ship. They boasted not only sitting rooms but they each had their own private fifty-foot promenade deck so that their occupants might take the sea air in private and not have to suffer the indignity of having to share it with those, they at least, considered their inferiors. For among the very rich there were deep divisions and social lines that were not crossed. Those who considered themselves to be at the very top of the social echelon very often had little contact with those who were on a lower rung of the social ladder even if they were members of their own class. Frequently, a member of the highest order would be more apt to speak or otherwise have contact with a person of the middle class, or even the lower class, than with a socially inferior constituent of his own class.

One of the deluxe parlor suites, Lord Bainbridge had found out, was occupied by J. Bruce Ismay, managing director of the White Star Line, the company that owned and operated the vessel on which they were sailing. Lord Bainbridge had seen him a number of times throughout the voyage, and though they had never been officially introduced, Ismay always smiled and nodded to him as they passed. But Lord Bainbridge never failed to notice that Ismay's smile vanished the instant they were apart only to suddenly reappear with equal brightness when he encountered another passenger. It also seemed to Lord Bainbridge that Ismay was all over the ship, poking his head into every nook and cranny. A couple of times, Lord Bainbridge came upon him engaged in a heated conversation with a member of the ship's crew. Once, most surprisingly, it had been the captain himself who Ismay appeared to be berating. This time there was no smile of formal cordiality from the managing director though the captain had caught Lord Bainbridge's eye and conveyed to him, with a simple downturn of his lips, his apology for the unseemly scene. Mr. Ismay, Lord Bainbridge was quick to surmise, was a man who was considered important by none more than himself. Lord Bainbridge found him as unsavory in appearance—with his thin wavy hair, full handlebar mustache, and pale anemic-looking skin—as he did in manner—filled with the kind of arrogance that denoted a man of action but only when the action benefited himself. *Not one I would want to have around me in a crisis*, Lord Bainbridge had concluded in an observation that was to prove quite prophetic in the days to come.

The occupant of the second parlor suite, the one closest to his own stateroom on the starboard side of the ship, was unknown to him by name. Actually, the lady in question's true identity was a mystery to most everyone on board as she was for some obscure reason traveling under an assumed name. Lord Bainbridge had heard that she was an American. He had caught sight of her on occasion parading disdainfully through the ship's first-class public rooms, always dressed in the latest Paris fashions, and usually clutching a little dog of undeterminable breed, undeterminable especially to Lord Bainbridge who, never having been a dog fancier himself, had no head for deducing the various breeds of canine. There appeared to be no husband or other male companion trailing in the lady's wake, which would have obviously been the proper place for such a man should he have existed. The lady did however, Lord Bainbridge could not fail but notice, have a very large retinue of servants, especially for one person traveling alone. He counted three maids, possibly four but he wasn't quite sure, and two young men, one quite striking in appearance, dark and mysterious and very Continental looking. All six of them, or five, always seemed to be coming and going from her suite in great haste, rushing about almost as if the ship were on fire. Curious as to the reason for all their frenzied activity, Lord Bainbridge resorted to one of the oldest adages among the rich. "If you want to know something, ask the servants." Alfred, who Lord Bainbridge suspected had a fancy for the striking young man and often took tea with him in the lounge reserved exclusively for the maids and menservants of the first-class passengers, did not disappoint his master's curiosity. He relayed the following:

It seems the lady had come aboard the ship with what could only be described as a mountain of luggage. Now, Edwardian ladies, and gentlemen too for that matter, did not travel lightly. One titled English lady had famously remarked, "A very large fraction of our time each day is spent dressing and undressing." Thus traveling abroad necessitated the bringing along of substantial amounts of baggage, for many did travel for extended periods of time and certainly had to have the proper clothes available for any climate or occasion. Lord Bainbridge was accompanied on the ship by three trunks and various smaller suitcases and valises. In contrast, according to Alfred's informant, the American lady had brought along sixteen trunks, numerous suitcases and smaller pieces of luggage, and at least a dozen packing crates. Alfred had more news. It seems the striking young man was employed as the lady's bodyguard. It was not that she feared an assassination attempt, but rather he was along solely to watch over her jewelry. Apparently, she had an expensive and extensive collection that she preferred to keep in her suite instead of locked up in the purser's safe. The young man even carried a gun, which he proudly displayed to Alfred, frightening an elderly nursemaid sitting near them into flight. As to the reason for all of the servants rushing to and fro from the lady's suite, this was because of her very demanding and often capricious nature. Because even in her spacious luxury suite there was hardly enough room to accommodate a fraction of her luggage, most of it had to be stored down below in the first-class baggage compartment on G deck. And the lady was constantly deciding that she just couldn't live a moment longer if she didn't have a particular item from below, so one of the servants was instantly sent on the long trek down five decks. Trips often became hourly. And a number of times it got so bad, the young man had told Alfred, that two of the servants would pass one another in the passageway or on the stairs, and the one having just been to the baggage compartment would pass on the item they had just retrieved and then return to the compartment for the item the second servant had been sent for.

Lord Bainbridge had found his own stateroom most adequate and surprisingly comfortable although he had done a bit of rearranging when it came to the room's furniture. The sofa, he had quickly decided, would be much more comfortable before the fireplace, particularly on the cold nights they could expect. He also moved a small table with a lamp, along with a sturdy chair, to one corner of the room to give himself a private area for his writing. On the table, he placed his writing instruments, the notes he had begun on his second book, and a small tintype of his father, the father he had never known. But other than these changes, he found the stateroom's original setup as well as its decor very pleasing. The room's dark mahogany paneling reminded him of a den or a room in one of London's exclusive gentlemen's clubs. The dark blue upholstery of the furniture with its splashes of red was matched by the drapes that hung at the two windows, actually square windows not portholes, that looked out onto the deck and the sea beyond. The big double bed, which he had found more pleasing than most beds he had encountered outside of his own home, stood beside the door to the wardrobe room and was generously supplied with crisp sheets, warm blankets, and topped off with a rich satin comforter. All in all, the stateroom was first rate in Lord Bainbridge's opinion, and with his own personal items scattered around, it almost seemed like home, especially coming in late at night after an invigorating day at sea.

It was Friday night, their third night at sea, and Lord Bainbridge was eagerly awaiting the arrival of his guest. The little clock on the fireplace mantel chimed out the hour of ten. Its chimes were discretely tuned to a gentle tone so as to neither startle or irritate only to inform. The lamps in the stateroom were turned down low, and in the fireplace, the electric heater glowed, spreading its warmth throughout the room.

The door to the corridor opened, and someone stood there framed in the doorway, hesitating as if reluctant to enter, his features momentarily concealed in the dim lightning.

Behind him, Alfred grew impatient. "Well, go ahead, go in. He ain't gonna bite you," he snapped.

The young Irishman walked into the stateroom. He grinned at Lord Bainbridge and immediately doffed his cap. He had obviously dressed in his best clothes, shirt and tie, trousers, waistcoat and jacket.

Lord Bainbridge, after much deliberation and having laughed at himself for dithering like a schoolgirl on her first date, had selected for his own attire a simple pair of gray slacks, not too tight, and a collarless white cotton shirt.

Now he stepped forward and offered his hand, "Jeremy Bainbridge."

"Tom Kennedy," the other responded, taking his hand and giving it a firm, manly shake.

Having made his delivery, Alfred had already disappeared, not into his own room, but back out into the corridor, closing the door behind him. *Probably gone to chat up the young bodyguard again,* Lord Bainbridge thought to himself.

A moment of silence followed, uncomfortable but not unexpected. "This is quite a place," Tom said, glancing around the stateroom.

"It's cozy and comfortable," Lord Bainbridge agreed.

"The whole ship is rather splendid," Tom went on. "I never thought I'd get to see this part of it." He laughed a bit. "I'm afraid your man got a little put out with me. When we passed the first-class dining saloon, I had to have a look inside. It was all lit up, I guess they were readying the tables for tomorrow's breakfast." He shook his head remembering. "God, what a sight, like a palace! I've never seen the likes of it before!"

"Would you like to have dinner there tomorrow night?" Lord Bainbridge suggested on the spur of the moment, enchanted by the young man's enthusiasm.

"I can't imagine myself eatin' in such a place," Tom said. "It would be like I'd died and gone to heaven."

"Oh, I don't think the food's quite that bad," Lord Bainbridge joked.

Tom didn't immediately get the jest. He smiled shyly. "I doubt they'd even let me in the door," he said.

"Of course they would, you'd be with me," Lord Bainbridge responded rather self-righteously.

Tom's smile deepened, "Well, if you really mean it."

"That I do," Lord Bainbridge answered. "Good, it's all set then, tomorrow night."

"What a grand adventure that will be!" Tom exclaimed with excited anticipation.

"Well, we don't have to stand around as if we were waiting at a trolley stop," Lord Bainbridge laughed. He indicated the sofa before the fireplace to which they both then crossed and took seats. A bottle of wine and two glasses sat on a little table beside the sofa.

Lord Bainbridge poured them each a glass. As he passed one of the glasses to Tom, he asked a question. "What shall we drink to?"

"To new friends," Tom suggested after a moment's thought.

"Perfect," Lord Bainbridge agreed. And as their glasses clinked gently, their eyes met for just a second before they each took a swallow of wine.

Lord Bainbridge offered a cigarette from his case, which Tom accepted with thanks and then thanked him again when Lord Bainbridge struck a match and lit it for him before lighting his own.

His good manners reminded Lord Bainbridge that two nights before, on their first night at sea, another young man had sat in that very same spot. But Marco Borsalino, the Italian, had shown far less proper deportment. Unbid, he had helped himself to a cigarette and then scooped up a handful and stuffed them into his pocket. "For later," he had smiled. His actions at the time had amused Lord Bainbridge, for he certainly did not expect to find good manners, or fine etiquette, among the companions he sought. But he was enough of a snob to be pleased when he did.

Thus armed with wine and cigarettes, the two items that Lord Bainbridge often considered essential to carry on a conversation, especially when he found himself in the type of situation he was presently engaged in, the two of them sat back on the sofa. They looked at one another, smiled, and then for a long moment, neither of them could think of a word to say.

Finally, Lord Bainbridge decided a compliment would break the ice. "You look very nice," he told Tom. "Most handsome."

Even in the dim light, Tom's blush was detectable. "I put on my best clothes," he returned, and then he quickly found something of great interest on the tip of his cigarette.

"How's your head?"

"Beg pardon?"

"You got beaned with that football," Lord Bainbridge reminded him.

"Oh that!" Tom grinned. "It was nothing."

"Did you win the game?"

"Of course!" Tom answered proudly.

Lord Bainbridge poured them each a little more wine. "So you're going to America?"

"Is that where this ship is headed?" Tom asked, his head cocked mischievously to one side.

"I'm afraid so, my friend," Lord Bainbridge assured him.

"Well, sure then," Tom said, "I guess that's where I'm going."

"And what will you do in America?"

Tom took a few moments and a couple more sips of wine before he answered this one. "What I would like to do is paint," he finally replied.

Lord Bainbridge wasn't quite sure exactly what he meant, and he was not about to be so indelicate as to ask if he meant painting houses, so all he said was, "Really?"

"I like to paint landscapes," Tom explained. He frowned. "I'm not sure I'm any good. Though my mother thinks I'm very talented, my father less so."

Lord Bainbridge was both amazed and delighted. "I'd like to see some of your work," he suggested.

Tom's frown deepened. "I'm afraid I left everything behind in Ireland, even my paints and brushes. I'll have to buy some new ones when I've earned the money."

Lord Bainbridge nodded, knowing that now the door had been opened and the next move was up to him. It was a familiar narrative, and he knew what to do next. He reached out and touched Tom's thigh tentatively. He felt him give a little start as if he had not been expecting the touch, but he did not pull away. His next words did not surprise Lord Bainbridge.

"Your man mentioned that you would be giving me some money."

Lord Bainbridge got quickly to his feet. "Of course"—he nodded—"we can take care of that right now if you like." He felt a momentary wave of sadness overtake him as he moved toward the dresser where he kept his money. It was not that he found Tom's request unusual; they most always wanted money, some even rudely demanding it. It was, he knew, the basis of nearly every relationship between men of different classes, a practice that went all the way back to ancient times. Some, being crude, would call it prostitution, while others of a gentler nature would simply refer to it as patronization. Lord Bainbridge always saw it as an exchange, a bartering of goods—what one has he gives to the other in trade for what he desires. But this one time he had thought, even dared hope, it might be different.

Before he had reached the dresser however, Tom called him back.

"No!" he cried out anxiously, obviously extremely agitated that he had been misunderstood. "I don't want your money," he told him.

Lord Bainbridge returned to the sofa and sat down beside him. And it was Tom who took his hand. "Do you always give them money?" he asked.

Lord Bainbridge nodded, and for a moment, he felt ashamed and deeply troubled as if Tom had looked inside of him and seen his soul.

"But why?" Tom asked. He reached up and stroked Lord Bainbridge's cheek. "You should never have to pay for love," he said simply and most eloquently.

"Why . . . why did you come here?" Lord Bainbridge asked, stammering and stumbling over his words, his mind turning in confusion, and feeling ecstasy and horror both at the same moment as if were whirling around on a merry-go-round gone out of control.

"To get to know you," Tom answered. "I saw your face, I liked it. I wanted to get to know the man behind it."

Lord Bainbridge was completely astonished. "You shouldn't paint, you should write books," he said.

Tom laughed, shaking his head. "Nah, I've no great head for words."

"The hell you haven't," Lord Bainbridge murmured.

Tom looked at him for a moment as if he were taking a silent measure of the man who was sitting across from him. "I've done this before," he confessed. "It's not my first time." And then as if to prove his boast, he leaned toward Lord Bainbridge and kissed him full on the mouth.

It was only a fleeting kiss, but it was on the lips, and the instant it happened, like an echo from two nights before, Lord Bainbridge heard the voice of the Italian. "On the cheek only, not on the lips."

That was the normal. They would let you kiss them on the cheek but hardly ever on the mouth. It was their cardinal rule, and if it was ever broken, they seemed convinced it would diminish their manhood, shame them in their own eyes no matter what else they let you do to them.

Reacting to the rather shocked look on his companion's face, Tom offered a quick apology. "Forgive me, I'm afraid I'm being too forward. It's the wine."

Lord Bainbridge had at last pulled himself together, and he immediately held out the wine bottle. "More?"

"I think we've both had enough wine," Tom told him.

He took Lord Bainbridge's hand, and wordlessly, they slipped down before the fireplace, feeling the warmth from the electric heater on their faces, warming faces that were already feverish with desire. They sat like that for some time in silence, wrapped in each other's arms, their backs against the sofa. Lord Bainbridge remembered another scene before a fireplace, another defining moment in his life that now seemed like it had happened a hundred years ago.

Tom turned his head, and they kissed once again on the mouth but still gently, still as if testing. Then he pulled back, and they stared at one another for a long moment, each searching the face of the other as if looking for some answer to a question not yet asked.

Lord Bainbridge watched as Tom took off his tie and unbuttoned his collar. Then he slipped off his jacket and waistcoat. His shirt followed, and in the semidarkness, his naked chest gleamed like marble, the marble of a statue seen long ago in a museum. Tom got to his feet, kicked off his shoes, and unbuckled his trousers, letting them fall to the floor. He stood before Lord Bainbridge wearing only a pair of cotton underdrawers, their snowy whiteness proudly proclaiming their newness. Then Tom knelt and began touching him, caressing him through his clothes, his face hovering over Lord Bainbridge, his incredible grin replaced by a shy smile, the smile of a boy, the smile of a man. Their mouths met again, brushed gently at first and then forced themselves roughly against each other, parting lips and giving roam to searching tongues. Quickly, Tom helped Lord Bainbridge out of his own clothes.

And as they reached for each other, Lord Bainbridge knew at that exact moment all the endless sordid beds and squalid embraces he had endured up until now were suddenly swept away. Here, with this young Irishman, he was being both initiated and reborn.

As if to remind them that time stands still for no man, the sky above the boat deck suddenly came alive with light, and the day was upon them. Exquisite mauves and pinks and blues spread across the heavens as if someone had decided this day, above all other days, was to be most splendid.

"It's going to be a beautiful day," Tom observed.

"Oh yes!" Lord Bainbridge agreed, but he was still looking at him, not to the sky. "We've been up all night. Shall we go below?" he suggested, remembering with much delight the previous night they had spent together, making love, falling asleep in his bed, and then wakening in each other's arms. Obviously, he was certainly hoping to repeat the experience.

But Tom begged off, "I'm exhausted. I just want to fall into bed and sleep for hours."

"We needn't do anything," Lord Bainbridge persisted. "We could merely sleep together—that would be nice."

Tom smiled, trying to be gentle, "Let's make it tonight. I'll come up, and we'll spend the whole night in your cabin."

Lord Bainbridge nodded, swallowing his disappointment. "Tonight it is then." A frown quickly crossed his face. "I'm having a special dinner with some friends tonight. But I'll be free by eleven. I'll send my man for you," he proposed.

"Don't bother," Tom responded. "I can find my own way. Besides, I don't think your man likes me."

"Oh, Alfred's all right," Lord Bainbridge assured him. "He can be a bit standoffish at times. But honestly, I don't know what I'd do without him."

Tom gave him a strange quizzical look. "Really?" He considered this for a moment, his deep brown eyes seeming to travel away to some far distant place as he concentrated on the matter. "I got the impression he was jealous of me," he said finally. Now, it was Lord Bainbridge's turn to look puzzled, his opportunity to turn something over in his mind. But before he could respond, Tom spoke up and put the matter to rest at least for the time being. "It was a momentary feeling I had, nothing more. I'd better be off," he added.

They shared a final smile, staring into each other's faces like comrades who had been through a battle together. Lord Bainbridge had the awful feeling that there was something very important he had forgotten to say, something of the utmost urgency that had been left unsaid. They were only parting for hours, but he felt like their separation was to be eternal.

He hadn't realized Tom had left his side until he suddenly saw him halfway down the deck. Then the young man turned around, and Lord Bainbridge thought with a leap in his heart, *He's going to come back!*

But Tom only called out to him. "I forgot about the clothes," he said, indicating the suit of evening clothes he was still wearing.

"You can return them tonight," Lord Bainbridge called back.

Tom nodded. "They might not let me back into third class dressed like this," he added, his smile indicating he wouldn't mind letting a few of his fellow third-class passengers see him dressed up so impressively. He waved his hand as he walked away. "See ya!"

"See ya!" Lord Bainbridge returned, watching him until he had disappeared from sight.

Then Lord Bainbridge turned away from the rail to head down to his own bed, hoping that perhaps some of the fragrance and the warmth of the young men that had so recently shared that bed might still linger there. He knew sleep would come to him quickly and without a struggle. And he also knew it was now destined to bring with it such wonderful dreams.

On his way below, he passed one of the ship's lifeboats lashed to the deck, the name of its ship painted boldly on its bow: *Titanic*!

Chapter II

November 1904

If he looks back at me one more time before he goes inside, Lord Bainbridge thought to himself, *then I'll know he feels the same way I do.* The object of his observation had just sprinted across the quadrangle, hurrying to catch up to his classmates, the robes of his undergraduate gown flapping around his thin legs, and his arms overflowing with schoolbooks. Lord Bainbridge leaned against the gate and stared hard in the noonday sun across the rich green lawn of the quadrangle. The bells from the chapel on the far side of the quadrangle started to count out the noon hour, but he was deaf to their noise. Then just as the crowd of boys started piling up the steps of the science building to be funneled through the one front door, his prey looked over his shoulder and smiled back at him. It was a glance that lasted only a second, but like a single drop of rain falling on parched earth, that gesture nourished Lord Bainbridge and made his spirits soar. He leaned weakly against the gate, his own schoolbooks spilling unnoticed to the ground at his feet. He had waited so long for this one moment, this one look. And in spite of the fact that this look had been no different than the hundreds of others they had shared, he had convinced himself, because he wished it so, that this was the look that had revealed to him the other boy felt as he did. As he slumped there against the gate, he kept whispering the boy's name over and over as if it was a magical chant, an incantation that would grant him, if not eternal life, at least eternal joy. "Denham Granville-Smith! Denham Granville-Smith!"

Lord Bainbridge, who was now in his second year, had entered Winchester, a preparatory school, at the age of fourteen. By then the wheel of sexual choice had already spun for him. As in all public schools of the period, Winchester had its underbelly of vice and bullying, where the older boys victimized the younger boys, in all manner including sexually. But most often, the boys they picked on were the pretty ones, the ones with blond hair and rosy cheeks, often timid and shy, or others whom they perceived as spoiled little rich boys who needed to be taken down a notch or two. Lord Bainbridge did not conduct himself in a manner that anyone would find offensive, and he certainly could not have been counted among the pretty ones, so as a result, he was left alone by those boys who practiced their various forms of intimidation. Thus, he was free to make his own friendships, without having another forced upon him, and he could play the game of schoolboy homosexuality on his own terms. Most of the boys at Winchester, as in other boarding schools, passed through a period of active homosexuality. Then after they left the school, they moved on to eventually marry, father children, and lead a normal life. Lord Bainbridge knew from the start that his road would lead in a much different direction. His school friendships he divided into three separate categories. The first were his everyday companions, those whom he went to classes with, dined, and studied with and regarded quite unsentimentally. Second were those he was more intimate with, an-arm-around-the-shoulder types but still purely innocent. These were the ones who very often proclaimed to each other that they were tremendous friends and would be for life. And thirdly were the ones whom he regarded as neither pure nor innocent and whom he had either already been with sexually or, as in the case of Denham Granville-Smith, he ached to do so. In fact, Lord Bainbridge had ached for Denham for two full terms, and they had not even done so much as spoken a single word to one another. It had been an intolerable situation that had almost driven him mad, but at last, he was now convinced that the Rubicon had been crossed. The gates of Thebes had been thrown open, and he was about to enter paradise.

The object of his intense adoration was a boy his own age who came from a well-to-do if unremarkable family. His father had once been a member of parliament, and his mother had borne seven children and was well-known for her splendid needlework. They were conventional in all respects, and that they should have produced such a son was, at least in Lord Bainbridge's estimate, a miracle indeed. There was no denying the fact that Denham Granville-Smith was good-looking. He had the requisite blond hair and blue eyes all done up in a choirboy's face. But he also had a cocky smile, a self-satisfied expression befitting one sure of his own desirability. Lord Bainbridge was quite certain Denham knew he was desired by many and was rather pleased about it. And though he always seemed to have a crowd of boys around him, almost like courtiers, and though almost every boy who saw him instantly and fervently declared they were mad for him, no one knew anyone who had actually been with him in a carnal manner. In fact, no one even claimed to have been whether it was true or not even though a boast of such a conquest would have greatly raised one's standing throughout the whole school. Instead, Denham Granville-Smith sailed through his days at Winchester apparently untouched, molested only in the dreams of other boys.

Lord Bainbridge, for his part, also dreamt of Denham, almost nightly, and he spent a good deal of his daylight hours dreaming about him as well. As luck would have it, bad luck, in the two terms since Denham had arrived at Winchester, they had taken no classes together. They each had a completely different circle of friends, with not a single individual overlapping from one group to the other who could have served as a go-between or at least provided an introduction.

Their rooms were at opposite ends of the school, and they even took their meals in separate dining halls. All Lord Bainbridge ever saw of Denham were fleeting glimpses in the hallways or on the grounds, momentary quick flashes of his face, his smile, which would both delight and torture him for hours, for days, afterward. He couldn't bring himself to just go up and speak to him for two reasons. The first being that it was something that was just not done. The unofficial rules of etiquette that governed the social world of the boys of Winchester frowned on members of one group chumming around with those from other groups. Everyone was expected to find his own niche, secure his own circle of friends, and stick with them. The second reason, and the one that prevented him the most from acting on his desires, was the normal inferiority that a less attractive person often feels toward one of a more favored appearance. At sixteen, Jeremy Bainbridge had come to realize he was no great beauty and was never destined to become one. Hours spent before his mirror, struggling with various hairstyles, had left him only frustrated and looking no better than when he had started. He knew he wasn't ugly, but he also knew he was far from a head turner.

Lord Bainbridge had made one attempt to get closer to Denham, and it had turned into a disaster of, as far as he was concerned, epic proportions. In keeping with his angelic looks, Denham was a member of the school's choir, and they practiced every afternoon at four in the chapel. Now, though he had never sung a note before, doubted he could carry a tune, and in fact was tone deaf, Lord Bainbridge was so desperate to get close to the boy he so passionately desired, he decided to audition for the choir.

This brought him into contact with one of Winchester's legendary masters. Cecil Asquith was a fussy little queen of a man, and if ever a name befitted its bearer, it was his. Hardly anyone could keep a straight face when he introduced himself in his customary lilting lisp. And their amusement was only intensified by the toupee he wore to cover his little bald head. It was, to begin with, of a terrible color, an unnatural shade of brown that looked more like something one would step in in the street rather than something one would intentionally put on their head. But its worst transgression was its fit—it didn't! It seemed to almost be a living thing. For every time you looked at the poor man, the toupee seemed to be sitting in a different position, not just day by day, but minute to minute as if it shifted with every turn of his head. Once in a high wind, it had taken flight as he was crossing the quadrangle, and much to the delight of the boys who witnessed this calamity, the choirmaster had sprinted after his fleeing hairpiece, his skinny arms thrashing in a frenzy, screaming out to it, "Come back! Come back this instant!" The students giggled amongst themselves and told the most lascivious tales about him, often mimicking his trembling affectations complete with hands waving madly about as if he were being set upon by a swarm of angry bees. Most of these tales involved his obvious fondness for his students, his little angels as he called them. He had what the students referred to as busy hands—always adjusting their robes, patting a shoulder here, pinching a cheek there. The choirmaster lived alone in a little cottage behind the chapel, and those who had been inside reported that it was adorned with paintings, drawings, and statues all of joyous naked boys. In the summer and spring terms, the choirmaster insisted that all his students take a weekly compulsory nude swim in the nearby river. He would sit on the riverbank in a state close to ecstasy, watching them frolic in the water. Perhaps even more bizarre was another of his edicts that mandated that all members of his choir wear nothing under their choir robes. "Tight undergarments inhibit and restrict the body and so the voice," was his reasoning. "The voices of angels must be free to soar up to the heaven so that God himself might hear and be enchanted by them." But in spite of all this, Cecil Asquith had never once been accused of a single impropriety, and though many boys thought he had the potential, most considered him merely a dirty old man, a voyeur at worst.

The choirmaster held auditions for the choir in the sitting room of his cottage, and it was there that Lord Bainbridge was summoned to on a cold and damp midweek morning. He entered the room to find it almost exactly as it had been described to him, images of naked youths peered at him from every conceivable location. In fact, the room was so overstuffed with paintings and drawings on the walls, statues, big and small, filling the tables, the fireplace mantel, and even the windowsills, it reminded him of the cluttered sitting room of one of his numerous maiden aunts although her obsession was cats, not naked young boys.

Lord Bainbridge found himself immediately plunked down on a stool, and with Cecil Asquith hovering anxiously over him, he was commanded to sing the scale.

Now young Bainbridge had, for some reason known only to himself, never expected to be asked to sing at his audition. He had figured the choirmaster would ask him a few questions such as, "Why do you want to be in the choir, young man?" "Because music is my greatest love," was to have been his prompt prepared response. Then with a quick pinch on the cheek, the choirmaster would announce he was in the choir. And after that, every afternoon at four he would spend blissfully at Denham's side.

"The scale?" he stammered.

"Yes, come! Come!" To help things along, the choirmaster blew a note on the pitch pipe he wore on a chain around his neck.

"I . . . I don't know the scale," Lord Bainbridge finally had to admit, hanging his head as he felt a blush of embarrassment start to darken his cheeks.

Cecil Asquith's hands fled to his chest as if he were suddenly in the midst of a massive coronary attack. On top of his head, his wandering toupee appeared to slump forward over his forehead as if it too was shocked by the boy's confession. "Impossible!" the choirmaster cried out in the same horrified tone one might have used in the middle of a church service had the reverend suddenly announced their was no God. "Everyone knows the scale!" the master insisted. "Now, come on!" And once again to prompt the reluctant boy into compliance, he blew a note on his pitch pipe. Actually, he blew a number of notes and hit various keys on the piano beside him as well as if desperately hoping at least one chord might strike a familiar note with the boy.

Miserable with mortification, Lord Bainbridge shook his head. "I don't know it. I really don't!" And before Cecil Asquith could say another word although at the moment he had turned so blue in the face it was doubtful he would have been capable of any form of communication, Lord Bainbridge leaped from the stool and fled from the choirmaster's cottage never to return.

But more humiliation was to follow for Lord Bainbridge, and this time, it was destined to be played out before the whole student body. However, at least this time, his shame would produce a happier ending. The occasion was a lecture by the headmaster, a tradition that took place midway through each term. It was held in the great lecture hall, a drafty old pre-Victorian building that leaked buckets when it rained, always seemed to smell as if something had just died and, many years before, had been the setting for a traumatic incident when one boy had stabbed another to death in the front row. Their quarrel, not surprisingly, had been over another boy. Nowadays, the only crime committed in the hall was that which was perpetrated by the hard wooden seats with their uneven slats that would cruelly pinch young bottoms whenever they squirmed or merely readjusted their positions.

As Lord Bainbridge filed into the hall with his mates, he looked anxiously around for a glimpse of Denham. But in a sea of over three hundred faces, he couldn't find him although in such a crowd, it would have been easy to miss him. As he took his seat with his friends, about halfway down the hall toward the front, he had to admit to himself that perhaps he had been wrong to try and interrupt the look Denham had given him across the quadrangle the previous day. And more depressingly, perhaps all the looks they had shared through the last two terms, all the secret smiles, had, as far as Denham was concerned, meant nothing. Perhaps he smiled that way to everyone, and perhaps given the fact that no one had ever come forth and said they had been to bed with him, perhaps Denham Granville-Smith was nothing more than a tease. This thought, this startling revelation, so distressed Lord Bainbridge, he slumped down in his seat and refused to be roused by the high jinks of his friends around him. Then as if God had finally taken pity on him, there appeared right in front of him the answer to prayers. Denham, leading his own group of friends, was filing into the row of seats just forward of his own. They came practically face to face for a moment, and when Denham lifted up his eyes to look at him, Lord Bainbridge was convinced he saw in their depths a look of desire. This look so unnerved him, he wiggled about in his seat, and though his bottom took a merciless beating, he hardly felt it. Could it be that Denham Granville-Smith felt as he did? It was too good to be true! Denham and his friends had settled into their seats, and whether by design or accident, Denham had stopped one seat short of the end of the row, so that the seat beside him was empty. With incredible longing, Lord Bainbridge stared at that empty seat. He had to force himself to stay in his own seat and not climb over the back of the row in front of him and claim the prized sacred place beside the boy he so worshiped. But the more he stared at that empty seat, the more he knew it had to be his.

Glancing up at the stage, he saw that the headmaster had risen from his chair and was gathering his notes as he conversed with one of his colleagues. His lecture would begin any moment. Throwing all caution to the wind, all sense of propriety, Lord Bainbridge jumped to his feet and began to push his way down his own row, past his friends.

"Bains, where are you off to?" one of his friends challenged as Lord Bainbridge stepped on his toes in his haste.

"I've forgotten something," Lord Bainbridge answered, still struggling to get clear of the row of seats.

The commotion he was making attracted the attention of a goodly number of the boys in his vicinity. Even Denham turned around to see what was going on. Another boy theorized aloud to the loud guffaws of his companions that obviously, "Bains must have to take a wicked tinkle." At last, Lord Bainbridge found himself in the aisle, and then he looked around in confusion, not sure what to do next. Many boys were looking at him with amused grins on their faces, and though he didn't know it at that moment, even the headmaster had spotted his antics. Taking the only course open to him, Lord Bainbridge turned and trudged up the aisle to the back of the hall. But reaching the closest exit door, he turned around, and with determination spread across his young face like jam, he marched back down the aisle.

This was too much for the headmaster, and stepping up to the podium, he addressed the situation, "If the boy running up and down the aisle will be so kind as to take a seat, we may begin."

Now, everyone in the lecture hall turned their heads, craning their necks to see the cause of the disturbance. But Lord Bainbridge had not come this far to turn back now. In spite of the fact that he knew every eye in the place must be upon him, he took his courage in hand and once again made his way down a row of seats. However, this time it was not his own row, but rather the row in which Denham sat. Behind him, his own friends hollered and hooted to him that he was in the wrong row, but he pretended not to hear them. Finally, after what certainly had seemed to him to have been the longest journey of his life, Lord Bainbridge slipped into the vacant seat beside Denham. But he was so embarrassed by his actions, he could do nothing but stare down at his shoes.

"Well done!" the headmaster remarked rather sarcastically, having no idea how well done indeed it really had been.

It was some time before Lord Bainbridge could force himself to raise his eyes, and when he glanced over at Denham, now sitting beside him, he saw an amused grin on the other boy's face and what he was quite certain was a look of keen admiration.

The subject of the headmaster's lecture that day was "The Responsibilities of Today's Students," and as he droned on, Lord Bainbridge felt his heart race. It was not the headmaster's words that were making his heart pound faster and his head swim, but rather, it was because Denham was ever so gently, but persistently nonetheless, pressing his knee against Lord Bainbridge's. And as Lord Bainbridge returned the pressure, feeling the heat of Denham's body pass into his, he felt as if he would burst with happiness. Then Denham let his hand slip down to his thigh, and ever so gently and inconspicuously, he rubbed his knuckles along Lord Bainbridge's leg.

The headmaster's lecture came to an end much too soon as far as Lord Bainbridge was concerned. He could have listened to him all day though in reality, he had heard not a word the man had uttered except at one moment when Denham's movements had aroused him to such a fever pitch, Lord Bainbridge had actually let out a little moan. And it was at that precise instant that he thought he distinctly heard the headmaster utter the word *sodomites*! Not merely uttered it but thundered it out directly at him and Denham. Of course it hadn't really happened, but he had been unnerved enough by the whole situation to think it had or at least it might have.

As the students were making their way out of the lecture hall, Lord Bainbridge was set to go off with his own group. But Denham came up to him, boldly grabbed his hand, and held him back. And that was the true beginning of their relationship. From that moment on, they spent as much time as possible together, each breaking Winchester tradition and abandoning his own friends to be with the other. They would walk arm in arm across the campus or often stroll about the school with arms casually thrown over one another's shoulders. Even in their unflattering school uniforms—a Norfolk jacket of gray tweed, knee breeches, and thick woolen stockings—Lord Bainbridge was convinced Denham looked like a god. And walking beside him, Lord Bainbridge felt a thrill, precipitated as much by Denham's presence as by his own position at his side. They found they had much in common. Neither took much to sports; both were impossible at cricket and avoided football altogether. Denham did a spot of rowing every now and then, and Lord Bainbridge had always been an avid swimmer. At the other end of the spectrum, they both held in marked disdain males who in any way conducted themselves in a feminine manner. Even among the young boys at Winchester, there already were those who pranced about, wore makeup, and genuinely acted the woman's part. They also studiously stayed far away from the school's aesthetes, mostly older boys who displayed airy manners and spouted endless dialogues on the meaning of beauty. They always thought of themselves as actors in some flamboyant play, and Lord Bainbridge and Denham found them boring and ridiculous in their pretentiousness. As the weeks passed and they spent more and more time together, everyone around them knew they had become intimate friends, but few suspected that they had not yet been intimate as well. They had touched frequently, fleeting caresses that aroused and then dashed within seconds. And once Denham had even kissed Lord Bainbridge quickly on the cheek. Often studying together, they would lay one with his head against the chest of the other. But to Lord Bainbridge it seemed as if Denham had willingly taken their relationship to a particular point and then drawn back and would go no further. He didn't sense that Denham was forbidding deeper familiarities outright, only that he was hesitant about taking the final step. True, they both had roommates, Denham had two in fact, so they had to be very careful when they were alone in one another's rooms, for others were always popping in and out. And the schoolboy code at Winchester clearly stated that though two boys might be doing it, they must never be caught doing it.

But Lord Bainbridge was by now so consumed and so convinced that he was deeply in love for the first time in his life that he could think of nothing but getting his beloved into bed. So intense was this desire that he was willing to risk everything and anything to achieve it. He was even willing to risk losing Denham forever if that was the unfortunate outcome. So he laid out careful plans to seduce him.

His opportunity arose much sooner than he had anticipated. As the Christmas holiday approached, Denham informed him, rather gloomily, that his parents had written him that they would be going to Bavaria for Christmas to be with his older brother who had married a German girl who had just given birth to their first grandchild. Whether Denham had not been invited to accompany them or had chosen on his own not to go, Lord Bainbridge was never clear. Hastily, he wrote a letter to his own mother, seeking permission for Denham to join them for the Christmas holiday. He dreaded her response; knowing her contrary nature, he feared she might refuse. But by return post, permission was received. Denham was overjoyed that they would be spending the time together, and Lord Bainbridge wondered, with a shiver of delight, if his friend perhaps had plans of his own.

Two days before Christmas, a motor-cab from Victoria Station dropped them off at the entrance to Belgrave Square. Motor vehicles of any type were forbidden to enter the square itself for fear they might disturb the tranquility of its residents. Carrying their cases, the two boys strolled down to the very end of the square and stopped before number 124. Denham's reaction was typical of many when they first set eyes upon Bellington House.

"It's a castle!" he exclaimed, tilting his head backward to take it all in.

"And it's as cold as a bloody tomb all year round," Lord Bainbridge informed him.

Bellington House stood in its own private little park at the far end of Belgrave Square surrounded by a high iron gate. It did indeed bear strong resemblance to a castle with its impressive stone facade that stretched up five stories and towered ominously over all the other buildings in the square. To some of the Bainbridges' neighbors, the building was considered an eyesore, and only the previous year, a petition had been passed around the square suggesting that the house be torn down and replaced with something a bit more subtle. But the Bainbridge name still wheedled its share of influence, and the petition was quickly and quietly abandoned. Though this was the family's main residence, they also had a seaside retreat at Brighton, a country estate in Surrey, and various scattered rental properties in both town and country.

Lord Bainbridge had not even reached for the bell when the front door swung open, and a smiling face greeted them. This was William Hodges, the family butler. He had only been with them for two years, but he was already a valuable and trusted member of the household. Tall and dignified, he was always very proper in his manner and attire, a black mourning coat and stiff collar. Although he was considered young to be in such a prestigious position, he was only in his midthirties, he was of the old school in the way he conducted himself. And most important of all, he seemed to have found favor with the hard-to-please mistress of the house.

His greeting was friendly but within the bounds of propriety. "It's good to have you home again, Your Lordship. You're looking well."

"Thank you, Hodges," Lord Bainbridge responded. "This is my friend Mr. Granville-Smith."

Hodges quickly turned his attention to Dehham. "Welcome to Bellington House, sir. I hope you enjoy your stay."

Denham smiled and nodded, but he was still too in awe of the building they had just entered to speak. The entrance hall, in which they now stood, seemed to be cathedral in size, and its ceiling rose four stories above their heads. From the first floor landing, which was directly opposite them, the unsmiling portraits of Bainbridge ancestors peered down at them with what could only be called haughty indifference.

Meanwhile, Lord Bainbridge was making an inquiry. "How is Mr. Keys faring these days?"

Hodges frowned and then quickly twisted it into a patient smile. "As well as can be expected, sir," he answered. "You know, he'll be ninety-six come next March."

Keys was his predecessor, and it was probably natural that Hodges might feel a tug of resentment toward the man whose shoes he had to fill. For Keys had been something of a legend, having stood in faithful service in the Bainbridge household for over seventy years only finally stepping down when he had become practically blind and deaf and thus severely limited in the duties he could perform. Reluctantly, he had been sent off to live in a small house in the country with a middle-aged couple to care for him through his remaining years. Though most all the members of the household missed him when he finally left, it was the young lord who missed him the most of all. Keys had been the nearest thing to a father Jeremy had ever known. Even though Keys was already an old man when Jeremy was born, he delighted in the child, spoiled him outrageously, and spent endless hours entertaining him. Jeremy would follow him around like a puppy. And it was Jeremy who had given him the name *Keys* because of the great ring of keys, one for every room in the house, that he wore at his waist.

"And Mrs. Foxworthy?" Lord Bainbridge asked, mentioning another favorite.

"I'm afraid she's no longer with us, sir," Hodges replied.

Lord Bainbridge was taken back, "She's dead?"

"No, sir, relieved of her position," Hodges informed him.

Lord Bainbridge nodded. That was not unexpected. Housekeepers flew in and out of this house faster than drafts.

"Your mother is in the morning room, sir. She's expecting you," Hodges told him. The two boys followed him across the parquet floor, polished to such a high degree they could actually see their reflections in it.

As Hodges's hand reached out to turn the knob of the door to the morning room, Lord Bainbridge nudged his companion. "Brace yourself," he told him with a wink.

Lady Sybil Bainbridge sat on a sofa covered with a hand-painted tapestry of green and gold depicting knights and their fair ladies. The sofa was positioned in the exact center of the room so that the eyes of anyone coming through the door from the entrance hall would immediately fall on it. And of course on Lady Bainbridge. This was not some mere chance of interior design. Every room in the house, except the servants' quarters that were tucked up under the eaves on the fifth floor and where Lady Bainbridge would never have ventured even if the house was on fire and that was the last refuge, had been meticulously arranged down to the last detail by Lady Bainbridge herself. Every item of furniture, every painting or other work of art, every carpet and drape, even the fresh flowers, which were replaced every morning, were set out in her precise and prescribed manner. And woe to the poor, misguided servant who, through error or negligence, moved or otherwise altered a single item. Lady Bainbridge had taken great pains to assure that the rooms of her home reflected her tastes, her preferences, and even her beliefs. But most importantly of all, whichever room she was in, she must always be the center of attention in that room. Everything around her was a stage, and she was the leading actress. Everyone else was at best a bit player.

"Here you are at last," she said to the boys as they came into the room. "I'd almost given you up," she added, which was rather a strange remark since there had been no exact time set for their arrival and it was hardly past noon.

"Hello, Mother," Lord Bainbridge greeted her, leaning down to place the expected peck on her cheek that was briefly offered.

"I think we'll have tea and cakes now," Lady Bainbridge instructed Hodges who nodded and quickly left the room.

"Mother, this is Denham Granville-Smith," Lord Bainbridge announced, giving his friend a little nudge toward the sofa.

Denham smiled, took Lady Bainbridge's hand, and made a nice little bow, which Lord Bainbridge found quite impressive. "I'm very pleased to meet you, Lady Bainbridge," Denham told her. "And thank you so much for your kind hospitality."

Lady Bainbridge exhibited a most gracious smile and gave him a quick glance of appraisal. "You're welcome, Denham. I'm happy that you were able to join us for the holiday."

The two boys took chairs opposite the sofa, and for the next few minutes, they answered Lady Bainbridge's questions about how things were progressing at Winchester.

As they talked, Lady Bainbridge remained sitting on the edge of the sofa, her body leaning slightly toward them, her legs crossed, her hands folded out in front of her. She always sat on the edge of whatever piece of furniture she was occupying. Not as if she were about to take flight but rather as if she feared she might be instantly called away to rectify some misdeed or miscalculation that had befallen her household. This afternoon, she was wearing a long flowing dress of white and silver with just a thin thread of red woven through the material. She put as much thought into her wardrobe as she did into the rooms of her home, and as a result, her dresses changed hues as the seasons of the year changed their colors.

Even in middle age, Sybil Bainbridge retained a youthful beauty. Fair, with skin like fine porcelain and blue-gray eyes that were hard and knowing and had no need of spectacles, she had the look of a woman far younger than herself. But with this beauty, there also came vanity. She could never pass a mirror without an appraising glance, and most always, a hand would reach out to smooth away a touch of unwanted moisture or push back an errant curl. She had been brought up in a proper Victorian home where, as a young girl, she had been taught all the graces. As an adult, she painted delicate little scenes of flowers and birds, played the piano delightfully, and sang in a pleasant contralto. The center of Lady Bainbridge's life was her home where she entertained frequently, giving fabulous dinner parties and afternoon teas that were talked about for weeks afterward. Outside of her home, she was a completely different person—shy, retiring, one almost completely lacking in personality. She therefore only ventured outside her home on rare occasions to visit her small circle of friends or to attend to a bit of charity work. She much preferred to stay in her own home where she was mistress of the hearth and queen of the castle.

Their conversation about Winchester was interrupted by the reapperance of Hodges. This time, he was accompanied by a young maid in a starched uniform pushing a tea trolley that contained, in addition to a silver Georgian teapot and cups and saucers of flowered porcelain, delicate wafer-thin slices of raspberry and lemon cake. Though the job of pouring the tea and serving the cake would normally have been that of the hostess, Lady Bainbridge was perfectly content to let Hodges and the young maid fulfill that duty. Of course, she watched them carry out the task with a critical eye, but she made no comment except to remind Denham that all boys loved cake.

Lord Bainbridge took no cake himself, and he drank little tea, for he had observed that the young maid, as she went about her business, was flirting rather blatantly with Denham. *God,* Lord Bainbridge thought to himself with jealous indignation, *he's so incredibly good-looking no one can resist him.* He noticed that his mother also had not missed the maid's misconduct, and a single raised eyebrow told him, most assuredly, that the unfortunate girl would be gone by morning. This immediately eased his discomfort, and he finally reached for a slice of cake himself.

Though Lady Bainbridge was commonly known as a mild-mannered woman who never raised her voice and had never been known to lose her temper, at least not in public, when it came to the servants in her household, she could be and often was nothing less than a tyrant. Servants came and went through the back door of Bellington House with stunning regularity. Governesses, grooms, gardeners, maids, and especially housekeepers were dismissed on a regular basis. Many did not even last beyond their first day. Lady Bainbridge was so demanding in her expectations that a number of the agencies that handled domestic workers reached a point where they would no longer send her candidates to be considered for employment. And she could be devious too. She was not above setting traps to see if her servants were properly carrying out their daily duties. One of her favorite snares was to purposely discard a handkerchief behind the sofa pillows in the morning room, and if it was still there the next day, the parlor maid would instantly be given the sack. Among Lady Bainbridge's most persistent crusades when it came to the perfection of her home involved the salvation of her expensive carpets. More than one young and inexperienced girl had been let go because she had committed the cardinal sin of raising the window shades to their full extent and thus exposing Lady Bainbridge's precious carpets to the full damage of the day's sun.

Of course, there were exceptions—servants who managed to survive the rigors of employment at Bellington House although there number certainly was small.

Keys was one of those. He had been with the family since long before the current
Lady Bainbridge had arrived, and she had kept him on because of his devotion
to the family and only made him retire when his infirmities got the best of him.
Hodges, the new butler, too seemed to be working out well. And then there was
the seemingly indestructible Ms. Sprauge. She was Lady Bainbridge's personal
maid and had been for over thirty years. All the other servants called her the
Angel of Mercy, not only because she had survived so long in what surely must
have been the most difficult and demanding job in the whole household, but also
because she would, on occasion, try and intercede on behalf of a servant who had
fallen into Lady Bainbridge's bad graces. But Ms. Sprauge would only go to bat
for a servant whom she felt stood a chance of becoming a valuable employee.
Most of those who fell into disgrace, she agreed with her mistress, were hopeless
cases and should be cast out immediately without references.

Besides Keys, the old butler, the one other servant Lord Bainbridge remembered
fondly from his childhood days was Lizzie Manners, the family nanny. She had
taken care of him from the age of three until he was almost ten. A big-boned
North County woman, she always smelled of talcum powder and jam. And Lord
Bainbridge's fondest recollections were of the times Lizzie would hoist him up into
her large lap and tell him fairy stories, ones that she had made up herself. She
would spin wonderful fantasies filled with brave heroes, dastardly villains, and
amazing creatures like dragons and unicorns. Her stories would often continue for
days at a time with her little charge eagerly awaiting the next exciting installment.
Lord Bainbridge had wept for weeks after Lizzie too was inevitably dismissed,
most probably over some minor infraction. Later, when as an adult he wrote his
first book, he found himself often wishing Lizzie was still there so he could show
it to her. He knew she would have been proud of him and happy for him.

After the tea things had been cleared away and the three of them were alone
again, Lord Bainbridge remained for the most part silent, listening to his mother
and Denham carry on a conversation. He liked to watch Denham when he was
talking to someone else—his face lit up, and he became very animated, and as far
as Lord Bainbridge was concerned, this made him even more attractive if that
was humanly possible. Denham wore his blond hair long, almost down to his
collar, and parted in the middle. When he talked excitedly, which he was doing
at that moment, his hair kept falling into his face, and he would throw it back
with a toss of his head. It was a simple gesture but one that so entranced Lord
Bainbridge—he had tried to mimic it himself, standing before his own mirror.
But unfortunately, he quickly found out that his own rather limp brown hair was
not made for such spontaneous carefree gestures.

Lord Bainbridge couldn't also help but notice how utterly charming his
mother was being to Denham, laughing at his amusing school stories, chastising
him gently like a fond parent when he confessed to some minor misdeed. *She's*

playing the gracious hostess to the hilt, Lord Bainbridge thought sourly. For he knew she really wasn't listening to a word Denham was saying. Oh, she was nodding and smiling and making all the appropriate comments, but what he was actually saying held no interest for her. Lord Bainbridge could see the telltale slightly glazed look in her eyes, the same look they had when she was speaking to one of the servants. Lady Bainbridge had not asked Denham a single question about his home, his parents, or anything else about his personal life. She had not because the fact was these were things she didn't care about. Denham was her son's friend, and as such, he was welcome in her home; beyond that he didn't exist as far as she was concerned.

In due time, Lord Bainbridge's two sisters presented themselves to meet his school chum. Although they were dressed alike in white lace, the two girls were a study in contrast. Helen, the eldest, was seventeen. She was dark in coloring and plain in appearance. And where as a sunny smiling demeanor would have greatly softened her looks and made her more attractive, as it did for her brother, her mood was always sullen and unresponsive. She went and sat down at the opposite end of the sofa from her mother, folded her arms, and frowned. Her opposite, Amber, was thirteen and very pretty. Fair, she was a carbon copy of her mother and as merry as her sister was despondent. Her name had originally been Hazel, but when at the age of four, her mother determined that she was going to grow up to be a beauty, Lady Bainbridge had her rechristened Amber. And Amber she remained except when Lord Bainbridge resorted to teasing his younger sister by calling her Hazel, which never failed to send the child screaming in tears to her mother. Amber placed herself on a footstool at her mother's feet and rested her arm in her mother's lap as if the two of them were posing to have their portrait painted.

Watching his two sisters, Lord Bainbridge reflected on the sorry fact that there was no natural bond of affection between the three of them. They were his sisters; that didn't make them his friends. But it went deeper than that, and as expected, it all went back to Lady Bainbridge as most things did. Of her three children, Amber was the one who mattered to her. Certainly not her son, for she had never wanted a boy, and not her firstborn daughter who to be sure had not turned out to her expectations. It was not that she abused Jeremy or his sister, she simply denied them that which all children want most from their parents—attention. Amber was the one who had her undivided attention, and Amber was the one person she truly cared about besides herself.

After they had visited for about an hour, Lady Bainbridge suggested the boys might want to go to their rooms and get themselves settled in. "I've had the servants open up one of the bedrooms in the west wing for your friend," Lady Bainbridge told her son. "It's a nice room with plenty of light."

Lord Bainbridge felt his heart fall into his shoes. All the plans he had made were about to come undone. The west wing was on the far side of the house, seemingly miles from his own room. She might just as well have put Denham on the moon. Lord Bainbridge thought fast. "It'll be like a barn in there even with a fire," he protested. "I thought we could share my room. There's plenty of space. And it will give the servants one less room to clean," he added, thinking that in turn would give his mother one less room to have to check to see that the servants had carried out their duties to her high specifications.

Lady Bainbridge gave this suggestion a few moments of thought, and then she nodded her approval. "Yes, we must always think of ways to lighten the servants' burden," she added with just a thin veil of sarcasm in her tone. As the two boys prepared to leave the room, she issued a reminder. "Dinner is at seven sharp."

Once outside the morning room, Lord Bainbridge led the way across the entrance hall to the lift. He opened the door, and the two of them stepped inside the tiny box. Its wooden walls were decorated with carved scrolls and bunches of grapes. There was hardly room for two people inside as the lift had originally been designed to carry a single person at a time. Lord Bainbridge closed the door, pushed a button, and they began their ascent. They were crushed tightly together, which he didn't mind at all. And in his excitement, he boldly wrapped his arms around his friend. From the look on his face, Denham didn't seem to mind either.

"Well, what did you think of my family?" Lord Bainbridge asked. "Were they as horrible as I made them out to be?"

"Not at all," Denham assured him. "Your mother especially was very cordial."

Lord Bainbridge frowned. "Yes"—he nodded—"mother is nothing if not cordial."

The lift came to a sudden jerky halt, pushing them even closer together and prompting their bodies to come into intimate contact. This action startled them both and embarrassed Lord Bainbridge so much he quickly pushed open the door, causing them both to tumble out of the lift as if there had been a wreck and they had been thrown free.

Unable to look at his friend, Lord Bainbridge hurried off down the long corridor toward his bedroom. He was embarrassed both by what had happened and by the way he had reacted to it. At that moment, he seriously doubted his abilities as a seducer.

They reached his room without further incident. Once inside, they found a fire had been started in the fireplace, and the room was warming up nicely. The room, like all of the rooms in the house, was of stark dignity with a high ceiling, lots of carved moldings, and tall windows that reached to the floor and looked, especially at night, like ominous dark portals leading to another world. Through the years, these same windows had been the source of many a fearful nightmare for the room's young occupant. The furniture was all heavy Edwardian stained in dark mahogany. The bed was gigantic, and it sat up on a raised platform that made it look even bigger.

Denham was impressed, "That's one hell of a bed!"

"I've slept in that bed all my life," Lord Bainbridge told him, relaxed now, having got over his near fright in the lift.

"That bed could easily sleep twenty," Denham added.

"Two will be plenty," Lord Bainbridge said, smiling at him and once again making his plans.

Denham smiled back at him, his devastating smile that Lord Bainbridge knew so well and that had tortured him so since the first moment they had set eyes upon one another. Perhaps Denham was about to say something, but they were interrupted by a brisk knock on the door.

Before Lord Bainbridge could respond, the door swung open, and a footman came into the room carrying their cases. He paused, glancing from one to the other. "Where do you want these, sir?" he asked.

The footman was young and quite good-looking with dark eyes and a fine nose. Lord Bainbridge had never seen him before, and there was something about the way the young man was looking at them that he found offensive. He could only have been a couple of years older than they were, and yet the grin on his face, said he considered them both to be mere children and, worse than that, children who had been up to some naughty play. "Put the cases over there," Lord Bainbridge said curtly, pointing to the foot of the bed.

The footman obeyed and then turned back to them. This time, he spoke directly to Lord Bainbridge. "Will there be anything else, sir?" The knowing grin was still spread across his lips.

Lord Bainbridge was aware that Denham was staring at the footman with interest. "You're new here, aren't you?" Lord Bainbridge asked the servant.

The footman nodded eagerly. "Yes, sir, just started this week. Pip of a house if I might say so."

Well you needn't bother to unpack your own bags, Lord Bainbridge thought to himself, sure that his mother had already marked this one down as most unsatisfactory and he'd more than likely be out the door by daybreak. "That will be all," he said aloud to the footman who nodded and left the room.

"Cheeky bounder," Lord Bainbridge muttered under his breath.

"Did you ever do it with a servant?" Denham asked as the door closed behind the retreating footman.

Shocked, Lord Bainbridge spun around to look at him. "What?" he exclaimed.

"Well some of them are quite attractive," Denham went on. "That one, for instance," he added, referring to the recently departed footman.

Lord Bainbridge was so appalled by Denham's suggestion he could barely find the words to express his indignation. "I would never—not with a servant! Why it's just not done!" he said, seeking refuge in the den of propriety and proper etiquette.

But Denham seemed completely oblivious to the little storm he had blown up. He merely shrugged and began to move casually about the room, inspecting this and that.

While poor Lord Bainbridge stood there, all the color gone from his face and still so horrified by Denham's suggestion that for a moment, if only a moment, he was even put off by Denham himself and wondered if he had made a mistake bringing him home with him.

"Are these your toys?" Denham asked innocently. He had stopped before a low table on which an army of toy soldiers were on display, some engaged in fierce battle, others in smart parade.

"Yes." Lord Bainbridge nodded, and as he watched Denham out of the corner of his eye, he tried to figure out if he was more upset at what Denham had suggested or because he had obviously been attracted to the footman.

"Most impressive," was Denham's opinion of the military exhibit and then something else caught his attention. Crossing to a bureau, he picked up a photograph in a silver frame. He stared at it for a long moment before he asked the inevitable. "Who is this?"

Coming up beside him, Lord Bainbridge stared down at the photograph in Denham's hand. It was very old, a tintype, and it was of a young man hardly into his twenties. The young man was handsome, with a thin mustache, wavy dark hair, and a stare into the camera that was so intense, it almost made one nervous to stare back at it.

"That's my father," Lord Bainbridge told him. "It's the only photograph that was ever taken of him."

"What happened to him?" Denham wanted to know, still staring at the photograph in his hand.

"He died," Lord Bainbridge answered. "My mother said it was the influenza. I never knew him. I was only about three when he died."

"Do you remember him at all?"

"No, not a memory. I've tried very hard, but there's simply nothing there. He's like a ghost to me," Lord Bainbridge said. And at that moment, he thought of something else that he always did whenever he thought of his father, which he did a lot especially when he was melancholy.

And the thought was this: was it because he had been brought up almost exclusively with women that he was as he was? Growing up, he had often thought of his house as a nunnery, surrounded as he was by women: his mother, his two sisters, all the female servants and, of course, the never-ending parade of maiden aunts. He had been almost completely devoid of any male influence except for the occasional male servant such as Keys. Moreover, he had been kept in this perhaps unhealthy atmosphere for longer than most boys of his class normally were. Most upper-class boys, their parents guided by the rather brutal and exclusively British system of educating its young sons, were torn away from the family hearth at the tender age of eight or nine and shipped off to boarding schools. But instead, Lord Bainbridge at that age became what was called a day boy, meaning that his mother sent him to a nearby school every morning, and he returned home every evening. He was fourteen before he left home for the first time to attend Winchester. If his father had not died but had been there all the years he was growing up, would he have turned out to be what everyone else referred to as normal? It was a question that haunted him every time he looked at his father's photograph.

"Your father was very handsome," Denham commented.

"Yes," Lord Bainbridge agreed. "And my mother is very beautiful. So I wonder what happened to me."

"Oh, I'd say you turned out quite all right," Denham said with a smile as for a moment their hands touched together on the photograph. And the footman was banished from both their minds forever.

They spent the remainder of the afternoon unpacking their things, and Lord Bainbridge showed Denham his books and some of the things he had written. As they began to dress for dinner, Lord Bainbridge turned up the lamps.

"Did I tell you I'm afraid of the dark?" Denham said as he fiddled with his shirt collar. "I have to have a light on when I sleep."

"When I was a child, I had such a terrible fear of the darkness I couldn't sleep without a candle in my room," Lord Bainbridge said. "Then one night, my nanny sat me down and explained to me that there was nothing in the darkness that was not there in the light. 'After all,' she said to me, 'Darkness is only the absence of light.'"

"Is that supposed to make me feel better about the dark?" Denham asked, raising his eyebrows.

"It worked for me," Lord Bainbridge told him.

"I'll keep the candle, thank you very much," Denham said, playfully throwing a pillow across the room at him.

Dinner that evening was, as far as Lord Bainbridge was concerned, an interminable affair that he feared would go on until dawn. Ever the correct hostess, Lady Bainbridge saw to it that each meal presented under her roof lived up to the fabulous expectations of the Edwardian appetite. Taking their cue from their monarch, Edward VII, a man of ample girth who loved his food, Edwardian ladies and gentlemen likewise loved to eat. In an age known for its extravagance, each Edwardian meal was an event, and dinners in particular were sumptuous affairs that could run to as many as eleven courses. Servants completely cleared away the dishes from one course before setting down the next. This meant that meals could go on for hours. No one rushed. Food was intended to be digested at a leisurely pace, savored, and enjoyed, not tossed down one's gullet as if everyone at the table was in a race to see who could be the first to clear his or her plate. But all of Mrs. Sheffield's, the cook, efforts on this particular evening, and she was one of the best at her art in all of London, were lost on Lord Bainbridge. So nervous and keyed up with anticipation was he that he plowed through everything—the barley soup, the poached salmon, the filet mignon, the asparagus salad, even the chocolate eclairs, which Mrs. Sheffield had prepared especially for him, knowing they were his favorites—tasting nothing. It was a wonder he didn't give himself a severe case of indigestion.

When the meal was finally over and they were excused from the table, it was almost ten. The two boys retired to Lord Bainbridge's bedroom where they sat before the fire for some time—Lord Bainbridge sprawled in a wicker chair, Denham at his feet, his knees drawn up. Watching the fire, they spoke softly about everyday things, mostly school things, other boys at Winchester, and the schoolwork they would have waiting for them when they returned in two weeks.

As they sat there, it seemed like such a natural thing for Lord Bainbridge to reach down and stroke Denham's hair. Like a cat being petted, Denham appeared to luxuriate under his touch. He threw back his head, and a sound, not unlike a purr, murmured forth from his lips.

After a while, Lord Bainbridge got quickly to his feet. "I think it's time for bed," he announced with a nervous quake in his voice.

"Right you are!" Denham agreed, also standing up.

As they both started to undress, Lord Bainbridge crossed to one of the room's two large mahogany dressers. "Did you bring pajamas?" he asked over his shoulder. "If not, you can borrow a pair of mine."

"I don't wear pajamas," Denham answered.

And when Lord Bainbridge turned quickly back to him, he received an even greater shock. For Denham stood before him stark naked, his clothes in a pile at his feet, a mischievous grin on his face.

Of course, Lord Bainbridge couldn't take his eyes off Denham's body, which was just starting to pass from boyish thinness to a more manly development. His limbs were just starting to take on a thickness and become more defined while his whole body glowed in the firelight, all golden but as if it was lit not by the fire but from within. Lord Bainbridge could also not help but notice that there wasn't a hair on his young body save the few scattered almost apologetically around his groin.

"It's cold!" Denham shivered, and he leaped into bed, pulling the covers around him. "Come on," he encouraged. And when Lord Bainbridge, who was still only half undressed, continued to hesitate, Denham began to tease him. "Don't stand there like a dolt. What are you shy about?"

What Lord Bainbridge was shy about was the fact that the sight of Denham's nakedness had aroused him like their closeness in the elevator had, and he feared letting him see the result which was so angry and defiant, he feared it was about to poke a hole through the trousers he still wore. But a threat from Denham that he was going to go to sleep then, roused him into action, and tearing off the remainder of his clothes, Lord Bainbridge slipped naked into bed beside his friend.

Now that they were in bed together, even Denham suddenly seemed to have lost his boldness. They both lay on their own side of the bed, close to the edge, and as far away from each other as possible. When he had been a child, Lord Bainbridge had loved the vastness of his bed and roamed about it nightly in boyish adventures. But now, he cursed its size, feeling as if he were adrift on some endless sea, miles away from civilization, miles away from Denham.

"I'm still cold," Denham said after a few moments of silence.

It was Lord Bainbridge who went to him. Their arms wound around each other, the breath of each boy warming the cheek of the other. And Lord Bainbridge had ample proof that Denham's passion had likewise been aroused. Then there followed a dreadful moment when neither boy seemed to know what to do next. But the moment quickly passed, and they kissed. At first tentatively and then, as if they both realized all caution had already been thrown to the wind, with much feeling as if each were trying to suck the very breath of life out of the other. When the moment of decision came, the moment to decide who would play which part, Lord Bainbridge was content to let Denham have his way. And as he felt Denham behind him and he bent to his will, he surrendered everything he had, his body, his soul, and his heart, to his lover.

"I love you," Lord Bainbridge whispered softly not even sure if Denham heard him. But it didn't matter. He knew. That was enough.

Chapter III

Sunday, April 14, 1912

The *Titanic's* swimming pool, one of the first ever on a seagoing vessel, was located far down in the bowels of the ship on F deck. While not Olympian in size, it still measured an impressive thirty-two feet by thirteen feet and was over six feet in depth. It also boasted heated changing cubicles so that no one would catch a chill changing into their bathing costumes. From the first day of the voyage, a steady stream of passengers, first-class only of course, had enjoyed this unique facility. To many of them, the idea of swimming in a heated pool in the middle of the cold North Atlantic held a perverse sense of delight as if they were doing something that was almost forbidden, something that was contrary to all the rules of man and nature. Since mixed bathing was considered socially unacceptable, the pool was reserved for ladies in the morning while gentlemen had use of it in the afternoon.

On their second lap of the pool, Lord Bainbridge pulled ahead and easily outdistanced his competitor. As they reached the end of the pool, they both took a moment to catch their breath. Then the other swimmer shook his head in admiration. "You're too fast for me, mate," he confessed.

Lord Bainbridge smiled. "Oh, I don't know, you were right there with me 'till the end," he acknowledged graciously.

"Another go at it?" the other man suggested.

"Some other time," Lord Bainbridge told him. "I'm going to find some food. I've worked up a fine appetite."

"How about if we meet here same time tomorrow for a rematch?" his rival suggested.

"Done!" Lord Bainbridge agreed good-naturedly. His fellow swimmer gave him a wave before he plunged off across the pool again.

Lord Bainbridge climbed out of the water, up the iron steps to the pool deck. Grabbing a towel, he began to vigorously dry his hair. He had been swimming since he was a child and had become somewhat of an expert. In fact, when he moved on to Oxford University from Winchester, he could have easily made the Oxford swim team had he not been otherwise occupied. Swimming had become his preferred form of exercise, and it pleased him to some extent that here was at least one manly pursuit that he was good at.

After having slept soundly for a good six hours, although alas no pleasant dreams had entertained him, he had risen and dressed and come down here for an invigorating swim. And now, as he had mentioned, he was starved. He would go up and see if his friend Maude would join him for luncheon. He made his way along the blue and white tiled walkway, passing the Greek columns that seemed to be part of every swimming pool he had ever known and was about to head into his changing cubicle, where he had left his clothes, when he looked up to see a familiar face. He frowned for a second, acknowledging it was not a face he was terribly pleased to see.

The American was leaning on the iron railing that encircled the complete circumference of the pool. But he was not watching the spirited actions of those still in the water rather he was staring directly across the room at Lord Bainbridge. And his lips were twisted into that annoying smile, a smirk really, that he was so famous for—half mocking, half licentious.

To say that Ronnie Standish was of favored appearance was like saying the *Titanic* was a big ship. He was a very handsome young man, in his midtwenties prime, whose olive complexion, dark animated eyes, high royal cheekbones, full lips, and slightly long black hair, which he wore combed down over his forehead, all combined to give him a distinctly Mediterranean look. Ronnie's features would have been captivating enough on one of a melancholy nature, but he always seemed to be smiling, laughing, or joking in a very exhilarated manner, which made him appear even more attractive. He seldom frowned, but when he did, it was with much displeasure that caused the lines at the corners of mouth to turn very cruel. Well-built, of average height with slim hands that were surprisingly strong, he carried himself with a confident almost haughty air. Although his dark good looks were not to come into popular vogue for another ten years, when the still infant silver screen would provide an endless parade of Latin lovers, Ronnie Standish still managed to rouse feminine passions. Perhaps the women of 1912 were not quite ready to admit it to themselves or to anyone else for that matter, but the slightly menacing look he gave off was often what increased their heart rate. He looked somewhat evil, the type of man that might—heaven forbid!—force himself upon a woman. But in truth, there was something rather sad about all these eager young women, and there were many of them, who pursued him merely because of the way he looked. It was made even more pathetic by the fact that he had no interest in them. To him, they were of no more importance than the flies that buzzed around his head on a hot summer's day.

As usual, Ronnie was dressed to the nines. He wore a light gray wool suit with a bright red tie underneath a stiff collar, a darker gray wool overcoat draped over his shoulders, and a soft gray fedora on his head. One pearl-gray gloved hand clutched an ebony walking stick.

"You seem to have recovered nicely," Ronnie said as he strolled leisurely across the walkway to join him. He offered a cigarette from a gold case that Lord Bainbridge accepted.

"Recovered?" Lord Bainbridge questioned.

Ronnie struck a match. "When I saw you last night, or rather early this morning, you and your young friend were headed up on deck. And you did not appear to be feeling any pain," he explained.

"I was not drunk," Lord Bainbridge said with stiff indignation.

"No?"

"No!"

"Well then, congratulations on an impressive impersonation," Ronnie told him. He indicated the lighted match in his hand. "Do you mind? I'm about to set my thumb on fire."

"Sorry," Lord Bainbridge said, leaning down to take his light. Raising his head, he found himself staring straight into Ronnie's dark smiling face, his lively eyes seeming to take in everything missing nothing. Nervously, Lord Bainbridge shifted his own eyes away. "Did you come down for a swim?" he asked.

Ronnie seemed horrified by the suggestion as if he considered swimming to be an occupation only to be indulged in by the lower classes. "Heavens no!" he protested. "I can't swim a stroke."

"Just to look then," Lord Bainbridge suggested, the malice in his voice intended.

But Ronnie seldom took offense at anything that was said to him. He gave Lord Bainbridge's red-and-white-striped bathing costume a casual glance and, smiling, shook his head. "Hardly that either."

At their first meeting, which had taken place at a pub called the Crown in Charing Cross Road, it had been quickly established between them that, in spite of the fact that neither of them preferred the company of women, there was no danger of them coming together in a sexual manner. Ronnie had made it known that he also fancied lads of the working class. "Sex with one's own class is very tedious," he had told Lord Bainbridge at the time. "There is no mystery about it, no delightful air of the unknown. And most importantly, there is no danger."

Thinking back to that first meeting between them, Lord Bainbridge recalled how it had been just a chance encounter that might never have happened had he arrived at the pub an hour later or an hour earlier. He couldn't quite remember when it had taken place, but he had a feeling it had been sometime in the previous December. The Crown was a place that Alfred had first taken him to. Its clientele consisted of young out-of-work rogues and soldiers struggling to exist on their meager wages as well as gentlemen of more substantial means who desired the company of such needy youths and were more than willing to help supplement their earnings. But even before their first encounter, Lord Bainbridge had heard stories through the grapevine about the extremely good-looking American and his outrageous doings such as driving a motor car madly through the streets of London, that moment's favorite renter, a name often applied to those boys or young men who made themselves available for a price, sitting boldly at his side, or appearing in a box at the London Pavilion with another for-hire escort. After that first night, Lord Bainbridge kept running into Ronnie at various pubs and clubs throughout the city. They would often sit together for a couple of hours, smoke and drink and check out the young men who would parade before them. Their relationship remained casual and in no way intimate. Though Ronnie seemed to think of them as friends, Lord Bainbridge considered them as merely acquaintances who shared a common lifestyle, which a great deal of the rest of society would have considered quite uncommon. On a couple of occasions, Lord Bainbridge was certain, though he had no proof, that Alfred had procured a young man for Ronnie and, in exchange, received payment for his services. But if it was so, Lord Bainbridge shrugged it off, unwilling to begrudge Alfred a few extra pounds.

From their time together, Lord Bainbridge learned a little of Ronnie's history. He was apparently from a wealthy proper Bostonian family who proudly claimed to be able to trace their lineage in a direct line all the way back to the *Mayflower*. This to not a few Englishmen he encountered seemed a rather petty boast at best, given the fact that there were many of their own countrymen who could make such an ancestral journey all the way back to William the Conqueror. Ronnie was just finishing up a European grand tour, which had also included Egypt and Greece. And Egypt, Lord Bainbridge had to remind himself, was the very first place they had ever set eyes upon one another, even before that first meeting in the pub, though they had not exchanged a single word and their time together had been but a moment. It had taken place the previous spring, and Lord Bainbridge had always thought of the whole affair as that terrible business in Egypt. There was one other fact concerning Ronnie that he could not forget: this grand tour was also his honeymoon. Before setting out on his European tour, Ronnie Standish had taken a wife.

Upon first hearing this news, Lord Bainbridge had surmised that he had done so for respectability. Certainly, there were enough rumors constantly swirling around Ronnie's head to perhaps persuade him that a touch of respectability certainly could do him no harm. His manner, the way he conducted himself in public, in itself was enough to give one pause. He was very flamboyant, not in a feminine airy manner, but more in an exaggerated loud way as if everything he said and did was of the utmost importance not only to himself but to everyone else within earshot. If he saw a young man he thought was attractive, he was not reluctant to say so no matter who else might be in his vicinity. In a time when pride in what they were was not a trait shared by others who lived as he did, he was certainly not ashamed of who he was. And somehow he got away with it. Perhaps it was his charm and wit, both of which he had in abundance, that made people overlook the outrageous things he often said and did. He amused them, so they forgave him. But then poor Oscar Wilde had been amusing, and he most assuredly had not been forgiven. Perhaps it was Ronnie's good looks then that pardoned him. How could anyone so attractive be guilty of such horrible things? Maybe if Oscar Wilde had been one to set hearts aflutter, then he too might have been spared. Or perhaps it was the simple fact that there were few outside of the know who got Ronnie Standish. Many passed him off as a spoiled, at times annoying, young man, at worst a dilettante, but most were too ignorant when it came to his way of life to recognize it. They smiled uneasily and shook their heads, but few realized the true sense of what most of society would refer to as his depravity.

"I came down here looking for you," Ronnie told Lord Bainbridge.

"How did you know I would be here?" Lord Bainbridge questioned.

Ronnie chuckled. "Ships' stewards are like servants, they know everything, and for a small fee, they're quite willing to tell what they know. I simply asked your stateroom steward."

"And why would you go to so much trouble?"

"To chastise you," Ronnie answered.

Lord Bainbridge raised an eyebrow and stared back at him. "Really? And what have I done that would deserve a reprimand?" he asked, just the slightest trace of irritation slipping into his tone.

Ronnie shook an elegant finger at him. "Jeremy, one sleeps with them of course, but one does not dine with them, at least not in a first-class establishment," he answered, seeming to brush aside, at least for the moment, his own parade of indiscretions.

Lord Bainbridge feigned innocence and looked away. "I don't know what you're talking about."

"In the dining saloon last night," Ronnie reminded him. "Having dinner with your young friend. You thought you were safely tucked away in a corner, but everyone saw you."

"So I was having dinner with a friend, so what?" Lord Bainbridge challenged with bravado he did not feel.

"A steward saw your man bring your friend up from below decks, from steerage no less!" Ronnie informed him. "Though I do have to admit that, even from a distance, all spiffed-up he did look quite presentable."

Lord Bainbridge fell into a moody silence. He resented Ronnie's remarks although he knew what he said was all true. He had committed a social blunder, and worse than that, he knew he had treated Tom in a condescending manner.

It had all begun innocently enough when Tom had expressed his wonder at the sight of the first-class dining saloon. Wanting to do something to please him, and yes impress him as well, Lord Bainbridge had impulsively invited him to dine with him there the following evening. But almost immediately after he had extended the invitation, he regretted having done so. His reasons for regret were entirely selfish, and he knew they did not reflect well on himself. But they were concerns he could not ignore. What would people think who saw them together? Would Tom know how to conduct himself in such a place? What if some of his friends came upon them? How would he explain Tom to them? He had made up his mind to cancel the whole thing when Tom showed up at his door as eager and excited as a child at Christmas. He had put on a clean shirt and shined his shoes until you could see your face in them.

"Do I look all right?" he asked hopefully, standing in the doorway.

Lord Bainbridge pulled him into his stateroom, closed the door, kissed him on the mouth, and then steeled himself to tell him that evening clothes were required to take dinner in the first-class dining saloon. A little detail he should have thought of before now. But the look of innocent anticipation on Tom's face almost broke his heart, and he knew he couldn't disappoint him. The only thing left for him to do was try and find something suitable for him to wear. His own clothes would have been much too big as would have Alfred's. Then he remembered Sebastian Renoir and, leaving Tom for a moment, he slipped down the corridor to the Renoirs' stateroom, which was only a few doors down from his own. Madame Renoir, an old friend, was happy to oblige, and she loaned him one of her son's formal evening suits that he had outgrown. It proved to be not a perfect fit, for at fourteen, Sebastian Renoir was already taller then Tom, but it was close enough.

"You sure these clothes are necessary?" Tom asked, fidgeting in the unaccustomed suit. "I'd feel much more comfortable in my own clothes."

Lord Bainbridge assured him they were necessary, and then he pulled him into his arms and kissed him again because he looked so damn handsome all dressed up.

They took the lift down to the first-class dining saloon on D deck, and as they passed through the spacious reception room, Lord Bainbridge nodded to a number of acquaintances, but he did not stop to speak with any of them. They did pause for a moment to listen to the ship's orchestra, which was gathered around the room's large grand piano and entertaining those in the room with a lively selection of American ragtime. The music brought an instant and broad grin to Tom's face, obviously indicating he had never heard such gay toe-tapping music before. It was all Lord Bainbridge could do to pull him away from the music and through the large iron and wood doors that led into the dining saloon. They arrived just at the height of the dinner hour and were greeted by a buzz of activity. The tables were crowded with elegantly attired diners while among them waiters in smart white tunics moved with professional precision, seeing to their every need.

The *Titanic's* first-class dining saloon was one of the ship's crown jewels. It was the largest room afloat, over one hundred feet in length and stretching the entire width of the ship. Five hundred people could be accommodated at one sitting. Done up in the Jacobean style, its richly molded white walls and ceiling, along with ornate leaded glass bay windows, created a light and airy room of understated splendor while the warm oak furniture only added to the feeling of luxurious comfort.

Lord Bainbridge took the headwaiter aside, and in a low voice, he declined his usual table and asked for a more secluded table in one of the room's recessed alcoves that lined both sides of the room and gave one a sense of intimate coziness. He did this in the hope that he and Tom might dine in private and not be disturbed. That he also hoped they would not be discovered by anyone he knew was also in his mind, a fact of which he was not very proud. They were shown to a table for two at the far end of the room as remote a location as was possible in a crowded room capable of holding five hundred people. Their table was set, as all the tables in the room were, with snow-white linens and napkins, a centerpiece of hothouse-grown red roses, polished flatware, each piece adorned with little stars to remind each diner they were on a White Star ship, crystal water goblets and wineglasses, and china dinnerware of blue and gold with the distinct White Star pattern.

After they were seated and the waiter had filled their water goblets and then discreetly withdrawn to give them a few minutes to look over their menus, Tom spoke up from behind his menu, "I promise you, I wouldn't embarrass you."

Lord Bainbridge put down his own menu. "What do you mean?" he asked.

Tom smiled at him. "I know you asked the waiter to put us someplace where we wouldn't be noticed. I'm not stupid," he added.

Lord Bainbridge was instantly filled with guilt and shame. He shook his head. "I'm sorry," he said. "I was being an ass."

"It's all right," Tom told him. "I'm not offended. I can see where you might be worried that I wouldn't know how to behave in a place such as this. But you'll be pleased to learn that my mother taught me proper table manners. She actually did more than that. Although we were poor, she saw to it that I knew how to conduct myself even in surroundings as elegant as these." He winked at Lord Bainbridge. "I even know which fork to use."

The rest of their evening improved from that moment on. As they enjoyed a sumptuous meal, Tom told him about his life back home in Ireland, the life he was leaving behind forever. He related that he had been born in a tiny village on the coast with the quaint name of Cuddy Rook. His father was a fisherman, and his mother did laundry for an Englishman who owned a big manor house and miles of land nearby.

"My first memory," Tom said, "was of the sheets my mother washed and bleached by hand pinned to the clotheslines outside our cottage and flapping in the wind off the ocean like the sails of great ships." He had seven brothers and sisters. "I'm the baby of the family, the last to leave home." One of his sisters had immigrated to America, married, and started to raise a family. She had sent Tom the money for his passage.

As he continued to tell his story, it was obvious to Lord Bainbridge that Tom had great pride and affection for his family. "We were poor, it was true," he admitted. "But when I was growing up, I never realized it. My parents made sure of that. We had plenty to eat, it was warm at night, and we were loved." A deep sadness came into his face when he spoke of the parents he had left behind. "They're getting old now, and they're all alone. They wouldn't let any of us stay behind to take care of them. They insisted that we all must go out and make our own way in the world. 'Each of you must make your own mark no matter how small that mark is,' my father told us." Tom instantly became exuberant again when he spoke of his brothers. "Two of my brothers went to Belfast and took work in the shipyards." He grinned across the table at Lord Bainbridge as if he felt that what he was about to reveal next was just unbelievable beyond words. "They even worked on this ship! They'd write letters home, telling us what a grand ship she was, grandeur even than the one they had just finished building the *Olympic*."

Lord Bainbridge spent most of the meal listening to Tom tell his story, enchanted at the way the young man seemed to find delight in everything. He seemed to see life as a gift that was meant to be opened and enjoyed. And he appeared to have an endless reserve of happiness.

As Lord Bainbridge had hoped, they were not disturbed during the course of their meal. He knew that those of his friends who had become his companions during the voyage, Madame Renoir and her son, dear Maude Manchester, and Alonzo and Lucianna Fraboli were having dinner that night in the restaurant. He had of course been expected to join them, but because of Tom, he had begged off at the last moment. For one disturbing instant, he had spotted Ronnie Standish across the crowded room, but though he certainly must have seen them, the American made no move to come over to their table.

For dessert, they had chocolate and vanilla ice cream, a treat Tom had never sampled before and one he could not stop marveling about. "Do you think they will have this in America?" he asked eagerly.

"I'm sure of it," Lord Bainbridge promised him, smiling. "I think they may have invented it," he added.

As they were finishing their ice cream, an English couple whom Lord Bainbridge knew slightly—they were actually acquaintances of Lady Bainbridge—stopped before their table to exchange a few words. The two young men got to their feet, and after Lord Bainbridge had made the necessary introductions, they exchanged pleasantries and complimentary remarks about the ship. Watching Tom out of the corner of his eye as he conversed easily and even made a little joke that the English couple found terribly amusing, Lord Bainbridge was amazed and greatly relieved. And at the same time he realized that while Tom had conducted himself with grace and even nobility, his own part in this evening's events had been far less noble. He had played the villain, and he was not very proud of himself.

Over their after-dinner coffee and cigarettes, Tom suggested they go back to Lord Bainbridge's stateroom.

But Lord Bainbridge shook his head. "Not yet, my friend. We're going to take brandy and cigars in the smoking room and listen to the millionaires tell each other outrageous lies and exaggerations. Then I'm going to give you a complete tour of the *Titanic's* first-class accommodations."

And that is exactly what they did, wandering for hours through the smoking room, the lounge, and stopping to listen to the ship's orchestra playing in the Palm Court. This time, they were playing waltzes by Strauss, and a number of couples were dancing to the lilting, flowing music. Finally, the two young men ended up on the boat deck to greet the dawn.

Still feeling ashamed of his behavior from the night before, especially in asking for a secluded table in the dining saloon where he and Tom might not be observed by anyone who mattered, Lord Bainbridge questioned Ronnie Standish's own rather hypocritical stance.

"Didn't your idol Oscar Wilde take many meals at the Cafe Royal with his young friends?" he asked, knowing how Ronnie often went about quoting Wilde and likewise thought of himself as equally witty.

Ronnie nodded. "Sadly yes. 'Feasting with panthers,' he called it, and it led to the poor man's downfall."

But Lord Bainbridge disagreed. "Oscar Wilde's downfall was not because of what he did, but because he insisted he had not done it."

"A moot point at best," Ronnie shrugged in indifference. "I hardly think, however, that you should compare yourself to Oscar Wilde," he added as a mild reprimand.

Nor should you, Lord Bainbridge thought to himself, slightly perturbed. He turned away from the pool, tired of the whole conversation. "I have to meet someone for lunch," he said abruptly.

"I'll wait while you change, and we can go up together," Ronnie suggested. Lord Bainbridge's back was to him, so Ronnie didn't catch the grimace that crossed his face as he headed for the changing cubicle where he had left his clothes.

A few minutes later, Lord Bainbridge emerged wearing a navy blue blazer and white flannels. At the same moment, another person also came out of one of the other cubicles. He was a very large man, and he wore a white beach robe, the material of which looked to be straining with great difficulty against the mounds of flesh it was struggling to contain. In sharp contrast to his body, his head looked tiny, and it appeared to sit on top of his thick neck with extreme delicacy as if a simple jar might send it toppling off. His dark hair had streaks of gray, and he wore a mustache and beard, both neatly trimmed.

As the two younger men continued to watch, the newcomer moved to the edge of the pool, stared down at the water for a moment, and then slipped out of his robe, letting it fall at his feet. Underneath his robe, he wore absolutely nothing. He stood there hesitating a moment longer, the folds of his enormous expansion of flesh resting in unflattering naked repose. Finally, he took the plunge into the pool.

"My god," Ronnie exclaimed in shocked disbelief, "did you ever see anything quite so disgusting!"

"That's Benjamin Chamberlin, supposedly one of the richest men in America," Lord Bainbridge informed him. "I saw his picture once in one of the London newspapers."

"Apparently not rich enough to afford a bathing costume," Ronnie observed.

They watched for a few moments as, with expert strokes and surprising agility, Benjamin Chamberlin made his way swiftly through the water. "The paper said he was a champion swimmer in his college days," Lord Bainbridge added.

"Athletic prowess is hardly a worthy substitute for proper decorum," Ronnie sniffed, still deeply offended. "Come along although I for one have lost all appetite for lunch. I may never be able to eat again," he said with a sad shake of his head.

Amused by his reaction, Lord Bainbridge followed him through the door and out into the long corridor of F deck. They had only to wait a moment before the lift appeared in response to their summons. The liftboy, who opened the wrought iron door for them, could not have been more than twelve or thirteen at best, and as they stepped inside the cage, Lord Bainbridge frowned and wondered why a boy so young was so far from home and working. *He should be in school or playing with his friends,* he concluded with a righteous sense of propriety. That the boy's family's economical needs probably necessitated his employment did not occur to him.

As they ascended, Lord Bainbridge noticed that Ronnie had taken an interest in the boy and was chatting quietly with him. Lord Bainbridge couldn't overhear their exact words, but the boy seemed to be responding to Ronnie's questions with a brisk affirmative nod of his head. Once they laughed together over some remark, and for an instant, the boy turned to look over his shoulder at Lord Bainbridge, who was standing slightly behind them. The boy's stare was almost impudent, and from underneath his cap, his eyes regarded Lord Bainbridge with a knowing glance that appeared to far outdistance his young years. Lord Bainbridge quickly turned his own eyes away.

They reached their destination, and the boy slid the door open for them. Lord Bainbridge stepped out of the car, and turning back, he noticed Ronnie slipping a couple of cigarettes into the boy's willing hands. Then the door of the lift closed, the machinery whirled into motion once again, and the lift began its descent.

Standing in the middle of the magnificent A deck foyer with its polished oak wall paneling and elaborate gilded balustrades, Lord Bainbridge stared hard at Ronnie. His words, when they finally came out, were spoken with an edge to them. "Wouldn't you say he was a little young?"

Ronnie seemed unconcerned by his suggestion. "Perhaps a little," he admitted, "but he knows all the ropes. Trust me, he's your typical English renter. Only this one works the deck of a ship instead of a pub or a street corner in Piccadilly." He quickly shrugged off the whole incident and announced that he was off for a brisk walk up on deck. He trotted up the grand staircase toward the boat deck. Halfway up the stairs, he stopped and looked down at Lord Bainbridge. "Jeremy, you really need to loosen up a bit, you're in great danger of becoming a terrible bore like everyone else," he warned him. Then he turned and continued up the grand staircase, whistling a popular air.

Watching the American as he passed an ornamental wall clock on the uppermost landing with its two bronzed classical nymphs symbolizing Honor and Glory crowning Time, Lord Bainbridge reflected on the fact that Ronnie could both amuse and infuriate him. He seemed to be a master at both. And for some reason, he also seemed to have latched onto him as if their friendship had been one of long-standing. During the time when Ronnie had been in London, they had been nothing more than casual acquaintances, denizens of the same pubs, in search of the same game. But since their first day out of Southampton when they had encountered one another quite unexpectedly on deck, Ronnie had acted as if their friendship had always been intense, and he took every opportunity, as he had done this afternoon, to seek him out. And while it is true that intense friendships often take full bloom out on the open sea only to wither and die once land is sighted, Lord Bainbridge feared Ronnie meant to make him his boon companion for life. This he knew he would not be able to abide, and he was honest enough to admit to himself, that part of the reason he would not be able to tolerate Ronnie Standish's constant presence was because he, Lord

Bainbridge, was a coward. Ronnie, he had to admit, for all his faults lived his life boldly. His outrageous behavior seemed scandalous to some, but to others, it appeared admirably fearless. He went about being obvious, but he went about being himself. And that was something Lord Bainbridge could not bring himself to do. As much as possible he tried to conceal his own sexual preference, at least from those who might disapprove, and this meant most of society. He certainly would never have propositioned an underage liftboy the way Ronnie had obviously just done. But was his way of sending his manservant to make his assignations for him any less improper? Was it even more discreet? Wouldn't anyone with half a brain be able to figure out what he was up to if they had a mind to try and figure it out? He knew that Maude Manchester, his dearest friend and mentor, though she never mentioned it and seemed quite content to let it all remain unspoken between them, harbored suspicions about his true nature. Madame Renoir and her son, Sebastian, on the other hand, both let him know that they knew about his other life, and neither was troubled by it. But then they were French, and the French, Lord Bainbridge had observed, did not let themselves get into a tizzy about another's sexual choice as their English cousins so often did. But still, Lord Bainbridge did not feel comfortable revealing his true identity to the world in general. There might come a time in the future when he wouldn't care what others thought of him or his behavior, perhaps when he was ninety and on his deathbed. But at the moment, the risks were too great, and he wasn't brave enough to take that giant step. Still, he couldn't help but admire Ronnie's stance. And yet at the same time, he worried that if he were seen constantly in Ronnie's presence, he would be painted with the same brush. "You're known by the company you keep," one of his enumerable maiden aunts was forever reminding him when he was a child as if he had spent his childhood consorting with disreputable playmates. So while he could admit, at least to himself, that he admired Ronnie Standish's boldness, Lord Bainbridge sometimes wished he could admire it from a distance.

His friend Maude Manchester's stateroom was just off the A deck foyer, and he reached it in minutes. His first knock went unanswered, but his second, a louder double rap, received a brisk command to enter. As he walked through the door, he was greeted warmly. "Ah, Ducks, there you are. I wondered where you'd got to."

Her use of the nickname, which she had christened him with at their first meeting, always made him smile while the sight of her, as it always did, filled him with warmth and affection. "How are you today, Maude?" he asked, throwing himself into a convenient armchair.

"I'm in a bit of a muddle," Maude confessed. She was standing in the middle of the stateroom, and all around her was clutter. As Lord Bainbridge well knew, this was not unusual, for Maude's world was one where clutter always seemed to have the upper hand. Not one prone to pick up after herself, she left her possessions strewn about like debris from a whirlwind. Given the fact that she was also quite absentminded and could never remember where she had left anything, her daily life often lurched from one domestic crisis to the next. She absolutely refused to hire a maid to help pick up after her, which she could well afford, claiming such women were gossips and spies and one was not safe from their prying eyes not even in the lavatory. Every piece of furniture in the stateroom was covered with clothing as if she had gone through her entire wardrobe, found every item unsuitable, and abandoned it to the first available resting place. A small table in one corner overflowed with her books, her writing instruments, and the pages of her current unfinished manuscript. Elsewhere, bureau drawers and closet doors were popped open as if the room had been riffled by burglars.

Facing Lord Bainbridge with her hands on her hips, Maude demanded an opinion. "Well, what do you think?"

Lord Bainbridge paused, uncertain as to what he was expected to comment on. He stared back at the woman standing before him, taking in her full appearance and trying to figure out what was supposed to have captured his attention.

Maude Manchester was a formidable-looking woman, tall and big boned, with a more-than-ample bosom. And while no one would ever have referred to her as fat, her figure had, as she liked to put it, a "well-fed" look to it. Her face had the appearance of a scrunch-faced English bulldog, and as she neared sixty her hair, which she wore in a set of confused curls that were as disorganized as her nature, had already turned completely gray. Possessed of a number of chins, she had recently commented disparagingly about them to Lord Bainbridge. "My chins trouble me. They seem to have taken on a life of their own, and I think I've lost complete control of them. Heaven knows where they'll wander next!"

Given the multitude of articles of clothing that were tossed about the room, Lord Bainbridge deduced that it must be something she was wearing that Maude was trying to call his attention to. He could see nothing unusual about her dress. It was the same type she always preferred—a high-collared, long-skirted satin in a dark hue, which, along with her sensible shoes, allowed her to move about in a brisk and forthright manner as was her custom. This afternoon, her dress was of a deep violet, and there was some simple but elegant beadwork along the collar and the length of the sleeves. Lord Bainbridge finally decided that it must be her hat that warranted his consideration although he couldn't quite remember if he had seen it before or not. It was made of black velvet and had a broad brim, which was decorated with black-and-white ostrich plumes. *The hat it must be,* he told himself with shaky confidence and plunged ahead. "That's a splendid hat. Did you pick it up in Paris?"

Maude shook her head with impatience. "No, no, Ducks, that's not it at all. Now pay attention." She turned to give him a profile view, throwing back her shoulders and thrusting out her rather intimidating bosom.

But her action only confused Lord Bainbridge all the more, and he shook his head. "I'm sorry, Maude, I haven't a clue as to what I'm supposed to be looking at."

With a sigh, Maude gave up. "That's all right, Ducks. I should have known that you of all people wouldn't know a thing about ladies' undergarments. I'm wearing a brassiere," she confessed, lowering her voice to a whisper as if she were revealing a state secret.

Startled by her admission, Lord Bainbridge struggled to light a cigarette. "Oh really?"

"You do know what that is, don't you?"

"I've a general idea," Lord Bainbridge answered, burning his finger.

"It's the latest thing," Maude went on, keeping her voice low. "It's all very dernier cri. I bought it in Paris, and I must say it's far more comfortable than my old whalebone corset."

"Indeed," was about all Lord Bainbridge could manage in response.

"But I'm now having second thoughts," Maude continued as she turned this way and that before a full-length mirror. "I fear it might be too daring."

"Well, why don't we go and have a spot of lunch, and you can give it a sort of trial run," Lord Bainbridge suggested, having recovered and now feeling slightly amused.

"Oh, do I dare?" Maude pondered, still staring into the mirror. "Yes I do!" she quickly decided. "And let the world be damned!" She threw a fur wrap around her shoulders and pronounced herself ready.

Before settling down for a bite of lunch, they decided an invigorating walk on deck was in order. Reaching the boat deck, they found that many other passengers had had the same idea. The afternoon was clear and sunny though the temperature seemed to have dropped markedly from the day before. Maude took Lord Bainbridge's arm as she often did when they walked together, and they took a hearty turn around the deck, their pace in keeping with Maude's philosophy that one always moved at a respectable rate of speed as though one had a clear destination in mind. To stroll, or worse to dawdle, was in her mind quite unacceptable. Children walked in that manner as well as lazy and ineffectual adults who had no purpose in life. While responsible adults, those who lived a worthwhile and productive existence, in the view of Maude Manchester, moved in an energetic and forthright manner.

Almost every passenger they passed they greeted with a smile and a nod, and a number of times, they even stopped for a few friendly words. For although the first-class passenger list was populated predominately by Americans with only a handful of their countrymen and a sprinkling of Continentals added like spice to a dish already over cooked, nearly everyone they encountered was someone they knew even if just casually or in the least by reputation. For the world of the Edwardian rich was very intimate indeed, and the popularity of transatlantic travel had seen to the successful mingling of Old and New World aristocrats. But whatever their nationality, they all seemed to turn up at the same place at the same time; wherever was popular at that particular moment was where they went. Almost like lemmings, they streamed after one another, heedless of their destination, only wanting to be part of the crowd. And the crowd considered the maiden voyage of the largest most glorious ship in the world the current place to be.

At one point in their travels, Maude stopped their progress and asked in a whisper, "Do you think people can tell I'm wearing it?" This was followed by a rather suspicious glance down at her bosom as if she feared the brassiere had somehow mysteriously popped into view. Lord Bainbridge assured her no such mishap had occurred, and her secret remained secure.

Among those they passed on the boat deck was Ronnie Standish, who nodded and tipped his hat to them. Maude returned his nod, almost curtly, and Lord Bainbridge did not fail to notice the way the muscles of her face rearranged themselves into a look of marked displeasure at the sight of the young American. Benjamin Chamberlin as well appeared in their path, obviously much refreshed from his vigorous swim, and with his tiny wife attached to his arm almost like a handbag. For a perilous moment, he and Maude, like two sailing vessels under full power, were in great danger of a major collision as they came face-to-face. But at the last moment, the large man, once again displaying his amazing graceful agility, made a gallant side step and neatly pulled out of her way.

"I hear he's one of the richest men in America," Maude said as soon as Benjamin Chamberlin was out of earshot.

And one of the fattest too, Lord Bainbridge thought to himself. *I for one certainly have ample proof of that.*

Just before they headed below, they paused beside one of the ship's lifeboats, and Lord Bainbridge poised a question. "I wonder why a ship that's reported to be unsinkable needs to carry lifeboats?"

"Ducks, you don't really think any ship's unsinkable, do you?" Maude protested.

Lord Bainbridge shrugged. "Everything I've read about this one claims she is. Something about the captain being able to flick a switch, and all these watertight doors will come crashing down and securely seal off all her compartments."

"I'll tell you something," Maude said. "When I was boarding the ship at Cherbourg, I asked one of the crewmen handling the luggage if this ship was truly unsinkable. And do you know what he said to me?" she asked Lord Bainbridge.

"He said to me, 'Lady, God himself could not sink this ship.'" Maude shook her head with disapproval. "A direct challenge to the Almighty if I ever heard one. God could not have been pleased to hear such blasphemy!"

Now Lord Bainbridge knew that Maude was hardly a deeply religious person. She only appeared in church for weddings and funerals. Still, the crewman's words had struck a chord and obviously offended her deeply. He wondered to himself if they also worried her, perhaps even given her a premonition that something was going to happen to this ship they were on. He would have asked her about that had not, at that moment, the ship's bugler, announcing the last sitting for luncheon, let out a sharp blast on his instrument not six feet from where they were standing, rendering them both deaf for a moment.

"Great Scott!" Maude thundered in response. "That man should be thrown overboard this instant. Why, I've never been so startled in all my life!"

Lord Bainbridge could not help but laugh at her reaction, and as he did, he forgot all about ominous words and premonitions. Instead, he remembered watching Maude board the ship at Cherbourg. She had huffed and puffed her way up the gangway with great effort. When she had finally reached his side and caught her breath, she had suggested to him that in her opinion it would be a lot simpler if passengers could be lowered onto the ship from above with ropes and pulleys like they did with cargo. She had joined the *Titanic* at Cherbourg, one of the ship's three stops to take on passengers—the others being Southampton, where Lord Bainbridge himself had boarded the ship, and Queenstown in Ireland, where the majority who embarked were young emigrants like Tom Kennedy—because a week before their sailing date, she had decided to nip across the channel to Paris to pick up a few things for her trip to America. "I'll catch up with you at Cherbourg," she had told Lord Bainbridge. "You'll easily recognize me. I'll be the rather large English woman overburdened with hundreds of parcels."

A few minutes later, Lord Bainbridge found himself once again in the same lift that had earlier taken him up from the swimming pool. Now, as they descended to the dining saloon on D deck, he was somewhat unnerved when the liftboy, the same one as before, turned toward him, offering him a broad and, worst of all, knowing smile.

"And how are you this fine afternoon, sir?" the boy asked, letting his eyes drop, briefly but unmistakably, to Lord Bainbridge's crotch.

My God! Lord Bainbridge thought, *the little bugger's actually flirting with me.* He muttered some confused response and turned his head quickly away, feeling a flush creep up his neck underneath his stiff collar. He hoped Maude hadn't observed the boy's actions. But one glance at his friend, who was staring straight ahead and seemed to be deep in thought, assured him he was safe at least on that account. They reached D deck, and the boy pulled open the door. As they stepped out into the foyer, he spoke again, "I hope you enjoy your lunch, sir."

Deeply offended that the boy had had the presumption to behave in such a manner toward him, Lord Bainbridge turned back to reprimand him severely. But the boy had already started the lift up again although he could still see his mocking grin through the grillwork.

Well I shall report him, Lord Bainbridge told himself with righteous indignation. But as he thought about the matter, he couldn't figure out who he should report him to. The captain perhaps? Captain Smith and Maude were old friends; surely he would be the man to tell. But then, what would he tell him? "Captain Smith, I'm sorry to have to report this, but one of your liftboys behaved in an outrageous manner toward me." That, he quickly decided, sounded pretty ridiculous and could, if he wasn't careful, open up a whole other can of worms. No, better to let the unsavory matter drop and be forgotten.

"Hurry along now, Ducks, or they'll be closing the doors on us," Maude prompted as he remained staring after the ascending lift.

Lord Bainbridge quickly caught up to her, and passing through the white-paneled reception room, they arrived in the dining saloon just in time for the final luncheon sitting. The headwaiter saw them to their usual table near the center of the room. As he settled into his chair, Lord Bainbridge could not help but cast a glance toward the little alcove in the far corner of the room where he and Tom had had dinner the previous evening. This afternoon, the table was occupied by a young couple, and given the amount of billing and cooing that was going on between them, Lord Bainbridge could only surmise that they were one of the numerous honeymoon couples who he had heard were on board the ship. That they were now sitting at the same table, displaying their love for all to see, where he had spent two delightful hours listening to Tom tell him about his life irritated him and made him quickly turn his gaze away. That coupled with the improprieties of the liftboy had, he decided, put him in a right sour mood. But as she had done so often in the past, Maude immediately made him smile in spite of himself.

Handing him her menu across the table, she explained her latest predicament. "I haven't a cat's whiskers of a clue where I've left my spectacles, so you'll have to order for me." She considered this for a moment and then shook her head. "Won't matter much though what you order for me," she lamented, "because I won't be able to see what I'm eating anyway."

The disappearance of Maude's spectacles was an ongoing drama. It happened at least once a day, and given the way she left her possessions scattered around, it's surprising it didn't happen more often than that. She misplaced other things as well, but it seemed to be her spectacles that vanished with the most frequency. Often after an exhausting search, she would throw herself into a chair and demand of Lord Bainbridge, "They're not on top of my head are they?" And when he invariably assured her they were not, she would always chuckle and make the same remark. "They could be, you know, and I'd never know it." Inevitably, her spectacles would always turn up, trapped between the pages of a book to mark her place or stuffed onto the pocket of a coat or dress she had discarded hours ago. Maude's endearing absentmindedness was one of the things Lord Bainbridge loved best about her.

After he had ordered a light lunch for both of them, they sat there in comfortable silence, waiting for their food to arrive. They were so in tune, so compatible, that unnecessary chatter, prattle just to fill the time as Maude called it, was not required. As they sat there, Lord Bainbridge reflected on the fact that this dear woman across from him was his best friend in the whole world. And it didn't seem strange to him that he, a young man of twenty-four, should count as his best friend a woman more than twice his age. They fit well together, and her friendship he considered a gift, a gift beyond all measurable worth. When he thought about it further, he realized that the other good friends he had, Madame Renoir and Lucianna Fraboli, were also women of advanced years. For a moment, he wondered if perhaps he saw all three women as replacements for the mother who had shown him only indifference. It was a thought that occurred to him from time to time, but he never dwelled long on it.

It had been the written word that had initially brought he and Maude together; her words first and then later, his. For Maude Manchester was quite a well-known novelist. She was one of the first of the wave of lady novelists that sprang up at the beginning of the century, women like Elinor Glyn and Baroness Orczy. Maude was widely popular on both sides of the Atlantic. In fact, the reason she was on the *Titanic* was because she was on her way to America to take part in another tour to promote her latest novel. This would be her fourth American book tour; one had even taken her to what she liked to refer to as the American Wild West. The tour now before her, however, was far less adventurous, being confined to the more civilized cities along the East Coast. Although the works of female novelists were quite popular, especially among women, the world was still old-fashioned enough to think that women who wrote for a living, in particular novels, were somehow not quite respectable. Or as Maude herself liked to put it, "Being a lady novelist is sort of like being a circus acrobat, neither is the type one is eager to take home to mother." Maude's books were all light and frothy, filled with beautiful pointless characters living beautiful pointless lives. One critic complained that her books had no more depth than a lily pond. But Maude herself was the first to deride her own work and even more so those who fawned over it. "I could produce a book with completely blank pages, and there would still be fools who would declare triumphantly, 'Maude Manchester's done it again!'" she had said to Lord Bainbridge one day when she was feeling especially besieged by her fans. But in spite of what the critics said and her own feelings, she could tell a good story, and her books flew off the shelves almost the moment they hit the booksellers. And if she held a secret desire to write something of a more serious nature, she never mentioned it and seemed content to work within her own limitations. Maude had certainly not come from a literary background. Both of her parents, hardworking middle-class people, had spent their entire lives in Baisewater, their daily existence as dreary and dull as the name of the town where they dwelled. Neither of them had ever had the desire to read a book let alone write one.

Lord Bainbridge himself had never planned on becoming a writer although he had always known he had some ability in that direction. When he was at Winchester, a number of amusing short stories he had written were published in the school paper, and one of the masters had referred to them as quite good. But even that encouragement did not lead him to pick up his pen and apply it in a serious manner. After his failure at Oxford University and his return to Bellington House if not in disgrace, then certainly in exile, he still had no serious thoughts about becoming a writer. In fact, he spent the next couple of years with no serious thoughts at all, caught up in an endless search only for pleasure. He led what he would later call a less-than-honorable existence. Finally growing weary of the prurient life he was living with its nightly pub crawls, which invariably led to an endless parade of tough cockney youths and other ruffians, some no better than parasites and petty criminals finding their way into his bed, he stopped going out altogether. But after only a week of abstinence, he found himself climbing the walls of his forced confinement, and one night, he headed back out into the streets. But in spite of the fierce fire that burned in his loins, a fire he had long ago come to the conclusion would never be put out until he was lying in his grave, he was determined to seek out entertainment of a higher calling. And although his footsteps and his heart longed to direct him to the Crown, the pub Alfred had introduced him to, where he knew at that hour all sorts of young men with disreputable reputations were starting to gather, he kept to his resolve and continued his search for a more moral, a more uplifting and proper, way to spend his evening.

Quite by chance, he came upon the Victoria and Albert Museum where a sign announced a lecture by a lady novelist of whom he had never heard. "Well," he decided, "what could be more moral and uplifting than that!" So he went inside, bought a ticket, and slipped into the back of the lecture hall. Finding a seat in the very last row, he turned his attention to the speaker who appeared to be about halfway through her talk. She proved to be a rather large gregarious woman who spoke in a clear, well-enunciated tone and kept her audience in good humor with a continuous flow of terribly amusing anecdotes that poked fun at both herself and the state of the modern novel. Lord Bainbridge found her presentation so entertaining he was very sorry when it came to an end to enthusiastic applause. On impulse, he bought a copy of her book, which were conveniently on sale in the back of the hall, and got in line to have the author sign it. He had almost reached the front of the line when the person ahead of him, a rather silly young female, ridiculous in both dress and manner, began gushing on and on to the lady novelist. Since her words were uttered in a tone one might more properly use to announce there was a fire, not only Lord Bainbridge but everyone else in the room was privy to them. And it was not the work of the author before her she was praising, but rather she was going on about an idea she had for a novel of her own. This continued for some time as she told of an endless tale with a convoluted plot and clichéd characters that were already old when time began.

Out of the corner of his eye, Lord Bainbridge watched as the lady novelist nodded and nodded and nodded. Finally, even she couldn't take anymore, and reaching out, she grasped the young woman's hand, obviously gripping it tight enough to cause pain, for the young woman had to stop talking and gasp in discomfort. The lady novelist kept hold of her and spoke to her in words dripping with insincerity, "Yes, dear, you must put all your wonderful ideas down on paper straight away. You can send them to me in care of the Belgian Congo. I leave tonight!" She released her hand, giving her a little push away from the table. "Now hurry off and get to work at once before you lose your train of thought."

All atwitter, the young woman hurried off in ecstasy, dreams of literary stardom buzzing around her head like fruit flies.

"You're not really going to the Belgian Congo, are you?" Lord Bainbridge asked as he stepped up to the table and presented his book for her to autograph.

Maude Manchester looked up at him, a decided twinkle in her eye. "Good heaven's no! Can you imagine me in the African jungle? Why I'd be scared to death!" She glanced to where the young woman was making her way across the nearly empty hall. "Perhaps I shouldn't have been quite so cruel to her," she mused. "Undoubtedly, she'll send a manuscript of hundreds of pages to the Congo." She laughed at this thought, a hearty throaty laugh that was in character with her appearance. "Some poor native will be stuck with a pile of indistinguishable gibberish, which even if it were in his own language, he still wouldn't be able to make heads or tails of it." She reached for the book in his hand. "Everybody thinks they can be a writer," she added, glancing at him curiously from behind her spectacles.

"I enjoyed your lecture immensely," Lord Bainbridge told her.

"And the book?" Maude asked.

"Well I haven't actually read that yet," he had to confess. "But now I most definitely will."

Maude smiled and nodded. "What's the name?" she asked, her pen poised over the first page of the book.

"Jeremy . . . Jeremy Bainbridge."

Maude signed his book and passed it back to him. She glanced up at him again. "I know you."

"Beg pardon?"

"I know you," she repeated. "Well not you exactly, but I know that name," she amended. Then she began to pour through the stack of books and papers on the table beside her, which true to her nature, were arranged in complete disarrangement. "Here it is!" she cried out triumphantly a moment later, so excited that she bolted to her feet.

Lord Bainbridge instantly recognized a copy of the Winchester school paper. He watched as Maude thumbed quickly through its pages. Coming on what she had been seeking, she thrust the paper under his nose. "You wrote that?" she asked.

"Yes," Lord Bainbridge acknowledged, glancing for a second at one of the short stories he had written for the paper.

"Damn good," Maude pronounced. "Damn good indeed!" And then, in answer to the puzzled look on Lord Bainbridge's face, she explained how she had happened to be in possession of a school paper of such limited circulation. "One of my nephews was at Winchester a few years back, and from time to time, he would send me copies of the paper. Most of it was hardly worth reading, but this story is different. It is so good in fact that I often use it in my lectures to illustrate how a story should be written."

Lord Bainbridge was quite dumbfounded, "Really?"

"What else have you written?"

"Nothing," he answered with a shrug. "Oh, there were a couple more stories I wrote at Winchester."

Maude's large jaw dropped in incredulous disbelief. "Nothing since then? Unthinkable! You've a talent, Ducks. You shouldn't be wasting it." She noted something down on a slip of paper, which she handed to him. "My address. Come and see me when you've something to show me."

"I will," Lord Bainbridge stammered, still in somewhat of a state of shock.

"Well go on get home and start writing," Maude urged him, gathering up her books and papers. "I'll expect you to call before the week is out."

That then was the beginning of their friendship and the beginning of Lord Bainbridge's writing career. He had gone home immediately and sat down at his desk, and with a kind of carefree abandonment and Maude's almost daily encouragement, he produced a six-hundred-page novel in less than five months. It was a rather biting satire on the manners and morals of high society, and he chose for its title, words he remembered that his beloved nanny, Lizzie Manners, had soothed him with when he was a child, *Darkness Is Only the Absence of Light*. An obliging fellow who, as those in the know liked to say flew the same flag, was in the publishing trade and was able to see the book quickly into print. Then to everyone's surprise, none more than the young author himself, the first edition sold out in a matter of weeks. A second edition was quickly ordered. The critics too came on board and greatly praised the work. While a few members of society, whose primary occupation in life was to be outraged, campaigned unsuccessfully to have the book banned, which of course guaranteed a third and even a fourth edition.

Among those closest to him however, Lord Bainbridge found there was far less enthusiasm for his efforts. On being presented a copy of his book, his mother thanked him but said she only read French novels. And Alfred as well declined to read it, complaining it had far too many pages. Alfred's refusal was hardly surprising for he rarely read at all, and when he did, he preferred the *Penny Dreadfuls*, the weekly newspapers that contained sensationalized accounts of gory crimes committed mostly in London's poorer districts and were always accompanied by graphic drawings that left little to one's imagination.

Maude finished her consommé and put down her spoon. "Have you started work on your second book?" she asked.

Having been caught off guard by her question, Lord Bainbridge took time to wipe his lips with his napkin and glance around the dining saloon, which was almost empty save for themselves and their attentive waiter who stood not far off. "I have some notes and an idea," he finally answered.

Maude nodded, reassured. "The second novel is very important," she told him, "even more important than the first. Many a good writer was never able to write that second novel."

Lord Bainbridge watched idly as the waiter cleared away their empty soup dishes and brought them their salads.

I do have an idea, he thought. *Dear God, I do have an idea!* His first novel had obediently towed the line of traditional heterosexuality though in places he had carefully skirted the issue of homosexuality like a dog circling strangers. Now, he knew he wanted to write a book that would more closely resemble his own life. He wanted to write a book about the love that dare not speak its name. Perhaps this would be his way of announcing himself to the world. But then once it was written, would he have the nerve to show it to anyone let alone submit it for publication? His publisher friend was already eager for his next book. But if he lacked the nerve to present it to the public, then it would probably lay locked away in some drawer only to be discovered years after his death. His lost work, they would call it, and finally after he was gone and it no longer mattered, everyone would know his true nature.

Lord Bainbridge's fork slipped from his fingers and landed with a clank onto his salad plate.

Maude was instantly alert. "What's wrong, Ducks?"

Lord Bainbridge shrugged it off. "Nothing," he said, "for an instant I had a glimpse of my own immortality."

"How chilling," Maude remarked. Then obviously relieved he was not ill, she returned to her own salad with gusto.

Chapter IV

May 1907

Lord Bainbridge did not miss the ever so slight touch of irritation in Hodges's voice as the butler opened the door to greet him. "Why, Your Lordship, we didn't expect you until tomorrow."

Yes, I know, Lord Bainbridge thought to himself, hardly in a charitable mood that morning. *My arriving today has, I'm sure, thrown the whole household into complete chaos.* "I decided to come down a day earlier," he said aloud. He indicated the pile of luggage that the motor-cab driver had left at the curb. "Will you have someone see to that please." Times had changed, and the increasing popularity of motorcars now allowed them to even enter the once forbidden grounds of Belgrave Square.

Hodges nodded. "Of course. Are you home for good, Your Lordship?" he asked as Lord Bainbridge walked into the entrance hall of Bellington House.

Lord Bainbridge took a long moment to gaze around the hall, and its familiarity did nothing to comfort him. "Yes, I'm here to stay," he finally answered. And as Hodges held his gaze for a moment longer as if he half expected him to say something more, Lord Bainbridge continued his foul thoughts, picking on poor Hodges as if he were the source of all his misery. *My Oxford career is finished. I didn't even make it through the first term. There, Hodges, that should give you something to whisper about below stairs with the rest of the servants.*

Hodges smiled uncomfortably and informed him that both his sisters were out but were expected home shortly. "And I'm afraid Lady Bainbridge is not at home either. She's gone to one of her committee meetings." Having completely recovered from this unexpected arrival and being the efficient and resourceful servant that had allowed him to keep his position under Lady Bainbridge's exacting demands, Hodges once again picked up the reins of his command. "Your room has been aired, and there are clean sheets on the bed, Your Lordship. I'll tell Mrs. Sheffield you're here and have her prepare you some lunch. Will you be requiring anything else?"

Already feeling ashamed of the mean thoughts he had had, Lord Bainbridge could only shake his head. And as Hodges headed off to have a word with Mrs. Sheffield in the kitchen, the young man walked toward the lift. But then, remembering what had once taken place there between him and Denham, he drew back as if he had been suddenly slapped in the face. He hurried up the stairs instead, taking them at a hearty clip, almost as if he were running from something or someone.

When he reached his room on the second floor, he had to pause a moment in the doorway until his breath found its way back to him. Then he stepped over the threshold, but the moment he did, he realized he had made a terrible mistake. The room, the whole house in fact, was filled with memories of Denham. Not just memories of that first visit over Christmas, that in itself would have been enough to haunt him, but there had been many other visits during their final two years at Winchester. He stared across the room at his big bed standing before him like an immense lonely island. They must have frolicked and made love on that bed at least a dozen times. And now he was doomed to spend his nights alone on it like some castaway banished into solitary exile. No, he should never have come back here. But where else could he have gone? And even if he had found some other sanctuary, memories do not need a specific location to stir and break the heart. He could have hidden himself away in a dark cave in some lost range of mountains in Madagascar, and still memories of their time together would have assaulted him with their poignant and painful reminders. There was no place to run to when what you were running from dwelled, and would dwell forever, in the deepest recesses of your heart and soul. No, this house, this room, was no greater hell than any other place on earth would have been.

Movement behind him stirred him, at least for the moment, from his melancholy thoughts. He stepped aside as two footmen, struggling with his mountain of luggage, came into the room. Neither man was the same young man whom Denham had been so taken with on his first visit. In fact, as Lord Bainbridge had so rightly predicted, that unfortunate young man was already long gone when he and Denham returned for their second visit together three months later. The footmen deposited their burdens and departed silently and discretely as Lady Bainbridge had obviously taught them to do.

So despondent, he couldn't even decide what to do next, Lord Bainbridge flung himself down into a chair before the fireplace. He kicked off his shoes and unbuttoned his collar. The weather had been mild, even for May, and there had been no need for a fire in the fireplace. Lord Bainbridge stared into the empty cold hearth, and tears rolled rapidly down his cheeks as he remembered the first time he awoke and found Denham asleep at his side.

It had just started to turn light, and from somewhere deep inside the house discrete noises indicated the servants were already up and about their daily tasks. The bed was a mess, sheets, quilts, and pillows had been thrown about in a chaotic manner, some even tossed to the floor. This destruction was no surprise to Lord

Bainbridge. After all, he told himself rather proudly, they had made intense love four times. It was a wonder the bed itself was still standing!

Leaning over, he stared into Denham's still sleeping face just as the morning light hit it. His lips were parted slightly, and as he slept, a sound like a whimper or a sigh kept coming from his mouth as if he were having a dream. Watching his friend sleep, Lord Bainbridge could see no sign on his face of what they had done the previous night. There should be a trace, he thought to himself, something to mark the passion that had so gripped them both. But on Denham's face, he saw nothing. In fact, there was such an angelic expression of innocence on his blond features that he looked to be nothing so much as a virginal child, fresh and untouched.

This unnerved Lord Bainbridge somewhat, and he jumped out of bed. Walking across the cold floorboards, he went to stare at his own reflection in the mirror above his bureau. Again, he saw nothing; his own face stared back at him, looking no different than it had the day before. *How strange,* he thought, his hand reaching up to touch his cheek, *how strange that neither of us has changed a bit.* It was almost as if it had never happened between them, but he knew it had. And if it had not changed his appearance, it had certainly changed everything else about him. And he knew he would never be the same again.

Quickly, he hopped back into bed and spent the next few minutes trying to arrange himself so that when Denham awoke he would find him lying there in a most flattering poise. But then Lord Bainbridge began to worry that, in the cold light of day, Denham might be embarrassed by what they had done the night before, or worse he might be cold and indifferent.

His concerns however proved unfounded. For a few minutes later when Denham did awake, he kissed Lord Bainbridge on the cheek and then flung himself out of bed, obviously in high spirits. But then Denham was always in high spirits. Even when he was depressed, which in truth he rarely was, he seemed able to maintain a humorous outlook. He had an impertinent sense of fun, and being much less inhibited than Lord Bainbridge, he was always on the lookout for, as he called it, jolly fun!

One afternoon during his first visit to Bellington House as they were walking home from Regent's Park, Denham spied a bicycle, which an unsuspecting delivery boy making his rounds had left momentarily unattended outside a shop. Denham immediately appropriated the vehicle, and calling for Lord Bainbridge to jump on the handlebars, he hopped on the bicycle and took off like they were fleeing a robbery. With whoops of boyish delight, Denham pedaled them furiously up and down sidewalks, scattering pedestrians right and left. While a terrified Lord Bainbridge could only hang on for dear life. Their joyride ended when Denham crashed them into a fruit stand. But neither boy was injured, the bicycle was not damaged, and Denham had the good character to return the bicycle to where he had found it.

On another day, they planned an excursion to Regent's Park to go ice-skating. The two of them were all set to take off when Lady Bainbridge, coming upon them in the entrance hall with their skates slung over their shoulders, insisted that they should take Lord Bainbridge's two sisters along with them. This, Lord Bainbridge thought a very unpleasant suggestion, but Denham didn't seem to mind. As it turned out, the excursion was less than memorable, at least from Lord Bainbridge's viewpoint. He spent most of the time sulking because he and Denham couldn't be alone together. Meanwhile, his older sister, Helen, skated around in moody indifference, which was her standard outlook on life. While Amber, his younger sister, spent her time frequently falling on the ice. And each time Amber fell, she insisted that only Denham be allowed to pick her up.

"Didn't Denham come down with you?"

Her voice so startled him, intruding as it did on his misery, Lord Bainbridge leaped out of his chair. Then angered and embarrassed both, he lashed out at his sister. "Why are you always creeping about like a cat? Do you find great pleasure in spying on me?"

Amber shrugged, not being one who ever gave a thought to anything she did and caring even less about how anyone else might perceive anything she did. "Isn't Denham here?" she asked again.

"No, he's still at school," Lord Bainbridge answered, glancing away from her inquisitive if rather blank stare.

"Then why are you here?"

"I've left Oxford," he said. "I'm not going back."

"Did you flunk out, or did they ask you to leave?"

His eyes shot back at her, and if they had been bullets, they would have certainly killed her. "I just left," he said, and as he returned her stare, he realized that she probably had a pretty good idea of the true nature of the relationship between him and Denham.

Now sixteen, Amber had kept her childhood promise of beauty, blossoming into a very attractive young woman; a halo of long golden hair surrounded a slightly full face dominated by a pair of big blue eyes. Now, if only she had had a disposition to match her appearance. But unfortunately, she was a variable little minx—snide, manipulative and, not surprisingly, spoiled. Even Lady Bainbridge sometimes lost patience with her, and she of course, normally adored her youngest.

"Well at least now Denham will have more time for his studies," Amber rationalized before she glided out of the room as silently as she had come into it.

If he had had something in his hand at that moment, Lord Bainbridge would have thrown it at her, hoping in the very least to knock her unconscious. But his hands were empty so all he could do was throw himself back down into the chair in front of the empty fireplace and once again take up his brooding as if it were a tapestry or some other piece of needlework that he had momentarily laid aside.

Following their return to Winchester after their first visit together to Bellington House, Lord Bainbridge and Denham began two years of an intense and yet often playful, relationship. Their classmates all regarded them as tremendous friends, and many assumed that they were also lovers as they were. This was a blissful time for Lord Bainbridge, for he believed with all his heart that he had found the one and only love of his life. And although Denham returned his passion and was often even more demonstrative than he was especially in bed, Lord Bainbridge always had the feeling that his lover was not quite giving up everything to their relationship. While he had given all he had, even his soul, he sensed that there was a last little bit of himself that Denham was refusing to surrender.

One night as they sat talking, Denham asked Lord Bainbridge when he first realized his true nature. For Lord Bainbridge, it was an easy question to answer because there were two incidents in his childhood that he considered road signs that pointed in the direction his life was to take. The first incident had taken place when he was nine. Lizzie Manners had taken him and his older sister for an afternoon's outing to the British Museum. Momentarily slipping the leash of her authority, Lord Bainbridge had drifted away on his own. His solitary wanderings took him into a room filled with Greek and Roman sculptures. The boy instantly felt as if he had entered one of his own dreams. He stood transfixed in the center of the room, slowly turning his head to take in the sights before him. Most were complete statues, but some were only parts of bodies: a headless torso, a heavily muscled arm holding aloft a sword in triumph. All those depicted were male, and all were naked. A colossus, a young athlete caught in a moment of deep reflection, towered above everything else in the room. Lord Bainbridge moved closer to get a good look at this giant. The athlete's great stone face stared down at him; his features were molded into almost a look of sadness as if he was remembering past glories that were long gone never to be repeated. There was a wooden railing in front of the statue with a sign that read No Admittance. What it meant of course was No Touching. Feeling quite daring as he proceeded to break both the law of nature and the law of man, young Bainbridge reached out to touch one of the statue's thighs. Amazingly, he found the marble warm under his fingers as if it were alive and blood was flowing freely beneath its stony surface. But he quickly realized it was the bright midday sun that was trying to bring the young athlete back to life as it poured down on the statue from a skylight situated directly overhead. Lord Bainbridge remained there for a long time, staring up at the statue and wondering how many other young lads had had their true sexual preference revealed to them as they gazed at the naked statues of the British Museum.

The second defining incident had taken place about two years later, and though it lacked the drama and the intensity of his visit to the British Museum, it supplied the last piece of the puzzle, and in Lord Bainbridge's mind, it sealed his fate forever. In addition to the swarm of maiden aunts that periodically descended on Bellington House like locust, there was one male relation who turned up regularly once a year for Easter Sunday dinner, one of Lady Bainbridge's yearly culinary triumphs. Lord Bainbridge was never quite clear what exact relation Uncle Ned was to the rest of the family. Although the rumor was that he was Lady Bainbridge's second or third cousin. A connoisseur of antiques and fine works of art, Uncle Ned lived alone—an unmarried gentleman of discretion in his midfifties. The joke among the members of the household, both above and below stairs and which made the rounds every Easter Sunday, was that you could plunk Uncle Ned down into the middle of the pack of maiden aunts, and you would not be able to pick him out. It was a joke Lord Bainbridge heard often as he was growing up. This second incident had taken place as they were all seated for one particular Easter Sunday dinner. The long dining room table was crowded with women: Lady Bainbridge, her two daughters and, of course, a sea of aunts. And there in the middle, sitting across from one another and looking like two pieces of flotsam washed up on an unfamiliar shore, were Lord Bainbridge and Uncle Ned. At one point in the meal, with feminine chatter both assaulting and ignoring them from all sides, the two males looked across the table at one another. And at the same exact moment, they both realized the unspoken bond they shared. It was just a quick look, the passing of a second no more, but in that silent instant, volumes were spoken. Of course, the incident was never mentioned between them. They never once spoke of the heritage they had suddenly realized they had in common. It was as if to acknowledge it had been enough. The torch had been silently passed from one generation to the next.

As their final term at Winchester drew to a close, Denham announced that he had been accepted into Oxford University. Of course, Lord Bainbridge immediately decided he too would be going to Oxford. It was not quite that easy. He had never been much of a scholar, and except for some creative writing courses and the stories he had written for the school paper, he had gone about his schoolwork in a rather desultory manner. "If only he would apply himself," had been his masters' constant refrain in their end-of-term reports to Lady Bainbridge. But at Winchester, Lord Bainbridge applied himself to little else besides Denham. In the end however, he was finally accepted at Oxford because his father had been an Oxford man, and thus the Bainbridge name had some pull although almost everyone involved in the decision, and this included Lady

Bainbridge herself, held little hope that the candidate would turn his acceptance into a scholastic triumph.

At Oxford, the two young men took rooms in High Street—the same rooms, in one of those amusing coincidences that make life so interesting—that had once been occupied by Lord Alfred Douglas, Oscar Wilde's young friend and, some might add, the purveyor of his downfall. Their first few weeks at Oxford passed as their days at Winchester had except now they had private rooms of their own where they could indulge themselves as often as they liked. But soon, Lord Bainbridge began to notice a change in Denham. He began to grow distant, seeming to spend every moment hunched over his books. When they did make love, which became less frequently, Denham appeared to be driven by a desperate urgency to complete the act as quickly as possible. No more did they sleep the night away in each other's arms.

Lord Bainbridge was in despair, his world had stopped spinning, and he didn't know why. He could feel Denham slipping away from him, but he didn't have the courage to confront him, fearing that he would hear things he didn't want to hear. Miserable at midterm, he went home alone to London. He returned to Oxford for the rest of the term to find Denham so completely changed—it was as if he had a different roommate altogether. He was now so remote he might easily have been a stranger.

Finally, one cool and damp evening with darkness already descending and the lamps in their study room lit, Lord Bainbridge could stand it no longer. He flung himself out of his chair as if it were on fire and crossed the room to confront his friend.

"Denham, talk to me!" he pleaded in anguish.

Huddled over his books, Denham at first refused to look up at him, and he kept on with his work.

"Denham, please tell me what's happened to us!"

Denham sighed loudly, and his shoulders heaved. He turned slowly around to look at Lord Bainbridge, flipping his hair out of his face with a toss of his head in that way he did. "Jeremy, we're older now. We have to change," he began carefully, repeating words he had obviously given much thought to.

But if Denham could be rational, Lord Bainbridge was so worked up, so filled with despair, he could hardly think straight. "I don't want to change!" he practically screamed.

"There's a whole world outside those windows that disapproves of what we do together," Denham told him, keeping his own voice calm. "We have to live in that world."

"I don't give a damn what the rest of the world thinks!" Lord Bainbridge shot back.

"What we do is a crime," Denham reminded him.

"But we love each other!" Lord Bainbridge cried out as if that were the answer to everything, and he was young and innocent enough to think it was.

"Jeremy, society won't let us love each other," Denham said.

A thought occurred to Lord Bainbridge, and in his desperation, he flung it out as if to a drowning man. "We could go away together, to France or Italy! Someplace where people don't know us."

"I won't run away," Denham said with a trace of indignation at the very suggestion. He hung his head, and this time when his long hair fell into his face, he did not toss it back. "I must deny my true self," he added. "I am not brave enough to live my life as I would prefer." He paused a moment as if gathering courage to speak the words he knew would hurt the most. And because he was a decent chap, he raised his head and looked Lord Bainbridge straight in the face when he spoke. "After I graduate from Oxford, I intend to find a wife and start a family. I intend to be respectable."

"You can never be respectable, you're a bugger!" Lord Bainbridge snapped, not meaning the words only wanting Denham to feel some of the pain he was feeling.

But Denham took no offense at his outburst. He merely smiled and shrugged. "We'll always be the best of chums forever," he assured Lord Bainbridge.

At that moment, Lord Bainbridge knew it was over between them; a door had been shut and the key lost forever. Denham had made up his mind. He had chosen a different path. And it was a path Lord Bainbridge knew he himself could never walk. After that, there was nothing left for him to do but pack his things and leave. Denham protested that at least he should stay until the end of the term. They could get separate rooms, he suggested. But Lord Bainbridge knew that to still be in sight of Denham and not be able to touch him would have been worse than being away from him altogether. No, leaving was the only thing he could do. That was his path.

For the next six months, Lord Bainbridge moped around Bellington House, keeping to his room as much as possible and torturing himself with his memories. Lady Bainbridge did not appear overly distraught that he had left Oxford probably because she had had no great expectations to begin with. She made no demands on her son, content as she had always been to let him find his own way. His two sisters avoided him as much as they could. And although Amber seemed to be secretly amused by his grief, which he did little to hide, even she had enough sense to stay out of his way, and not further antagonize him.

Then Lady Bainbridge made a decision that although she would never come to realize it changed her son's life forever. Innocent of what was to come, Lord Bainbridge walked into the morning room one day early in November to find a stranger standing before his mother, his cap respectfully in his hands. A casual glance revealed a young man, certainly no older than himself with rumpled dark blond hair and full lips that, at his entrance, rolled back into a smile that was almost, but not quite, a smirk.

From her usual tentative perch on the edge of the sofa, Lady Bainbridge spoke to her son, "Ah, Jeremy, I'm glad you're here. I want you to meet Mr. Watkins." The two young men nodded to one another. "I've just hired Mr. Watkins to be our chauffeur," his mother concluded.

"But we don't even have a motorcar," Lord Bainbridge felt obliged to point out.

Lady Bainbridge smiled with measured tolerance. "I know that, Jeremy. But since none of us know anything about motors, I thought it prudent to have someone who has such knowledge help us to make our first purchase."

Although motorcars had been in popular use in London since soon after the turn of the century, and had recently gone from being used mainly for sport or gallivanting about to being a vehicle of convenience even necessity, Lady Bainbridge had up until now resisted their temptation. Her reluctance may have somewhat been influenced by a mishap she had been involved in as a young woman. Along with a number of other young ladies, she had been bicycling along a gentle country road one balmy afternoon when from out of nowhere a monstrous steam-billowing motorcar, one of the first of its kind, had suddenly appeared right in front of them, barreling down on them at the unbreakable speed of nine miles an hour. Terrified, most of them had never even seen a motorcar before let alone come face to face with one, the poor women, to a female, fell off their bicycles in a panic. Fortunately, the motorist was able to swerve into a dense thicket of shrubs and avoid the bicyclists sprawled in the road before him although three bicycles were severely mangled. But at last when Lady Bainbridge decided it was time the family possessed a motorcar; her decision, not surprisingly, was precipitated by yet another row with one of her servants. This time the unfortunate recipient of her displeasure was the coachman, who had been with the family for as long as Lord Bainbridge could remember. Like so many others before him, his transgression was never completely defined, at least not to his own satisfaction, still he was dismissed. Once he was gone, Lady Bainbridge took the reins into her own hands, so to speak, and decided to make a clean sweep. She got rid of their horses and carriages as well, deciding it was time they moved into the modern age. After all, it was now the twentieth century, and Lady Bainbridge, of all people, certainly didn't want to be left behind.

"Mr. Watkins has much expertise with motors," Lady Bainbridge told her son. "His references are simply glowing," she added, indicating the pile of papers spread out on the coffee table before her. "How long have you been driving, Mr. Watkins?" she inquired.

"Four years, ma'am."

Looking at the young man out of the corner of his eye, Lord Bainbridge suspected his expertise did not lie in the area of motorcars. Although he was dressed well, his clothes neat and unsoiled, there was a toughness about him that was unmistakable. Lord Bainbridge had seen the look before in the faces of some of the boys at Winchester—the ones who had come from poor families, the ones whose lives had been much more of a struggle than his own. But this Mr. Watkins had something else in his look as well. There was in his eyes, as he returned Lord Bainbridge's glance, a glimmer of what Lord Bainbridge could only describe as lust. It unnerved him immensely, and he quickly turned his own eyes back to his mother.

"My son will take you down to the kitchen and put you into Hodges's hands," Lady Bainbridge was saying. "He'll show you to your room and explain the rules of Bellington House."

Mr. Watkins's head bobbed in response. "Thank you, ma'am. I'm sure I'll find it a great pleasure and privilege to be working for you."

Lady Bainbridge smiled but said nothing further. And that look of glazed indifference that she was so famous for slipped down over her features, indicating the interview was over.

As he made his way down to the kitchen with Watkins trailing after him, Lord Bainbridge felt slightly uneasy having the young man behind him. He wasn't quite sure why he felt this way, but he was glad when they finally reached the kitchen, which was actually divided into two rooms and took up one whole half of the basement level of the house. Hodges was waiting for them, and when Lord Bainbridge turned his new charge over to him, the butler gave the newcomer an up-and-down appraisal. The frown on his face informed Lord Bainbridge that he was hardly impressed by what he saw.

"I'll leave you in Hodges's care then, Mr. Watkins," Lord Bainbridge said, anxious to be away.

"It's Alfred," Watkins corrected, still smiling that teasing annoying smile.

Looking back at him and also seeing Hodges's scowl of disapproval, Lord Bainbridge nodded. "Alfred it is then," he agreed. Then he hurried as fast as he could out of the kitchen.

That night, Lord Bainbridge found himself pacing nervously about his bedroom, unsure what he was so worked up about. In truth though, he knew damn well what was perturbing him, and that made him try and deny it all the more. For he found that the harder he tried not to think of Alfred Watkins's knowing smile and his eyes, which shone with such naked impure desire, the more vivid his features became in his mind, mocking and taunting him.

Finally, unable to stand it any longer, Lord Bainbridge slipped out of his room and crept up the three flights of stairs that led to the top floor of the house. The servants' quarters were tiny, almost cell-like rooms tucked well up under the eaves, but at least they were warm and dry. As he passed each door, Lord Bainbridge held his breath and prayed he wouldn't step on a squeaky floorboard. It was past ten now, and he knew all of the servants should at least be in their rooms, if not already fast asleep. Their days began before dawn, so early retirement every night was a necessity. He passed Hodges's door with extra caution. The butler had ears like a cat; the other servants said he could hear a mouse even before the mouse had made up its mind to move. Safely past Hodges's room, Lord Bainbridge suddenly realized he didn't know for sure which room Alfred had been given. There were a number of vacant rooms along the corridor since at the moment, the house was understaffed. Deciding that the logical decision would have been to give Alfred the room that had belonged to the departed coachman, Lord Bainbridge stopped before that door. But then another moment of panic struck him as he considered the possibility that he had misread Alfred's looks. Perhaps the young man's teasing smile and randy eyes had not been an invitation after all. Perhaps he was making a terrible mistake that was about to blow up in his face with a bomb blast that would be felt throughout the whole house. He had almost made up his mind to creep back to his own room when he noticed the shaft of light coming from under the door before him. If Alfred was in that room, then he was still awake. Lord Bainbridge knew he couldn't knock, for even a light tap on the door wouldn't be missed by Hodges. Feeling his heart pound in his chest as though it surely would break through its confinement, he reached out and turned the knob. The door swung open easily.

Alfred was lying on his narrow bed, his arms locked behind his head. He was wearing only his trousers, and the first thing Lord Bainbridge noticed were the tufts of hair under his arms. They were much darker than the hair on his head. The other thing that he could not help but notice was that Alfred's upper body and his arms were more muscularly developed than they looked when he was clothed.

His heart now in his throat, Lord Bainbridge babbled out an explanation for his sudden appearance. "I came up to make sure you were all settled in. Do you need anything?"

Alfred remained on the bed for a moment, smiling his mocking smile, his gray eyes dancing with the delight of the moment. *He knew I'd come,* Lord Bainbridge told himself. *He's been lying up here waiting for me.*

Then Alfred bounded off the bed, and coming up to Lord Bainbridge so quickly it gave him a start, he grabbed his face and kissed him hard on the mouth. "That's what I needed," he told him with a broad grin.

And then before Lord Bainbridge could offer any resistance although he had none planned, Alfred took his hands and placed them on his body, making Lord Bainbridge touch his chest, his nipples, and then, with an almost angry thrust, between his legs. As this was happening, he whispered to him hoarsely, "I knew you was one. I spotted you the first moment you walked into the room." His own hands began to work on Lord Bainbridge's clothes, and none too gently either, ripping off at least two buttons and tearing his shirt collar to shreds. Then he got rid of his own trousers and underwear, and as they stood naked before each other, Alfred issued a command. "Kiss me, kiss me hard!" Their mouths came crashing together, and Lord Bainbridge kissed him like he had never kissed anyone before, certainly not Denham. At one point, he tasted blood in his mouth, but he couldn't tell if it was his or Alfred's. First slipping the latch on the door to make sure they were not disturbed, Alfred then half dragged half carried Lord Bainbridge to the bed. As they fell amongst the bedclothes, there was no mistaking who was in charge. They wrestled about on the bed for a bit in a playful prelude to the more serious lovemaking that was to come. Their activity became so spirited they both ended up tumbling off the bed and landing on the floor with a hard thump. With their hands over each other's mouths to suppress their giggles, they both held their breath and listened intently to see if anyone else in the house had heard the noise. But there wasn't another sound to be heard, so they quickly climbed back into bed.

Alfred wrapped his arms around Lord Bainbridge in a powerful bear hug and made him a promise. "You ain't ever gonna forget me." And then he went on to prove, at least in that respect, he was a man of his word. An hour later, both worn out and satisfied, the two of them fell asleep. Lord Bainbridge awoke later to find Alfred gently snoring at his side. He had decided to slip back to his own room when one of Alfred's arms fell across his chest, pinning him to the bed. Glancing over at him, Lord Bainbridge saw that he was still asleep. As Alfred's arm continued to hold him captive, Lord Bainbridge felt that it was also protecting him. And so, feeling safe and contented, he willingly dropped off to sleep again.

They both awoke later to the pounding of Hodges on the door. "Watkins, are you awake? It's past seven! You should have been downstairs half an hour ago!"

Alfred bounded out of bed, almost dumping Lord Bainbridge once again onto the floor. "I'm on my way!" he called out.

"Well, see that you make haste!" were Hodges's final words before they heard his footsteps disappear down the hallway.

"Damn!" Alfred cursed as he scrambled into his clothes. "Late my first day on the job. Your mother'll give me the boot for sure!"

"No, she won't. I won't let her," Lord Bainbridge said confidently from the bed.

Alfred paused a second to look over at him, and he shook his head. "I don't imagine you'd have much to say about it," was his blunt opinion. Then he was out the door, still pulling on his shoes.

He didn't get the boot. But although his prowess in the bedchamber had proven impressive, his foray into the world of motorcars was far less successful at least initially. Things started out well enough at first though. Lady Bainbridge provided Alfred with a smart chauffeur's uniform of royal blue, complete with a pair of high black boots and a black leather cap that Alfred took much delight in wearing pulled down so low, it almost reached his eyes. Apparently wanting to get into the spirit of their new venture and at the same time always wanting to be at the height of fashion, Lady Bainbridge procured a motoring outfit for herself. This consisted of a long woolen motoring coat called a duster, a cap, and goggles. Whenever Lord Bainbridge saw his mother dressed in this manner as if she herself were about to get behind the wheel, he never failed to be greatly amused. Lady Bainbridge also had workmen come in and remodel their former stables behind the house. But although the word *garage* was in use by some, Lady Bainbridge, like many other English women, considered the word rather vulgar, it was French after all, so she preferred to call the new facility a motor stable.

The day their first motorcar was delivered, Lord Bainbridge, his mother and his sisters, and many of the servants poured excitedly out of the house. Alfred, proud as a peacock in his uniform, climbed in behind the wheel and mimicked the motions of a real driver. The motorcar was a Rolls-Royce, a beautiful impressive machine with silver trim and painted a vivid claret red. Watching Alfred's pantomime behind the wheel, Lord Bainbridge was quite convinced he had chosen the car because of its color.

Unfortunately for the new chauffeur, Lady Bainbridge, since she was already suitably attired for motoring, decided that she and her children should be taken for an immediate spin that very moment. They all piled into the motorcar. Sitting beside his mother, Lord Bainbridge noticed the flush of red that began creeping up the back of Alfred's neck as he struggled to start the engine.

Lady Bainbridge too sensed that all was not well. Using the speaking tube that connected the passenger cab with the driver's area in front, she made her inquiry. "What seems to be wrong, Watkins? Why aren't we moving forward?"

Alfred's mumbled response through the speaking tube made Lord Bainbridge smile and also made him wish he could hug him at that moment. "I'm not sure what's wrong, ma'am," Alfred reported. "But I think the gears must be foreign."

Lady Bainbridge was both sympathetic to his plight and properly vexed. "You'd think the least they could have done was given us one with English gears," she complained.

But somehow Alfred managed to start the engine, and they actually took off at a crawl down the street.

"We're moving!" Amber cried out in delight.

But her joy was short lived, for starting the engine and steering the car were two different things, and after traveling a few feet, they ran off the road and into a tree. It was only a minor accident, and no one was even scratched.

Lord Bainbridge leaned into the front seat. "What happened?" he asked.

The sweat was pouring down Alfred's face, and he shrugged helplessly. "I've never driven a car before in my life," he whispered.

Sitting back in his seat, glancing at his mother who was adjusting her cap and goggles, which had become slightly dislodged when the car hit the tree, Lord Bainbridge feared the worst. This was obviously the end of Alfred! He'd be gone by morning.

But Lady Bainbridge didn't blame her young driver at all. "It's clearly a faulty machine," she declared. "We'll send it back tomorrow and demand they send us one that works properly."

That night after Lord Bainbridge had snuck into Alfred's room, which he had come to do almost nightly, Alfred confessed to him that not only had he never driven a car before but all his glowing references were forgeries. "I wrote them myself," he boasted proudly.

Delighted that Alfred had put one over on his mother, she who rode her servants so mercilessly, berating them over the most minor infractions, Lord Bainbridge was nevertheless worried that when the new motorcar arrived and Alfred had the same difficulties, Lady Bainbridge would not prove to be so charitable. So he arranged for Alfred to take some driving lessons from the chauffeur of a friend of his who lived across London. By the time their second motorcar was delivered, a Renault, painted a more dignified dark blue, Alfred was able to slip behind the wheel and take them for a leisurely and uneventful motor. Lady Bainbridge was impressed, and Lord Bainbridge greatly relieved. For he would have been most distressed to have Alfred leave. He knew he wasn't in love with him, not the way he had been with Denham, but he certainly loved going to bed with him. Most of the details of Alfred's past remained a mystery—he revealed very little. He did tell Lord Bainbridge enough to give him the impression that he had been involved in more than one shady deal. Or perhaps this was just more of the false boasting that Alfred often indulged in. He had been born in the East End of London, where the worst slums of the city were located and where only a few years before, that notorious fiend Jack the Ripper had searched for his victims among the most desperate of the desperate. Alfred spoke of no family and said only that he had left his home at the age of thirteen and never looked back. Though he was very articulate and could read and write proficiently, his education had been rudimentary at best, gleamed apparently more from the streets than the schoolroom. And although he was not material for any university or other institution of higher learning even if he had had the money, he was determined to make his way in the world. He was equally determined not to spend his days at some menial backbreaking labor that would leave him old and spent at forty clutching a few coppers.

As to the circumstances that brought him to Bellington House to apply for the chauffeur's position, he was more forthcoming. It seems he had seen the position posted in the window of an agency that placed domestic help. He had decided that instant that he wanted to be a chauffeur and drive a fancy motorcar all over London. After all, how difficult could driving a motorcar be? He had returned immediately to the shabby room where he was staying and written out his clever forgeries. Appearing at the agency first thing the next morning, he had been interviewed by the owner himself who had been so impressed by the letters of recommendation he had presented, he took them on face value and never even bothered to have them verified. Alfred boasted to Lord Bainbridge that this was because the man had been hot for him, and he let the old geezer squeeze his knee a couple of times under the desk. Before agreeing to send him out for an interview however, the owner first gave him a stern warning regarding the demands Lady Bainbridge made on those she employed.

"I was shaking in my boots when Hodges ushered me into meet your mother," Alfred told Lord Bainbridge. "But she was actually very pleasant to me. I think the flowery letter of praise that the owner of the agency sent along with my references certainly softened her up a bit." He gave Lord Bainbridge a licentious wink. "And then you walked into the room, and I knew I'd made the right choice."

Alfred had been with them about a month when one morning as they shared a cigarette before he went down to work, he made a statement that had been on both their minds. "You know, we can't keep going on like this in this house. Some of the other servants are already suspicious, and Hodges is spying on me all the time."

"Do you think they know about us?" Lord Bainbridge asked anxiously.

Alfred shook his head. "Not yet, they don't. But Hodges is bound to sniff it out sooner or later."

"Thank God my mother is as oblivious as ever," Lord Bainbridge said.

"Your mother's not stupid," Alfred told him almost as a reprimand. "If she doesn't suspect anything, she certainly hears the gossip of the servants."

"So what should we do?" Lord Bainbridge asked with a shrug.

Alfred got up off the bed and stood with his back to him, the neat lines of his chauffeur's uniform showing off his figure to good advantage, a fact he was not unaware of. "You could take rooms of your own," he suggested.

Lord Bainbridge nodded. "Yes, it's something I've been considering of late. It is probably time for me to be out on my own."

"And I could move in with you," Alfred suggested, his back still toward him. "Of course, I'd have to give up my position here, and then I'd have no income," he added. Then before Lord Bainbridge could respond, Alfred kissed him roughly on the cheek, declared he was bloody late for work, and bounded out of the room, slamming the door behind him.

Smiling to himself, Lord Bainbridge lay back on Alfred's bed, quite aware that the chauffeur had obviously given this whole idea very careful thought.

Money was something he himself had never given much thought to. Never having had to struggle for it or even work for it, he had hardly ever considered it. His father had left him a perpetual annuity that would last him his lifetime. And his mother also provided him with a generous monthly allowance, which he did not suspect she would withhold should he move out. In fact, he thought with a little grin, knowing her, she might even double it when he left. No, money would not be a problem. He would have enough to support himself and Alfred in comfort. But then another thought occurred to him. Perhaps Alfred wouldn't want to be supported that way. Perhaps he would not be keen to be seen as a kept man. One of the things he had learned about him in the short time they had been together was that he was very proud. "The most important thing for blokes like me, working-class lads, is to always save face," Alfred had told him one time. And then he even issued a warning, "We must never be made to look the fool." Well then, Lord Bainbridge thought, perhaps he could take him on as say his manservant. That way they could live together in properly acceptable terms agreeable to society, and Alfred's vanity would also be soothed.

Later that night when they were again alone, he proposed his solution to the chauffeur and was greatly relieved when Alfred embraced it wholeheartedly. And then the young man embraced him, looked into his eyes, and spoke words that Lord Bainbridge found quite touching and never forgot. "I'm gonna look out for you. And I ain't ever gonna let anyone hurt you. Never!"

Lord Bainbridge made plans to move out in two weeks while they decided that Alfred should wait an additional two weeks before giving his notice so that, at least in appearance, they were not seeming to be leaving together. As Lord Bainbridge suspected, his mother was not dismayed that he was leaving home. "He was of age now," she said. "And it was a proper decision." Two weeks after he had left Bellington House, Alfred joined him and reported that Lady Bainbridge had been quite outraged at his departure, accusing him of being an ungrateful wretch and practically having Hodges throw him out of the house. Apparently, Lord Bainbridge thought to himself highly amused, the loss of a chauffeur was a greater tragedy than the loss of a son. At least to Lady Bainbridge.

Alfred had brought his chauffeur's uniform along with him. He had become very attached to it and very pleased with the way he looked in it. Of course they had no motorcar, but a number of times when they made love, Alfred wore the chauffeur's cap and boots and nothing else. So at least parts of the uniform were put to good use.

They had found suitable rooms in Margaret Street, off Regent Street, close to the park. There were two bedrooms, a dining room and a kitchen, a sitting room, and a smaller room, which had been a dressing room at one time but which they decided could be turned into a study where Lord Bainbridge could take up the writing he had begun at Winchester if he ever so desired. The rooms were neatly if not impressively furnished. Obviously, the previous tenant must have had a longing for the Orient, for there were bulrushes in Japanese vases, Japanese screens, and bamboo chairs in nearly every room. A woman came in daily to cook and clean. So they set up housekeeping; to the casual observer they were merely a proper upper-class gentleman and his servant.

Though their lovemaking continued after they had moved in together, to some extent, their passion for each other began to slowly burn itself out. It had burned furiously at first, but as they grew more accustomed to one another, it began to cool. But this didn't seem to be of great concern to either one of them, and they both were content to let their relationship wander where it may.

One night as they were lying in bed, Alfred made an interesting observation. "I've spoiled you for your own kind now, ain't I? No more fancy aristocratic types for you! Now you want to frolic with the lower-class ones, the rough lads like me!" he added rather proudly.

In spite of his boasting, Lord Bainbridge had to admit that Alfred was right. Though he still thought about Denham and on occasion, he would remember with a pang the times they had spent in each other's arms, looking back on it now, their lovemaking seemed pallid, almost chaste, especially when compared to what he and Alfred had shared. And he knew he would never be satisfied with that type of relationship again. Now, it was the working-class type he found himself attracted to—the young men he saw every day in the streets, the laborers, the road workers, the deliverymen.

"I know places we can go, places where you can find what you're looking for," Alfred whispered into his ear. He pinched his cheek playfully. "Don't you worry, my pet, I'll keep you supplied."

The Crown was a pub in Charing Cross Road in London's West End. "It has a reputation for being lively," Alfred assured Lord Bainbridge with a wink as they entered the pub around ten on a midweek night.

The place was crowded with bodies packed tightly together. As Lord Bainbridge followed Alfred into their midst, he was quite certain he felt a hand brush across his buttocks. Startled, he complained to Alfred that he had been touched.

Alfred grinned and nodded knowingly. "Oh yah," he said, "there's always stray hands here trying to get a free feel."

He bought them a couple of pints at the bar and then once again led the way through the crowd. They at last reached a vacant table near the back of the room and settled in without further incident. They lit up cigarettes and then Lord Bainbridge sat back and took in the Crown.

The pub, on first glance, looked no different than any other pub he had ever been in. Its windows were made of stained glass, and behind the long mahogany bar, there was a gilded mirror that reflected the faces of the bar's patrons over and over again as if there were a thousand rather than merely a hundred crowded into the room. Not having yet been wired for electricity, the pub was lit by gas lamps along the walls and two gas chandeliers that hung from the low beams of the ceiling. Over everything and everyone, there hung a blue cloud of cigarette and cigar smoke. Between the bar and the tables and chairs placed toward the back of the room, there was a large expanse of open floor space. And it was in this area that a goodly portion of the crowd was congested. They were not stationary, but rather they surged to and fro, ebbing and flowing like a giant tide. Lord Bainbridge sensed there was a great restlessness in their movements. They all seemed to be searching for something. And everything they did or said—their gestures, their conversations, their laughter—seemed heightened and overdone. As if, he concluded, they were all actors playing out their parts on a mammoth stage.

Beside him, Alfred got to his feet. "Stay here," he instructed. "I'm going to have a look around."

Watching him walk away, strutting proudly in his chauffeur's uniform, Lord Bainbridge suspected this was probably not the first time he had worn his uniform here. As they were getting dressed to come out that night, Alfred had suggested to him that if anyone asked him he should inform them that he was his chauffeur.

"We don't have a motorcar, Alfred," Lord Bainbridge was quick to point out.

Alfred shrugged. "They don't have to know that. We can tell them it's in the shop."

As to the choice of his own wardrobe, he had been prepared to dress casually. But Alfred had other ideas. "It's important you look your part," he had told him, insisting that he wear a tie and stiff collar along with an expensive cashmere coat.

Continuing to follow Alfred's progress as he made his way through the crowd, Lord Bainbridge observed that he seemed to know a goodly number of the pub's clientele, young and old alike. He watched him laughing and joking with them, slapping this one on the back, accepting a cigarette from another. Alfred seemed right at home. Observing Alfred's actions, Lord Bainbridge also noted that the patrons of the pub were divided into two distinct groups. There were many men who it was easy to tell by their attire—custom-made suits, a flash of a ring, or an expensive watch, even a few walking sticks—were well-off. They were almost to a man, except for himself and one or two others, at least middle-aged, and quite a few were elderly. The other group, of which there was an even greater number, were young men of, to put it gently, obviously meager means. Their wardrobe among themselves was also very similar, loose trousers, worn jackets or waistcoats, cloth caps, and collarless open shirts. And between the two groups, he could not help but note, there was being played out a constant dance.

Feeling rather conspicuous and alone, Lord Bainbridge shifted uneasily in his chair as he rubbed out his cigarette. Looking up for Alfred, who seemed to have disappeared for the moment, he found himself staring directly into the face of a young man who was intently staring back at him. Startled, Lord Bainbridge looked quickly away, but a moment later, he glanced back again. The young man was still leaning against the wall, watching him with a broad smile on his face. His hands were shoved into the pockets of his trousers so that just his thumbs were exposed, and they were positioned so that they met just above his crotch, obviously and purposely calling attention to what lay below.

Their gazes held a moment longer, and then the young men broke away from the wall and strolled over to him, his walk a confident, almost joyful, swagger. Reaching Lord Bainbridge's table, the smile still broad on his face, he pushed his cap back on his head. "How you doing, sport?" he asked. "I'm Bobby Marsh," he added, offering his hand.

Lord Bainbridge stumbled to his feet. "Jeremy," he returned as Bobby took his hand and pumped it vigorously.

"May I sit with you?" Bobby asked.

"Of course," Lord Bainbridge agreed, returning to his own chair.

But Bobby remained standing for a moment longer so that his crotch was directly in Lord Bainbridge's line of vision. Then he slipped easily into a chair across from him. "Got a cigarette?" he asked, still smiling broadly as if he were in on the most wonderful secret and was just bursting to tell it to someone.

Lord Bainbridge offered him a cigarette from his case, and as he lit it for him, Bobby held his hand just a moment longer than was necessary to complete the action. Looking at him now under the gas lamp, Lord Bainbridge was shocked to see he wasn't quite the young man that he had appeared to be from across the room. Though his face was handsome enough, broad with lively brown eyes and a smile that just wouldn't quit, there were unmistakable lines at the corners of his mouth and around his eyes. *He must be at least forty,* Lord Bainbridge thought to himself.

"I noticed you eyeing my bundle from across the room," Bobby told him matter-of-factly.

"I'm sorry?" Lord Bainbridge said, not quite sure what he meant.

"My friend," Bobby explained, glancing coyly down at his lap. "I wear special underwear made in France," he went on. "It makes it stick up more. Though I don't need much help. I'm known to have one of the biggest in the whole of the West End." His words might have sounded offensive to some, but they were delivered in a light and cheery tone as if he were discussing everyday things such as the weather or football scores.

Thankfully, Lord Bainbridge was saved the embarrassment of asking for further clarification by Alfred's return. Seeing him, Bobby jumped to his feet, and they embraced warmly, pounding one another heartily on the back.

"I figured you'd be here someplace," Alfred said.

Bobby shrugged good-naturedly. "One should never stray far from home. So you two know each other?" he asked as they took their seats.

"We live together," Alfred told him.

Bobby's eyebrows shot up, "Really? Well then," he said to Lord Bainbridge, "since you're a friend of Alfred's, I'll go with you for free."

"Free?" Lord Bainbridge asked, puzzled.

"Jeremy's never been here before," Alfred told Bobby. "He doesn't know the score."

"Well, why don't you explain it to him while I go get us a round," Bobby suggested. And when Alfred made a move as if to reach for his billfold, Bobby assured him, "I've got money."

"What I neglected to tell you," Alfred began when they were alone, "Is that lads who come here all expect to be paid for their time. That's why they come to the Crown, to make money."

Lord Bainbridge took a few minutes to digest this news, letting his eyes roam around the pub and now seeing the young men gathered there in a different light. He was not completely oblivious to the fact that male prostitution existed. He had heard the occasional story, and one night when he had been going to a party, he had passed through Trafalgar Square and seen the young men loitering around the fountain. A couple of them had even called out to him.

"Most of 'em ain't even got the money for a pint," Alfred went on, leaning across the table, so their faces were closer. "There's a lot of lads out there who can't find a job, and this beats going into the workhouse." He shrugged, and the corners of his mouth turned up. "Of course some of 'em are just right layabouts, and this seems to them an easy way to make money. And another thing," Alfred added, his voice becoming more intense, "most of 'em ain't inverts like you and me."

Lord Bainbridge winced at his use of the word *invert*. He knew it was the popular slang used to refer to men who preferred men, but he always thought it had a derogatory connotation to it. Of course, he had to admit that when most of society thought at all—which they rarely did—of those who were like Alfred and himself, their thoughts were invariably derogatory.

"Many of these lads have girlfriends or wives they go home to every night when they're through with business," Alfred told him. He paused to light a cigarette. "Remember what I told you, the most important thing with working-class lads is that they don't lose face."

Bobby returned to their table with three pints and a funny story to tell. "See that old poof over there by the bar"—he nodded—"the one with the dyed hair. He pretended he didn't know me. But just yesterday afternoon, I was in this public loo in Leicester Square taking a piss, and this old darling's standing right next to me, eyeing my friend as if it were a big juicy steak. So's I kinda shook it at him.

Well the poof was so startled he almost fell into the urinal, and then he ran out of the loo so fast he forgot to button up his trousers. I never laughed so hard in my life," Bobby said, laughing now as he finished telling the story.

Alfred laughed too, and even Lord Bainbridge couldn't help but smile. For the next few minutes, Alfred and Bobby shared stories, mostly about mutual friends they knew.

At one point, a couple of effeminate young men, wearing tight trousers and fancy scarves draped around the necks sashayed by their table, flirting and making kissing sounds with their lips.

"Damn Mary-Annes!" Alfred snarled with contempt. Lord Bainbridge had learned early on in their relationship that Alfred, being a dedicated lover of men, had a strong dislike for all women, but he had an especially strong hatred for men who pretended they were women. These, along with lesbians, he considered the lowest forms of life.

Bobby finished off his ale and smiled across the table at Lord Bainbridge. "So what'd you say, sport, you want to have a go at it?"

And when all Lord Bainbridge could do was swallow hard and look embarrassed, Alfred stepped in. "I think he's still in shock, Bobby. He's gonna need a little time to come around."

Bobby nodded and bounced to his feet. "Well, I gotta be off. This place is way too quiet for me," he added in spite of the almost frenzied activity that was going on all around them. He and Alfred hugged again, and he winked at Lord Bainbridge. "See you soon, sport."

"Look out for yourself," Alfred called out to him as they watched Bobby make his way through the crowded pub, his steps once again a joyful swagger. Before he reached the door, he turned and waved to them, and then he was gone, swallowed up into the night.

Alfred sighed and shook his head. "Poor Bobby, he makes out better in the streets where it's dark, and no one can get a good look at him."

"And this is how he lives?" Lord Bainbridge asked.

"Pretty much," Alfred said. "Oh, I guess he takes the odd job now and again. But yeah, this is his life. He's past it now, too old, but he doesn't seem to mind. He goes where he knows he can still get it." He stared for a moment intently into his glass. "In the dark, nobody cares how old you are." He fumbled for another cigarette. "Bobby took me under his wing when I was all of fourteen. He was the first person in my whole life who was ever a friend to me." He took a long drag on his fresh cigarette. "Bobby is as straight as the day is long. He's the only person I've ever completely trusted."

"He seems rather sad, I mean his life," Lord Bainbridge observed.

Alfred shrugged. "Perhaps. But Bobby don't think so. He's the most carefree and uncomplicated person I've ever known."

They fell silent for a few moments, and then Lord Bainbridge asked a question. "So what do we do now?"

"It's up to you," Alfred told him. "You want to stay or leave?"

"I just never thought about paying for it before," Lord Bainbridge said. "It all seems so rude."

"If these are the types of lads you fancy, then you're going to have to pay for 'em, like it or not," Alfred said.

Lord Bainbridge took another look around the pub. More than one young man, feeling his eyes on him, turned to smile back at him. This time his gaze lingered on a young man of medium height who wore his cloth cap cocked to one side, revealing unruly strands of long blond hair. He had a broad baby face, and he sort of looked like Denham if Denham had come from the East End and if he had been scuffed and roughed up a bit.

"Which one?" Alfred asked, instantly alerted. And when Lord Bainbridge indicated his preference, he got to his feet. "I'll be right back," he said over his shoulder as he made his way through the crowd.

In the few minutes Alfred spent chatting up the blond, Lord Bainbridge, in his nervousness, managed to spill what was left of his ale and burn his thumb struggling to light another cigarette.

Alfred returned, bringing the young man with him. "This is Colin," he told Lord Bainbridge. "I think the two of you will hit it off," he added with a mischievous gleam in his eye. Then he took off again, leaving the two of them alone.

Lord Bainbridge smiled and held out his cigarette case, "Cigarette?"

"Thanks, mate," Colin said as he helped himself. "I could go for a pint as well," he added, pulling out a chair.

"Of course"—Lord Bainbridge nodded—"as many as you like."

Chapter V

Sunday, April 14, 1912

At exactly 4:00 PM that afternoon, Lord Bainbridge took tea alone in the Cafe Parisien, happy for a few moments of solitary contemplation. Adjacent to the restaurant on the starboard side of B deck, the cafe had been designed in the style of a sidewalk eatery one might encounter on the streets of Paris. Staffed by French and Italian waiters, adding their own Continental charms, it boasted large windows that gave sweeping views of the sea, ivy growing up the trellis-covered walls, and lest anyone should forget they were on a British ship, sturdy British wicker tables and chairs. Throughout the voyage, the cafe had proven to be a great success, especially among the younger passengers.

Maude had gone off for a last-minute consultation with Monsieur Gatti, the manager of the restaurant, in regard to the dinner party she was giving that evening in Captain Smith's honor. It was to be a small affair involving just their intimate friends, and it promised to be for them the highlight of the crossing. Lord Bainbridge was looking forward to the event even though it would be keeping him from meeting up with Tom until eleven, something he was also, understandably, looking forward to.

Unlike the dining saloon, the restaurant was not part of the White Star Line, but rather it was run by Monsieur Gatti as a private concession. It offered first-class passengers a menu even more varied and delicacies even more rare than those that were served in the dining saloon. The Cafe Parisien was also run by Monsieur Gatti, and the same Continental waiters served in both the restaurant and the cafe. When he decided to take his tea there, Lord Bainbridge had some concern that he might run into Marco Borsalino, the Italian, who worked for Monsieur Gatti. He had initially set eyes upon him on their first night at sea when he had waited on them as Lord Bainbridge and Maude had taken a late dinner in the restaurant after Maude had boarded the ship at Cherbourg. Lord Bainbridge, therefore, was greatly relieved when his afternoon tea was brought to him by a waiter he had never seen before. He certainly had no desire to see Marco again although he feared he was bound to turn up tonight when they ate once again in the restaurant. The whole episode with him had been a mistake, one he regretted almost from the moment it began.

But at least for now there was nothing to disturb him, so he sat there sipping his tea and gazing serenely out at the ocean. He wasn't positive, but he sensed that the ship was going faster than it ever had before on the voyage. *Someone must be in a damn hurry to get to New York,* he thought, amused at his own observation.

Then as if on cue, J. Bruce Ismay appeared in the doorway leading back into the restaurant. He paused, surveying the few passengers scattered about the cafe, obviously looking for someone in particular. Frowning and shaking his head as if it were somehow the fault of those gathered in the cafe that whomever he sought was not there, he withdrew and disappeared back into the restaurant. *Like a rodent scurrying back into its hole,* Lord Bainbridge thought as for a moment the intrusion of this unsavory little man threatened to spoil his contented frame of mind. But he quickly put him out of his thoughts and returned to other contemplations.

As he sat there at his little wicker table, sipping good hot English tea, he remembered sitting at another table in a far different establishment at a time that now seemed in the distant past although it was hardly more than four years ago that night he and Alfred had first gone to the Crown together. He could recall very little of that first visit. He did remember Bobby Marsh, but only because he and Alfred encountered him most every time they returned to the Crown, which they did with frequency. Bobby was as much a part of the Crown as the gilded mirror behind the bar and the stained-glass windows though, as he had done that first night, he almost always slipped out into the night to make his contacts. Of the first young man whom Alfred had brought back to his table, Lord Bainbridge could remember neither his face nor his name. He could recall however that the two of them had returned to his rooms and that he had paid him.

And that was the beginning. Straight on after that first night, Alfred had introduced him to a pack of sexually congenial young ruffians. Often they were petty criminals, dealers in stolen goods, pickpockets, and the like, youths who lived on the very margins of society and whose names never made it into the newspapers, not even when they died. And though they might let their bodies out for an hour or two, they would only go so far, and not a step further. "I am the man!" they would insist, and that was the part they played. As if to reinforce their masculinity, whenever a female happened to wander into their view they would, especially if they were in the company of a rich toff who had designs on them, follow her lustfully with their eyes, call out rudely to her, and whistle at her, making a big show of it. There was rarely any trouble between the young men and their benefactors as long as each kept to his assigned role and no one stepped over the bounds of his prescribed part. On occasion, blackmail would raise its ugly head when a young man felt he had not been given enough or he felt he could get more. Alfred was always there to make sure Lord Bainbridge didn't get mixed up with the wrong kind of lad. Once however, one ungrateful young man did threaten blackmail after their encounter, and Lord Bainbridge was about to pay him off when Alfred stepped in and said he would fix the matter. He returned to their rooms a few nights later, cut and bruised. He would never say how he had taken care of things, but that particular renter was never seen again, at least not in London.

There was another passing from the London scene, and this individual was much more soundly mourned. About two years ago, Bobby Marsh had taken his own life. Arriving home one evening from a visit with his mother, Lord Bainbridge found Alfred sitting alone in the dark. Turning up the lamp, he was startled by the face that looked up at him. Alfred had obviously been crying, and his face held one of the most wretched looks Lord Bainbridge had ever seen.

"What is it?" he asked, fearing the worst.

"They just found Bobby," Alfred said. "He killed himself."

Apparently, Bobby had tried to hang himself with a bedsheet in the little room behind the grocery store where he had lived alone for over twenty years. But the chandelier he had tied the sheet to came loose from the ceiling under his weight, sending him crashing to the floor. He died, not from the hanging, but from the blow his head received when it struck the stone floor.

"Poor Bobby, he knew it was over for him," Alfred said, his hands covering his face while his tears dripped between his fingers. "He told me a couple of days ago that he wasn't getting it anymore, not even out in the dark where no one could see his face. He knew it was time to go."

Lord Bainbridge was greatly moved by Alfred's grief. This was the first time he had ever seen him cry, and he made up his mind to do whatever he could to ease his suffering. Bobby had died as he had lived, destitute, and he was destined to be thrown into a pauper's unmarked grave. That was until Lord Bainbridge stepped in and not only bought him a grave plot with a small but tasteful headstone but paid for a lavish funeral as well. It was a gesture Alfred deeply appreciated and promised never to forget.

The day of Bobby's funeral, they joined a long line of mourners following behind his horse-drawn hearse as it rolled slowly down Charing Cross Road past the Crown, which in respect had closed its doors for the afternoon. Alfred was impressed by the turnout. "Looks like every renter in London is here," he whispered to Lord Bainbridge. There were also a fair number of benefactors in the crowd as well, those who dared to show their faces in public. As they neared the cemetery, the band that was leading them stopped playing their mournful dirge and broke into a spirited burst of American ragtime. It had been Bobby's favorite kind of music, and its gay bubbling sound exactly mimicked his carefree jaunty strut and provided a fitting accompaniment as he passed through the gates of Calvary.

Lord Bainbridge put down his tea and took a moment to light a cigarette. Beyond the wide windows of the cafe, the sea and sky passed by in a stunning panorama. Perhaps it had been Bobby's death that had made him take a serious look at his own life. Alfred had been right—he no longer desired slim young aristocrats like Denham, who now seemed almost feminine in their appearance when compared to the tough working-class lads. But though these were the ones he now preferred, the ones he sought out, he found with them that there was always something missing. For though he might thrill to their rough embraces, he knew what he was feeling was not returned. He might fall in love with them, but the chances of one of them falling in love with him was slim. Love was not what they were dealing in. And though his sexual encounters were numerous, he was still pure enough of heart to believe that he might find someone he could spend the rest of his life with. He continued to believe, as he combed through the seemingly endless supply of young men that came nightly through the doors of the Crown, that he would find the one he sought. He knew at times when it came to seeking out sexual gratification, he had been both reckless and irresponsible and often with no twinge of conscience. Being an aristocrat, he was indifferent to bourgeois morality and felt he had the privilege, no, the right, to amuse himself as he pleased. But after Bobby was gone, he began to question his own wanton behavior and wonder if there was not some other way. The writing of his novel helped take his mind to other areas for a while, and its unsuspected success both pleased and, to some extent, intimidated him. Maude, setting out on one of her book tours, had been the one to suggest they make the crossing together. Then when they reached New York, he would be on his own for a few weeks. And maybe in New York, maybe in the New World, he would find that someone special. Then quite suddenly, just two days ago, Tom Kennedy had dropped into his life. Lord Bainbridge knew without hesitation, without a moment's contemplation, that he was in love with Tom. It was like being struck by lightning or being hit on the head with something that stunned but did not injure. He wasn't sure how strongly Tom felt about him. He was worried that Tom's life had already been laid out for him, down a path that was straight and narrow and one from which he would not or could not deviate.

As he finished his tea, Lord Bainbridge resolved that he would tell Tom how he felt about him and propose that they spend the rest of their lives together when he saw him that night. He knew there was a fair chance he would be rejected, or perhaps to be more precise, the way of life he was offering Tom would be rejected, but he knew it was a chance he would have to take. After having searched for him so long, he could not let Tom just slip through his fingers as nothing more than that old cliché, a shipboard romance.

Leaving the Cafe Parisien, Lord Bainbridge felt good, flushed even with a sense of exhilaration as one often feels after settling on a course of action, determined to see it through come hell or high water. He might fail but, by God, he was going to give it a good shot.

Deciding to seek a breath of fresh air before retiring to his stateroom to dress for dinner, he wasn't supposed to meet Maude until seven, he took the stairs up one flight to the open promenade on A deck. Walking the highly polished deck floor, he passed a row of stacked-up deck chairs and then the lighted windows of the lounge. Looking up and down the deck, he saw that it was almost completely deserted save for a single seaman toward the bow walking his lonely watch. Most of his fellow first-class passengers, Lord Bainbridge assumed, had already headed inside to the warmth of their cabins and staterooms to prepare themselves for whatever evening festivities lay ahead of them. He could appreciate their flight, for the air had taken on a decided chill, and it smelled the way air smells just before it snows.

We must be nearing the ice fields now, he thought to himself, remembering the ship's officer's words.

It was at that moment that he noticed the young woman standing at the rail. She was wrapped in a white fur coat with the collar turned up, so that nothing was to be seen of her but the glance of her eyes as she watched him approach. Then as he drew along the rail beside her, she turned down the collar of her coat like a flower unfolding its petals. And Lord Bainbridge looked into the face of the most beautiful woman he had ever seen.

Now, not ever having been a connoisseur of feminine beauty, Lord Bainbridge had always been able to be objective when it came to defining a woman as beautiful. True to his nature, he found beauty in a man more readily and more often. So when he finally came upon a woman he considered to be truly beautiful, it was a pretty safe bet that she would turn out to be quite spectacular in appearance. And this one, who now stood beside him on the promenade deck of the *Titanic*, was certainly that. In fact, her beauty was so spectacular it gave him a start as if someone had just suddenly pounded him sharply on the back. It was, he thought, like looking at an exquisite painting and expecting to see something quite wonderful and in reality being startled by something so unexpectedly splendid it took your breath away, and even for a moment, made you dizzy. Her complexion was fashionably pale that gave even greater definition to the chiseled perfection of her oval face. The startling vividness of her eyes were made even more astounding by their shade of deep violet, a shade that Lord Bainbridge was quite certain he had never ever seen before. She was not wearing a hat, and her long hair, so black it had a blue sheen to it, framed her face but delicately and in no way intrusive. That she was bareheaded at a time when it was dictated that every woman, at least those of good society, should put on a hat before she set foot outside her door was in itself a novelty, and one that Lord Bainbridge found quite delightful. Then there was her smile, a tantalizing expression that lit up her whole face and seemed to promise wondrous untold secrets just waiting to be revealed.

"I've just had the most amusing experience," she said to him as a way of greeting.

To Lord Bainbridge, this spontaneity, this complete disregard for the formalities of introduction, was like a breath of fresh air. He could tell at once that she was American, and he wondered if all the Americans he would come to meet in the days ahead would prove to be so open, so unhampered by convention. He listened, quite enchanted, as she went on to tell her amusing tale.

"I was taking a walk up on the boat deck when I came upon this sign above a door that read, Gymnasium. Never having been inside such a traditionally male dominated preserve before, I was curious to have a peek inside." Her tone was light, slightly mocking, and most of the mockery was directed at herself. "As soon as I stepped over the threshold I was confronted with a whole room full of strange-looking apparatus, none of which I had ever seen before. I think I would have felt more at home if I had stepped into a medieval torture chamber. There were no other passengers there, only a spry little man in white flannels whom I took to be the gymnasium instructor. He seemed very pleased to see me, and as I walked slowly around the room, being very careful not to trip over anything on the floor, he kept nodding and pointing to various pieces of machinery as if encouraging me to try them out. This I had no intention of doing even if I had known the proper way to mount any of those mechanical monstrosities. So I kept slowly circling the room, staring intently and knowingly at everything as if I were studying paintings in an art gallery. And all the while, the little man is following discretely behind me, trying to encourage me. Then finally, I came upon something I recognized—a bicycle! The instructor came up to me, and smiling broadly, he offered his hand to help me mount the bicycle. 'Where do you ride it?' I asked him. The room seemed way too crowded to pedal a bicycle around. 'Where?' the little man stammered. I nodded. 'No, miss,' he said, 'you see, it's stationary.' 'You mean it doesn't go anywhere?' I asked. Now, it was his turn to nod. 'Then, what's its purpose?' I asked, quite convinced that if a bicycle didn't go anywhere, it was completely useless. I'm afraid at that point the poor little man became quite agitated. 'No, no, it's for exercise,' he explained. 'You see that clock there with the little red arrows tells you how far you've gone.' Well, I nodded and thanked him very much for his time and started to edge my way toward the door. I certainly had no interest in riding a bicycle that didn't go anywhere! Obviously greatly frustrated at his failure to convince me, the little man then leaped on the bicycle and began to pedal as if his life depended on it. 'You see!' he cried out to me. 'You see!' I thanked him once more and made a quick retreat out the door. For all I know, he's still pedaling madly," she added, laughing merrily.

Her laugh was equally delightful, and Lord Bainbridge was relieved that in spite of her youth, she could not have been more than twenty-two or three—her mirth was not displayed in that annoying tittering manner that he had observed most young women seemed to prefer these days.

For a few moments, they both stared silently out at the ocean as its calm, unruffled surface slipped easily past them. "It's so clear you can see right to the horizon," the young woman remarked.

"Our ancient ancestors believed the known world ended just over the horizon and any ship that sailed in that direction would certainly fall off the edge of the earth," Lord Bainbridge told her and then immediately became vexed with himself for uttering such an inappropriate statement.

But she just smiled at him and nodded politely as if she was not quite sure how she should respond to his words.

Watching her, Lord Bainbridge was quite certain he had seen her somewhere before. Although, he was equally sure that it had not been aboard the ship in the previous days. In fact, to him at that moment, it seemed as if she had dropped magically onto the ship in the middle of the ocean. But no, they had met somewhere else, and though the memory was vague and without definition, he had the uneasy sense that there had been something unsettling about their past meeting.

"I don't believe I've seen you about the ship before," he said.

She shook her head, which caused her dark hair to tremble slightly as if it had been stirred by a gentle summer breeze. "No," she answered, "I've kept to my stateroom. I've not been feeling well."

"But you're better now?"

"Much," she answered. "This little excursion up on deck has done wonders for me. I'm afraid I'm not a very good sailor," she confessed.

"It was Dr. Johnson who said going to sea was like going to prison with the chance of being drowned," Lord Bainbridge said. And then once again he wondered what possessed him to persist in uttering such pessimistic drivel.

"Is he your physician?" she asked, perfectly straight-faced.

"No," Lord Bainbridge answered, startled at her suggestion and wondering if she were quite serious. But her next words instantly relieved him.

"I was only kidding," she laughed with a twinkle in her eye. "I know perfectly well who Dr. Johnson is. Honest!"

He laughed too. "I'm sure you do. Do you like to read?"

"Yes, very much."

"What do you read?"

"Oh, let's see. There's Dickens and the Brontës. And of course Dr. Johnson," she added with a wink.

"Did you ever read anything by Maude Manchester?"

"Yes, I love her books. They're such fun."

"I'm traveling with her. I'll introduce you," Lord Bainbridge suggested.

"Really? That would be lovely," she responded with enthusiasm.

His vanity couldn't stop him from asking his next question. "Have you read *Darkness Is Only the Absence of Light?*"

"Oh yes," she replied solemnly, and her frown distressed him.

"You didn't care for it?" he asked rather anxiously.

"No, I did," she answered quickly. "It was just . . . well there were things in it that were not really said, but that I sensed were there, and they disturbed me. But it was very well written," she added.

"I'm Jeremy Bainbridge," he said. She smiled blankly at him, not immediately making the connection. "I wrote the book," he prompted.

"Yes of course," she remarked. "Now I remember."

"I'm afraid people remember the names of the books they read far more often than they remember the names of the authors who wrote them," he suggested.

"Yes, that's probably true," she agreed. "I did like your book though, enormously. You should be very proud of it."

"Thank you," Lord Bainbridge acknowledged. "That's very kind of you to say."

She held out her hand, "I'm Elaine Standish."

Taking her hand, Lord Bainbridge felt a little jolt, like a tiny electric shock, both from her touch and the revelation of her identity. Of course, this was Ronnie's young wife! That news in itself was enough to startle him—why did this beautiful and utterly charming young woman marry him of all people? As to their former meeting, that now came quickly back to him, and he remembered at once the look of devastation that he had seen on her face that day.

He spoke of that meeting but with caution as if he feared the wrong words might terribly offend her. "We have met before, you know."

She raised an unsuspecting eyebrow, "Really?"

"Well, almost," he clarified. "It was in Egypt, in the Valley of the Kings. You almost ran me down. It was hardly the time for proper introductions," he added, struggling to keep it light.

"You were there?" she asked in a tone of utter amazement.

"Yes." He watched her as for a moment she seemed to come all apart clutching the deck rail with both her hands while the deep violet of her eyes seemed to widen with what he could only describe as momentary terror. She was seeing a ghost, of that Lord Bainbridge was certain. But she quickly recovered and pulled herself together though a shudder passed through her body as if they had somehow suddenly hit a bump in the ocean.

"Are you cold?" he asked, instantly solicitous.

"Just a sudden chill," she answered.

"Come inside," he said, taking her arm.

Lord Bainbridge led her across the deck, and they slipped in through a door to the A deck foyer, and finding this even a bit chilly, they continued on until they reached the aft door leading into the first-class lounge. Once inside, they were greeted not only by the welcome warmth, but also by a goodly number of passengers as well.

So this is where everyone has been hiding, Lord Bainbridge thought to himself as the two of them paused to take in the room and its occupants seated in Edwardian splendor as they finished up their afternoon tea. It was probably only his imagination, but he felt as if everyone in the room had suddenly stopped their conversations to look up at them when they entered. *They're all undoubtedly wondering what the two of us are doing together,* he thought.

Beside him, Elaine must have had a similar uncomfortable sensation. "Not here," she whispered to him.

Nodding, Lord Bainbridge took her arm once again, and they passed quickly through the lounge and into the adjoining room. This was referred to on the ship's plan as the reading and writing room, and so it was equipped. Amid its elegant Georgian setting with its white walls and ceiling and thick carpet of dusty rose with complementary pink draperies, passengers could sit in comfortable armchairs and peruse the numerous books and current magazines that were laid out for their enjoyment. There were also numerous little mahogany desks filled with White Star Line stationery in case one cared to jot off a letter headed "From the *Titanic* at Sea."

The last of the day's sun was pouring in through the large bay window at the forward end of the room, painting everything with a golden hue. By mutual silent agreement, the two of them crossed to the window and sat down before it.

Lord Bainbridge watched as Elaine unbuttoned her fur coat and pushed it back on her shoulders. Underneath it, she wore a blue silk scarf around her neck and a deeper blue velvet suit trimmed in white satin. It was an outfit, Lord Bainbridge noted with approval, that was quite smart and made her look even more lovely. But he quickly concluded that she would look equally smart had she been dressed in nothing but sackcloth.

They sat together for a few minutes in silence, admiring the view. Lord Bainbridge purposely said nothing to allow her time to compose herself, for she still appeared slightly unnerved at his mention of Egypt, and at the same time, he was wondering how much he should tell her. If he told her he was acquainted with her husband, he didn't want her to get the impression they had been intimate. He couldn't quite explain why, but he knew it was very important to him that she did not think such a thing.

After a few minutes, Elaine appeared to have returned to the cheerful person he had originally come across on deck. She sat there, smiling warmly at him, the fading sunlight turning her all golden like the room. Once again, Lord Bainbridge was reminded of an exquisite painting, but this time, it was one that had been restored to its former brilliance.

"How kind you are," she said simply, still watching him.

Lord Bainbridge blushed slightly and sought a topic of conversation. "I understand this room was initially designed to be a place where the ladies could retire to after dinner while the men smoked and played cards," he explained. He glanced around the empty room. "I guess someone forgot to remind the White Star people that this is the twentieth century and ladies no longer wish to retire."

"I've no wish to smoke or play cards either," Elaine added with a mischievous smile.

"Your husband and I have met before," he said quickly. "We were introduced in London and ran into each other a number of times there and of course here on the ship." He shrugged rather helplessly. "He seems to fancy himself my friend."

Her eyes widened but only slightly. "And are you?" she asked.

Lord Bainbridge hesitated, feeling a greet need to defend himself. "We hardly know each other," he answered. "He is very amusing."

"Oh yes," Elaine agreed, "Ronnie is very amusing."

"Why did you marry him?" he asked, and then because he was so shocked by what he saw as his incredible rudeness, he stammered to take back the words. "I'm so sorry. I don't know what possessed me to ask such a question. We're strangers, I had no right."

But Elaine seemed neither offended or surprised by his inquiry. "It's a question I've been asked before," she said. "My husband's actions, his preferences, are hardly a secret. I heard the rumors even before we were married. I wasn't conceited enough to think I would be able to change him."

Lord Bainbridge, made miserable by what he considered an unpardonable indiscretion on his part, watched as a single teardrop paused in the corner of one of her eyes. "Forgive me," he barely whispered.

But the teardrop did not fall to her cheek but remained in the corner of her eye, waiting as if to be called upon another time. "I married Ronnie because I loved him," she said. "It's as simple and ridiculous as that." And because she sensed quite rightly that he was about to apologize again, she reached out and took his hand. "Do not be so concerned. You have done nothing to offend me. As I said before, you have been very kind." She got to her feet, gathering her fur coat about her. "Now, I must go and dress for dinner. This will be the first night I've taken dinner outside my stateroom. I'm quite looking forward to it." She winked at him, or perhaps she was merely brushing away that single tear. "I'm anxious to see what the rest of you have been eating. Perhaps I'll see you this evening," she suggested.

"Yes, perhaps."

"That would be nice," she said. And then offering him a final smile, she turned and walked away, gliding through the door to the lounge with the grace only a beautiful woman can manage.

Watching her until she disappeared from his sight, Lord Bainbridge felt a curious sensation stirring inside of him. So unexpected was it and so out of character for him, he first put it down to a touch of indigestion. But he could not deny the fact that Elaine Standish had touched something deep inside of him. Standing there in the middle of the reading and writing room, he took a few moments to try and analyze this feeling that had come over him and surprised the hell out of him. He lit a cigarette and then held it in his hand, staring intently at it for a long moment. He knew he wasn't physically attracted to the young woman who had just left his side. But still he had the feeling that if he had answered a different calling, if the road of his life had led in the opposite direction from the one he had taken, then he had just met the exact type of woman he would have picked to be his wife. But then after a moment of further reflection, he quickly amended that thought. No, she would have been the one he would have picked. It was as simple as that—if he had had the desire for a wife and family, then at some point, of course had she been free, he would have asked Elaine Standish to be his wife. The fact that she was married to Ronnie only added to the irony of the whole situation. With a final shake of his head as he marveled over the wondrous and complicated twists and turns one's life could take with just an innocent meeting, Lord Bainbridge walked out of the reading and writing room.

Sensing that a good slap of salt air against his face would quickly bring him back to reality from which he had strayed, if only momentarily, he walked out onto the open deck. He had only walked a few steps when one of the ship's junior officers fell into step beside him.

"Have a good day, did you, sir?" the young officer asked, smiling brightly.

Lord Bainbridge nodded. "Yes, quite. This is a remarkable ship," he added, feeling obliged to make a compliment.

"She's the best there is, sir," the officer said with unmistakable pride. "None like her ever before."

Lord Bainbridge smiled at the young man's enthusiasm. It was not the first time they had talked. They had encountered one another a number of times during the voyage, and each time, the officer had made a point of stopping for a few minutes of friendly chat. In fact, he had been almost too friendly as if very anxious to please, but there was also an innocence about him. Lord Bainbridge was quite certain the officer was flirting with him, but he was equally sure the young man had no idea he was doing so. Certainly, Lord Bainbridge found his attentions much more acceptable than the blatant overtures of the underage liftboy.

The officer was handsome enough in a very English sort of way with a milk-white complexion enhanced by rosy cheeks, thick brown hair, and narrow brown eyes that often looked as if he were squinting. *Perhaps he needs eyeglasses,* Lord Bainbridge had thought and then proceeded to wonder if this insufficiency of eyesight at all hampered his duties as a ship's officer on board the world's largest steamship. His attentions to him amused and flattered Lord Bainbridge the way another man of the opposite persuasion would be amused by the flirtations of a younger woman. Although in truth, there couldn't have been more than two or three years at best between them. And Lord Bainbridge did nothing to discourage his attentiveness.

"I've been keeping a sharp lookout for an iceberg," the young officer said, momentarily peering intently out to sea. "I sure am keen to see one, never have before." He was the same officer who had informed Lord Bainbridge the previous day that they should encounter the ice fields today. Now, he gave him an update. "They say now we won't reach the ice much before nightfall."

"We seem to be going faster than ever before," Lord Bainbridge noted.

The young officer nodded. "We are. Though I heard the Old Man, beg pardon, sir, I heard Captain Smith, tell the first officer we weren't going to try for a record run this trip. But you never know, especially with Mr. Ismay on board," he added. His enthusiasm pumped up again. "Would be a cocker though if we did get in a record run!"

"Indeed it would," Lord Bainbridge agreed.

"Can't wait until we get to New York," the officer went on eagerly, his face bright with anticipation. "It will be my first time there. We've got a few days before our return trip, so I plan to see as much of the city as I can. Someone told me it was very lively."

Lord Bainbridge stopped dead in his tracks, staring back at the young officer. He had just used the same code word Alfred often used to describe a place where they would be sure to find kindred spirits. Had it been intentional or merely a random word selection?

"Something wrong, sir?" the officer asked, obviously hoping he hadn't somehow offended.

"No, everything's fine," Lord Bainbridge assured him. "I too have heard that New York is very lively," he added.

The officer stared at him for a moment with a blank look on his face. "I sure hope so," he finally responded. "Well, I'd better shove off, I'm due on the bridge shortly," he said. He offered a broad smile, waved his hand, and was away, walking briskly down the deck, his steps a somewhat exaggerated display of what he obviously considered was the proper way for a ship's officer to stroll the deck of a ship but which unfortunately made him look as if he were still struggling to find his sea legs.

Lord Bainbridge watched him depart with amusement. He realized that though they had spoken several times, they had not exchanged names. He suspected the young officer was shy about introducing himself, perhaps because such intimacy between members of the crew and their passengers, especially first-class passengers, was probably not proper White Star policy.

Back in his stateroom, Lord Bainbridge found that Alfred had lain out his clothes for dinner and was ready to draw his bath. Stripping off his clothes as Alfred prepared things in the bathroom, Lord Bainbridge reflected on how necessary, how indispensable, Alfred had become to his life. Alfred took care of everything: he ran their household, even kept their books. If Lord Bainbridge wanted to go to the theatre, or the music hall, which was more to Alfred's liking, it was Alfred who bought the tickets and who hailed the motor-cab when it was time to go. Lord Bainbridge never carried any money with him when they went out. Alfred always paid for everything; of course it was Lord Bainbridge's money he paid with. It was as if, Lord Bainbridge concluded, they were an old married couple who had settled comfortably into their individual domestic roles.

Alfred popped his head out of the bathroom. "Water's ready," he announced.

Lord Bainbridge walked naked into the bathroom. It was a small room, but in keeping with the *Titanic's* luxurious first-class accommodations, its walls were sheathed in marble, and all of its fixtures were gold-plated. Slipping gratefully into the tub, he found the water to be the exact temperature he always desired. Feeling relaxed and at ease with the world, he leaned his head back and closed his eyes. He must have fallen asleep, probably just for a few minutes, because when he opened his eyes again, Alfred was leaning in the doorway, his arms folded, watching him. "Be careful of this one," he advised as Lord Bainbridge vigorously soaped himself.

Lord Bainbridge knew at once that he was referring to Tom. He didn't respond at first but concentrated on cleansing himself. "What do you mean?" he finally asked.

Alfred shrugged. "I don't think he has any bad intentions. And those are the ones you have to look out for," he added before disappearing into the next room.

A short while later, Lord Bainbridge stood before a full-length mirror which was situated in one corner of his stateroom. He was partially dressed for dinner, wearing his underdrawers, a white starched shirtfront with a stiff collar, and black silk stockings held up by black garters. Alfred stood close behind him, his hands reaching around to tie his black bow tie. As he worked, Alfred's body kept pressing tighter and tighter against Lord Bainbridge, his state of arousal unmistakable.

"What are you doing?" Lord Bainbridge asked, catching his eye in the mirror before them.

"Helping you with your tie," Alfred answered in mock innocence.

"No, the other."

Alfred's face grinned in the mirror. "I never could resist a bloke in his knickers." He laughed. Then finished, he stepped away, and they both had a good laugh.

They were no longer intimate, that part of their relationship had run its course, and they had curtailed it by mutual agreement. Now, they had something more.

Lord Bainbridge reached out and caught Alfred's hand. "Whatever happens with Tom is not going to change our relationship," he told him. "I don't want you to feel threatened."

Alfred cocked his head to one side. "That right? I don't feel threatened," he added still grinning at him, looking slightly sinister. "If I did, I'd have to get rid of him."

Lord Bainbridge finished dressing by himself, and when he was done, he stepped back from the mirror to take in his appearance. He tugged down the corners of his white pique waistcoat, adjusted his stiff collar and, in spite of Alfred's strenuous efforts, took a few additional moments to industriously redo his tie. Picking up a brush from the dresser, he gave the silk-faced lapels of his double-breasted dinner jacket a couple of good sweeps. And then satisfied, at least with his wardrobe, he turned his attention to the man. Taking up one of his hairbrushes, he began brushing back his short brown hair, pushing it first that way and then the other, attempting to achieve a look he knew he never would. Sighing in defeat, he put down the brush and stared back at his face in the mirror. There were times when he wished he had been drop-dead handsome like say, Denham. For a moment, he did wish he looked like Denham and that it would be Denham's face Tom would see tonight when they met. Then, he was sure of it, Tom would be quickly won. For who in their right mind or right senses could ever have said no to the likes of Denham Granville-Smith? Lord Bainbridge smiled and shook his head at his own foolish thoughts as he turned away from the mirror.

Alfred was gathering up his coat and hat. "Where you off to, then?" Lord Bainbridge asked.

"To grab a bite to eat myself," Alfred answered, opening the door to the corridor.

"And then a visit to the bodyguard?" Lord Bainbridge suggested with a sly wink.

Alfred paused in the doorway. He shrugged noncommittally. "Perhaps. I haven't done it with him yet if that's what you're asking. But I'm working on it," he added just before he shut the door behind him.

Left alone, Lord Bainbridge smiled to himself. Alfred liked to say things like that every once in a while. He liked to shock for the sake of shocking as if to remind everyone, himself included, that he came from the East End, and nothing was ever going to change that.

Pulling out his watch, Lord Bainbridge saw that he still had plenty of time before he was expected to pick up Maude, so he decided to have a brandy and a cigarette. He had just settled into the sofa before the fireplace, and was swirling the brandy in his glass, when there was a knock on the door leading to the corridor. Before he even got to his feet, there was a second knock, sounding more urgent than the first.

He opened the door to find an anxious face, followed by equally anxious words. "Hurry let me in before someone spots me!"

Lord Bainbridge stepped aside, and then he quickly shut the door. "What are you doing here?" he asked, both surprised and annoyed.

Marco Borsalino grinned and shrugged his shoulders as if it were a question whose answer was obvious. "I came to see you, of course," he answered.

"But how did you find your way back here?" Lord Bainbridge wanted to know.

Marco shrugged again. "I know this ship like the back of my hand," he boasted. "I've been all over it like a rat since we left Southampton." Spying the brandy and cigarette that Lord Bainbridge still clutched in his hand, he nodded approvingly. "Ah, just what I need." And without further ado, he crossed to the sofa, flung himself down, lit up a cigarette, poured himself a generous glass of brandy, and put his feet up.

"Well you can't stay here," Lord Bainbridge told him. "I'm going to dinner."

Marco said nothing for a moment, taking time to blow a contented puff of smoke from his cigarette. He looked up at Lord Bainbridge, smiling like a child, a devious child up to no-good. "I can make smoke rings, would you like to see?" he asked.

"Not particularly," Lord Bainbridge returned, still standing as if he were waiting to be asked to take a seat.

"I know you are having dinner in the restaurant tonight, but not until seven," Marco said. "I should be there now, getting the tables ready. They'll be looking for me soon," he added, but he didn't seem overly concerned about his tardiness.

"How did you know I'd be having dinner in the restaurant tonight?" Lord Bainbridge asked, beginning to feel uneasy and wondering if Marco had somehow been spying on him.

"I overheard your friend, the big English lady, talking with Monsieur Gatti. She was planning a party for the captain. She mentioned your name in particular," Marco answered.

Lord Bainbridge came around the sofa and sat down beside him but keeping his distance. "Now look, Marco."

"Are you not please to see Marco?" the other asked, leaning toward him. He often did that—speak of himself in the third person. "Did you not say I was to be the love of your life?" he added even flickering his long eyelashes coquettishly the way a young woman might do.

Lord Bainbridge was quite certain he had made no such declaration, not even in the heat of passion when one's tongue is apt to slip and then later be misquoted.

"The other night," Marco prompted. He took a long swallow of his brandy. "When we made love," he added, wiping the drops of liquor from his lips with the back of his hand.

Lord Bainbridge certainly needed no prompting to remember the night, their first night at sea, though he would have hardly referred to their encounter as making love.

It had all began because Maude, having compared the menus of both the dining saloon and the restaurant, had decided that the food in the restaurant looked to be vastly superior to that being offered in the dining saloon. "The food in the restaurant," she had announced with a firm shake of her head, "has a more Continental flair to it. While the dining saloon is obviously catering to the majority of Americans on board and my stomach, which you know is never on its best behavior when at sea, certainly could not stand the shock of American food on our first night out." So they had dinner that night in the restaurant.

Lord Bainbridge couldn't remember when he first became aware of the tall young waiter. He was quite certain he hadn't been there during the beginning of their meal. But later, he looked up casually as his plate was being cleared away and stared right into the face of one of the most remarkable-looking young men he had ever seen. First of all, there was his height. At nearly six feet, he was tall and spindly as a tree, and his arms were so long they poked out some distance from the sleeves of his waiter's uniform as he reached for Lord Bainbridge's plate. Underneath his thick black curls, the hollows of his cheekbones had hollows of their own. He had a laughing face, his dark features always twisted in amusement, sometimes mocking, sometimes teasing, but always, at least on the surface, amused. If you looked closely into his green eyes, as Lord Bainbridge did for a fleeting second, you saw flecks of gold. The young waiter instantly caught onto Lord Bainbridge's interest, almost as if he had been expecting it, and first offering him a broad and knowing smile, he then proceeded to pick up his tray of dishes and walk away from their table toward the kitchen. But it was the way he walked that instantly caught Lord Bainbridge's attention. The best word he could have used to describe it was saucy. It was neither effeminate or mincing although it was exaggerated and obvious and most decidedly done exclusively for Lord Bainbridge's benefit. The waiter's uniform the young man wore consisted of a very short black jacket with gold lapels and tight black trousers that stretched enticingly across his buttocks, leaving very little to Lord Bainbridge's imagination. Later when they were alone back in his stateroom, Marco would reveal to him with mischievous glee that he had purposely selected a pair of trousers two sizes too small for himself. They hurt like hell to wear, he had confessed, but they got him the attention he desired. As Lord Bainbridge watched Marco walk away from their table in the restaurant, putting every ounce of concentration and effort into his stride, he marveled that the young waiter was able to carry it off while burdened with a full tray of dishes. But Marco made it to the kitchen without a mishap and doing no damage except to Lord Bainbridge's nerves.

Sitting across the table, Maude, bless her heart, noticed none of this, or if she did, she was discrete enough to pretend she didn't.

From the first moment he set eyes on him, Lord Bainbridge knew he wouldn't be able to resist Marco's obvious charms. Even though a little voice inside of his head warned him this was a relationship that held no promise and might even prove to be unsavory. But as it had been so many times before with him, it was Lord Bainbridge's loins, not his head, that ruled the day. And so later that night, he sent Alfred to the restaurant to arrange a rendezvous. He did not have long to wait. Within the half hour, Alfred returned with a most willing and eager Marco in tow. True to his nature, Alfred treated the Italian with the contempt and disdain he felt for anyone who belonged to a non-English-speaking nationality.

Once they were alone in Lord Bainbridge's stateroom and money had been exchanged, as both the giver and the receiver had known it would be, they settled down before the fireplace with cigarettes and brandy. Lord Bainbridge quickly discovered that Marco Borsalino loved to talk, and what he loved to talk the most about was Marco. In fact, he was so obsessed with himself that all other beings were excluded from his realm, and so he became, by default, the center of his own universe. He told Lord Bainbridge many stories of his past, conflicting tales that often refuted one another. Many were obvious exaggerations while others could only be outright lies. With Marco, it was impossible to separate fact from fiction. It wasn't that he was ignorant, he just seemed to find much delight in spinning fanciful tales as long as they were about himself. One moment, he would say that he came from poor parents who lived in the slums of Rome. Then almost with the next breath, he would claim to be descended from a distinguished family of minor nobility from Ravenna. He liked this story a lot because it also claimed that he had the right to be called a prince. He told Lord Bainbridge that he was nineteen. But the Englishman sensed that he was a bit older, probably twenty-one or—two. Nineteen, he reasoned, was a convenient age to be when you were up to no good or in the very least playing for sympathy. Lord Bainbridge learned that Marco had signed on with Monsieur Gatti to work in the ship's restaurant only to get a free passage to America. He planned to jump ship when they reached New York. The one flaw in this scheme, which he didn't find out about until he was already on board ship, was that Monsieur Gatti would not be paying his employees any of their wages until they had completed the return trip. Marco Borsalino and the other waiters, cooks, and cashiers would not be paid a penny until the *Titanic* docked once again in Southampton. Since he had very little money of his own, Marco would therefore be arriving in New York nearly destitute. This distressing situation only momentarily weighed heavily on the young Italian, for Marco was one of those individuals who refused to brood about a misfortune, choosing instead to spend his time coming up with alternate solutions to his problems. Marco's solution to his monetary woes was to seek out willing contributors to his cause like Lord Bainbridge. That this was something he had done before, and not infrequently, was fairly obvious. In fact, Lord Bainbridge speculated that for Marco, it was a common practice not unlike the young men he had encountered at the Crown. But in addition, Marco revealed that he had even more ambitious plans. Apparently, he had heard from some of his fellow waiters, these being more seasoned ocean travelers, about the card games that went on in the first-class smoking room, games that would continue for the whole voyage and where fortunes turned hands, sometimes in the blink of an eye. "There's a lot of money eagerly waiting to be lost on this voyage," one of them had told him. Marco had boasted to Lord Bainbridge that he was going to find a way to get in on one of those games during the *Titanic's* trip. He explained that another Englishman he had known years before had taught him to play cards, and Marco was convinced he could play good enough to win a tidy bundle. Lord Bainbridge remained skeptical of Marco's ability to find a way into one of the card games in first class although he had already realized the young man was both bold and opportunistic.

Now as they once again sat before the fireplace in Lord Bainbridge's stateroom, Lord Bainbridge, annoyed by Marco's abrupt intrusion, found a certain amount of pleasure in inquiring if Marco had indeed managed to take part in any first-class card games.

"Regrettably no," Marco admitted. He didn't seem fazed by his failure. In fact, he now seemed indifferent to the whole idea of the card game. His mind, Lord Bainbridge reasoned, was probably already working on another scheme. Schemes were Marco's lifeblood, and Lord Bainbridge quickly realized that he would try anything to get his way, and if that didn't work, he would merely shrug his shoulders and try something else.

Marco hadn't articulated to Lord Bainbridge his precise reasons for going to America, but it was obvious that his goal was similar to that of probably almost every passenger on board the ship who was traveling third class—a better life. But while the others dreamed of someday owning a fruit farm in the Midwest or a tailor's shop in Boston or Philadelphia, Marco dreamed on a much grandeur scale. He saw himself living in a mansion with servants and motorcars and, most importantly, money to burn. And while the other emigrants in third class were prepared to use hard labor as a means to their hopeful ends, Marco was quite prepared to use anything, honestly or dishonestly, to achieve his dream. And this included his body.

Marco thrust his glass out for more brandy, which Lord Bainbridge reluctantly filled, realizing it was not going to be easy to get rid of him. The young Italian helped himself to another cigarette from Lord Bainbridge's case, which lay open on the table in front of them. Then Marco turned to Lord Bainbridge with a broad smile on his face and turned on the charm.

"I was sure you would have sent for me before now," he said. He was flickering his eyelashes again in that way he did, which he must have thought was flirtatious but on a young man looked rather ridiculous. Then he did something quite unexpected, at least Lord Bainbridge certainly was not prepared for it, he reached out and rested his hand on Lord Bainbridge's knee.

Lord Bainbridge actually recoiled from his touch as he stammered out an excuse. "I've been very busy with my friends." He even laughed a little although it was a hollow and empty sound. "At sea, time seems to go by so quickly," he added.

Marco's touch had unnerved him because of its unexpectedness. It was not that he found the young man unattractive or repulsive. Quite the contrary, there was no denying the fact that with his striking features, he was very handsome. His flashing smile and eager-to-please manner could be charming. And he actually spoke well, if mostly of himself. Their first night together, when finally Marco had talked himself out and they had gone to bed, Lord Bainbridge had found his body almost breathtakingly beautiful. His skin was a golden brown as if he had spent every waking hour in the sun. Each cheek of his small delicately formed posterior had a faint blush to it like fruit newly ripened. But the love making that followed, if that's what it could have been called, left much to be desired. Marco lay stiffly on the bed, his arms tight at his side, taking no active part. His role was entirely passive, and he made that abundantly clear. His body could be used, even abused, but in its surrender, he would not participate. At one moment, at the height of Lord Bainbridge's passion, Marco presented his full lips enticingly as if for a kiss and then turned them away at the last moment so that Lord Bainbridge's lips fell on his cheek. "Not on the mouth," Marco had hissed in a whisper. It had been Lord Bainbridge's experience that many of the lads he had encountered, especially those commonly referred to as rough trade, had a great fear of losing their masculinity or at the very least compromising it. After all many of them had women, wives, or sweethearts, whom they returned to after their "business" had been completed. So when they went to bed with other men, they always set boundaries, restrictions, lines over which they would not cross. This almost always meant that they would take the male role when it came to sex. "I am the man," was their favorite and often spoken maxim. But at least they took part in the act. Seldom before had Lord Bainbridge come upon a young man who would just lay there in the bed, refusing to contribute. But that was Marco. And had his body not been warm, it might easily have been a corpse. This had been a huge disappointment to Lord Bainbridge. His earlier travels to Italy and the south of France had exposed him to the pleasing sights of young Mediterranean males strolling about with their arms around each other's shoulders and even holding hands. This had convinced him that Mediterranean males often had intense friendships and were not afraid to be demonstrative when it came to showing affection for one another. But Marco at least proved otherwise. Of course, his night with Marco had occurred before he met Tom. Now that he had, he realized that even if Marco had proven to be a lover of the greatest expertise he had ever known, a concept that in itself now seemed pretty ridiculous, it would have not been enough to stir his thoughts from Tom. Now, as the minutes dragged on and they continued to sit there before the fireplace, all Lord Bainbridge wanted from Marco was his departure.

Marco must have sensed his disinterest for he quickly withdrew his hand and his charm, turning the latter off like an electric switch. He was staring sullenly into the coils of the electric heater in the fireplace when he suddenly made a startling statement. "I killed a man once."

Lord Bainbridge shot him a quick glance, wondering if Marco had decided to now try intimidation. "Oh really?" he responded, careful not to let even a hint of apprehension seep through his tone.

"Yah." Marco nodded. "An Englishman," he added with intended emphasis. Then still gazing moodily into the fireplace, he told his story. "When I was fifteen, he came to our village."

Now it was a village, Lord Bainbridge noted, no longer the slums of Rome or a palace in Ravenna.

"The Englishman was a photographer," Marco went on. "And he paid me a few coins to help him lug his camera equipment around when he went out to take pictures of the ancient ruins or the sea. He also liked to photograph people, especially boys and young men," he added, casting Lord Bainbridge a brief but knowing glance. "Some of them he would take back to the little house he had rented and take photographs of these boys without their clothes on. When we weren't taking photographs, he would teach me English and how to play cards." True to his nature, Marco couldn't resist a boast. "I was soon speaking English as good as him and beating him at cards every time. One day, he offered me more money if I would let him photograph me with no clothes on. It was more money than I had ever seen in my whole life, so I said yes. But as soon as I was naked, the Englishman began to go all crazy. He wrapped his arms around me and began to whisper words in my ear, words of love. His breath was hot and unsavory, and though I struggled, he wouldn't let me go. Finally, I managed to break free of him, and I warned him to stay away from me. But he came at me again, so I picked up one of his glass camera plates, and I smashed it into his face as hard as I could. Even with blood streaming down his face, he still tried to grab me, so I hit him with the plate again and again. Until at last he fell in a heap to the floor. I knew he was dead. I pulled on my clothes and got out of there as fast as I could. Later, the police questioned me, but they soon let me go. 'Murder and robbery by an unknown intruder' was the official police report. Though I don't know how they could say robbery since I had been too scared to steal anything from him, not even the money he had promised me."

"But why did you have to kill him?" Lord Bainbridge asked, troubled.

"I told you," Marco insisted, "he wouldn't back off. He wouldn't stop touching me. No one had ever touched me that way before." Then he lowered his voice to a whisper, a troubled whisper that was haunted by what had happened that terrible day, that terrible day when he, Marco Borsalino, had been responsible for the ending of another man's life. He had taken away that Englishman's last breath. "I was scared," he whispered. "I was scared to death." Then he hung his head and said nothing more on the matter.

So much for intimidation, Lord Bainbridge thought to himself.

But Marco was not quite done yet. He raised his head, looked over at Lord Bainbridge, and smiled devilishly at him. "I could perhaps tell your friends about what we did together," he suggested.

So now it's to be blackmail, Lord Bainbridge thought, highly amused. "My friends already know about me," he lied.

"Ah yes, but what about the rest of the world?" Marco said. "When we reach New York I could tell my story to the newspapers. About how I, an innocent young boy, was seduced by a famous English writer."

"I'm not that famous," Lord Bainbridge reminded him. "No one would care."

"I will go to the ship's captain," Marco insisted rather absurdly.

Lord Bainbridge was quite certain Marco was bluffing and that he wouldn't do any of these things. But, he reasoned, you never know for sure what Italians will do. They were such an unpredictable race even more so than the French. Watching him and seeing on his face every conceivable course of action as it tumbled through his brain as he struggled to glean something more from a relationship that even he must have known was over, Lord Bainbridge was quite certain that twenty years from now, even ten, when his features had hardened into a mask, Marco would still be scheming and plotting, still searching for his pot of gold. And because he would be no longer young, no longer so pretty, his search would become more desperate, and he would take chances and do things he had never done before. And then, and this was something Lord Bainbridge was quite sure of, as if he had seen it clearly in a dream, on some dark street at some unspeakable hour Marco would be killed. It was such a vivid vision of the future that he had sensed, it made Lord Bainbridge shiver in the warm room.

Feeling sympathy for him because of what he had just imagined lay ahead of the young Italian, Lord Bainbridge tried to be gentle as he got to his feet. "I'm sorry, Marco, it's getting late. I must meet my friends."

Nodding, Marco got to his feet as well. He stared silently back at Lord Bainbridge for a moment, took a last puff on his cigarette, and expelled the smoke on purpose into Lord Bainbridge's face. Underneath his thick black curls, his green eyes danced with childish delight at a prank well conceived.

He let Lord Bainbridge escort him to the door, and as he stepped out into the corridor, he turned back to him. "You're not done with me yet," he promised, a broad smile lighting up his dark face and making him look, indeed, like a child. Then he was gone, loping off down the corridor at a high rate of speed as befitting one who suddenly realizes they are late for work.

Watching him go, Lord Bainbridge could only hope Marco wouldn't cause any kind of scene in the restaurant. At the very least, he could only pray that he wouldn't be serving at their table. Cursing himself for having got himself into this whole mess in the first place, he closed the door to his stateroom and hurried off to collect Maude, who surely must be thinking he had abandoned her.

Chapter VI

Sunday, April 14, 1912

In the restaurant that night, Lord Bainbridge's worst fears were unfortunately realized. Marco Borsalino was indeed assigned to their table although only as a junior waiter, which meant he only cleared away their dishes when they were done. To the senior waiters went the honor of serving. Still given the fact that Maude's little dinner party was in honor of Captain Smith, Lord Bainbridge found it surprising that Monsieur Gatti had given the plum assignment of waiting on their table, even as a junior waiter, to Marco. Surely, there were other junior waiters on his staff who had much more experience waiting on tables than Marco's few days worth. But then knowing Marco as he did, Lord Bainbridge surmised he probably had wheeled and charmed his way into the position. Of course, Lord Bainbridge was not vain enough to think that Marco had secured this coveted position just in order to harass him. Undoubtedly, he had another goal in mind, and it could only be that he hoped to impress Captain Smith and perhaps catch his eye. Though to what benefit, Lord Bainbridge didn't have a clue and perhaps neither did Marco, seeking only to impress someone who impressed him with his title and authority. But at least initially, Marco seemed barely to notice Lord Bainbridge as he concentrated on his duties. And although their eyes did meet once or twice over the heads of the others at the table, he seemed in no hurry to exact any sort of revenge. The presence of his boss, Monsieur Gatti, likewise probably kept him momentarily in check.

Monsieur Luigi Gatti was an elegant little balding man with an impressive mustache who overflowed with Continental charm. Having been previously employed by two of London's most renowned eating establishments, the restaurant at the Ritz Hotel and the ultra posh Oddenino's Imperial Restaurant, he had brought to the *Titanic* all his skill and expertise. Monsieur Gatti was known as something of a taskmaster and a perfectionist. No detail of his operation was too small for his attention. Only that very afternoon, he had paid a call on Thomas Andrews, managing director of Harland & Wolff Shipyard in Belfast, builders of the *Titanic*, who along with eight of his associates was making this trip to work out any kinks that might occur on the *Titanic's* maiden voyage. Monsieur

Gatti's complaint to Mr. Andrews was about the restaurant's galley hot press that seemed to be having difficulty maintaining an even temperature. It was a minor concern, but Thomas Andrews, being perhaps even more of a perfectionist than Monsieur Gatti, assured the restaurant's proprietor he would have one of his men check it out straight away. Other than the galley hot press, Monsieur Gatti had found everything else in his new establishment to be in first-rate order. The restaurant, as befitted its special status, had its own kitchen, and this had been equipped with all the latest culinary contraptions from electric potato peelers to bains-marie used exclusively for cooking delicate items such as custards. There were numerous giant refrigerators, their larders filled with everything from game birds of every variety—a particular favorite of Edwardian palates—to hothouse grapes, fresh asparagus, and hundreds of quarts of ice cream. If the dining room area of the restaurant was a calm and tranquil oasis where passengers took their meals in a relaxed and congenial atmosphere; the kitchen, by contrast, was a beehive of frenzied activity. Noisy and hot despite the fans. So hot in fact, that a kitchen boy armed with towels was placed by the door to the dining room. His one task was to wipe the sweat from the faces of the waiters before they emerged into the dining room with their heavily laden trays. In such a heated atmosphere, inevitably there were clashes of temperament between personnel, especially between cooks and serving persons. And given that these individuals were all of Mediterranean descent, volatile outbursts were to be expected. But a stern reprimand from Monsieur Gatti always instantly brought calm and a return to strict discipline.

Monsieur Gatti managed it all like a mammoth stage production. Every dish, skillfully prepared in the kitchen, was brought to its intended table at just the right moment and with just the right amount of flourish. And at every meal, Monsieur Gatti, elegant in his frock-tailed coat, was there. He could be seen flitting around the tables and in and out of the kitchen, seeing to every detail, adding something here, taking something away there, always knowing just the right touch to make one's dining experience sumptuous and unforgettable.

Of course, the stage setting for his production was in itself equally sumptuous. Beneath the crystal chandeliers, the tables, each set with a centerpiece of pink roses and services of green and gold Royal Crown Derby china, were spread out across a deep-pile carpet of a delicate Rose duBarri hue. The walls were covered with fawn-colored paneling of French walnut while the large bay windows were hung with rich rose silk draperies. It was a splendid scene that could have easily rivaled any five-star restaurant in London or even Paris for that matter.

In fact, even a Parisian had been impressed. When the members of Maude's dinner party had first gathered and been seated, Madame Renoir had turned to Monsieur Gatti, hovering nearby to see that all was well, and stated her admiration. "Monsieur, these surroundings are *tres elegant.*"

Maude, who was already an eager convert to the restaurant's many charms, agreed wholeheartedly. "It's every bit as impressive as the Cafe Royal in London," she added enthusiastically.

Monsieur Gatti thanked them both for their compliments and then hurried off to the kitchen to see to their first course. And during the rest of the evening, his eyes never strayed far from their table.

Meanwhile, Lord Bainbridge, who after taking his seat had let his mind wander way with pleasant thoughts of Tom and their meeting to come, came quickly back to the present at the mention of the Cafe Royal. He instantly recalled the words he and Ronnie Standish had had earlier in the day regarding Oscar Wilde and his frequent visits to the Cafe Royal with his constant parade of young renters. "Feasting with panthers" were the words Wilde had used to describe these meals, and Wilde had learned, as Lord Bainbridge had also on occasion, that panthers do have sharp claws and often are not reluctant to use them. Feeling slightly mischievous and, having already downed a before-dinner cognac along with the brandy he had consumed in his stateroom as he had dealt with his own panther, Lord Bainbridge toyed with the idea of offering his little Wilde tidbit up for general conversation. It would be quite naughty of him for sure, but as he glanced around the table at his dinner companions, he decided he should perhaps hold his tongue. Besides, no one discussed Oscar Wilde anymore except Ronnie Standish.

In addition to Captain Smith, his dinner companions were to number five. Of course, there was Maude and then Madame Renoir and her son, Sebastian. And to complete their party, Count Alonzo Fraboli and his wife, Lucianna, an Italian couple in their mid-sixties. Lord Bainbridge and Maude had visited Count Fraboli and his wife the previous spring in their family home in Venice and then traveled with them to Egypt. After they had all come on board the *Titanic*, they had become one of those unique groups that often come together during sea voyages where the chemistry between members is just right, and they all become good friends. Maude had nicknamed them Our Little Group. And the six of them had spent my pleasant hours in each other's company, taking meals together, strolling the decks and, many nights, enjoying the concerts provided by the ship's orchestra. It was all great fun and made a delightful ocean crossing even more of a treat. Now here they were about to begin what surely would turn out to be the highlight of their trip.

Their guest of honor had not yet joined them, and Captain Smith's absence had begun to concern Maude. She fidgeted nervously in her chair. She was wearing a black taffeta evening dress with a taffeta cape lined with black fur. Her one adornment of jewelry was a magnificent string of pearls that cascaded down her equally magnificent bosom. This evening, she wore her spectacles dangling from a silver chain around her neck. This arrangement however in no way guaranteed that she would be able to find them should she have need of them. She had also confessed to Lord Bainbridge before they left her stateroom that she had put her corsets back on. "It seemed the proper thing to do," she had told him, "Captain Smith, you see, is of the old school."

Now she voiced her concern about his late arrival. "I hope there's nothing wrong with the ship."

Seated to her left, Count Fraboli shook his finger at her and chided her gently. "Dear lady, what could possible go wrong with a ship as magnificent as this one?"

But Maude, though a seasoned Atlantic traveler, always remained slightly apprehensive when she was out on the ocean, and perhaps the crewman's blasphemous challenge to God still stuck in her mind. "Any number of things could happen," she answered but declined, to most everyone's relief, to offer specifics.

Count Fraboli smiled back at her with the kindly forbearance that was his nature. He had a way of looking at people as if he alone were standing on some Olympian heights, watching the human follies being enacted below. It wasn't done in a condescending manner, but rather in a detached gentle way as if he found all of mankind worthy of both his attention and amusement. He was over six feet tall, and in spite of his advanced age and poor health, he carried his height with the ramrod stiffness of a Prussian military officer. His sunburned and lined face, like his body, had a thinness, a trimness, to it, ending in a very determinedly pointed chin that was concealed by a fine thick gray beard. Like Maude, he too had a problem with his spectacles. His were a rimless pair that he always wore on the very end of his prominent patrician nose. This precarious position often placed them in great jeopardy of being flung off into space with any sharp turn of his head, a not infrequent occurrence. The descendant of Venetian nobility, he could effortlessly trace his lineage all the way back to the fourteenth century. He had inherited a title and wealth that had greatly simplified his life's struggle.

At the age of seventeen, the count went off on a trip to Egypt with other young blades of his class. While his companions spent most of their time larking about, drinking and chasing the dark Egyptian girls, he became intrigued by the work being done by a group of his countrymen in the desolate Valley of the Kings where the ancient Egyptians had buried their royal dead. Alonzo approached his countrymen and announced himself ready to help them with their excavations. They were greatly amused, to say the least, at the sight of this skinny young dandy standing before them in a brushed frock coat, complete with top hat and walking stick, offering to join them in their dirty and, more often than not, unrewarding labors. But he seemed enthusiastic, and they were shorthanded, so they took him on for his keep and put him to work at the lowest tasks that even the natives shunned. The frock coat and top hat were soon replaced by proper digging clothes, but the walking stick remained. And Alonzo Fraboli, the elegant young Venetian nobleman, found his true happiness grubbing in the red Egyptian clay underneath an unrelenting sun which turned the hollow valley into a merciless incubator. At night, after a full day's exhausting toil, he would wander alone through the length of the valley while from the craggy limestone cliffs above him, he was sure he heard voices, snatches of conversations from the far distant past. He was enchanted by it all, and he knew he would never be able to leave this place. He returned year after year, and as he worked, he learned. These were the early years of what would become the field of modern archaeology, and most of the men practicing it were concerned with finding only treasure. At the beginning of every digging season, the human locust descended on the land of the Nile, men and women, fortune seekers, most of them untrained, many uneducated, rich and poor alike, seeking their fortunes or at the very least an amazing trophy or two to dazzle the folks back home. The Egyptians themselves were no better; corruption was universal from the lowest digger to the highest official—a little baksheesh and the eye looked the other way. Gradually, a new breed of men began to appear in the valley, and Count Alonzo was one of these, men who were concerned with the systematic retrieval and accurate recording of the objects they found. For them, the acquisition of knowledge was more important than the gathering of spoils. As the years passed, the sight of this tall thin man, with his walking stick always poking at things in his path, looking like some large specimen of stork, became a familiar part of the valley landscape. After his marriage, Lucianna came with him to Egypt every year and worked at his side, always protected from the sun by a wide-brimmed hat and a colorful sunshade held over her head by an Egyptian lad. While most other archaeologists had to depend on the whims of the wealthy benefactors who financially supported their work, Alonzo was in the unique and enviable position of being his own patron. He had the money to hire his own diggers, and after having acquired the necessary licenses from the Egyptian government, he could decide where they would dig. As his skill and knowledge increased, so did his finds, starting with a couple of small insignificant tombs that had belonged to a pair of royal princes all the way up to the tomb of the important pharaoh Tuthmosis III. But as his career progressed, one discovery escaped him as it did all the others working the valley—the uncovering of an intact tomb. So much had already been lost, plundered away by both ancient robbers and their modern counterparts that every new discovery revealed hardly more than an empty sepulcher with sometimes an overturned sarcophagus and some debris scattered about the floor. All the gold and other precious items that each pharaoh had been prepared to enter the after life with had long since disappeared. And as time passed, and tomb after tomb was opened and its long dead occupant checked off on the list of pharaohs prepared by the ancient priests, the chances of finding an unplundered burial became less and less. Many archaeologists gave up on the valley and moved on to more promising sites, convinced that any area that had been dug over since the time of Napoleon had nothing left to yield; like a gold mine, it had been played out. In spite of this, Alonzo remained convinced that somewhere in the valley, an ancient ruler still slept undisturbed. He was certain that there still lay hidden at least one untouched pharaonic tomb. But if this was so, he was not destined to be the one to find it. The 1911 digging season was his last in the valley.

Although the doctors could not identify it or its cause, Count Fraboli could diagnose the illness that had begun to plague him and would soon kill him. He and his wife spent the summer at the fashionable Winter Palace in Luxor, close to the valley. Then in the beginning of October, he took one final trip to the valley for a last look around. Even though so many now declared the area exhausted, new excavations were starting, and Alonzo renewed his acquaintance with an energetic Englishman named Howard Carter, whom he had known for many years and one of the few like himself who continued to believe an unopened tomb might still be found. With envy, Alonzo wished him luck and then left the valley forever, leaving behind as he later told his wife, "Most of my heart and all of my spirit." They spent the holidays in the family home, the seventeenth century Palazzo Bernardi on Venice's Grand Canal, and from there, they retired to the south of France for a few month's rest. Now here they were off to America, to Boston to be exact where Count Frabolii was to be feted by the Museum of Fine Arts for his years of tireless duty to the science of Egyptology. His long career, like his life, was coming to its end.

Lord Bainbridge was keenly aware that as soon as Count Fraboli had offered Maude his mild chastisement over her concerns about the *Titanic*, his wife, Lucianna, had fixed him with a look from across the table. And knowing them as intimately as he did, Lord Bainbridge was aware that they were able to communicate with each other without words, with nothing more than a look, a simple glance. As he turned slightly toward Lucianna, sitting beside him, Lord Bainbridge knew as well that the look she was giving her husband, while gentle and loving, was urging him not to offend.

And so it was that Count Fraboli after his mild protest fell silent and presented Maude with nothing more than his kindly smile. It was not that he was ruled by his wife, but rather that they were so in tuned, so aware of each other after forty years of marriage, that each could think for the other, and each sought continuously to keep the other from harm even from something as minor as a misspoken word.

"Sometimes Alonzo gets a little carried away," Lucianna said, turning now to her table companion. She spoke English in that beautiful Continental modulation that was almost musical and made the language, with just a tiny trace of accent, sound as if it were being spoken the way it was meant to be spoken without the jarring distortions added by both the English and the Americans.

Lucianna was tall and stately like her husband, with silver gray hair that had turned to its flattering shade when she was in her early thirties. Her features, which some might have labeled as severe even haughty, were immediately tempered by a warm and generous nature. Both she and her husband were part of the Old World, part of the old European order that now at the beginning of the new century was fast slipping away. They spoke of a time of courtly manners, gracious smiles and emotions that were kept tightly in check and only unleashed when one was alone. Lucianna Fraboli was a fastidious dresser, and having both a private fortune and a private dressmaker in Florence, she was able to indulge this whim to her heart's content. For this special occasion, she wore a gold and silver brocade evening dress with an overlay of gold lace and a train of gold lamé. Her long silver hair, swept up on her head, was held in place by a gold band inlaid with precious stones. Her husband had been suitably impressed by her appearance and had declared, somewhat appropriately that she looked like a pharaoh's treasure. Even Madame Renoir, who was, as has already been noted, from Paris, the undisputed fashion capital of the entire world, had murmured her approval. One other item of Lucianna's attire should be mentioned. She wore long white gloves. In fact, she always wore gloves of some kind whenever she went out in public. Years spent working at her husband's side had destroyed her hands and nails, and rather than let them be seen by others, she chose to conceal them. And while some might say this spoke to the woman's vanity, others would be quick to point out that it spoke more to her devotion and love for her husband.

Lord Bainbridge smiled back at Lucianna. "Usually it's Alonzo's work that stirs his passion so," he said. And then quickly realizing his mistake, his eyes sought hers as his hand momentarily covered hers on the table between them. "Is there no chance he might be able to return to it?" he asked.

"No chance at all," Lucianna answered quickly. She glanced across the table toward her husband and then back to Lord Bainbridge. "The doctors have said," she began and then with a sigh and a shake of her head she repeated the prognosis. "No, no chance at all."

"How is he taking it?" Lord Bainbridge asked.

Lucianna sighed once again, and her elegant shoulders shrugged. "Some days he rants and raves, other times he sits for hours, brooding. With all that he's done," she went on, "he still feels his work is uncompleted." She stared intently into Lord Bainbridge's face. "You know, the one goal that escaped him, the one find he never made."

Lord Bainbridge nodded, knowing as he did that Alonzo Fraboli's whole life had been his work. And now that that work was forbidden to him, he could only imagine what a crushing blow that must be for the man even more so given the fact that he felt that his work was still uncompleted.

It had been Alonzo's work that had brought them together, but in a strange twist, it had begun with the father Lord Bainbridge had never known. In the early years of his adulthood, his father, Owen Bainbridge, had had a passion for archaeology, Egyptian archaeology in particular. And after having read every book on the subject he could lay his hands on, he had one day taken off quite unannounced for Egypt. This was of course before he had any responsibilities such as marriage and a family to contend with. In fact, he was actually in that heady, wondrous moment when a young man stands at the crossroads of his life and, looking both right and left, debates his future. As luck would have it, one of the most eminent archaeologists of the day was, that season, digging in the Valley of the Kings. Having nothing to lose, and filled with the bold and brass confidence of the young, Owen presented himself and offered to work with him. At first glance, Count Alonzo Fraboli saw little promise in the handsome young Englishman with the thin mustache and the dark wavy hair. But perhaps remembering his own far-from-auspicious start, and probably with the urging of his wife, he finally agreed to take him on. It turned out to be a bargain well made, for Owen Bainbridge proved a willing and enthusiastic worker, never complaining of the hard labor, always filled with the wonder of what they were trying to accomplish. Added to this was a charming, easygoing personality that captivated both husband and wife. But at the end of the season despite the success of their companionship, both Owen and the Frabolis knew it would not be repeated. He was obliged to return to England where arrangements were already being made for his coming marriage and a life that would preclude any future trips to Egypt. It was a sad parting, but a link had been formed. And over the next few years, monthly letters were exchanged that kept Owen informed of the continuous work in the Valley that he had loved so much and taken to with such zeal. After his death, for a long while the letters kept coming, only to pile up on the table in the entrance hallway, unopened and unanswered, until finally they stopped altogether. Then one day, quite out of the blue, and many years later when the new Lord Bainbridge was ten years old, Alonzo and Lucianna, who happened to be in London on business, came to call at Bellington House. Lady Bainbridge received them in her polite if distant manner. The Frabolis were shocked and saddened to learn of Owen's untimely death. But they were delighted with his son, who had read almost every one of his father's books on Egyptian archaeology and showed a keen interest in the subject. Lady Bainbridge, of course, had no interest in archaeology or archaeologists, or Italians for that matter. But that hardly mattered, for the link had been reformed, and once again there was a busy exchange of letters between Bellington House and the Frabolis' palazzo in Venice as well as from Egypt. When he was a little older, Lady Bainbridge even permitted her son to journey by himself to Venice although she absolutely forbid his frequent requests to travel to Egypt as well. Undoubtedly, Lady Bainbridge was reluctant enough to let her son travel to a place where he would be surrounded by nothing but Italians, but the very idea of him going to land infested with Egyptians was beyond even her easygoing attitudes on child rearing. So it was not until the previous year that Lord Bainbridge finally got to Egypt, and then what he found when he got there were matters that had little to do with archaeology.

Captain Smith at last joined them, taking his place at the head of their table like a benevolent patriarch and apologizing profusely for his unforgivable tardiness that he assured them was due to minor ship's business that, no matter how insignificant, could not be ignored.

From the opposite end of the table, Maude made introductions to those the captain did not know personally, and pleasant greetings were exchanged.

Monsieur Gatti appeared and handed the captain a slip of paper. "From the wireless room, sir. They said you should see it at once," he announced.

Captain Smith nodded, and smiling at his table companions, he unfolded the piece of paper and read it casually as if he were doing nothing more then scanning the daily newspaper.

Meanwhile, some of those gathered around the table shared apprehensive glances, but their looks were not caused by undue alarm, but rather they were the expected reactions of those who found themselves in an unfamiliar environment.

The captain, certainly not one unaccustomed to such reactions, sought to quickly put them at ease. He waved the piece of paper before them as if to indicate its insignificance. "From the *Californian,*" he informed them, "telling us of ice ahead."

"Is that a problem, Captain?" Madame Renoir asked.

"Oh no, no," Captain Smith told her, shaking his head. "But we shall keep a sharp lookout."

"Shouldn't we at least slow down our speed?" Lord Bainbridge heard himself ask, a little surprised to hear his own voice poise such a question. Certainly, he had no knowledge of ship navigation and no reason to question the judgment of someone so much more experienced. It was just that it seemed like a practical suggestion; they were headed into ice, so they should slow down. To his uneducated mind, it seemed elementary.

On his left, he noticed Maude was frowning at him, and he knew instantly what that was all about. Despite the fact that only moments before she had been if not prophesying doom, at least suggesting its possibility, he knew she was a great friend of Captain Smith and considered him the best at what he did. In fact, his presence on the *Titanic* had been the deciding factor in her mind when it came to choosing which ship they should take. The *Titanic's* sister ship *Olympic* had had an earlier sailing date and would have got them to New York in time for Maude to enjoy a full two weeks' leisure before her first speaking engagement, but the *Olympic* was not to be captained by E. J. Smith, so it was out of the question. Now, Lord Bainbridge could tell by her look that Maude was upset with him for questioning Captain Smith's judgment. She was worried that he might have vexed her friend and perhaps even soured the mood of the whole evening that was intended to be festive.

But Captain Smith was in no way vexed. In fact, behind his neatly trimmed white beard, his lips formed an even deeper smile, and his sharp deep blue eyes actually twinkled as they often did. "We will be able to see anything in time, Lord Bainbridge," he assured him. "It is a clear night. If it becomes at all hazy or overcast, then I think we will reduce our speed. But until then"—he shrugged amicably—"we are fine."

Lord Bainbridge nodded, and Maude, obviously greatly relieved that her little dinner party had not gotten off to a rocky start, let out a great sigh of relief and beamed approvingly at Captain Smith as if he had just successfully navigated the most treacherous of waterways.

At that exact moment, Monsieur Gatti emerged from the kitchen leading a parade of waiters each one carrying a silver tray. They bore their first course: plover eggs topped with caviar and set in aspic. This was only the beginning of the nine-course Edwardian banquet that Monsieur Gatti, in consultation with his head chief and of course Maude, had prepared for them. The eggs were an artistic as well as culinary masterpiece, and they generated much comment as they were placed before the appreciative diners. In addition, the wine butler made his way around the table, filling their glasses with either White Burgundy or White Bordeaux, whichever was preferred. And so the meal got off to a delightful start.

As the guest of honor, Edward John Smith, or EJ as he was affectionately known by many, was in a relaxed mood and filled with his customary good humor. Sitting there in his long navy-blue coat with two medals over his heart and four rings of gold on each sleeve, he was a majestic comforting figure. And although he was not tall, only of medium height, he always gave one the impression of much greater height and solid dependability. Now sixty-two, he had gone to sea at the age of twelve as a cabin boy on a square-rigged sailing ship plowing the coast of Africa. Since that start, he had made a swift climb up the nautical ladder, joining the White Star Line in 1880 and taking his first command in 1887. He was now commodore of the line and as such was given the privilege of taking each new White Star liner on her maiden voyage. Captain Smith was a great favorite with his crewmen who found him authoritative but always fair and one never known to raise his voice in anger. They admired him for his expert handling of his ships, and many of them were not above frequently boasting of their master's expertise to those of their brethren who had the misfortune to sail under lesser skippers. He was equally popular with the wealthy first-class passengers who frequently traveled on his ships. And there were many of them, like Maude, who would book Atlantic crossings only on ships he commanded.

"We've traveled together across the Atlantic at least eight or nine times," Maude told the others at the table. "Isn't that so, EJ?"

Captain Smith smiled at her and nodded. "Oh yes, Maude, at least that number."

"Well, let's see, there was the *Oceanic*, the *Baltic*, the *Republic*," Maude began, counting them off on her fingers.

But Captain Smith, laughing, stopped her in protest. "Maude perhaps it's better if you cease before you reach the *Nina*, the *Pinta*, and the *Santa Maria*."

His remark caused much laughter around the table, and none laughed harder than Maude herself.

Watching the two of them interact, really for the first time, Lord Bainbridge could see the deep affection that existed between the two of them. It was more than just what would have been expected between a ship's captain and a favorite passenger. He remembered the story Maude had told him of her first crossing on one of Captain Smith's ships. The sea had been so storm tossed, she had been deathly seasick and unable to leave her cabin. When Captain Smith had learned of her unfortunate plight, he had seen to it that the ship's surgeon had visited her twice daily and had a special broth prepared in the kitchen and sent up to her cabin. On the final day of the voyage when the waves had subsided and Maude had found her sea legs, or what was left of them, EJ had made sure she was seated at his side in the dining saloon on her first and only appearance in public during the whole trip. Perhaps, years ago, there had been some sort of romantic attachment between them, Lord Bainbridge surmised. Like all lovers in the first throes of their newfound passion, he wanted to believe that others too had had or were having the same glorious experience. But then, he remembered Maude telling him also that at their first meeting EJ had made a great point of revealing to her how much his wife absolutely loved her books and simply couldn't put them down. It was his way, Maude had confided to Lord Bainbridge, of setting the ground rules for their relationship and, at the same time, telling her that he was an honorable man, who would do nothing to hurt his wife or his relationship with her. *So it must be,* Lord Bainbridge thought, *that Maude and Captain Smith had remained only friends all these years.*

Lord Bainbridge was aware that there had been one great love in Maude Manchester's life, and its circumstances were as colorful and as tragic as those found in any of her popular novels. It had happened many years ago even before Lord Bainbridge was born. Maude's lover had been a Balkan prince, and Maude had described him to Lord Bainbridge as "a big dark man with a drooping mustache and a combustible temper who was ready and eager to challenge all of mankind to a duel in the name of honor." From what Maude had told him, Lord

Bainbridge gathered that theirs had been a fiery and passionate courtship. One little anecdote that she revealed, he found very touching. On many occasions, Sasha, that was the prince's name, would take Maude's face in his hands and whisper over and over again that she was beautiful. This, Maude had confessed to Lord Bainbridge, was somewhat of an exaggeration, for even then, as a young woman of twenty, she was far from comely. But when Sasha told her she was beautiful, she believed it herself, at least for a little while. They had been together less than six weeks when on a Sunday morning in Paris, Sasha had been cut down by an assassin's bullet. His murderer was one of many misguided anarchists who had popped up around the end of the nineteenth century, convinced that if they shot or blew up enough members of the nobility and holders of high office, they could change the world order. Sasha had been killed, not because he was of any importance, but only because there had been a prince in front of his name. It was a blow from which Lord Bainbridge knew Maude never completely recovered.

As the waiters began clearing away the soup course, Marco—who Lord Bainbridge had been trying to ignore, for he had been hovering around their table like an avenging sprite for the past few minutes—leaned into his face to take his plate away and whispered a single word at him. And though it was spoken in Italian that Lord Bainbridge did not understand, there was no mistaking by his tone that it was something quite unflattering.

Lucianna Fraboli had also heard the word, and she, having the advantage of comprehension, turned quickly to Lord Bainbridge. "That waiter just called you the vilest of names," she told him, her shocked tone indicating her revulsion that not only had such a word been spoken but it had been spoken in a first-class establishment.

Lord Bainbridge, feeling a redness creep up the back of his neck, tried to shrug it off as a joke. "Perhaps he was upset that I didn't finish my soup," he suggested.

"We should make a complaint," Lucianna said, watching Marco's retreating back as he returned to the kitchen. For a second, it looked as if in her outrage, Lucianna was about to leap from her chair, overtake Marco, grab him soundly by the scruff of the neck, and give his face a good slap.

"It's nothing really," Lord Bainbridge assured her with a weak smile.

They were distracted by Madame Renoir asking a question of Captain Smith. "I understand this is to be your last trip, Captain?"

The captain took a moment to wipe his lips with his napkin, and then he responded, "Yes, when we return to Southampton, I shall hang up my uniform. I've a wife and a daughter, a little house, and a garden that all need my attention. I shall not mind retirement at all," he added.

"Retirement is not always the heaven one dreams it is going to be," Alonzo Fraboli stated rather flatly.

Captain Smith, giving an example of the tact and understanding of people for which he was so well-known and that had carried him so far in his career, nodded in sympathy. "How difficult it must be for you to give up such exciting work as you engage in, Count Fraboli. I have followed your career over the years with the most profound interest. You must have many wonderful stories to tell," he prompted.

Alonzo flushed and then smiled. If there was one thing he loved almost as much as his work, it was talking about it. And he talked of his work with such passion that no one was ever bored listening to his tales even if, like Lord Bainbridge, they had heard them many times. But this night, perhaps because the talk of retirement had slipped him into a melancholy mood or perhaps because he was haunted by his own mortality, he spoke, not of some fabulous experience he had had in the valley, but rather of his own coming demise.

"I am dying," he announced to those gathered around the table, most of whom were aware of this fact. For so renowned was this man and the work he had accomplished that the previous year many of the world's leading newspapers had reported that Count Alonzo Fraboli was spending his last season working in the Valley of the Kings. Declining health, they explained, was forcing him to retire.

Startled by his pronouncement in such a public place, his wife spoke his name softly but urgently, "Alonzo."

But this once, Count Fraboli ignored her intervention and went on. "I am dying," he repeated. "And none of the foolish doctors can tell me why. But I know why!" he insisted, his voice rising as if the errant physicians were present in the room and could hear his denouncement of their medical skills.

Glancing at Lucianna out of the corner of his eye, Lord Bainbridge saw such a distressed look on her face that once again his hand reached out and covered hers on the table between them as her husband continued.

As he spoke about something that he had obviously given much thought to and felt very strongly about, the craggy lines of Count Fraboli's face, weathered and sunburned like the limestone cliffs of his beloved valley, seemed to shift and displace themselves. "About two years ago, I came upon a tomb in the valley that had been the final resting place for a priest of the sixteenth dynasty," Count Fraboli told them. "As tombs went, it was small and insignificant, with little decoration. It certainly in no way compared to the immense royal tombs where the pharaohs were laid to rest. Like all the other tombs I had come across, this one too had been stripped of most of its contents." He paused for a moment, knowing like a good storyteller always does, that he had their rapt attention. "Above the door that led into the burial chamber," the count went on, "there was an inscription in hieroglyphics. It read, 'Whoever enters my tomb, whoever desecrates my mummy, the Sun-god shall punish him. He shall have no rest and the fires shall burn inside of him until he is consumed from within.' Although the tomb had obviously been sacked by ancient grave robbers, the priest's body still lay in its sarcophagus. We of course removed the mummy. I believe it ended up in the Cairo Museum."

"Alonzo, please," Lucianna said, trying once again to silence him.

Her husband gave her a gentle smile. "There's more," he said to her, "more that I've never even told you, my dear." He took a sip of wine and then a moment to catch his breath, for he appeared to have become winded. "After my illness began, and the foolish doctors could not tell me what it was that was killing me," the count continued, "I began to do some research on what had happened to the others who had been with us the day we opened the priest's tomb. Some we already knew what their fate had been." He looked to his wife again. "Remember the young Scotsman, whom we hired only a week before we discovered the priest's tomb?" Lucianna nodded. "What happened to him?" Alonzo reminded her.

"He died," Lucianna answered softly, "the day after we opened the tomb.

"How did he die?" someone at the table inquired. They were all caught in attitudes of engrossed attentiveness. Even one of the waiters, who was serving the next course, had paused a moment to catch the details of the count's story, that is, until Monsieur Gatti cast him a stern eye, and he quickly resumed his duties.

"A stone block from the tomb fell on him as he was emerging back out into the daylight and crushed him to death," Count Fraboli answered. He shook his head. "That poor young man, he was so eager to learn and willing," he added, casting Lord Bainbridge a glance that held just a hint of recrimination.

Lord Bainbridge knew that Count Fraboli had always been keenly disappointed that neither he nor his father had followed him in his beloved profession. Never having had any sons of his own, the count had hoped he might be able to pass on his knowledge, his passion, to first the father and then later the son. But it had not worked out that way in either case, and it was a double loss that still pained the elderly Italian.

"And what about the foreman of the dig, Said Ahmed?" the count asked urgently.

"He was a delightful man with a wonderful smile," Lucianna remembered.

"Two weeks to the day when we removed the priest's body from his tomb, poor Ahmed went for a swim in the Nile and was pulled under by a crocodile and instantly devoured," Count Fraboli informed them in grisly detail.

"Alonzo, that is hardly appropriate dinner table chatter," his wife admonished him.

But the count had now really warmed to his subject, and he took off on a torrent of words, his rimless spectacles trembling on the edge of his long nose, threatening any moment to hurl themselves off into space. "On every dig I have been involved in, I have always kept a meticulous list of the men working for us. This, along with the fact that most of the same men worked with us for many years and most of them came from the same village, enabled me to quickly establish the fate of almost every single one of the men who were with us on that particular day. And do you know what I found?" he asked his fellow diners who, much to Monsieur Gatti's profound dismay, were for the moment completely ignoring the fabulous food being set down before them. "Every man who had been there when we removed the priest's body had died. And not by natural causes either!" Count Fraboli rushed on. "Many of them, like the young Scotsman and Ahmed, had suffered terrible accidents. One was reported to have been struck by lightning, another bitten by a poisonous asp, and at least three were murdered, one by his wife who had apparently gone mad. Others died mysteriously, healthy one day, dead the next. Two years ago, I was as healthy as you are today," Count Fraboli said to Captain Smith. "And now in a year or less, I'll be dead," he added.

"And you think it's the priest's curse that is killing you?" Captain Smith asked.

Count Fraboli shrugged. "What other possible explanation can there be? To the best of my knowledge, I am the only one left alive who two years ago defiled his tomb and carried off his mummy."

"And what about me, Alonzo?" his wife asked. "I was there too. Am I also to be struck down by this foolish curse of yours?" Though there was a hard edge to her tone and it was obvious that his story had upset her, one could still sense the affection, the love, she had for the man.

The count smiled back at her, his face instantly relaxing as if a flood of tension had suddenly left him. "Not all the curses throughout all of eternity would dare lay a hand on one so divine," he answered, blowing her a kiss from across the table.

"You know," Captain Smith began thoughtfully, "maiden voyages too are looked on by some people as a curse."

This certainly caught everyone's attention, and their eyes that had been so eagerly fixed on Count Fraboli now turned to the captain, and their excited buzz encouraged him to go on. "On this trip, we're hardly more than half filled passenger wise," Captain Smith explained. "First class is not even that. We had quite a number of last-minute cancellations, prominent names too. Someone had a premonition or another's mother had a bad dream. Whatever the reason, many people seem to avoid maiden voyages." Captain Smith's blues eyes twinkled mischievously. "I'll tell you another little story although I really shouldn't. This one is more of a legend than a curse," he told them. "They say this ship was built so fast that two men were accidentally sealed inside her steel hull. And sometimes down below, you can hear them tapping frantically to get out."

Maude shivered in the warm room, "Oh dear, now I know I won't sleep a wink tonight."

Young Sebastian Renoir spoke up for the first time. "Then do you think, sir, the ship might be haunted?" he asked of the captain.

Captain Smith chuckled. "Could be, lad. I've always felt that out here in the middle of the ocean, things aren't quite as normal as they are back on dry land. One never knows," he added with a wink.

"I should like to check that out for myself," Sebastian suggested rather boldly.

"Tell you what," Captain Smith offered, seeming to find delight in the boy's enthusiasm, "why don't I have one of the officers take you on a tour of the engine rooms first thing tomorrow. Then you can see what makes the ship run, and perhaps if you listen very closely, above all the clamor, you might hear something."

"That would be super, Captain," Sebastian said eagerly.

"Thank you, Captain Smith," Madame Renoir put in. "That is very generous of you. I'm sure Sebastian will greatly enjoy it."

"You bet I will!" the boy exclaimed.

But now, all conversation came to a halt as their main course, quails with cherries, appeared before them, and much to Monsieur Gatti's great relief, everyone was suitably impressed and once again turned their attention back to the food.

Over the quail, Lord Bainbridge happened to look up and catch a smile from Sebastian, sitting across the table. A gentle-looking brown-haired lad of fourteen with fabulous facial bone structure, which he had obviously inherited from his mother, Sebastian had a delicacy of appearance that in no way signaled frailty. At one time, Lord Bainbridge had suspected that he might, when he was a little older, become a fellow traveler, but he quickly learned that Sebastian had a very French and a very hearty appreciation for the ladies even at his young age. They had first met, quite by accident, three years ago in of all places the British Museum, where Lord Bainbridge often went to relieve the dreadful tedium brought on by his endless almost nightly visits to the Crown. They had stuck up a conversation over some piece of artwork, a painting or a statue long since forgotten, and Lord Bainbridge had been so taken by young Sebastian's, he was then only eleven years old, poise and intellect, not to mention his wonderful sense of humor, that on the spur of the moment he had asked him to lunch. Not being Ronnie Standish, he had no designs on the boy save the enjoyment of his company. After lunch, Sebastian had taken him around to the hotel where he was staying to meet his mother. And such was the agreeable afternoon that the three of them spent together that like Alonzo and Lucianna Fraboli before them, the Renoirs, mother and son, were so instantly taken with Lord Bainbridge, they invited him to spend the coming summer with them at their summerhouse in the countryside of Provence.

Now watching them as they sat side by side across the table, conversing softly together in French as they often did, Lord Bainbridge remembered that summer warmly. In particular, he recalled one evening at twilight when he and Marguerite Renoir were sitting alone on the veranda, watching a flock of songbirds flying through the last of the day's sunlight, their tiny wings beating furiously as if they were trying to race the sun to its nightly resting place.

Madame Renoir had turned to him and said most naturally, without hesitation or preamble, "I know about your other life." There was neither chastisement nor criticism in her voice. By her tone, she might just as easily have said she knew he was English or that his hair was brown.

"But how . . . ?" Lord Bainbridge stammered, caught off guard.

"We French sense these things," Madame Renoir answered. Then she had smiled at him. "Tonight when we went out to dinner, I twice watched your eyes follow a good-looking young man when he passed our table."

"I guess I'm not as subtle as I thought I was," Lord Bainbridge acknowledged. He had been startled by her revelation, accustomed as he was to the tight reserve of his countrymen who hardly ever spoke of such things, and when they did, it was only to deny them. But at least, he had the presence of mind on this occasion not to issue a hollow denial on his own behalf. In fact, he would later think of his response as having been quite worldly, quite cosmopolitan. "The French have a much better take on this sort of thing than we English do," he had said.

Madame Renoir had smiled again and nodded. "With us French it is no big deal. We do not struggle with it as you English do."

As far as Sebastian was concerned as the days of that first summer together passed, Lord Bainbridge came to look upon the boy as the brother he had never had but had always wished for. Instead, he had been stuck with two sisters, whom he had absolutely no affection for, and who both returned his feelings in kind. Lord Bainbridge and Sebastian spent their time together swimming, hunting for frogs and rabbits, and engaging in other boyish pursuits that Lord Bainbridge had never taken part in during his own rather sad boyhood days. Later, he would look back on that time as perhaps the best summer of his life.

One incident that had happened toward the end of August made Lord Bainbridge realize that Sebastian's intuition was as sharp as his mother's. He and the boy had gone on an overnight fishing expedition. That night as they sat around the fire cooking their day's catch, Sebastian had revealed an incident that had taken place at the private boarding school his mother had sent him to just outside of Paris. It had happened only a couple of months ago. And the gist of it was that Sebastian and another boy, a couple of years older, had been intimate one night after the lights had gone out.

Lord Bainbridge had listened to Sebastian's rather bold unabashed recitation with a slight smile on his lips, remembering the nights he and Denham had spent at Winchester.

"I didn't care for it," Sebastian had confessed to him. "I concluded it was not for me. But," he quickly added, catching Lord Bainbridge's eye, "that doesn't mean it can't be right for others."

That was all that had been said about the matter between them, but Lord Bainbridge would always remember the night, not so much because of Sebastian's revelation, but because the boy had wanted him to know that he knew about him as his mother did, and although he found that way of life not to his own liking, he didn't want Lord Bainbridge to think he was rejecting him as well. He wanted them to be friends, and he had taken great pains to make sure he had in no way offended him.

Still watching mother and son as they continued to converse softly together, laughing at some private joke between them, Lord Bainbridge knew there were many who considered this type of behavior no less than rude, especially when Madame Renoir and Sebastian chose to talk to each other in French when many of those around them did not speak the language. Others went further and declared with righteous indignation that their actions spoke of an intimacy that was unnatural. Their condemnation was additionally fueled by the frequent sight of Madame Renoir and her son walking or sitting with their hands intertwined, and the many times, it was noticed that Madame Renoir stroked her son's hair or reached out and brushed it back from his face. But Lord Bainbridge knew the Renoirs did not intend to be rude nor were they involved in any form of forbidden intimacy. Sebastian had told him that his father had deserted them even before he was born, and from that moment on, there was just the two of them. In the whole world, they had only each other. They had always depended on each other for everything, and in addition to the natural bonds between mother and child, they had developed a steadfast friendship. They were that rare duo indeed, a parent and an offspring who not only loved each other, but liked each other as well. Lord Bainbridge felt privileged that they had taken him into their private little world and made him feel so welcome.

One other aspect of Marguerite and Sebastian Renoir should not go unmentioned. And that was the remarkable resemblance between them, which transcended even the normal similarities that often identified kinsmen. Theirs was a shared likeness that was uncanny; looking into the face of one, you always saw the other. They had the same remarkable high cheekbones, the same almost almond-shaped eyes, which spoke of an Asiatic heritage somewhere back in their family history, the same finely textured medium brown hair, and the same prominent nose with a slight downward hook to it. This last, on another person might have looked ungainly even unflattering, but on mother and son, the Renoir nose, as some persisted in referring to it, gave their individual faces strength and character. Sebastian was already showing promise of someday obtaining his mother's height. Madame Renoir was tall like Lucianna Fraboli, but while the Italian woman was full-figured even slightly hefty, Madame Renoir was very thin with a long graceful neck that gave her the look of a Modigliani sculpture. On this evening, she wore a tight red velvet dress with long sleeves that clung to her body, emphasizing her marked slimness. The dress also had a very low cut neckline, which Maude had whispered to Lord Bainbridge was "very French." Her one piece of jewelry she wore was a small gold medallion on a chain around her neck.

Maude had immediately taken a liking to Madame Renoir and her son when Lord Bainbridge had first introduced them. Her friendship was returned, especially when the Renoirs found out that Maude had once visited what she liked to refer to as the American Wild West. This was to be their own destination, and Sebastian in particular had eagerly plied her with questions about her experience.

"Did you see any bloodthirsty savages?" he had wanted to know.

"Indians, you mean?" Maude inquired. Sebastian nodded eagerly. "Yes, I did," Maude answered. "Though I must confess they seemed pretty docile, mainly sitting around weaving these gorgeous baskets."

"Then, they weren't on the warpath?" Sebastian asked with a decided trace of disappointment.

"Not that I noticed," Maude responded.

This trip to the American West was just the latest robust adventure the Renoirs had embarked upon. Marguerite and Sebastian had traveled all over the world together on their private yacht. They had circumnavigated the globe twice, calling into exotic ports in every corner of the world. They were both avid big game hunters, having safaried in both Africa and India. They had also climbed the Himalayas and gone dogsledding across Canada. Now, they were off to the American West, hoping to find it as wild and lawless as they had heard and read about.

By now, they had reached the ninth and final course of their meal, assorted fresh fruits and cheeses, accompanied by champagne, and everyone at the table agreed they had enjoyed a culinary masterpiece. Maude asked one of the waiters to have Monsieur Gatti come to their table. Immediately, the proprietor came from the kitchen, almost at a run, his face covered with distress as if he feared something must have gone terribly wrong with his special dinner party. But his expression instantly melted into a beaming smile of pride when everyone at the table rose from their chairs and gave him a hearty round of applause.

"Monsieur Gatti, the meal was perfection," Maude told him.

"Everything was all right, then?" he asked as if making sure.

"Outside of my own dear wife's home cooking, that was the best meal I have ever eaten," Captain Smith declared.

Monsieur Gatti nodded, still beaming. "Good, good. Thank you all for your kind praise. My staff worked very hard. They knew how important this occasion was."

"Be sure and give them all our thanks," Maude said.

"Yes, I certainly will," Monsieur Gatti assured her.

And thank Marco for remaining in the kitchen if you would, Lord Bainbridge thought as he took his seat again. For the Italian had not been seen for some time, and Lord Bainbridge wondered if Monsieur Gatti might not have banished him to kitchen duty for some infraction. He could envision Marco scouring pots and pans with his sleeves rolled up and plotting some suitable revenge.

The attention of everyone at the table was momentarily distracted as the American lady, the one with the disdainful demeanor who occupied one of the ship's most expensive parlor suites, strolled by on her way out of the restaurant, her eyes staring straight ahead, glancing neither to the right or the left. As usual, she carried her little lapdog, and this time, there was a man trailing in her wake. This, Lord Bainbridge knew to be the young bodyguard. And dressed in evening wear, he was indeed quite handsome. Dark with slick-backed hair, he had the look and manner of European royalty. But Alfred had told him that he was definitely an American who spoke with a broad American accent and, when he was not in the company of his employer, swaggered around with a typical American strut. He certainly was in no way as high-toned and elegant as he pretended to be. Lord Bainbridge felt there was something strange in seeing the two of them together in of all places, the restaurant. Obviously, the American woman had just finished her dinner. But what was the bodyguard doing there? The woman did appear to be wearing a goodly number of pieces from her fabulous jewelry collection, including a diamond-encrusted tiara. It was the bodyguard's job to protect her jewels, Alfred had said. But he certainly couldn't have taken a meal with her. Servants, no matter how exalted their position, would never eat at the same table as their master or mistress. Perhaps she had made him stand guard behind her chair while she ate. This, Lord Bainbridge found slightly amusing. But knowing something of the eccentricities of the American rich, he did not put it beyond the bounds of possibility.

Meanwhile, while he was concentrating on the bodyguard, the others at his table had much to say about his companion.

"I don't think I've observed her speaking to another passenger during the entire voyage," Maude said as the woman passed their table.

"Most aloof," was Madame Renoir's observation.

"As silent and mysterious as the Sphinx," Count Fraboli added.

Captain Smith, given his calling, was a bit more discreet. "Yes, I believe she has kept pretty much to herself. She's traveling under an alias, you know."

Maude became excited, "Oh, EJ, can you tell us her real name?"

Captain Smith put his finger to his lips, "I'm sorry, Maude, captain's secret."

Maude shrugged with disappointment and passed her final judgment as the woman exited the restaurant. "I've always felt very strongly that neither children nor dogs should be allowed in eating establishments."

Behind his napkin, Lord Bainbridge chuckled to himself for he knew what was coming. Maude's dislike for children and dogs was well known, and it was a toss-up which she disliked the most. But she certainly loathed to see either of them in places where she felt religiously they did not belong, such as restaurants and zoos. Yes, zoos! The tale that he knew she was about to begin was one he had heard before, a number of times in fact, and though he found it amusing, he was not sure how it would be received by the rest of his table companions. But there was no stopping Maude. She was already off and running.

"I remember a visit to the zoo in London's Regent's Park that I took one fine summer's day," Maude began. "What should have been a delightful afternoon of animal contemplation was completely ruined for me by hordes of beastly little children running amuck all over the place. Their screams were unbearable, and they appeared to be completely devoid of parental supervision or restraint. I took refuge on a bench in a secluded arbor where I fell into conversation with one of the zookeepers. He seemed a kindly old man, and he told me the zoo had fallen on hard times. Apparently, some weeks there was barely enough money to provide food for all the animals." A mischievous gleam came into Maude's eyes as she came to the meat of her story. "It was at that moment," she continued, "that divine providence struck me, and I had a revelation. At that instant, I came up with a way for the zoo to solve its financial shortcoming. It was quite simple! All they had to do was make proper use of the wild packs of little kiddies running and ranting all over the place. Certainly, if they bound enough of the little mites together, they would make a substantial, not to mention nourishing, meal for even the most demanding of the zoo's carnivores. And in the end, the zoo's animals would be properly fed, and the zoo itself would be restored to the tranquil oasis it was always meant to be."

A rather stunned silence followed Maude's recitation. Her table companions shared uneasy glances as each one of them tried to decide if she had actually been serious with her suggestion, or if it had been just some of the rather outrageous humor that often crept into her books.

Even Captain Smith, accustomed as he was to reacting to all sorts of situations as well as to words that were spoken, sometimes in jest, sometimes in anger, appeared at a loss for words of his own. He cleared his throat nervously a couple of times and spent a long moment studying his large hands as if he had never seen them before.

It was left to Sebastian Renoir to be the one to comment on Maude's idea. And with the innocence of youth and the practical mind of a fourteen-year-old, he responded, "Beg pardon, Mademoiselle Manchester, but I greatly fear that the merits of your plan would quickly be extinguished when supply was overtaken by demand." He shrugged his shoulders and shook his head in the French way.

"Sooner or later, there would be no more children, but there would still be plenty of hungry animals."

Now, everyone at the table suddenly felt an urgent need to clear his or her throat, and Madame Renoir said something to her son in French, which no one else caught.

"Jeremy, I just finished reading your book, and I enjoyed it immensely," Lucianna Fraboli said a little too loudly, but at least it managed to effectively and quickly change the subject.

Lord Bainbridge thanked her and glanced across the table where Maude was beaming approvingly at him like a proud parent.

"Yes, Ducks has a great career ahead of him if he buckles down and applies himself," Maude told the others.

Lord Bainbridge cringed at her use in public of her favorite nickname for him. Still, he basked in her praise and remained greatly relieved that the critical acclaim his book had received had in no way tarnished their relationship. When the first reviews came out and he found his work praised to the level of Dickens and Thackeray, he had instantly been worried that Maude, whose books despite their immense popularity had never attained such glowing comparisons, might be jealous of his achievement. But he should have known better. Maude's generous heart and spirit plus her deep affection for him could never have held his success against him. Instead, being Maude, she praised him, encouraged him, and nagged him constantly, into greater effort.

It was already past nine, and Captain Smith indicated with regrets that he must return to the bridge. Maude brought what had been a delightful evening to a close. She offered a toast to the captain, saluting both his years of devoted service to the White Star Line and its passengers and the years of happy peaceful retirement that lay ahead of him.

As their party started to break up and leave the restaurant, Lord Bainbridge found himself thinking not of Tom, who had been in his thoughts most of the night, but rather of Egypt. For Count Fraboli's words had reminded him of his own visit to that ancient land. And when he remembered Egypt, he had no choice but to remember Denham as well.

Chapter VII

March 1911

The *Orient Express* was scheduled to leave London's Victoria Station at exactly 3:45 PM. Above its platform the station clock read 3:43. The train's whistle blew twice, signaling departure was eminent.

Lord Bainbridge leaned his head out of the window of his compartment and scanned the platform, quite convinced, at that moment, that he would be traveling alone. Maude was nowhere in sight, and he was afraid she was about to miss their train. He knew that in spite of the fact that his dear friend was such a frequent traveler, because she was so disorganized, her preparations for departure were often scenes of total chaos. Traveling from room to room for her was a traumatic experience, so when she was called upon to make a more extensive journey, the resulting muddled confusion often left her quite ready for hospital.

Finally, he spotted her charging down the platform toward the train, huffing and puffing as if she herself, like the train, were under steam power. All Lord Bainbridge could think of was the stories she had told him of the great herds of American buffalo that she had seen stampeding across the Western plains. Behind her came at least half a dozen railroad porters struggling with the various suitcases, hatboxes, and valises that made up her luggage.

Seeing his face, Maude began frantically waving her arms and calling out to him. "Stop the train, Ducks! Stop the train! Pull the cord!"

This action hardly seemed necessary to Lord Bainbridge since the train had not yet started to move. Indeed, though the platform clock now distinctly read 3:45, they were as yet not under way. Obviously, someone in authority, perhaps even the engineer or at least the stationmaster, had spotted this late arrival and held up their departure until she was safely aboard. This was accomplished with much pushing and tugging, but finally Maude was seated opposite Lord Bainbridge in their compartment, her baggage piled up on either side of her like two great walls. The train gave two final whistles as if to announce that all at last was ready, and with a lurch, they were off. The train started slowly down the track, but greatly picked up speed as they emerged out of the dark cavern that was Victoria Station and into the almost blinding daylight.

"Well, we're on our way, Ducks!" Maude declared with much excitement.

"Yes." Lord Bainbridge nodded, showing far less enthusiasm. He knew he should have been as excited as Maude was, perhaps even more so, for he was making the trip he had dreamed about and wished for practically his whole life. After a two-week stay with Count Fraboli and his wife at their palazzo in Venice, which Lord Bainbridge had visited once before when he was a young teen, they were to accompany them to Egypt just in time for the beginning of the spring digging season. The count had promised them an exclusive tour of a tomb he had just finished working on the previous season that contained, he assured them, the most magnificent wall decorations. They were to linger in Egypt a number of weeks and then make a leisurely trip home by sea, leaving the Frabolis to continue their work in the valley.

Initially, the idea for their trip had been Maude's. About to start work on her next romantic novel—the story of a lovelorn young English woman who, one moonlit night while walking through the Valley of the Kings, meets a handsome young man who might be either real or the ghost of an ancient Egyptian prince—she was convinced that she needed some on-site research and inspiration. Lord Bainbridge eagerly embraced the idea and wrote at once to Count Fraboli in Venice. Then after all the details and itinerary for their trip had been laid out, invitations made and accepted, reservations posted, and tickets purchased, Lord Bainbridge received a bit of news that had the potential to quite ruin the whole trip for him and put him off it completely.

Somehow, it seemed most fitting that this unwelcome information should be supplied to him by none other than Lady Bainbridge. She had revealed it to him during one of the infrequent afternoons after he had moved in with Alfred, that he had returned to Bellington House to take afternoon tea with his mother. It was a ritual he did not especially enjoy but one he felt was his duty. Lady Bainbridge, he was certain, viewed their get-togethers in much the same light. On this particular afternoon after Lady Bainbridge's famous tea and cakes had made their appearance, his mother had announced that she had had a letter from his sister. Frowning as he bit into a tart, Lord Bainbridge knew at once that of course she was referring to Amber. Poor Helen was still living at home and showed no signs of ever leaving. Thus, she had no reason to write her mother a letter, and even if she had, Lord Bainbridge knew his mother would hardly think the contents of such a letter worthy of repeating.

"Amber said to tell you that they will be in Egypt on the exact same dates you will be there," Lady Bainbridge told him almost excitedly and apparently having accepted, if reluctantly, the reality that two of her offsprings would be visiting a foreign land that she still considered a place of heathen inhabitation.

This piece of news was so unexpected and so unwelcome, Lord Bainbridge immediately dropped his plate and half-eaten tart to the blue-green pile carpet underfoot. "Sorry," he apologized, thankful he at least hadn't been holding his teacup and saucer.

"Jeremy, in heaven's name, what's got into you?" Lady Bainbridge inquired, quite startled by his reaction to her news but relieved that her china plate had survived its fall unscathed. She at once rang for a maid to come and clean up the mess. Then she folded her hands in her lap, eyed her son inquisitively, and made what could only be described as a major understatement. "One would think you aren't pleased that you'll be seeing your sister in Egypt."

I'd sooner drown in the Nile than come face to face with that little wretch anywhere on the face of the earth, Lord Bainbridge thought. But it wasn't the idea of meeting up with Amber in Egypt, distasteful as he might find that to be, that had so upset him. Oh no, it was the rest of it that had so unnerved him, and the rest of it had to do with the "they" Amber had mentioned in her letter to her mother. For Amber was with her new husband, and they were on their honeymoon, a grand tour of Europe and the Middle East that had already lasted four months. But there was worse, much worse to come. For Amber had married Denham Granville-Smith.

How this bizarre and unnatural coupling, as Lord Bainbridge could not help but think of it, had come about he still wasn't completely sure. He and Denham had not communicated since he had left Oxford, and the scraps of information he had received about him—that he graduated from Oxford, had taken a job with a law firm, and settled outside of London—had come to him secondhand. Later, it would suddenly dawn on Lord Bainbridge that it had been Amber who had supplied him with this information on Denham. Again, looking back even further to the times when he and Denham had visited from Winchester, Lord Bainbridge remembered that Amber always seemed to be underfoot. She was always trailing after them, eyeing Denham adoringly. This, Lord Bainbridge of course found quite annoying, but decided it was nothing more than a schoolgirl's crush on her older brother's chum, a not unusual occurrence. When at another of their afternoon teas Lady Bainbridge had informed her son of his sister's engagement to Denham and their pending wedding, Lord Bainbridge was, as would be expected, dumbfounded by the news. Thankfully, that time he was not holding any of his mother's precious china crockery, which he might very well have flung against the wall if he had. For the next few months, he purposely avoided Bellington House fearing, not unreasonably, that he might run into Denham there. He did return one month before the wedding date set for the happy couple to retrieve some notes in his room that he planned to incorporate into his second novel. Feeling somewhat like a spy on a secret mission, Lord Bainbridge managed to get into the house observed only by Hodges, the butler, who of course missed nothing.

For some moments, he bent over his desk, selecting the papers he needed. Then suddenly conscious of a chill on the back of his neck as if someone had opened a window and let in a cold draft, Lord Bainbridge looked up to see Amber standing in the doorway of his room. He had no idea how long she had been standing there, but it was something she had done all their lives—lingering in his doorway, not speaking while silently and critically observing him.

"What do you want?" he asked in irritation, shoving the papers he had wanted into the pocket of his coat.

For a long moment, Amber didn't answer, and she was so still, it was hard to tell if she was even breathing. Two long delicate fingers of one of her hands twirled a strand of her radiant golden hair between them. This was often her most strenuous and thought-provoking activity of any given day. Then she smiled her delicious golden smile that made everyone, who didn't know her, think she was much nicer than she actually was. "I'm not as stupid as you think I am," she said to her brother. "I know Denham doesn't love me, not like I love him. I know he's only marrying me because he can't marry you."

Lord Bainbridge's head shot up, and he spun around to confront her, quite prepared in his rage to leap upon her and beat her into unconsciousness. But he was spared that rather extreme reaction, for Amber had already vanished. Having shot her poisonous arrow, she had slithered away, smiling with smug satisfaction.

"Really, Ducks, by the look on your face one would think we were headed for a funeral, rather than setting out on a glorious adventure," Maude gently chastised him, bringing him back to the present.

Lord Bainbridge managed a weak smile, which then immediately broadened and spread across his whole face as he took in his friend's appearance, in particular her choice of headgear. For in spite of the fact that they were in the grip of a spell of typical late March London weather, cold and damp, and the fact that Lucianna Fraboli had written that the weather they would find in Venice was much the same, Maude wore a pith helmet with a veil made out of mosquito netting drawn down tightly across her face as if she expected they would be in the tropics by morning.

His own wardrobe, which Lord Bainbridge considered somewhat vainly to be quite the proper attire for an upper-class young Englishman going abroad, consisted of a charcoal-gray three-piece suit with a thin white stripe, a black wool overcoat, and a snap-brim leather cap. He also had with him a silver-handled walking stick that had once belonged to his father that he had recently taken to carrying both for sentimental reasons and because he felt it lent him an air of sophistication.

They left the train at Dover to cross the Channel and resumed their journey on the *Orient Express* at Calais. They reached Venice exactly twenty-four hours after they had departed from London's Victoria Station. As soon as they disembarked from the train, they were bundled into a gondola and, like spirits, they glided almost silently through the canals. There was hardly a sound except for the slap of the water against the side of their vessel and an occasional hail of recognition as one gondolier recognized another in passing. It was very cold. There were even spits of snow in the air, a thick fog hung low over the canals, and that inevitable and constant curse of Venice—dampness—was so heavy it seemed almost a visible presence.

Dusk was just starting to gather when their gondolier pointed through the fog. "Palazzo Bernardi," he informed them.

Both Lord Bainbridge and Maude strained their eyes to see where he pointed. At first, they could make out nothing. But as they drew nearer and the wisps of fog gave way, if somewhat reluctantly, what came into their view was a towering building looking to be at least six stories high and fairly dripping with ornamentation, so that it looked like nothing more than a giant wedding cake covered with layer after layer of frosting.

Count Fraboli himself was out on the landing to greet them as their gondola pulled up alongside. Bareheaded and in his shirtsleeves, he waved excitedly to them. "Welcome! Welcome! Forgive me for the weather. It's abominable! But then the weather is always abominable in Venice. Today it snows, tomorrow it rains." He spread his arms and shrugged. "But what can one do?" He assisted them from the gondola, hugging Lord Bainbridge warmly and bowing and kissing Maude's hand with a great flourish. Then after giving instructions to the two servants who had followed him out onto the landing to see to his visitor's luggage, he hustled them toward the palazzo's entrance. "Quick, inside where it's warm."

Inside, it was not much warmer. The count led them through what seemed to be a labyrinth of high-vaulted chambers, most of which looked to be used for storage. Moisture dripped from the walls, and from somewhere close by, came the distinct sound of water lapping against stone. Once they passed through an inner courtyard where sea nymphs frolicked in an ornate fountain, Maude let out a sudden squeal of terror, "Oh my!"

"What is it?" the count asked, stopping their progress.

"Something ran across my foot," Maude cried out.

"Oh don't be concerned," Alonzo said to her. "It's probably only a water rat."

"A rat!" Maude protested.

"The rats never go above the ground floor," Alonzo added, seeking to reassure her.

"How damned decent of them!" Maude muttered to herself as they continued on.

Taking a stone staircase, they traveled down a long corridor, which seemed to be winding back on itself. All around them, servants were quietly lighting the evening lamps.

"How many rooms are there altogether?" Maude asked.

Over his shoulder, Count Fraboli answered, "I've never been quite sure myself. At least four hundred, I should imagine. Of course my wife and I only live in a few of them," he added. He stopped them before a fresco depicting angels ascending to heaven. The painting was peeling and very faded. "As you can see, everywhere there is decay," the count pointed out. "The whole palazzo is falling into disrepair. There is not enough time or help or money to keep it up."

"What would it take to fix it up?" Lord Bainbridge asked.

"A major restoration project," the count answered. "The kind that an individual could never undertake. Only a government could finance such a project." He shook his head, for a moment looking very defeated. "It will last us the rest of our lives and then"—he shrugged—"and then sadly it will eventually all fall into ruin."

"Such a pity," Maude said, gazing up at the scarred walls.

The count studied her for a moment, his head cocked to one side. "Yes, dear lady, such a pity indeed," he agreed. Then he took her arm. "Come, my wife is most anxious to meet you."

He led them into a drawing room where on the far side of the room comfortable leather armchairs were drawn up in front of a giant fireplace made of Sienna marble from which a welcome fire burned brightly, casting flickering fire shadows that stretched all the way up to the room's cathedral ceiling.

Lucianna rose from her chair and came across the room. Smiling with much warmth, she held out her hands to them. "Ah, here you are." The necklace at her throat twinkled in the firelight while the long multicolored silk dress she wore rustled softly like leaves in a gentle breeze as she moved.

After dinner that night in the dining room, which overlooked the Grand Canal, the four of them gathered at one end of the long wooden table. The meal had been superb, and now they were relaxing in candlelight, sipping champagne. Their conversation was relaxed as their mood, and they found, with no strain on anyone's part, that the four of them were able to converse easily, each one sharing their experiences with the others.

"Jeremy, I bought your book," Lucianna told him.

"And?" he inquired.

"I'm afraid I haven't had a chance to read it yet," she confessed, somewhat embarrassed.

Lord Bainbridge smiled. "Then, I can hardly ask you for a review."

"You won't be able to put it down once you start it," was Maude's observation.

"I shall start it soon," Lucianna promised.

"Tell us about your latest work," Lord Bainbridge suggested of the count.

Alonzo threw up his hands in mock protest. "No, no, you don't want to be so bored," he insisted.

His wife laughed, a lilting merry sound. "Just try and stop him," she said.

"Lucianna, how unkind," the count said, pretending to be terribly insulted.

"You love to talk about your work, and you know it," she answered, giving his cheek an affectionate pinch.

"I will tell you a story, a true story," Alonzo consented. He took a sip from his champagne and began. "Four seasons ago, we discovered the tomb of a royal noble in the valley. As soon as we entered the antechamber, we could tell the tomb had been pilfered in ancient times. But in the main chamber, we came upon a curious sight." He paused for dramatic effect, looking at the expectant faces of his two guests.

"Please go on," Maude urged eagerly.

"He's such an actor," Lucianna scolded good-naturedly.

"We found," the count continued, "the mummy in its proper place but stripped of all its jewelry and other finery. But just inside the door, there was another corpse, nothing more than a skeleton, for it had not been mummified. Beside it lay a broken tablet. When we pieced the tablet back together, we found the following inscription: 'the spirit of the dead will wring the neck of a grave robber as if it were that of a goose.' The tablet had been placed so it would fall on whomever was the first to enter the chamber, the first to disturb the sleeping noble. So through thousands of years of eternity these two, noble and thief, had slept together. Most probably strangers in life, they had shared death."

"But," Lord Bainbridge asked thoughtfully, "if the grave robber was killed the instant he entered, then what happened to all the jewelery and other artifacts?"

Count Fraboli shrugged. "A good question. Perhaps at a later date, another robber came along and saw the way had been cleared for him. Or perhaps, and this is the theory I like best, perhaps the first robber had accomplices who probably knew there would be some sort of trap set for them, so they were more than willing to let their poor friend enter the tomb first. Or perhaps he was just the most greedy of the bunch and insisted on being the first through the door. Either way, it cost him his life."

"What a thrilling story!" Maude exclaimed. "You just have to let me use it in my novel."

The count bowed his head to her. "But of course, dear lady, the truth is never copyrighted." He got to his feet. "Come, let me show you something." He led his three companions into the next room. From a glass case, he took a small carved figure that he passed to Maude.

"How exquisite," Maude said, holding it up to the light and examining the tiny birdlike creature with its human face. "What is it?" she asked.

"It's called a *Ba*," the count explained. "The face is an exact replica of the prince to whom it belonged, and it's supposed to represent his soul." He showed them other items from the glass case: the bust of a princess, scarred and missing her nose, an alabaster vase, and a perfume spoon in the shape of a crocodile. "I'm not really a collector," Alonzo went on. "It's the history I'm after, the human story." He turned to look at them gathered around him. "After all these years of digging in the valley, I still believe that somewhere there still rests undisturbed the tomb of a noble, perhaps even a pharaoh. The ancient Egyptians buried their royal dead with everything they would need in the next world. To uncover such a burial would be fantastic! In that respect, I guess I am a selfish man. I wanted to be the one to find such a tomb."

Lucianna looked away for the briefest of moments as a wisp of sadness came into her face. It was a change of expression that only Lord Bainbridge caught. But it vanished almost instantly as Lucianna leaned toward her husband and whispered a few soft words in Italian to him.

Later, before they retired for the night, Lucianna drew Lord Bainbridge aside. She took his hand, hers felt like ice. "Jeremy, this coming season will be Alonzo's last in the valley. His health is rapidly declining."

Lord Bainbridge was shocked. "I had no idea," he said. Lucianna glanced down at their clasped hands, and a moment later when she raised her eyes to him, they were wet. "I'm so sorry," Lord Bainbridge added, not knowing what other words of comfort he could offer. "What can I do?" he asked.

"Just be our friend," Lucianna responded.

"Always," Lord Bainbridge promised.

That night, Lord Bainbridge slept fitfully, disturbed about the sad news of his old friend. Early the next morning before anyone else in the household was awake, he stole from the palazzo, seeking the quiet solitude of the city of Venice. During the night, a substantial snow had fallen, so that now all the city's buildings were covered with a mantle of white, looking like ancient courtesans adorned in coverings of new finery, trying hard to conceal the decay and rot underneath. As he slipped quietly through the narrow huddled streets, Lord Bainbridge encountered few other early risers. The air was cold and damp, and some of the lagoons were covered with a thin layer of ice. He came suddenly, as one often does in Venice, upon an empty little square. All the buildings that fronted the square were closed and shuttered. Lord Bainbridge paused a moment, leaning against a fountain in the center of which a lasciviously smiling satyr found himself frozen in place.

A young man suddenly appeared out of nowhere as if in answer to a silent prayer or a desire unfulfilled. He was a strikingly handsome Italian with lively dark eyes, the beginnings of a thin mustache struggling to grow above his upper lip and strands of thick blond hair escaping from underneath his wool cap. He paused and smiled invitingly at Lord Bainbridge. Knowing hardly a word of Italian, Lord Bainbridge was tongue-tied. But his hesitation was due to more than his linguistic insufficiency, for without Alfred there to intercede, to act as intermediary, Lord Bainbridge realized he alone could not complete the transaction. So accustomed had he become to letting Alfred arrange his assignations, he was lost and helpless without him. Seeing no response, not even a smile, the young Italian shrugged and disappeared quickly from the square.

Left alone and feeling, if only momentarily, like a spurned lover, Lord Bainbridge pondered over the wisdom of having had Alfred remain behind in London. It had been a decision they had reached through mutual agreement although at times when they were arguing it out, it had definitely sounded more like a disagreement. Given Alfred's disdain for everything foreign, especially foreigners, it was no great surprise that initially he had expressed no interest in taking part in the proposed trip. And Lord Bainbridge, knowing he would need Alfred's assistance when it came to making his arrangements with the Italian and Egyptian young men he expected and looked forward to encountering, found himself trying to convince him to come along. Then apparently after each of them had given the matter sufficient thought, they switched points of view, and each of them argued the reverse of their previous position. Alfred, perhaps deciding that Lord Bainbridge might get himself into trouble if he was not around and perhaps even worrying that he might find someone to replace him in his absence, decided he should accompany him. While Lord Bainbridge came to the reluctant conclusion that their proposed itinerary would leave little time and even less opportunity to pursue the "connections" he sought, and Alfred's presence, especially given the fact that he and Maude were less than compatible, might prove an encumbrance or even an embarrassment. But there was an even more important reason why Lord Bainbridge did not want Alfred to go with him to Egypt. Denham would be there, a fact that in itself had greatly unnerved him. But the thought of Alfred and Denham meeting each other was to Lord Bainbridge, the worst sought of catastrophe that he could imagine. He regarded both of them as important influences in his life but polar opposites that had pulled him in different directions. Denham had been his first love, and in those first weeks and months of blissfulness, Lord Bainbridge believed he had found his life's companion, and that he was destined to spend the rest of his days with someone of his own kind, his own class. But then when that didn't work out, he found Alfred. Or rather, Alfred found him. And although he was convinced he would never love Alfred, at least not as he had loved Denham, he had great affection for him and gratitude. For Alfred had opened a door to another world, a world Lord Bainbridge had never known existed, a world where he was convinced he had found his true self. He knew now that he would find his true love, his life's companion, not among the slim young white aristocrats with their blond hair and fine graces but rather among the rougher darker types of the underclass who had a decided lack of manners. "I want to be loved by a lad of the lower class," he often whispered to himself as if he believed that if he repeated the phrase enough times, it would happen. It hadn't happened yet. Though he had loved quite a number of them, none had ever loved him in return. But he was convinced it would happen one day. No, it would be quite impossible for Denham and Alfred to meet. If they did, Lord Bainbridge was quite convinced Denham would think he had fallen in with bad company, and Alfred, he was sure, would deride Denham and tell Lord Bainbridge he was well rid of him. But fortunately, it was not to come to that. Lord Bainbridge managed to convince Alfred that the coming trip was to be one of intellectual pursuits with daily visits to museums and other cultural haunts, leaving no time for excursions of a more sensual nature. With the added incentive of the already scheduled trip next spring to America, during which Lord Bainbridge assured him they would be able to go off on their own to seek their preferred diversions, Alfred surrendered any desire he had to accompany him to Venice and Egypt. It helped that he was currently involved in a romance with a young German sailor in port for an extended leave. And in addition, Alfred much preferred going to America rather than to either Europe or the Middle East. At least in America they spoke English. Or as he said to Lord Bainbridge, "A variation of the language."

As he was having all these thoughts, Lord Bainbridge had been walking aimlessly through the narrow streets and alleyways of the city. Then he crossed over a bridge and once again came unexpectedly into a square. But this was not just any square, for before him stretched Venice's most famous square, indeed one famous throughout the world: St. Mark's. So spectacular was the sight, especially coming upon it in the early morning light under a new fallen snow, Lord Bainbridge, like so many thousands of tourists before him, caught his breath and felt a shiver run down his spine. Passing underneath the tall colonnades that ringed three sides of the square, he came out into the open where he stared up at the towering campanile, the ancient watchtower. Nearby, close to the water's edge, on its stately column stood the Lion of St. Mark's, the city's symbol. Despite the lone pigeon that had momentarily settled on its head, the lion stared out at the city, proud and defiant. Turning his head just slightly, Lord Bainbridge's eyes fell upon the Basilica of St. Mark's. Lifting his eyes to the very top of the cathedral, he could make out, even through the low clouds and fog, the famous four giant bronze horses, looking as if they were prancing majestically through the sky unbound and unfettered. The whole view was so breathtaking that Lord Bainbridge stood there for a long time as though he was mesmerized. There wasn't a sound to be heard, and in this place, this solitude, it wasn't hard for him to imagine that some calamitous holocaust had befallen the rest of mankind, and he alone had survived.

But he was soon relieved of this rather macabre reverie by a sound that came to his ears. It was a gentle sound, a plaintive almost soulful male voice raised in song accompanied by the soft strum of a guitar. Even though it was sung in Italian, Lord Bainbridge could tell it was a love song, but one of love lost, not found. He turned his head from side to side, but he could not discover the source of the music. Whoever it was, they were hidden from his view. At first tempted to go in search of this mysterious troubadour, Lord Bainbridge instead remained where he stood, taking in the view and the music as if he were listening to a private concert arranged just for him and spread out before him on the most magnificent of stages. As he continued to stand there, the snow began to fall again, and the wind blew in a great gust from the water. Lord Bainbridge shivered and felt very much alone.

It was still early morning, but already the valley was like an oven. The insistent sun, a fiery fist jammed into the palm of heaven, reached downward and scorched everything, even the sands on which he stood. Lord Bainbridge wiped the beads of sweat from his forehead with a white silk handkerchief. Shielding his eyes, he glanced upward toward the craggy limestone cliffs that towered all around them, enclosing them and trapping them in this stifling crucible.

"My God, what a place!" he exclaimed, both in wonder and discomfort. This, his first view of Egypt's fabled Valley of the Kings, had not failed to greatly impress him. As he was growing up, fueled at first by his father's books and later by the stories and work of Count Fraboli and his wife, the valley had taken on in his mind an almost mythical connotation like Camelot or Atlantis. And now here he was standing on that very place. To Lord Bainbridge it felt almost as if he had stepped upon the moon.

As he stood there still mopping his brow, he could not help but recall with fondness any number of typical cold and damp London mornings. He let his eyes drop from the high cliffs above to the valley floor around him. Here, there was a beehive of human activity. The floor was covered with hundreds of people—endless groups of tourists parading in smart single file in and out of the numerous tomb openings cut in the faces of the rocks and cliffs, a half dozen different teams of archaeologists and diggers working separate sites, the workmen's chants ringing up and down the valley, and everywhere native boys and young men going about with hands extended, begging for baksheesh. But in spite of all this bustle, this hubbub that produced a tumultuous sound not unlike the din he remembered when their train was leaving Victoria Station, the impression Lord Bainbridge got was of a lonely and desolate place. He remarked on this to Maude.

"Well, after all, Ducks," she reminded him, "it is a graveyard, you know."

Seated on a large rock, her pith helmet and veil firmly in place, Maude was industriously scribbling away in her notebook. She had been hard at this labor ever since they first arrived in Egypt three days ago, recording her reflections and impressions for use in her forthcoming novel. As she told Lord Bainbridge, surely intending her words as a bit of a friendly jab at his own most unexpected literary success, "My books may never win great praise from the critics, but at least no one will ever accuse them of being inaccurate."

They had arrived by ship and, upon disembarking, had been ushered aboard a *dahabeyah*, a luxurious sailing vessel, one of many that had been built especially to transport rich foreign tourists. With their paneled cabins and lounges, they were as elegant as any first-class hotel. They spent twenty-four hours on a leisurely trip down the Nile lounging on the open deck under colorful striped awnings as the narrow strips of land dotted with palm trees glided past. At sunset, drinks were served just as they came upon the Temples of Abu Simbel with their four gigantic statues of Ramses II. Reaching Luxor the following morning, they found their rooms waiting for them in the palatial Winter Palace, a favorite watering hole of the wealthy traveler. Lord Bainbridge and Maude had connecting suites while Alonzo and Lucianna were just across the hall. Later when their English guests had left and they were ready to get down to the serious work of the spring digging season, the count and his wife would move to a little stone house on the edge of the valley that they rented every year. That second day in Egypt, Lord Bainbridge and Maude did the tourist things. This included, of course, a camel ride, and once Maude was finally hoisted aboard her rather unfortunate animal, little children ran alongside of her, hooting and laughing at the sight of this large imposing Englishwoman riding a camel. But Maude took it all in good strides, and when at last with equal hard labor she was returned to earth, she rubbed her backside vigorously and pronounced the experience quite invigorating. They also paid a visit to a teeming native bazaar where they passed stall after stall offering ancient souvenirs from the tombs of the pharaohs although they made no purchases, having been warned by Count Fraboli that anything found there was hardly authentic.

That night, they had dinner in the hotel's grand dining room where they talked excitedly about their first trip to the valley the next morning. And it was here, among the potted palms and rattan furniture with a six-piece native orchestra bravely pumping out distorted versions of American ragtime, that Amber and Denham Granville-Smith joined them for the first time. After introductions were made and handshakes exchanged, they all settled down to the meal being laid out before them by white-gloved waiters.

Lord Bainbridge's first impression of his former schoolmate was that though he still found him extremely good-looking, Denham appeared leaner and paler. And though he was still only twenty-three, he looked as if life had already begun to wear him down. Lord Bainbridge could also tell at a glance that the union between Denham and his sister was far from a happy one. Watching the interaction between them, he could see the many telltale signs of discord that even the most obtuse of observers could not have failed to notice. This knowledge gave him no sense of satisfaction, for no matter how much he disliked his sister and how much he resented Denham for having deserted him to embrace a life of respectability, he by no means wished his former lover an unhappy life. Lord

Bainbridge was still amazed that the two of them had come together at all. Another piece of this complicated puzzle did fall into place when he learned from his sister Helen who, though she had no life of her own, always seemed to be a fountain of information when it came to the lives of others, informed him that Denham had, on the death of one of his uncles, inherited enormous wealth and estates. This, Lord Bainbridge, knew would have certainly made him a much more appropriate candidate for Amber's hand as far as Lady Bainbridge was concerned then when he had merely been her son's school chum.

With the arrival of their food, conversation at the table was momentarily put aside. But it was quickly taken up again as the meal progressed. The topic was once again the next day's visit to the Valley of the Kings, which everyone was eagerly looking forward to. Everyone save one.

"I shan't be going with you," Amber announced, looking up from her plate to gaze around the table at the others with her well-known vacant little stare. "I have no desire to go down into some dirty smelly old tomb," she added.

Her declaration was greeted with a moment of stunned silence. Then the count put down his fork, and with his spectacles trembling dangerously on the edge of his nose, he addressed this, as far as he was concerned, heresy. "Why, my dear young lady, whatever are you saying? This tomb I am going to show you tomorrow is like nothing that has ever been seen before. It is in magnificent condition. Its wall paintings are so vivid with color you'd swear the paint was still wet. And no one except myself, my wife, and our diggers have seen it. You, my dear friends, will be the first."

"Why, I'd be scared witless to go into such a place," Amber told him.

Hardly a significant loss to our little group, Lord Bainbridge could not help but think sarcastically to himself. Glancing across the table, he saw the flush of embarrassment that covered Denham's cheeks. Their eyes met and held for a moment, and then Denham ducked his away.

Though clearly disappointed at Amber's defection, Count Fraboli struggled to play the perfect host. "The director of the Museum of Antiquities is a personal friend of mind," he told Amber. "I'll have him arrange a special tour for you. The museum has some fabulous pieces I'm sure you'll appreciate."

Amber shook her golden curls politely. "Thank you, no," she replied. "I find the weather here far too hot for going outside. I'll be perfectly content to remain here at the hotel. I shall sit on the veranda with a cool drink and wait for you all to return."

"My wife suffers terribly from the heat," Denham offered, displaying a loyalty he obviously didn't really feel.

But Count Fraboli was appalled and deeply offended. He stared incredulously across the table at Amber who, true to her fashion, had no idea how much she had upset him. "Why, my dear young woman, why did you bother to come to Egypt at all?" Alonzo asked, his voice trembling with indignation.

Amber smiled at him, a little amused smile of pity for his failure to understand what was so obvious. "Why, because everyone's going to Egypt this year," she answered.

As if he had been slapped, the count sat back in his chair, gripping its arms. He probably would have said something further, sputtered some response to her empty-headed babble, but his wife gently placed her hand on his arm and spoke to him softly in Italian.

Not content to leave a bad situation alone when she could make it even worse, Amber had one final observation. "I must say," she began, "I have been greatly disappointed in Egypt. Everything is so different, so . . ." She wrinkled her nose in thought, struggling for the word she sought. " . . . so foreign!" she concluded triumphantly.

Not long after that, their little gathering broke up, and they all scurried off to their beds like survivors fleeing the scene of some major disaster.

The morning brought more defectors from their planned excursion to the valley although these were quite unexpected. Just after dawn, word was brought to the count from the foreman of their latest dig that an important find had just been made at the site, which was at the far end of the valley, and his presence was required there immediately. Apologizing profusely to his guests, Count Fraboli promised them a tour of his prized find as soon as he and his wife returned. In the meantime, he put them in charge of the best guide in the valley who would give them, he assured them, a most splendid tour.

Maude was still seated on her large rock, writing furiously in her notebook as if all the sights and sounds of the valley before her were about to slip away before she could get them down on paper.

Looking around, Lord Bainbridge noticed that Denham was standing a few paces away, talking with a young couple. The woman's face was completely hidden by a large-brimmed hat that, while offering fine protection from the persistent sun, seemed to Lord Bainbridge would have been more appropriate at Ascot rather than in the Valley of the Kings. Her companion, on the other hand, was in full view, and even from a distance, Lord Bainbridge could see that he was extraordinarily handsome, as dark as Denham was light. The two of them appeared to be in an earnest discussion while the woman stood beside them momentarily forgotten. Watching the stranger as he conversed animatedly with Denham, Lord Bainbridge came to the very quick conclusion that he and the stranger obviously "went to the same church." This was a popular phrase he had learned from Alfred to denote those who shared the same sexual preference as they did. He wondered if Denham had caught on.

A few minutes later when Denham returned to where Lord Bainbridge and Maude were waiting, he told them of his encounter. "The fellow just came over and started talking to me all friendly like," he related.

I bet he did, Lord Bainbridge thought rather sourly.

Denham continued, "They're Americans. Their name is Standish, from Boston. They're also on their honeymoon. They want Amber and I to have dinner with them tonight." Then nudging Lord Bainbridge, and in a tone of voice that sounded far from genuine, he made an observation. "I say, I don't think I've ever seen a more beautiful woman."

But Lord Bainbridge was hardly impressed nor for that matter inclined to be so. He grumbled a vague response and walked away.

Shortly thereafter, their guide, a little Englishman with an enormous Adam's apple, a thin reedy voice, and a rather pompous manner gathered his group together. Most of their tour group was made up of a large party of Germans. There were a half dozen other British subjects, besides Lord Bainbridge and his two companions, and three bewildered-looking Spaniards, who had the stunned look of tourists who have found themselves not only on the wrong tour but, worse, in the wrong country. The German majority was all very large, noisy, and had apparently, Lord Bainbridge was quite convinced, all vowed not to bathe until they had returned to their native land. At least the English guide appreciated the proper order of things, for he first explained everything in English and then in German. The three dazed Latins were unfortunately left to supply their own narrative.

The guide proceeded to line them up in precise order as if they were starting out on parade, reminding them to keep in close formation and warning them to pay strict attention to every word he said. He carried a rolled-up black umbrella with a miniature British flag tied to its handle. Flourishing the umbrella high above his head and uttering a single command, "Rally!" he started them off with all the pomp of a drum major leading the Queen's Own Guard. The guide trooped them past piles of sand and past many entrances to subterranean tombs until they reached the desired sepulcher. They paused and gathered around him while he explained that the tomb they were about to enter had been the final resting place of a royal prince, a son of Ramses II.

After a few more minutes of scholarly discourse, the guide with another wave of his umbrella, led them down a series of steep stone steps and into a long corridor. They walked in single file, packed so closely together Lord Bainbridge could feel Denham's breath on the back of his neck. The air was stale and heavy, and it was almost pitch-black.

"You know, I've always been afraid of the dark," Denham whispered to Lord Bainbridge.

"Don't step on the bat guano," the guide warned them.

"What's that?" Denham asked in alarm, trying in vain to see where he was putting his feet down.

"Bat droppings," Maude informed him with a chuckle.

"Ugh!" Denham shuddered, making an appropriate face of disgust.

They finally emerged into what had once been the central burial chamber. Here, there were electric lights strung above their heads by cables, so that the whole room was illuminated. But sadly as the group moved into the room, there seemed little to see, certainly no wonders to marvel at. The chamber was completely empty, vacant of any trace of the treasures that must have been left there thousands of years ago. Even the great stone sarcophagus along with what was left of the young prince's mummy was gone, shipped off to the Cairo Museum. All that was left behind were the faded but still distinguishable wall paintings, a parade of gods and humans that surrounded the chamber on all four sides. Using the tip of his umbrella, the guide pointed out various features of the paintings as he made his way around the room trailed by his obedient followers.

"Look, that one looks like our old Latin professor at Winchester," Denham exclaimed.

"That's Anubis, God of the Dead," Maude explained. "He has the head of a jackal."

"Well so did Professor Ridgley," Denham added with a grin.

Lord Bainbridge looked at Maude. "How did you know that?" he asked.

"Research," Maude told him. "I've been researching ancient Egypt for months now. I've got enough material for two novels." She gave this a moment's thought. "Which might not be such a bad idea," she concluded.

They had made their way around to the fourth and final wall when Lord Bainbridge interrupted the guide's well-rehearsed dissertation with a question that had occurred to him as he remembered the words Count Fraboli had spoken with such an intense fervor. "Do you suppose there are still any undiscovered tombs in the valley? I mean, ones still filled with treasure?"

The guide gave out with a long sigh and shook his head. It was clear from his attitude that it was a question he fielded many times in the course of a single day. He fixed Lord Bainbridge with a rather unfriendly stare, his Adam's apple bobbing with what could only be called indignation. "Sir," he answered, "everything that was ever placed here by the hands of the ancients has been carried off either thousands of years ago by grave robbers or in modern times by archaeologists. Even though there are some who still persist in digging up the earth, let me assure you, it is a well-known fact that the Valley of the Kings has been completely exhausted." He paused a moment to mop his face with his handkerchief, for in the close confines of the tomb, it was quite hot, and his words had been spoken with the heat of passion. "There's nothing left here but the dust of the past," he added in conclusion. Then waving his umbrella about, he shooed them back toward the long entrance corridor. "Come along now, don't dawdle. We've got many more tombs to visit."

The Germans, jabbering away excitedly in their native tongue and using their considerable bulk, began to push themselves into the corridor as if they were all fleeing a burning building and each one had to be the first to reach the welcome fresh air outside. For a moment, it even appeared that two of the largest of them had got themselves wedged so tightly together in the narrow corridor that nothing short of a huge dynamite blast would ever free them. But then with more shoving and to the accompaniment of boisterous laughter, the way was finally cleared. Maude and most of the rest of the tourists followed the Germans out of the burial chamber.

But Denham held back, and just as Lord Bainbridge was about to enter the corridor, Denham reached out and grasped his hand, pulling him back into the chamber.

Lord Bainbridge turned to look back at him. "What is it?" he asked.

Denham pulled him deeper into the chamber, back against one of the decorated walls. He stared at him silently for a long moment, and then with a gesture Lord Bainbridge remembered so well, he swept his long blond hair out of his face with a toss of his head. "I've missed you," Denham told him, his full lips parted slightly, his eyes very alive, sparkling in the electric lights.

In a gesture of his own that spoke volumes, Lord Bainbridge tugged his hand free that Denham still held. "We'd better catch up to the others," he suggested quickly.

But Denham was not quite ready to let him go. "For months after you left Winchester, I felt like I was living in hell," he told him.

Lord Bainbridge instantly remembered his own pain, those long torturous days and nights he had spent during his lonely exile at Bellington House. He stared into Denham's eager face. "Funny, I never saw you there," he answered.

Denham leaned his face into his, and though he didn't quite kiss him, he brushed Lord Bainbridge's lips with his own. "It doesn't have to be over," he whispered.

For an instant, just a breath of time really, Lord Bainbridge was ready to reach out, wrap his arms around Denham, and crush their bodies desperately together. But the instant quickly passed, and as if someone had given him a sudden knock on the side of his head, he came back to his senses, back to reality. He knew the time for him and Denham to be together had long passed. And although he still held great affection for him and sweet remembrances of him as his first love, he knew he was no longer in love with him. His desires now answered a far different calling. Alfred and his band of rough rogues had seen to that. Furthermore, Lord Bainbridge knew that even if he found himself still attracted to Denham, the very thought of sharing him with the sister he despised was so off-putting, it would have doused any hint of desire that still burned inside of him. Denham had made his decision, and for better or worse, he now belonged to Amber and to her alone.

Lord Bainbridge ducked away from him and headed toward the corridor. At the corridor's entrance, he turned back to look at his friend. "We've both moved on, Denham. It's time to put it to rest," he said.

"We could meet at your place whenever I'm in London," Denham suggested, almost desperately.

They shared a moment's uneasy glance, and then Lord Bainbridge turned and ran headlong into the pitch-black corridor. He continued running down the long length of the corridor, stumbling but not falling, and not caring if he stepped in bat guano or anything else. Finally, he emerged back out into the open panting and gulping in gasps of fresh air. He turned and looked back into the tomb, but saw no sign that Denham had immediately followed after him.

Shielding his eyes with his hand, he let his gaze wander up and down the valley before him. But though there was plenty of activity and hordes of people within his sight, he didn't catch a glimpse of Maude and the rest of their tour group. He concluded they must have already descended down into another tomb. Having no great desire to follow after them, he decided to do some exploring on his own.

The valley spread out before him shaped like a giant human hand with its fingers splayed. An intricate web of footpaths, some ancient, others modern, extended across the valley floor and up into the cliffs. Lord Bainbridge chose one of the paths that led upward into the cliffs. He quickly came to realize that the path he was following was one that was obviously not meant for tourists. It was an arduous climb, and more than once, he tripped over a bit of fallen rock and had to catch himself to keep from falling. Added to this was the unbearable heat that made it seem as if each step upward he took was bringing him that much closer to the roasting sun. His white linen suit was soon soaked through, and perspiration dripped from his face as if he had been caught in a torrential downpour. But he kept on, determined to reach the top, although he had no idea why this goal had suddenly come upon him. As he climbed, Lord Bainbridge kept glancing back down to the entrance of the tomb he had run out of, but he did not see Denham emerge from the entrance. This concerned him, and he worried that perhaps Denham had fallen and hurt himself or suffered some other mishap inside the tomb. But he didn't turn back. He kept climbing until he reached the cliff's first ridge. Here, he paused to catch his breath, and glancing down to the floor once again, he was surprised to see how little distance he had actually covered. Although he felt as if he had been climbing for at least an hour, he could still make out the faces of those moving about on the valley floor below. And though there was still no sign of Denham, he easily picked out the other members of his tour group just as they descended into yet another tomb. He figured Maude was too intrigued with everything she was seeing and too busy scribbling it all down in her notebook to even notice he was missing.

Lord Bainbridge turned his eyes from the valley floor up to the cliffs towering above him. He felt a sudden cool rush of air on his face as if someone had opened the door to a giant icebox. For a fleeting second, he was positive he caught a glimpse of a figure standing above him on the next ridge. In the next instance, the figure had disappeared, perhaps having vanished into the large gaping black hole in the rock behind it. Intrigued, Lord Bainbridge continued his ascent. It took him twenty minutes to reach the next ridge. The large black hole he found to be the entrance to another tomb. There was a chain stretched across the front of the tomb with a little wooden sign that declared in English, Entrance Forbidden! About to disobey the command and step over the chain, Lord Bainbridge was confronted by a figure emerging from the tomb in great haste. It was a woman, and she came running out of the tomb at the same breakneck speed he had used in his own exit in the valley below. The chain stretched across the tomb's entrance, however, slowed the woman down, and she came to an abrupt halt, which at least spared her from tripping over it. With a gentlemanly and courtly gesture as if he were helping her step down from a carriage at Hyde Park Corner, Lord Bainbridge offered his hand, which the woman took, and assisted her smoothly over the chain.

Looking at her as she stood there for a half second, Lord Bainbridge recognized her as the young American woman who had been standing with the young man who had engaged Denham in eager conversation. She was the American's wife, he believed Denham had told him. Lord Bainbridge recognized the woman from her hat, a great plumed monstrosity. Now, the hat was cocked unfashionably to one side of her head while strands of her vivid black hair poked out from all sides. Her face, which he had not been able to see before, now looked back at him in what he could only describe as a look of terror. Her skin was pale, her eyes wide with fright, and there was either sweat or tears streaming down her cheeks. Obviously, he concluded, something she had seen inside the tomb had greatly upset her. She paused a moment longer to offer him thanks for his assistance, and then she was off again on a run. Holding her long white skirt up to a definitely unladylike length, she careened down the rocky path.

Lord Bainbridge could not prevent himself from calling out a practical warning to her. "It's quite mad to run around in this heat, you know!" But she paid no heed to his words, slipping and sliding on the treacherous footing but miraculously never losing her balance. He watched until she disappeared from his sight around a bend in the path.

Turning his attention back to the tomb the young woman had fled from, Lord Bainbridge quickly decided he needed to find out what had frightened her so. Carefully, he stepped over the chain and stared into the entrance. He could only hope she hadn't been startled by a snake. Ever since his childhood, he had had a pathological fear of snakes not even being able to look at the picture of one in a book. And their guide had warned them to be on the lookout for cobras that infested the valley, especially in the cool dark recesses of the tombs. Screwing up his courage and brandishing his father's walking stick like a sword, Lord Bainbridge strolled into the tomb.

He found himself confronted at once by a flight of steep stone steps. Enough light from outside enabled him to ease his way down the steps, clinging to the iron guardrail, certainly placed there by modern man. The steps led him deep into the tomb, and at their conclusion, he found a thick wooden door slightly ajar. He was able to squeeze his slight form through the crack without disturbing the door. He emerged into a very large chamber lit like the other tomb had been by electric lights strung from the ceiling. Although it took his eyes a few moments to adjust to the change from natural to artificial light, other impressions came quickly without hesitation. A rush of much colder air made his skin quiver while his nostrils were invaded by a damp moldy smell with a strange sweetness to it. Lord Bainbridge wondered if it was the smell of death. Once his eyes had become accustomed to the light, he was surprised and delighted with what he saw. For on all four walls of the chamber, animal and human figures danced in vibrant display—hippopotamuses twirled with bejeweled slave girls while Nile boatman cavorted with long neck cranes. And there was so much more—lions and little boys, fat matrons and slim gazelles, grinning crocodiles and haughty princesses. All of these figures were rendered much more lifelike and alive than the ones he had seen in the other tomb. But it was more than that. The figures in the other tomb had been stiff and solemn, obviously figures in mourning. These, on the other hand, were gay, filled with abandon, loving life and, as he looked a little closer, even slightly obscene. It was a wondrous display, and Lord Bainbridge spent many minutes taking it all in.

A noise pulled him reluctantly away from these frolicking creatures and drew him toward a tall arched doorway, which led into a second chamber. Whatever had so unnerved the young woman was undoubtedly in this room, Lord Bainbridge decided. Feeling his heart pound in his chest, he stepped through the doorway. The chamber he now found himself in had a high vaulted ceiling supported by numerous thick stone columns and was also illuminated by electric lights. The first thing he noticed was that all the walls were completely blank, and they looked as if they had recently received a thick coating of whitewash. *How odd,* Lord Bainbridge thought, *it's as if whatever was on these walls had been deliberately covered up.* Perhaps they had been paintings of a nature even more risque than the ones in the previous room. From his own readings, he knew that both the ancient Greeks and Romans had produced pornographic works of art. So why not the ancient Egyptians as well? How incredible, he thought, that some prudish government official should decide they were unsuitable to be seen by the public and, in doing so, had destroyed a piece of his country's history. Deciding that there was nothing in this room to detain him any longer, Lord Bainbridge turned his steps back toward the first chamber. But then he heard the sound again. He stopped in his tracks, and though he still could not identify it, to his ears, it sounded animalistic. And in spite of his surroundings, he somehow knew that whatever kind of creature had made that sound it offered him no harm. As he retraced his steps and moved deeper into the chamber, there was now only silence. His hand reached out and touched the cool, slightly moist surface of one of the giant columns. Directly ahead of him was another column, and from behind it, he sensed rather than saw movement. Drawing up to the suspicious column, Lord Bainbridge held his breath, having no idea what he would find behind it.

The first thing he saw was the smile—thick lips curled back, displaying prominent discolored teeth. It was the insolent smile of an Egyptian lad of perhaps seventeen, no more. The boy didn't seem startled by Lord Bainbridge's approach as he stood there leaning against the column, holding his single soiled garment up to his chest. Kneeling before the boy, his hands still clutching him, was the young American who had befriended Denham. He too seemed unfazed by this interruption. Getting to his feet, he smiled at Lord Bainbridge who could not help but notice that in spite of the fact that his own clothes were soaked thru with sweat, the American's clothes, a suit of starched white linen, appeared in perfect condition without a soil or stain. Even his knees where he had knelt in the dirt of the tomb's floor were without blemish.

The three of them stood there for a moment in what was, at least for Lord Bainbridge, a moment of awkward silence. Then the American, whose name at that moment Lord Bainbridge remembered Denham telling him was Standish, made a gesture that was unmistakable, a gesture that indicated Lord Bainbridge was quite welcome to share the boy who stood grinning between them.

It was a suggestion Lord Bainbridge found quite distasteful, both because he considered the boy quite unappealing and because he resented the fact that this Standish bloke had the presumption to assume he would be interested in such a proposal. What did the American see in him to suspect he would have such an interest?

But Lord Bainbridge had no intention of finding out. He quickly left the columned chamber and passed through the first chamber with its remarkable wall paintings. He trudged up the long flight of stone steps, emerging once again out in the daylight. He had to shield his eyes from the sudden hit they took from the insistent sun. Then he retraced his steps back down to the valley floor. Though he hardly traveled at the rate of speed the young woman had used on her decent, he found going down was much easier and much faster than his ascent had been. Reaching the valley floor, he looked around for the American woman, concerned about her condition now that he knew the scene she had come upon. He wondered if she had been so upset because she had never suspected such a thing or if what she saw merely confirmed that which she had already known. Either way, he felt a great sympathy for her.

A moment later, he looked around to find Denham standing at his side. "Where have you been?" Lord Bainbridge asked rather anxiously, still reacting to the fact that Denham had not immediately followed him out of the tomb.

Denham shrugged. "Nowhere. Just lingering about. I saw no reason to hurry after you," he added, regarding him with a hint of displeasure and disappointment.

Maude joined them, coming out from the middle of the crowd of German tourists. She gave Lord Bainbridge a startled look. "Ducks, what happened to you? You look like you fell into the Nile."

"I took a hike up there," he answered, pointing up toward the top of the cliffs towering above them.

"What did you find?" Denham asked him rather pointedly.

Lord Bainbridge stared back at him. "Nothing," he answered, "only the dust of what had once been and can never be again." Then he turned and walked away.

Chapter VIII

Sunday, April 14, 1912

The Palm Court, often referred to as the Veranda Cafe, was actually two rooms, one on either side of the *Titanic*, just aft of the first-class smoking room on A deck. Both rooms were bright and airy, done up in the Mediterranean style with lots of color. The furniture was white wicker, the walls were covered with ivy-adorned trellises, and the high arched bronzed framed windows, nearly seven feet tall, let in plenty of sunshine during the day and filled the rooms with moonlight at night. And though this could hardly have been the intent of the ship's builders, once the voyage was underway, the room on the starboard side of the ship was taken over by the first-class children on board and became their exclusive indoor playroom while the other room, on the port side, remained the playground of the adults. By day, this room was a welcome haven for those passengers coming in through the revolving door after a brisk and invigorating turn about the deck. Hot tea and coco served with smart little cream cakes and biscuits awaited them and brought instant solace. But it was at night when the Palm Court was seen at its intended perfection. With its lamps lit, its tables filled with exquisitely dressed ladies and gentlemen sipping their coffee or after-dinner drinks, and a quartet from the ship's orchestra led by Wallace Hartley—a virtuoso violinist, who could make his listeners weep one moment and then tap their feet furiously the next—playing the classics or the new and very popular American ragtime, the room had all the magnificence, all the grandeur, of a stage set. The whole scene could have easily been mistaken for a set from one of the great European opera houses that dotted the Continent. Indeed if someone had stood on the outside looking in, especially one who was not accustomed to such surroundings, the sense they would get was that everything they were looking at was not quite real, that everything they saw beyond the windows was at best only temporary. When the curtain came down, it would all be packed away in crates, the players would give back their costumes, the lights would be turned off, and the set would be plunged into darkness until the next performance.

So onto this stage, there now came the members of Our Little Group, fresh from their triumphant dinner in the restaurant in honor of Captain Smith. One of the Palm Court's slim young waiters helped them pull two of the small wicker tables side by side so the six of them could sit together. Then he took their order for drinks. Lord Bainbridge decided on a hot lemonade as did Sebastian Renoir with some insistence from his mother. For Count Fraboli, it was a hot whiskey and water. And the ladies had settled on coffee when Maude changed her mind and selected a whiskey and soda, declaring that she needed the stimulation as she intended to stay up late that night and work on her new novel.

The orchestra had been playing a ragtime tune when they entered, and the music immediately caught Lucianna Fraboli's attention. "It's 'Alexander's Ragtime Band,'" she informed them. "One of my favorites." The music was obviously delighting her, and she tapped her feet enthusiastically. "If only they had had music like this when I was a girl," she lamented.

But her husband was less impressed. "Too noisy," was his brief comment.

The orchestra began another tune, this one even more lively than the previous one. A number of young couples stepped out into the middle of the room where space had been left for dancing.

"Oh, what dance is that they're doing?" Lucianna asked eagerly as the dancers began their steps.

"It's called the cakewalk," Lord Bainbridge answered. "It's really lots of fun." He held out his hand. "Shall I show you how it's done?"

"Oh, I couldn't," Lucianna protested.

"Go on," Madame Renoir urged the other woman, smiling warmly at her. "Jeremy's a fine dancer."

"Really?" Maude inquired, somewhat startled to learn this about her friend.

Madame Renoir nodded approvingly. "But of course."

Lord Bainbridge smiled to himself, flattered by her praise and remembering a special dance that he and Madame Renoir had once shared.

It had taken place on one of the many times he had visited the Renoirs in Paris at their house on the Rue Saint-Maur. This was a beautiful structure, built in the late eighteenth century and containing more than a hundred rooms. The most elegant of these was undoubtedly the ballroom, a cavernous room with mirrored walls, gilded molding, and a hardwood floor made from six kinds of exotic woods. On a warm night in June, Madame Renoir had given a party for over two hundred guests. The party was a grand success, and after all the guests had left, Sebastian had long ago tumbled off to bed, and dawn was fast approaching; Madame Renoir and Lord Bainbridge found themselves alone in the vast ballroom. The musicians Madame Renoir had hired for the evening were packing up their instruments, having been paid and well fortified with food and wine.

Taking Lord Bainbridge's hand, Madame Renoir walked up to the musicians. "Will you play one more tune, a waltz?" she asked them.

Basking in her generosity, the musicians were only too happy to oblige. Retrieving their instruments, they struck up a moving and slightly melancholy rendition of "The Merry Widow Waltz." Holding out her hand to him, Madame Renoir made a little bow to Lord Bainbridge. "Will you be so kind, monsieur?" Lord Bainbridge took her into his arms, and they began a slow sweep around the floor, their pace increasing with the tempo of the music.

Never having considered himself much of a dancer, after all as Alfred had once said to him, "The companions you now seek are hardly known as demons on the dance floor," Lord Bainbridge was surprised at how well he and Madame Renoir moved together. This he attributed solely to her efforts and her ability and to something else as well. For though she had the natural elegance of manner and movement that he had observed in most European women, Madame Renoir's elegance went beyond that. Hers seemed inbred as if even if she had been poor and in rags, she would still have retained an elegance of movement. Even when she was walking, it was almost as if she were dancing.

As they continued to whirl around the room, Madame Renoir asked him a curious question. "Do you see them?"

"See whom?" Lord Bainbridge inquired.

"The ghosts of the Marquis de Collot and his young wife," Madame Renoir answered.

Lord Bainbridge smiled to himself, thinking perhaps his companion had had a little too much champagne. But because her face looked quite serious and she was obviously waiting for his response, he felt he must reply. "I'm afraid I don't," he answered.

"They're here," Madame Renoir stated emphatically. "Oh yes, they're here!"

"Indeed," Lord Bainbridge returned, baffled to say the least.

The music ended, and after Madame Renoir had thanked them for their indulgence, the musicians once again packed up their instruments, and this time, they departed.

When they were alone in the ballroom, Madame Renoir told Lord Bainbridge the story of the de Collots. "They were my ancestors," she began. "The marquis built this house. He was a man of forty-five when he met Louise Desmoulin who would become his second wife. Though she was only twenty-one, they were very much in love and hoped to raise a large family together in this house. But their dream was not to be," Madame Renoir said with a sad shake of her head.

"Why not?" Lord Bainbridge asked, intrigued.

Madame Renoir, whose eyes had been downcast, met his gaze. "History overtook them," she answered, the flickering candles from the chandelier above their heads casting strange dark shadows over her features giving even greater definition to the fine bones of her face. "Men do terrible things to each other even in the name of liberty," she went on. "The marquis and his young wife were caught up in the bloody throes of the Revolution, just two people among the thousands of innocents who found their way to the guillotine in the name of liberty and justice for all. They were denounced because they were of the nobility. At first, they were only placed under house arrest, which to them didn't seem so bad since they had come to love this place they had made their home. But then one afternoon as they sat in the garden, just as the fruit trees were beginning to bloom, they received word that the next day they were to appear before the Revolutionary Tribunal. Though the tribunal was supposed to function as a court of law," Madame Renoir said with scorn, "almost all of those who were called to appear before it ended up on the guillotine. The de Collots were well aware of this. And as dawn broke the next day, they put on their best finery and came here to the ballroom. A faithful servant, the only one who had not deserted them, came with them. And while the servant played a tune on his violin, the marquis and his wife danced in each other's arms around and around the ballroom. They didn't even stop dancing when they heard the Revolutionary Guards breaking down the door."

"And did they die?" Lord Bainbridge asked.

Madame Renoir nodded. "They went to the guillotine that very evening at sunset."

"How sad," Lord Bainbridge murmured.

"Sad?" Madame Renoir shook her head. "Not at all. Tragic, yes. But the marquis and his wife were very happy in the short time they spent in this house. I like to think of them being here still, waltzing here in the ballroom every dawn." She smiled at the young man standing at her side, and reaching up, she placed a hand against his cheek for a moment. "Your friendship has become very dear to both Sebastian and myself," she told him.

"As has yours and his to me," Lord Bainbridge responded.

Madame Renoir took his hand, "Come, we will have breakfast in the garden."

Lord Bainbridge got to his feet and once again held out his hand to Lucianna. "Come on," he urged.

Lucianna looked to her husband, "Oh dear, should I?"

"If you wish to make an exhibition of yourself," Count Fraboli grumbled, but there was a twinkle in his eye.

"Here I go then," Lucianna said. Rising, she took Lord Bainbridge's hand and followed him out into the center of the room where the dancing was continuing.

"Ready?" Lord Bainbridge asked, smiling at her.

Lucianna picked up the train of her gown and wrapped it over her arm. "I hope I won't embarrass you," she said.

"You'll do fine," Lord Bainbridge assured her. "Now, we put our hands out like this. And it's all quick steps. Let's try." They began to move around the floor. "That's it, quick, quick."

"Oh my," Lucianna lamented, struggling to follow his lead.

"No, it's okay. You're getting it," Lord Bainbridge told her. "Now to the side, quick paces."

"Oh, this is delightful!" Lucianna laughed as she caught on.

"It is fun, isn't it?" Lord Bainbridge agreed, laughing with her. "Now here's another step."

Around the room they two-stepped, a wonderfully pleasing sight—a tall and stately gray-haired woman and a pleasant-looking animated young man. All too soon for them, the music ended. And as they stood there, applauding politely with the other dancers, the orchestra began another tune. "Shall we?" Lord Bainbridge asked.

"I think once is enough for me," Lucianna told him, smiling. "But thank you so much, Jeremy. It was such fun."

Lord Bainbridge took her hand, kissed it, and bowed before her. "The pleasure, dear lady, was all mine."

Still amused, they returned to their friends. "Well now, Alonso, did I look like a fool out there?" Lucianna asked her husband, sitting down beside him.

Count Fraboli leaned over and kissed her cheek. "A vision, my dear, an exquisite vision," he beamed with pride.

The orchestra was now playing a lively tango, and there was but a single couple on the dance floor. The woman was very small and middle-aged and, as they made their way around the floor, seemed in instant danger of being enveloped in the massive folds of flesh of her much larger partner. The man Lord Bainbridge recognized at once as Benjamin Chamberlin, and having already witnessed his prowess in the swimming pool, he was now equally impressed with the expertise he was displaying on the dance floor. The American multimillionaire moved with that special blend of grace and weightlessness that many large people surprisingly seem to possess.

"My, he certainly is light on his feet," Maude commented with just a trace of jealousy, which befitted another rather large person who was quite aware that she lacked the same agility.

"I only fear for his poor wife," Count Fraboli chuckled. "She may never been seen again."

Perhaps seeking to divert everyone's attention from the display on the dance floor, Maude turned to Sebastian Renoir. "Why isn't a handsome young man like yourself out there dancing?" she asked. "I can spot a number of delightful looking young ladies, who I'm sure would be thrilled to have you ask them to dance."

Sebastian's young cheeks blushed, and he appeared to be about to speak. But it was his mother who responded to Maude.

"Sebastian is just getting over a love tragedy," Madame Renoir informed her. "I don't think he's quite ready to venture out again." And in answer to the looks from the others gathered around them, she simply added, rather bluntly, "The girl was not nearly good enough for him"

It was only Lord Bainbridge who caught the quick look that Sebastian gave his mother, and it was a look that he had never before seen pass between them, for it was a look of defiant displeasure.

Sebastian had confessed to Lord Bainbridge that this love tragedy, as his mother had so dramatically put it, was nothing more than a few shared kisses and an ending that was by mutual agreement, both parties having quickly lost interest in the affair. After all, he was only fourteen, hardly at an age when love matches were made. He had also told Lord Bainbridge that when he met the right girl, he would know it, and they would be together whether his mother approved or not. Lord Bainbridge sensed that in the years to come, the close relationship that Madame Renoir and Sebastian now shared would certainly be put to the test.

Lord Bainbridge looked up and spotted Ronnie Standish on the other side of the room, prowling through the edges of the crowd that filled the Palm Court. He appeared to be looking for someone. And to Lord Bainbridge, his face had the unsavory look of a predator. As he continued to watch him, Lord Bainbridge was suddenly reminded of the fact that his own face had often held a similar expression, especially during the many hours he had spent at the Crown. This comparison unnerved him completely, and he quickly turned his eyes and his attention back to those gathered around him, hoping only that Ronnie would keep his distance.

"Are you quite all right, Ducks?" Maude asked him. "You've a very startled look on your face."

"I'm fine," Lord Bainbridge assured her. *I just looked into the mirror and saw someone else's reflection,* he thought to himself.

"I think Jeremy has a wonderful new secret," Lucianna announced with a kindly teasing smile.

Lord Bainbridge gave her a startled look. "What do you mean?" he asked, struggling to keep both his composure and his voice from breaking.

"I've noticed a difference about you this evening," Lucianna told him. "There's a glow of happiness about you. I think you've met someone special," she added.

"Oh, for heaven's sake, Lucianna, leave the poor boy alone," the count protested. "Can't you see you've got him blushing?"

Lord Bainbridge, however, was quite sure he wasn't blushing; in fact, he was equally certain he had gone quite pale. Had Lucianna somehow found out about Tom and him? Perhaps someone had told her of seeing the two of them having dinner together in the dining saloon the night before. But then Lucianna's next words revealed that her information was but speculation.

"I'm quite certain Jeremy has met some special young lady on board this ship," she said to the others at their table. She smiled deeply at Lord Bainbridge and reached over and patted his hand. "A woman can sense these things," she added.

Lord Bainbridge smiled back at her, calmed and greatly relieved. But as he sat there looking around at the faces of his friends aware that they were waiting for him to respond in some manner, either deny or confirm Lucianna's suspicions, he was suddenly struck by a great desire, a great need to tell them everything, to tell them all about Tom. Inside his head, a thousand voices howled at him to admit the truth, to speak to these people, his dearest friends, of the love that dare not speak its name. Surely, they would understand and accept. Feeling both a little wicked and a little light-headed, he tested the waters.

"Actually, I have met someone," he confessed.

Out of the corner of his eye, he saw Maude's eyebrows arch up in sudden surprise, and he knew, without even looking at her, that Madame Renoir likewise was registering surprise on her face.

"I knew it!" Lucianna exclaimed, casting her husband a triumphant glance. "Tell us about her, Jeremy," she prompted.

Lord Bainbridge suddenly realized he had put himself in dangerous waters, for even with these people, his friends, some of whom already knew of his secret life, he knew he did not have the courage to announce aloud the true nature of his affections. But he was rescued from the dilemma he had got himself into by the sudden appearance of someone he never thought he would be relieved to see.

"Well, this certainly looks to be an amusing gathering," Ronnie Standish said, pausing before their table. "Jeremy, you must introduce me to your friends."

In a time when what men wore was dictated by rules almost as rigid as those that prevented one man from loving another, Ronnie Standish, as was his fashion, often chose to challenge those inflexible ordinances. And this night was no exception. Surrounded by a host of gentlemen properly attired in traditional black evening wear that no matter how well cut and tailored still unfortunately gave most of them the look of well-turned-out penguins, Ronnie stood there in the Palm Court wearing a suit made out of the finest white silk cut to perfection with wide lapels and a narrow waist. It was a beautiful garment made especially for him by a tailor in Florence, unique in workmanship and presentation, and completely unsuitable for evening wear. He would probably have caused less of a stir had he walked into the Palm Court stark naked. But a stir was what Ronnie Standish always wished to create, and he had purposely dressed this way this evening, being conceited enough to be convinced that his startling appearance would give everyone something to talk about for days afterward, the dramatic highlight of the voyage that they would all remember long after the ship had docked in New York. So of course, he remained standing before Lord Bainbridge and the others for a protracted length of time almost as if he were poising for his portrait, keenly aware that almost everyone in the room was watching him, and those that were not concentrating on his wardrobe, were most assuredly dwelling on his reputation, which swirled around him like a slap of cologne that was too strong.

Finally, feeling rather awkward but bound by the rules of polite society, Lord Bainbridge got to his feet and made the necessary round of introductions. Both Count Fraboli and Sebastian also rose and exchanged brief handshakes with the American. The older man's face registered perplexity while the youth showed a hint of curiosity as if the boy were trying to figure out the particularities of this strangely attired man who stood before them. The women remained seated, a nod of their heads and a brief fleeting smile their only greeting.

"You must let me join you," Ronnie said, smiling at them. "The rest of the room appears to be occupied exclusively by stiffs and bores."

Again, politeness dictated, and chairs were shuffled to make room for him among them. However, it was Ronnie who chose his own place, squeezing himself in between Lord Bainbridge and Sebastian.

A great sense of uneasiness now swept over Lord Bainbridge as Ronnie joined them. He feared Ronnie would say the wrong thing, make the wrong reference or, even worse, allude to their shared preference. The words *guilt by association*, a favorite phrase of his mother's, came quickly to his mind. But as he looked around the table, he was relieved to note that while most of his friends were simply puzzled by the American's manner and dress, they at least appeared like most everyone else, not to get him. Certainly, the count and his wife seemed not to have a clue, and even an observant novelist like Maude likewise looked to be in the dark. But when Lord Bainbridge turned to look at Madame Renoir, he could tell at once she knew the whole story. He should have expected that, for after all, she had uncovered him. The moment Ronnie had sat himself down beside her son, Madame Renoir had turned her glance on him, and her look was hard and cold, unforgiving and knowing. Lord Bainbridge knew that what she had accepted in him, even approved of, would not find her favor in someone like Ronnie Standish. And the fact that as soon as he had sat down he had engaged Sebastian in some intimate words in French that the others could not hear, only added to Madame Renoir's apprehension. She had suddenly become a lioness whose cub she feared was in great peril. And though a table separated them, the look in her dark eyes told Lord Bainbridge that a single pounce could easily land her on Ronnie Standish's throat.

But as it turned out, things got off to an innocent enough start, at least on the surface. "What part of America are you from, Mr. Standish?" Maude inquired.

"Boston," Ronnie answered rather abruptly, obviously reluctant to turn his attention away from the boy at his side.

"Well, that is a coincidence!" Maude announced enthusiastically. "Boston is to be the first stop on my book tour. Perhaps you might suggest some historical sites I would find interesting," she proposed, her large face beaming at him with anticipation.

Only now did Ronnie turn his full attention to her, and his own smile, though equally broad, was filled with a cruel glint that hinted at the mischief he was about to unleash. It was a look that only Lord Bainbridge understood, for it was of a kind that had been practiced and perfected mainly by those young men he and Ronnie socialized with.

"There is one particular place I think you might find of interest," Ronnie began, his voice lazy, almost hesitant as if, and this was in marked contrast to what he really felt, he were reluctant to divulge this special information to her.

"Oh, do tell me about it," Maude pleaded eagerly and in complete innocence, ignoring Lord Bainbridge's warning glance from across the table.

"It's a club on Broad Street," Ronnie revealed. "There's no sign on the door, and you have to be a member to be admitted." He winked at Maude. "But I think I can get you in if you like."

Maude was still uncomprehending. "Well, of what historical significance is this place?" she asked.

Lord Bainbridge closed his eyes, quite certain he knew what was about to come. He felt as if he were standing before a firing squad, awaiting the expected bullets. It seemed like an eternity before he heard Ronnie's answer.

"As far as I know, its the only place in Boston where men are allowed to dance with other men," Ronnie answered.

Opening his eyes, Lord Bainbridge was relieved that though the bullets had been fired, he himself had escaped them, at least for the moment.

The rest of the table was engulfed in a stunned silence except for Ronnie, who having accomplished his aim to shock, had returned his attention to Sebastian, speaking softly once again to him in French. The boy appeared to becoming more and more uncomfortable under Ronnie's rapt attention. Madame Renoir, for her part, was glaring across the table at Ronnie, her lips set tightly in a frown. The count and his wife were sharing an uneasy glance. While Maude sat there with her mouth hanging open, her heavy bulldog jowls fairly shaking with indignation, and her eyes fixing Ronnie with a look no on would have considered friendly. She seemed to have lost the ability to speak and was reduced to making little angry sounds in her throat as if she had just swallowed something that had lodged itself halfway down. Finally, she managed to sputter out a response.

"Mr. Standish, I hardly think I would be interesting in visiting such an establishment."

Ronnie offered her a quick glance and a shrug. "Well then, perhaps some of your friends might be," he suggested before quickly turning back to Sebastian.

That's it, Lord Bainbridge thought as he felt the bullets slam into his chest. But as he gazed apprehensively around the table, he could see that none of the others had connected Ronnie's insinuation to him. He had escaped free and clear. Then the next moment, everyone's attention turned to Sebastian Renoir.

Flushed and trembling, the boy leaped to his feet. He moved so quickly, and with such sudden force, he knocked his chair over backwards. Turning on Ronnie, he spoke his words in a low voice filled with emotion and an adolescent tremor. "If you ever do that to me again, monsieur, I swear I will kill you!"

Madame Renoir rose as well, and only Lord Bainbridge's restraining hand on her arm kept her from advancing furiously on Ronnie.

As it was, the American was wise enough to see the immediate need for a hasty retreat. Getting to his feet, he made an elegant little bow that was more sarcastic than polite, first to Sebastian then to his mother. Then Ronnie turned on his heel and made his way out of the Palm Court, exiting through the revolving door at the end of the room that led out onto the open deck.

Sebastian retrieved his chair and sat back down. Madame Renoir came and sat down beside him. And for perhaps the first time in his life, the son rebuffed his mother's attentions, telling her he was perfectly fine and not to fuss over him.

The others at the table once again fell into an uncomfortable silence. Taking out his pocket watch, Lord Bainbridge saw that it was nearly ten. He had told Tom to meet him at eleven, so he figured in order to have enough time to get ready for him, he should shortly be making his excuses to his friends.

Then at that moment, he looked casually across the room and spotted Elaine Standish sitting on the other side of the dance floor. She was seated alone, directly across from them and staring right at them. And although there was some distance between them and there was no way she could have overheard what Sebastian had said to her husband, Lord Bainbridge could tell by the set look on her face that she had certainly understood what had transpired between them. To him, it seemed as if she had suddenly appeared from out of nowhere. He was sure she hadn't been there when he first saw Ronnie prowling about the room. She must have entered the Palm Court sometime after Ronnie but in time to see and understand all that had happened.

"Excuse me a moment," Lord Bainbridge said, getting to his feet. While his companions craned their necks to see what had attracted his attention, he crossed the Palm Court, having to duck around the eager dancers, who once again had taken to the dance floor as the orchestra struck up a new tune.

When he reached her table, he found that her head was bowed, and he feared what she had witnessed might have reduced her to tears. But when she raised her head, he saw that her eyes were dry, and the only thing that was disturbing them was the intensity of their brilliant violet hue.

Earlier in the day when he had seen her out on the deck, her dark hair had hung long to her shoulders. Now she was wearing it up in a most becoming coiffure, and whether by accident or design, a single curl had come loose and fallen charmingly across her forehead. The evening dress she wore was of yellow satin with an overlay of pale yellow silk, and it reached down to her ankles as proper etiquette demanded. Around her slim neck, there was entwined a necklace of yellow silk embedded with diamonds.

"Well, hello again." Lord Bainbridge smiled as if once again they were meeting under casual and unexpected circumstances.

Elaine smiled back at him, obviously pleased to see him. "Yes, hello."

"May I join you?" he asked.

"Should you leave your friends?" Elaine inquired, nodding toward Maude and the others across the room, who were watching them while, of course, pretending not to.

"They're not used to seeing me in the company of a beautiful young woman," Lord Bainbridge said lightly. "Let's give them something to talk about."

Elaine nodded. "By all means. Shall I lean toward you and bat my eyelashes flirtatiously?" she asked, getting into the spirit of the moment.

"Anything but that," Lord Bainbridge said as he sat down beside her. "I didn't see you come in. I just looked across the room, and then suddenly there you were."

She looked away from him for a moment, appearing to watch the dancers on the floor before them, frowning as if she were disapproving of not only their movements but their happy flashing smiles as well. "I came in here to look for my husband," she said. Only then did her eyes swing back to Lord Bainbridge, and as they met his, Lord Bainbridge was quite certain he saw a trace of hostility in her stare. It was nothing more than a hint, a fleeting glance, but it was there, of that he was sure. "Obviously I found him," Elaine added quietly.

"About what happened . . ." Lord Bainbridge began, stammering in his embarrassment to explain.

"I know what happened," Elaine said quickly. "I don't need to hear the words. I've watched the scene played out a hundred times before. Do you have a cigarette?" she asked suddenly, leaning toward him, her voice hardly above a whisper.

"Yes, of course," Lord Bainbridge answered, somewhat startled at her request. Taking his cigarette case from his pocket, he flipped it open and held it out to her.

Her delicate fingers selected a cigarette. But instead of putting it to her lips, she held it aloft, twirling it between her fingers, examining it with great interest. "If I should smoke this, every tongue in the room would be instantly clicking away with disapproval," she said. "Actually, they already talk unflatteringly about me as it is," she added, placing the cigarette down on the table between them.

"Oh no," Lord Bainbridge protested.

"Not the English," Elaine assured him. "My fellow Americans are the ones with the loose tongues." She looked around the room as if she were trying to spot her tormentors among the assembled passengers. But the crowd in the Palm Court that night was gay and lively, and nobody appeared to be paying them any attention. Even Lord Bainbridge's friends, who had initially been watching them, were now engaged in a conversation among themselves and seemed to have forgotten about them.

"Surely people could never say bad things about you," Lord Bainbridge insisted, appalled at the very thought that this beautiful young woman before him could have been subjected to unsavory and malicious comments.

"Oh, they do," Elaine told him earnestly. "I've heard their whispers and seen the shakes of their heads. They condemn me because of my husband. They think that because Ronnie is different, I must somehow be different too." A hint of contempt crept into her tone. "Most of those fools don't realize how really different Ronnie is." Her eyes had been downcast as she had been speaking these words, her fingers toying with the cigarette on the table. Now she looked up at Lord Bainbridge and made a startling announcement.

"When we get home, I'm going to leave my husband. I intend to get a divorce." She searched his face. "Does that shock you? Or does it shock you more that I would confess this to someone I hardly know?"

"It doesn't shock me," Lord Bainbridge said. "It's what I think you should do. You deserve so much more, someone who can appreciate you. Someone who can love you," he added, ducking his own eyes away for a moment.

Elaine reached out and folded one of her hands over his. "How kind you have been to me. I feel like we've been friends forever." Her next words stopped his heart cold though he knew he should have been expecting them. "When it comes to love," she said cautiously, "you're like Ronnie, aren't you?"

At that moment, Lord Bainbridge had a great desire to deny his true self. It was something he had never done before. Although there were those who would say that by concealing his real identity he was thus denying it. He had not made a point of announcing himself to the world, but whenever he had been asked point-blank where his preferences lay, he had answered truthfully. And he had made a vow to himself that he would always do that no matter who was asking the question. Even if Lady Bainbridge herself had poised such an inquiry, he would have told her the truth. Of course, the very idea that his mother would ask such a question of him went well beyond the realm of preposterousness. Lady Bainbridge was so oblivious to her son's whole existence that whom he slept with held as much concern for her as the color of the shirt and tie he wore. In fact, if Lord Bainbridge had found reason to tell his mother about one of his lovers, undoubtedly she would have been more concerned about the individual's social standing than whether they were male or female.

But now, here was someone he had only known a short while asking him that same question, and he wanted desperately to lie to her. He wanted to swear to Elaine Standish that he was not like her husband, that his desires did not follow Ronnie's path. But he knew he couldn't. Staring back into her deep violet eyes with their almost hypnotic magnitude, Lord Bainbridge knew he would never be able to tell her anything but the truth.

"Yes," he answered, "we are the same." And then because he felt a need to do something with his hands, which he noticed were shaking, he lit a cigarette and sat back in his chair, waiting for her reaction.

"I thought so," she said.

This distressed him and he frowned. "Am I so obvious?" he asked.

"No, not at all," she hurriedly reassured him. "You have none of the ways, the mannerisms, that my husband has. It's just that I sensed something about you, something in what you said or didn't say. And then there was your book."

"My book?"

"Certain passages in it led me to suspect," she explained.

Lord Bainbridge smiled and shook his head. "And here I thought I was being so clever, dropping little hints here and there that only those in the know would uncover."

"You forget," she reminded him, "I am in the know." Then she brightened almost immediately. "I'm glad it turned out this way. We shall be friends always and never have to worry about all that other messy stuff."

"Good friends," he amended.

"Yes indeed!" she agreed enthusiastically.

The orchestra, which had been taking a break, started up another tune, and once again, eager dancers took to the floor.

"What's that song?" Elaine asked, humming along with the music. "I know it's familiar, I just can't think of its title."

"'The Tales of Hoffman,'" Lord Bainbridge answered.

"I think the waltz is the most beautiful and romantic dance ever created," Elaine said, watching the dancers.

Lord Bainbridge got to his feet and held out his hand. "Shall we have a go at it then?"

"You bet!" Elaine declared eagerly, jumping to her feet.

They moved out onto the dance floor and were immediately swept up by the music. Their young lithe bodies pressed close against one another, their faces but a breath away, they swirled around and around to the strains of the waltz. Their moves were so expertly and effortlessly coordinated, one would have thought they had been dancing together for years. Others, unknowing, would have immediately assumed they were lovers. After a few minutes, the tempo of the music slowed to a gentle lilting interlude before the next grand sweep would again send the dancers whirling around the room.

Their motion slowed down, and Lord Bainbridge and Elaine pulled apart, the distance giving them a clearer view of one another.

"You dance so well," Elaine said.

"So do you," Lord Bainbridge returned, surprised that once again, as with Madame Renoir and Lucianna Fraboli, he found himself to be a much better dancer that he had ever imagined himself to be.

"Some people might conclude we were professionals," Elaine suggested, glancing around the room. "Professional dancers," she mused. "That makes us sound slightly wicked."

"Yes it does," Lord agreed, highly amused.

The music picked up, and they were sent sweeping around the room once again with a speed and an intensity that made both of them dizzy. Then as it always does with a waltz, just as it felt like the music would go on forever, it came to one last crescendo and, with a final flourish that sent them spinning one last time, to its conclusion. For a moment, out of breath and with a floor beneath them that was still spinning, they clutched one another for support.

"Come and meet my friends," Lord Bainbridge suggested.

"I'd love to," Elaine responded.

In short order, introductions were made all around. Elaine was squeezed into a chair beside Maude with whom she fell immediately into an easy and friendly conversation.

Lucianna gave Lord Bainbridge a nod of approval, undoubtedly convinced that here at last was the special young lady he had been keeping all to himself.

Watching Elaine as she chatted animatedly with Maude, at one point laughing with a toss of her head that, for an unsettling moment, reminded him of Denham's famous gesture, Lord Bainbridge pondered once again over the fact that had fate dealt him a different hand from the one he held, then the beautiful young woman sitting across from him might easily have become his wife. And he could tell by the way his friends had instantly taken to her that his choice would have been as popular among them as he would have found it. But that would only have been if he had been a different person. His heart lay elsewhere. And with that little reminder like a jolt, he glanced quickly at his watch again and realized it was past time for him to make his excuses.

Elaine was telling Maude how much she admired her work. "I've read all your books, everyone," she confessed.

"Why, my dear, whenever did you find that much free time?" Maude asked, greatly flattered.

"I've nothing much else to do," Elaine answered, casting Lord Bainbridge a quick glance.

"Well, this has been a most delightful evening," Maude said, getting to her feet. "I hate to break up the party, but I must scurry off to get some writing done. My head is fairly swimming with creative thoughts."

The others pushed back their chairs, exchanged kisses and embraces, and all promised to meet the following day for luncheon after a good night's sleep. Or as count Fraboli put it, "Being lulled to sleep by the gentle motion of the ship like a baby in its bassinet."

Maude took Elaine's arm. "Walk me back to my cabin, my dear. I want to tell you all about my latest novel. It's set in Egypt, you know."

Lord Bainbridge was sure he saw a shudder pass through Elaine's slim shoulders at the mention of that far off place just as he took his leave.

He left the Palm Court through the revolving door that led outside onto the open deck. Immediately, he was struck with a blast of cold air that was so frigid, he figured the temperature must have dropped at least twenty degrees. Lord Bainbridge surmised they had probably finally arrived in the long promised ice fields. He went to the ship's rail and stared out at the sea, expecting to see a berg or two or perhaps even a field of ice. But there was nothing but the dark water, thousands of stars above, and the bitter cold. As he stood there shivering, he noticed one odd thing—there was no moon. The black sky was brilliantly lit with more stars than he had ever seen before in his lifetime, but even though there wasn't a cloud, the moon was not to be seen. It was as if it had simply vanished. Vaguely sensing that this was something of a dark omen, Lord Bainbridge turned to hurry below to his stateroom.

"Jeremy?"

Young Sebastian Renoir stood before him, obviously having followed him out of the Palm Court. The boy appeared slightly ill at ease as he shifted nervously from one foot to the other in that way adolescents do when they are unsure of the ground on which they stand.

"What is it, Sebastian?" Lord Bainbridge asked, smiling warmly at him.

"I don't want you to think," Sebastian began. But then he shook his head and started again. "It's just that I don't want you to think I had any intention of embarrassing you."

Lord Bainbridge was completely confused. He had no idea as to what Sebastian was referring. And the perplexed look on his face must have conveyed itself to the boy, for he quickly managed to straighten out both his thoughts and the words to express them. "Back there in the Palm Court, what happened between me and the American," he explained. "I was reacting to him, not because of his nature, but because he was forcing it upon me." He lowered his voice to a whisper although there was no one else about who could have possible overheard him. "He grabbed me intimately under the table," Sebastian revealed, blushing now even in the cold as he remembered the foul act.

"That bastard!" Lord Bainbridge fumed.

"Indeed," Sebastian agreed. "It startled me so I'm afraid I made a bit of a scene."

"I've a good mind to seek him out and give him a sound thrashing," Lord Bainbridge threatened. He didn't fail to notice the little smile that curled up the corners of Sebastian's mouth. "What, you don't think I could thrash him?" he challenged.

Sebastian looked embarrassed for a moment. "I'm sure you could," he responded. "I just don't think it's in your nature to thrash anyone, Jeremy. You're much too . . ." He struggled for a word. " . . . civilized!"

Lord Bainbridge recalled that night around the campfire when Sebastian had confessed his boarding school indiscretion. And now here he was again standing before him in the cold night air on board a great ship, making sure that his friend once again was not offended. Lord Bainbridge knew that Sebastian had somehow known all about him since almost their first meeting and had never held adverse judgment against him. He had accepted him as his friend and accepted all that there was about him. What is it about the French that makes them so perceptive and so without judgment? Lord Bainbridge had often asked himself. Maybe it was because, as many people often said, they were so worldly. Or perhaps it was, as Lord Bainbridge himself thought, it was because they were French.

Lord Bainbridge would have taken Sebastian into his arms and given him a great hug had he not thought better of it. Instead, he gave him a manly pat on the back, thanked him for his concern and told him it was much too cold for him to be standing out on deck without a coat and that he'd better get inside.

Sebastian nodded. "Yes, mother will be waiting." He had been leaning on the rail, facing the bow as they talked. Suddenly, something appeared to catch his attention and his whole body stiffened. "What's that?" he asked, pointing out to sea, his young voice trembling.

"Where?" Lord Bainbridge inquired, trying to follow his gaze.

Sebastian shook his head as if he were attempting to clear his vision. "For a second I thought I saw something up ahead in the water, off the bow. A large shape. There's nothing there now," he admitted. "It must have been my imagination."

"A phantom or a ghost perhaps?" Lord Bainbridge teased gently.

Above them countless stars watched them, twinkling with amusement. While beneath them the steel titan throbbed, pushing on faster and faster. While up ahead of them, quite close now, not a phantom or a ghost, but a titan of nature waited in patient silence.

Sebastian offered Lord Bainbridge a final smile and then strode off down the deck, his steps a curious mixture of man and boy, the boy he still was, the man he would soon become. He turned and looked back at Lord Bainbridge, giving him a little mock soldierly salute. "See you tomorrow," he called out to him. Then before he left the deck, he did some fancy footwork and jabbed the air with his fists at an imaginary opponent like a boxer. A second later, he had disappeared from sight.

Lord Bainbridge watched his antics with amusement. Then suddenly realizing he was going to be late, he took off on a run down the deck. He took the stairs down to the next deck two at a time, burst along the inside corridor, and arrived at the door to his stateroom quite out of breath.

As soon as he stepped over the threshold and closed the door behind him, Lord Bainbridge once again pulled put his pocket watch. It was almost eleven. Tom should be there any minute, for he knew that promptness was only one of the lad's many virtues.

Feeling almost a sense of panic as if the seconds were quickly slipping away from him, Lord Bainbridge hurried about preparing his stateroom for his visitor. First, he turned up the electric heater in the fireplace, for the chill that he had felt outside on the open deck seemed to have found its way like a thief into his stateroom. Next, he slipped off his dinner jacket and tie, throwing them casually across a chair. He unbuttoned the two top buttons of his shirt and adjusted the lamps in the room to an appropriate level. He considered setting out a bottle of wine but decided against it. It was most important that the two of them, at least initially, remain clearheaded. To this purpose, though he had a couple of glasses of wine at dinner, afterward in the Palm Court, he had stuck to lemonade. There were matters of the gravest importance that he needed to discuss with Tom, matters pertaining to their future.

As he continued moving about the stateroom, tidying up, he stopped before a small table in one corner of the stateroom. This had served as his writing desk, and spread out on it were the papers and notes for his second book. He glanced moodily through the pages, glimpsing snatches of conversations and descriptions of scenes not yet fully developed. Unimpressed, he laid the papers aside. Despite his already achieved literary success, Lord Bainbridge was often filled with doubts about his work. Sometimes he felt his scribbles were a waste of time and that he was less of a writer than a twelve-year-old boy who writes his mother once a week from boarding school. This was especially true now that he was struggling to begin his new book. Above everything else, it was its subject matter that had him filled with doubts. It would be his own life he was writing about this time, his own and that of his kind, and he wasn't sure he had the courage or the resolve to put all that down on paper for the world and himself to see. Perhaps he could deal with the world and its expected disapproval. But what if he disappointed those like himself who lived that life? And worst, what if once he saw his life written out before him, it didn't live up to the high expectations he had always held for it? What if his life on paper appeared as shallow and hollow as those who would mock it and disapprove of it had always held it to be?

Fortunately, these melancholy thoughts were timely interrupted by a knock on the stateroom door. His spirits immediately lifted, Lord Bainbridge hurried to answer it. Opening the door, he found Tom standing in the corridor, his fatal grin broad on his young face. "Hi!" he said, and Lord Bainbridge felt his heart fall into his shoes.

"Come in," he said, having to restrain himself from reaching out and pulling Tom into the stateroom with both hands.

Tom was once again dressed in the borrowed evening clothes, and he looked very smart except for his bow tie that hung at a crooked and uneven angle. "I thought I'd have an easier time making my way up here if I was dressed the part," he explained. "I had to give up on the tie though, it was just too much of a struggle."

Lord Bainbridge replied, closing the door to the corridor. "I always have a devil of a time with my ties as well," he confessed. "Alfred usually has to help me. He's an expert with them."

The mention of Alfred's name intruded upon them like a ghost for a moment, but like any proper spirit, it quickly vanished.

"I brought some of my own clothes to change into," Tom said, indicating the bundle under his arm. "I was afraid I was going to be late," he added. "I was reading your book, and I fell asleep. Thank you again for lending it to me."

"It's yours to keep," Lord Bainbridge returned. "It was a gift. I'm sorry it was so boring for you that it put you to sleep," he added with a bit of a chuckle.

"Oh no, not at all," Tom assured him. "I often fall asleep when I read. My eyes get tired, and I just nod off. But I like your book. I do. I have to read it slowly though, there's a lot to catch." He shrugged rather sheepishly. "I'm not sure I've caught everything that's in it as far as I've gone."

When they had parted Saturday morning, after having spent the night together, Tom had noticed the book with Lord Bainbridge's name on it on his writing desk. Lord Bainbridge had told him he was a writer, which impressed Tom greatly, and had given him the book to read. By the look of pleasure on Tom's face, one would have thought he'd been given the key to the vault where the Crown Jewels were kept.

"I've started another book," Lord Bainbridge told him impulsively.

"That's good. What's this one about?" Tom inquired.

"Us," Lord Bainbridge answered quickly.

Tom, who was putting his bundle of clothes down on the sofa, looked up at him quite startled. "You mean you and me?" he asked.

"Men who have feelings like us," Lord Bainbridge amended. Then he went on in a rush of words that revealed the torture and uncertainty he felt about his proposed book. "I know it is a subject which most of society is not anxious to see written about. If I do go ahead and write it, it will probably be banned in most of the civilized world except France of course."

"I think you should write it," Tom told him.

Lord Bainbridge was both surprised and greatly relieved. "Really?"

"Definitely," Tom assured him.

"I intend for it to have a happy ending," Lord Bainbridge added. "No one shoots himself on the last page."

"I much prefer books that have happy endings," Tom said, holding his gaze and then looking shyly away.

"I'm going to do it, then," Lord Bainbridge announced aloud. And as easy as that, he made up his mind and cast aside all his doubts, his fears, for he had the approval of the only person whose opinion mattered to him. If Tom had displayed the least hesitation, the least reluctance, then he would have abandoned the book and very possibly any future writing career. For Lord Bainbridge realized at that moment that if he could not write the book he really wanted to write, then it would be senseless and unforgivable for him to write anything else.

"Do you mind if I get rid of these fancy clothes?" Tom asked. "I'm afraid I'll never get used to them," he added, tugging at his shirt collar.

Lord Bainbridge smiled at him. "You're asking me if I mind if you get undressed?"

Tom laughed, "I guess that was a pretty stupid question." And he proceeded to pull off his clothes until once again he stood before Lord Bainbridge in nothing but his underdrawers.

A long moment passed while they stood starting at each other, a few feet apart, both breathing heavily. Neither one made a move toward the other. And they looked not unlike two actors in some risque French farce who, both having forgotten their lines, were standing on stage in a complete panic.

"Shall I get dressed then?" Tom asked after a bit, confused and wondering why Lord Bainbridge seemed suddenly to have grown so distant.

"Yes." Lord Bainbridge nodded with great reluctance.

Tom was surprised, "Are you sure?"

Finally, Lord Bainbridge came to him, and he touched him but gently and tentatively on his bare shoulder as if he feared that touch. "You'd better put your clothes on," he said. "We have to talk, and I won't be able to get a coherent word out if you continue to stand there like that."

Obediently, Tom pulled on the shirt and trousers he had brought with him. Silently, they walked over to the sofa and sat down before the fireplace. It was Tom who took Lord Bainbridge's hand. "You're shaking, Jeremy," he said. "What is it?"

"We need to talk about that happy ending," Lord Bainbridge answered.

"What happy ending?" Tom asked.

"Ours," Lord Bainbridge responded.

"Oh," Tom said, turning his face away to stare into the fireplace where the electric heater glowed with vivid intensity.

Lord Bainbridge took a deep breath and stared at the young man sitting across from him. They had made love only once, spent the night in each other's arms, dined together, and strolled about the ship—that had been the sum total of their interaction. And yet, here he was ready to commit himself to a lifetime together. He had had enough fleeting relationships, enough one-night stands, to realize when something better came along. But this was so much more. From the first moment he set eyes upon Tom Kennedy, he felt certain he was the one, the one he had been waiting for all these years. That he should have come across him on a ship in the middle of the Atlantic Ocean struck Lord Bainbridge as both the height of absurdity and romanticism. Shipboard romances were a well-known and well-worn cliché whether in real life or on the printed page. Certainly, Maude had sprinkled her various novels with enough of them to populate a good-sized passenger ship. And most of them, whether fact or faction, hardly ever lasted beyond disembarkation. What better chance had this one?

But still Lord Bainbridge knew he had to speak the words. "I want us to be together, Tom. Not just after we reach New York but forever." He paused a moment, staring at Tom's head which was still downcast. "You see, I love you," Lord Bainbridge added, knowing that those were the sincerest words he had ever uttered.

Tom looked up at him, very silent, very still. There appeared to be tears in his eyes, or perhaps it was his own tears that Lord Bainbridge was seeing.

"The first time I was ever with another fellow was when I was sixteen," Tom began, his voice softly modulated, his words coming slowly as if from a memory long repressed. "He was a mate of mine, the same age. We both had way too much to drink one night, and we went for a swim, naked. When we climbed out of the water, I was shivering, so my friend wrapped his arms around me. Then he kissed me, and I kissed him back. But I got so scared that I leaped up and ran away. I ran and ran until I got this terrible pain in my side and I had to stop. There's been three or four other times, but in someway, I think I'm running still."

"Tom, it's time to stop running," Lord Bainbridge said gently. "We could make it work. I know we could."

The indecision and confusion on Tom's face was unmistakable. He spoke his next words as if to himself. "I won't ever take money from you. I wouldn't live off of you. I would have to make my own way."

"If you come with me, I promise you can do whatever you want," Lord Bainbridge pressed urgently. "Get a job in a factory, drive a milk wagon, I don't care as long as we are together." He crossed himself rather dramatically even more so given the fact he wasn't even a Catholic. "And I swear to you, I won't lay a finger on you if you don't want me to. I'd be content just to be near you."

A hint of his famous grin broke Tom's features. "I never said I didn't want you to lay a finger on me."

Suddenly without warning, the door to the corridor was flung open with a bang that startled them both. Alfred lurched into the room. They could see at once that he was quite drunk.

"Ah, true love in bloom," Alfred mocked, "how touching!" He leaned over the back of the sofa and leered into their faces, the large amount of ale he had consumed reeking on his breath. "Well, I've had some lovin' of my own," he boasted, slurring his words. "I just did it with the bodyguard up on deck in one of the lifeboats. Christ was it cold!"

"You'd better go to bed, Alfred," Lord Bainbridge suggested rather sternly.

Before Alfred could respond, they all felt something unusual. It was like a tap or a bump rather gentle as if the great ship had nudged something or as if she were pulling up alongside a dock. It wasn't much really, just different enough from the everyday sounds and motions of the ship that they had become accustomed to that it attracted their attention.

In his inebriated state, Alfred came to a quick conclusion. "We must already be in New York," he mumbled. He staggered toward the other room. "I'd better go and pack up our things."

Lord Bainbridge quickly got to his feet. "No," he said, "we're certainly not in New York." He cast Tom an uneasy glance. "By no means," he added.

Chapter IX

At the exact moment that the three men in Lord Bainbridge's stateroom felt that rather curious motion, Lord Bainbridge glanced casually at the little electric clock on the mantel above the fireplace. He saw that it was exactly 11:40 PM. He wasn't quite sure why he had bothered to check the time, but later, he would look back at it as one of those curious random acts that burns itself indelibly into one's memory forever. The three of them stared blankly at one another for a moment, no one knowing quite how to react or what to say. Then in turn, their eyes fell on the door to the corridor, which Alfred had left wide open when he had stumbled rather ungracefully into the room. Their view of the corridor outside failed to offer a clue. There was no one to be seen, nothing to be heard.

"Let's have a look," Lord Bainbridge suggested, finally propelling them into action. He headed for the door with Tom at his heels.

Alfred started to follow them, but his coordination being definitely impaired, he managed only a few steps before his foot caught on the carpet, and he fell hard to the floor, getting a mouthful of expensive broadloom. The other two found this highly amusing, and they enjoyed a good laugh at his expense. Then Lord Bainbridge mildly chastised him. "Come on, Alfred, stop mucking about. This might be serious."

Grumbling and cursing, Alfred picked himself up, spit out a stray carpet strand or two, and followed after them.

Emerging out into the corridor, they still found it deserted and as calm and serene as if it were just another uneventful night in the middle of the Atlantic.

"Perhaps we were the only ones who noticed it," Tom suggested.

Lord Bainbridge shook his head, "No, I don't think so."

"Probably someone dropped something in the kitchen," Alfred mumbled, not in a mood to be helpful.

With Lord Bainbridge leading the way, the three of them continued down the corridor, turned left, and emerged into the B deck foyer. This too, they found completely deserted. As they started up the forward grand staircase, Lord Bainbridge suddenly wondered, only half seriously, if they were the only ones left on the ship. Had there been some sort of accident and everyone else been evacuated?

As if to prove the absurdity of such an idea, a steward suddenly appeared coming down the staircase toward them. He seemed in a bit of a rush and was obviously prepared to hurry right past them.

Lord Bainbridge's question brought him to a reluctant hault. "What has happened?"

The steward seemed as unconcerned as he was uninformed. "Don't know, sir. But I imagine it's nothing to worry about," was his brief reply. Then he hurried down the stairs and quickly disappeared down a corridor.

"Well, he certainly was a fountain of information," Lord Bainbridge observed in a tone of slight irritation.

They reached the A deck foyer. Above their heads, a huge wrought-iron and glass dome kept back the vast night sky. As Tom and Alfred made for the door leading out onto the deck, Lord Bainbridge called them back. "Let's go up on top," he proposed. So they climbed the final flight of the grand staircase, passing on the uppermost landing the elegant clock with its two classical figures symbolizing Honor and Glory crowning time.

As they emerged out onto the boat deck on the port side of the ship, they at last came upon other passengers. Not a great number, but a few and most obviously reacting to the same event that had disturbed Lord Bainbridge and his companions. Most, but not all. A couple, still elegantly attired in evening wear, strolled leisurely past them along the open deck. They passed so close in fact that Lord Bainbridge could not help but overhear their intimate conversation, which was unmistakably sprinkled with words of love. So enraptured were the couple, they were completely oblivious to anyone or anything that was happening around them.

And what was now happening, or rather not happening, startled Lord Bainbridge anew. "Why, we've stopped!" he exclaimed.

And indeed they had. The *Titanic* had come to a dead stop in the water. She sat motionless under a star-filled sky, three of her four funnels blowing off useless steam.

Among the little crowd gathered on the boat deck, no one seemed overly alarmed that their trip to New York had come to a sudden unexpected halt. They milled around, talking together in quiet unexcited tones or stood silently at the rail, staring out at the empty and placid sea.

Even Lord Bainbridge, though he had had a strange sense of foreboding ever since they had felt that jar back in his stateroom, seemed at the moment not to be greatly perturbed by the situation. "Perhaps we shall be delayed getting to New York," he said, flashing a smile at Tom.

"I shouldn't mind that at all," Tom responded.

At that moment, they were accosted by a large-built, red-faced man who spoke in a loud booming voice that easily carried over the roar of the ship's funnels. In addition, he spoke with a broad American accent, which the other three men found almost as annoying as the timbre of his voice.

"Hit an iceberg, we did!" the man informed them. "I saw the whole damn thing!" he boasted puffed up with pride as if this was an accomplishment to be much admired and marveled at. "It was taller then the ship's masts. Incredible! At first, I thought it was a windjammer under full sail that was bearing down on us. But damn if it wasn't a berg! There's still plenty of ice on deck," he added. "I'll be glad to take you fellows over to see it if you'd like."

"Sure," Lord Bainbridge responded with a shrug. "Why not? That would be right sporting of you."

"Okay then!" the American bellowed. He gave the three of them a hard stare and shook his head. "Boy, you English sure talk funny."

With that, he gave Lord Bainbridge a hearty slap on the back that almost made the young Englishman lose his breath and then proceeded to lead them off to see the ice. As if they were following a tour guide to some ancient ruin, the three men trooped after the American. First, they passed through the ship itself and came out on the other side, the starboard side of the boat deck. Then the American paraded them down the deck, forward toward the bow.

"There it is, then!" the American cried out, pointing down to the lowermost deck where it looked as if at least a ton of ice had been dumped.

That deck was part of the third class recreation area, and a number of young men were engaged in a spirited game of football using the chunks of ice as balls.

The whole scene reminded Lord Bainbridge of the moment two days ago when he had first spotted Tom involved in a similar rough-and-tumble game down on the same spot. Glancing at Tom leaning beside him on the rail, watching the players below, Lord Bainbridge could tell by the amused smile on his lips that he was remembering the same moment.

Of course then the American had to spoil the whole thing by opening his mouth. "I'd go down there and give 'em a hell of a game myself if they weren't steerage passengers and therefore unfit to associate with," he stated bluntly.

Lord Bainbridge felt Tom's shoulder, which rested against his, tremble. He was about to turn angrily on the American and berate him when Tom, perhaps sensing what he was about to do, spoke up. "It's cold," he said simply.

At that moment, Lord Bainbridge realized that in their haste, both he and Tom had come up on deck in their shirtsleeves. "Come on," he said, "we'd better get inside where it's warm."

But before they did, Lord Bainbridge couldn't resist asking the American a final question. "Do you think the iceberg did any serious damage to the ship?"

The American laughed and shook his head. "How could it have? After all, it's only a bit of ice. All of it would have melted away before it could do any real harm," he concluded.

Hardly convinced by this rather strained logic, Lord Bainbridge nodded, and thanking the American for showing them the ice, he facilitated a quick departure. With Tom and Alfred trailing after him, Lord Bainbridge took an outside set of stairs down to A deck. Halfway down, he stopped and made a rather unsettling observation to his companions. "These stairs don't feel quite right under my feet," he told the other two. "They seem almost as if they were slightly tilted."

Alfred was hardly impressed with this latest revelation. "I thought I was the one who was drunk, not you," he said rather smugly.

When they once again entered the foyer on A deck, they found a small crowd of passengers gathered there amongst the Edwardian splendor. Some of them were in evening dress, obviously still up and about and reluctant to bring an end to whatever gay festivities had filled up their Sunday night. A fewer number had thrown coats or wraps over their nightclothes and had just as obviously come from their staterooms. But no matter what their attire, each passenger presented a calm and unperturbed demeanor. They were curious, not panic-stricken. There was no sense of danger among them. They had only come up to see what was going on. Infested with the restlessness that seems to infect most people on board ships, they had been stirred from the warmth of their staterooms or the lavish public rooms, not so much by the jarring bump that to most had seemed of little importance, but rather by the silence as the ship glided to a halt and then lay motionless in the water. But even this development hardly disturbed anyone except perhaps one or two who feared it might delay their arrival in New York and who apparently had urgent business to conduct upon arrival. The very fact that these passengers had chosen to remain inside where it was warm rather than venture out into the cold night air on deck spoke to the degree of their concern. They wanted to know what was going on but were quite content to let someone else find out for them. There was certainly no need for them personally to get chilled to the bone.

"What do they say the trouble is?" someone asked as Lord Bainbridge and the others came through the door.

"Ice," was Alfred's blunt response.

"Anything to see?" another inquired.

"Loads of ice down on the steerage deck," Alfred elaborated. "Those idiots down in steerage are playing with it as if they'd never seen ice before," he added, failing to mention that it was the first time he too had ever seen ice.

"Could I get some for my drink?" an American asked jokingly.

"Sure," Alfred grinned, "if you want to ruin it."

Lord Bainbridge and Tom had walked over the grand staircase, and here they paused. "I'd better go below and check on my cabinmates," Tom said. The look on Lord Bainbridge's face disturbed him. "What is it?" he asked.

"I think we should stay together," Lord Bainbridge answered quickly. He lowered his voice to a whisper. "I've a bad feeling about all this, Tom," he admitted. "I think it's a lot worse than anyone suspects."

Tom's eyebrows shot up, "Really?" He looked about. "No one else seems terribly concerned," he pointed out.

Lord Bainbridge nodded. "I know." Tom was staring at him with not quite a smile on his face. Lord Bainbridge wanted desperately to take the young Irishman into his arms, crush him to his chest and, in doing so, blot out all the terrible persistent thoughts of doom he was having. "I'm awfully afraid I'll never see you again," he blurted out.

Now Tom did smile, his famous grin breaking from his lips and spreading across his whole face. "You'll not get rid of me quite so easily," he promised.

Then Lord Bainbridge did something he would never have dared to do had he not been so upset, had he not been so distressed. He reached out and touched Tom's cheek. In that very public place, with others milling around them, he threw all caution, all sense of propriety, to the wind and reached out and touched the face of the young man he loved. And though it was just a fleeting touch, more like a tap than a caress, it was bold and perhaps even foolish.

Tom, who very well might have been expected to move away at such a gesture in public, instead stood his ground and continued to smile back at him while Alfred, whose sharp eyes had not missed the indiscretion, became obviously annoyed by such a display, or perhaps he was to some extent jealous. Whatever his mood, he grunted his displeasure and walked quickly away. His steps were once again steady, and he appeared to have quickly sobered up. Perhaps it was the cold air out on deck that had revived him, or perhaps it was reality.

After Alfred's departure, they were quickly joined by another. It was the young junior officer who had befriended Lord Bainbridge. He came striding toward them through the foyer, his steps jaunty, his pace hurried but not in a manner that indicated anything dire was amiss. Spotting Lord Bainbridge, he waved him a friendly greeting before he even reached him.

"Oh, hello, bit of a lark, isn't it!" he joked as he joined them. "They say it was an iceberg. Never saw it myself, slept through the whole thing. Dash it all, I was so keen to see a berg!" His words came out almost in a jumbled tangle like those of a child who has so much he wants to tell and, in his excitement, can barely manage to get the words out. "There's tons of ice forward though. Have you seen it?" he asked. Lord Bainbridge assured him he had. "Got to report to the bridge, regulations you know," he told them.

"Do you think we're in any serious danger?" Lord Bainbridge asked.

At his question, others standing nearby turned their heads toward them, awaiting the officer's reply. For just a beat, an instant no more, a change of expression came over the officer's face. Like a dark cloud, it played across his features as he considered a possibility that truly, until that moment, had not occurred to him. But then, realizing he had an audience and because he really believed such a likelihood was unthinkable, he instantly brightened and shook his head. "Not a chance," he informed them. "I'm sure we'll soon be on our way again," he predicted confidently.

"Then why did we stop in the first place?" Lord Bainbridge asked.

The young officer had an immediate answer, which caused a number of those gathered around him to chuckle appreciatively. "I imagine we stopped so's we wouldn't run over the berg," he said. "Wouldn't want to do it any harm, would we?" Then giving Lord Bainbridge a wink, he turned and bounded up the grand staircase, taking the steps eagerly two at a time.

The officer's optimism had convinced at least one person. "See, there's nothing to worry about," Tom said to Lord Bainbridge.

Still, Lord Bainbridge clung to his feeling of uneasiness; like a man blindly groping in the darkness, he refused to light a candle no matter how many were held out to him.

"I'll be back as soon as I've checked on my mates," Tom promised. "Then we can spend the rest of the night together."

Lord Bainbridge had nothing left to say, no further protest he could muster. "Yes, all right," he managed with a shrug almost of indifference.

"Everything's going to be fine, Jeremy," Tom added. "I know it."

"Of course," Lord Bainbridge concurred.

Then Tom offered him a final grin and, with a wave of his hand, started down the grand staircase that led all the way down to E deck.

In a state akin to panic, Lord Bainbridge could not prevent himself from calling out his name. "Tom!" And when Tom paused on the stairs to look back up at him, Lord Bainbridge knew the only reason he had called out to him was because he wanted to see his face one more time.

Tom seemed to understand this as well, for he merely smiled at Lord Bainbridge and continued on his way.

Lord Bainbridge stood there in the middle of the foyer and watched him until he disappeared from his sight. Then with his heart and mind both still troubled, he made his way back to his stateroom. He found the corridors now more crowded with passengers emerging from their staterooms to find out what was going on. Two stewards passed him carrying life belts, that in itself was hardly reassuring.

He had reached his own door when the stateroom door across the hall opened, and Madame Renoir beckoned to him. Having obviously made ready to retire, she wore a kimono of Nile green, and her long brown hair, which she usually wore pilled high on her head, hung loose to her shoulders. To her appearing in public in this manner was no less than the height of impropriety, so instead of coming out into the corridor, she pulled Lord Bainbridge into her stateroom. Her hands that reached out to grasp his he found to be ice-cold.

"Jeremy, what is it?" she asked. "What's happened?"

"It appears we ran into some ice," he explained.

"Is there any danger? Are people alarmed?" Madame Renoir asked quickly, searching his face.

"I'm not sure," Lord Bainbridge said. "No one seems terribly upset," he added, thinking to himself, *No one but me, that is.*

"Should I awaken Sebastian?" Madame Renoir asked. "He's such a sound sleeper."

Struggling to put his own fears into perspective, Lord Bainbridge hesitated with his response. Finally, he counseled on the side of caution. "I think you should awaken him, and I think the both of you had better get dressed," he advised.

For a second, the fine features of Marguerite Renoir's face slipped into a mask almost of fear. But it was only a momentary change, and then her features relaxed like a vehicle going in the wrong direction suddenly making a quick and smooth direction change. "Yes of course, Jeremy," she said.

"It'll be all right," he suggested, and then offering her a reassuring smile that he did not really feel, Lord Bainbridge left her and slipped across the hall to his own stateroom.

Inside, he found Alfred standing before the fireplace, stripping off the last of his clothes. He straightened up completely naked and shrugged rather sheepishly as though he had been caught in the midst of some forbidden act. This act in itself was rather out of character for him as he had never before been shy about his own nakedness, often readily flaunting it before Lord Bainbridge in a teasing and amusing manner. "I'm going to bed," Alfred explained. "I see no reason not to," he added as if challenging Lord Bainbridge to disagree.

"I think you'd better put your clothes back on," Lord Bainbridge advised, turning away to light a cigarette.

"Oh, that's right, now that you've found your little mick, my body is repellent to you," Alfred said with a sneer.

Lord Bainbridge chose to ignore that remark, sensing, quite rightly, that there were other more urgent matters to contend with. As if to emphasize this, there was a knock on the door to the corridor, a brisk and official-sounding knock.

Lord Bainbridge looked to Alfred, who continued to stand there in his undressed state, now obviously determined to remain that way no matter who was on the other side of the door.

Lord Bainbridge called his bluff. "Come in," he called out unhesitatingly.

The door swung open, and a steward stepped into the room. At first glance, he didn't seem disturbed or even surprised by Alfred's lack of apparel. Most probably, the man has seen all sorts of sights opening stateroom doors, Lord

Bainbridge reasoned. And Alfred's little display wasn't probably even worth a second glance.

The steward came quickly to the reason for his intrusion. "Captain's compliments, gentlemen, all passengers are requested to put on their life belts and report to the boat deck."

"Life belts?" Lord Bainbridge said, momentarily both stunned and confused.

"They're on top of the wardrobe in the corner there, sir," the steward added helpfully.

"Is this ship going down?" Alfred asked bluntly.

The steward appeared deeply offended at the very suggestion of such a calamity. "Certainly not, sir," he responded quickly. "The *Titanic* wouldn't think of doing such a thing," he added as if the ship itself was capable of deciding its own fate. "It's merely a precaution, gentlemen, nothing else," the steward told them as he began to retreat, backing out of the room, smiling broadly as if it all had been nothing more urgent than a visit to replenish their bath towels. Before he closed the door behind him however, the man couldn't resist one last suggestion that he made to Alfred. "Warm clothes as well, sir, would be advised."

Left alone in the stateroom, the two Englishmen stared back at one another, neither wanting to be the first to react to the steward's instructions.

It was Alfred who was the first to swing into action. He left Lord Bainbridge standing in the middle of his stateroom and walked into his own room. Through the open door, Lord Bainbridge watched him pulling out his clothes and pilling them on the bed.

"What do you think we should take with us?" Alfred called out from the other room.

Lord Bainbridge ignored his question. He stubbed his cigarette out in a glass ashtray, being extra careful not to let any embers fall to the carpet beneath his feet. *This would be a hell of a bad time to start a fire,* he though humorously to himself.

"Should we pack our trunks or just an overnight case?" Alfred persisted.

"Alfred, we're not setting out for a weekend in the country," Lord Bainbridge called back to him, a bit impatient.

"I just need to know what to take with me," Alfred answered. And though Lord Bainbridge couldn't see his face, he knew his lips would be curled into a rather large pout.

"Whatever happens, I don't think it would be wise to encumber ourselves with luggage," Lord Bainbridge said.

Alfred appeared in the doorway to his room. He had at least managed to get into his underwear, a one-piece knitted cotton combination although in his haste he had mismatched the buttons, so that only half of them were properly fastened. "What about all my clothes?" he asked in distress.

Lord Bainbridge knew Alfred prized his wardrobe above everything else. The fancy clothes he wore were to him a true measure of his worth and an indication, at least in his own mind, to the rest of the world of the position he held in society, which was far above the normal standing for one from his humble beginnings. Lord Bainbridge had always been happy to indulge him in his desire for finery. It was one of the unwritten laws of the unique contract that bound them one to the other. And if need be, Lord Bainbridge was quite willing to refill Alfred's closets once again. He said as much, "Clothes can be replaced," to the figure standing in the doorway in his underwear.

"Damn!" Alfred swore. Then turning around, he stomped back into his own room where, to show his displeasure, he began throwing things around.

Ignoring this rather childish display, Lord Bainbridge turned his thoughts to his own clothes at least those that he should put on to journey up to the boat deck. He was much calmer now. All the forebodings of doom and dire consequences that he had previously held seemed to have, at least for the moment, disappeared. Strangely enough, it had been the steward's words that had reassured him, relaying the information that whatever the problem, Captain Smith had the matter well in hand and was taking whatever steps were necessary even if they were just precautionary. Obviously, Captain Smith was a wise and prudent man, Lord Bainbridge concluded with no small measure of comfort.

His mind thus greatly relieved, he stripped off his evening clothes and selected what he would wear on this unexpected, but now seen as rather exciting, trip to the boat deck. He began with a pair of wool trousers of charcoal gray and a simple collarless off-white silk shirt. Over this, he pulled on a heavy white wool sweater. Knowing it would be cold up on deck, he put on an extra pair of wool socks before slipping into a pair of ankle-length leather boots. The jacket he chose was also charcoal gray and double-breasted with a belt around the middle. It was commonly called a shooting jacket though Lord Bainbridge had never shot a thing save an occasional angry glance. He topped all this off with a gray felt trilby hat with a wide upturned brim. The hat was hardly proper with the jacket, but it was one of Lord Bainbridge's favorites, convinced as he was that it gave him somewhat of a roguish look.

He had just finished dressing when Alfred returned to the room. "That hat doesn't go with the rest of your outfit," were the first words out of his mouth.

"Yes, I know," Lord Bainbridge acknowledged, giving his hat brim a last little tweak. Observing his companion's attire, he couldn't resist a comment of his own. "Well, Alfred, what's it to be, a wedding or a funeral?"

Alfred frowned. He wore a three-piece wool suit of dark blue with a stiff collar and a blue-green printed silk tie. Over this, he sported a full-length wool overcoat. Leather gloves on his hands and a dark blue homburg on his head completed his ensemble. One of his gloved hands clutched that well-known symbol of the

English gentleman—a rolled-up black umbrella. This was the outfit that Lord Bainbridge knew Alfred had particularly chosen to impress the young toughs of American whom he eagerly hoped to encounter. Now, he tried to explain why he had chosen to wear it up to the boat deck of the *Titanic*. "Perhaps I ain't no gent, but if I'm gonna drown, at least I'll drown looking like one," he said.

"Don't be absurd, Alfred!" Lord Bainbridge snapped. "No one's going to drown!"

Alfred shrugged his shoulders. "I want to be prepared just in case."

Lord Bainbridge was staring down at his personal items that were scattered on top of the bureau beside his bed. Immediately, he picked up the miniature of his father and slipped it into the pocket of his jacket. Nothing else seemed worth bothering about.

"What about your jewelry?" Alfred prompted.

Lord Bainbridge opened the little silver box. There really wasn't much inside to see—a number of pairs of cuff links, a gold watch on a chain, which had been handed down through the generations of Bainbridge men but which no one could remember whom it had originally belonged to, a couple of rings, and his school pin from Winchester. None of the items held any special sentimental value to him except perhaps the pin. He never wore rings, convinced they made his slim hands look too effeminate, and he already carried a pocket watch. Just before he closed the box, he took out the pin and pinned it to his jacket.

"You can't leave the rest of that stuff lying around in here," Alfred protested. "All of the stewards have pass keys. Someone's sure to slip in and pinch it while we're all up on deck."

Lord Bainbridge shrugged. "If they want it, they're welcome to it."

"That ridiculous!" Alfred told him sharply. He picked up the silver box and shoved it into the pocket of his overcoat. "I'll keep it for you," he said.

"As you wish," Lord Bainbridge returned without protest.

It was Alfred who remembered the life belts the steward had recommended. He pulled them down from the top of the wardrobe. And as the two young men stared at the rather cumbersome belts, Alfred shook his head. "These won't do at all," he complained with a shake of his head. "They won't look good on us."

Lord Bainbridge agreed as he took one from Alfred. "Well, we probably won't have to really put them on. We'll just carry them with us to make everyone happy," he suggested.

Alfred nodded. "I wouldn't be caught dead in one," he added, obviously thinking more about his appearance than his life.

Thus finally ready, they headed for the door only to have Lord Bainbridge suddenly turn back. He went to the little table in the corner of the stateroom, and picking up his notes and the pages he had begun on his second novel, he placed them into the pocket of his jacket. Then he quickly followed Alfred out into the corridor. Before he closed the door to the stateroom, he glanced back one last time into the room, remembering the moments he and Tom had spent together there, moments when he had felt safe and secure and loved. With a sigh, he closed the door and locked it.

Crossing the corridor, Lord Bainbridge knocked twice on the door to the Renoirs' stateroom, but there was no response. "They must have already gone up on deck," he said to Alfred.

The corridor around them was filling up with people as more and more passengers headed up to the boat deck. Gently but firmly prodded along by the stewards, they paraded up in a variety of costumes. Some of them were still dressed in their elegant evening clothes, and others had merely thrown coats over their nightclothes while still others were turned out in impeccable style as if they were ready for arrival in New York. But whatever their attire, hardly anyone seemed upset or fearful although a few could be heard grousing about the inconvenience of having to be roused from a warm bed in the middle of the night. But there was much calling back and forth as friends greeted one another, much laughter and much amused banter, as if it all were nothing more than some mild diversion the White Star Line had thought up to entertain its passengers. Only here and there, on the fringes of the crowd, could there be detected a hint of panic.

At one point, Lord Bainbridge glanced at his pocket watch and saw that it was already past midnight. It was a new day: Monday, April 15.

Two young women suddenly stepped right into their path, coming upon them so fast that the four of them were just a breath away from a collision that, had it occurred, would undoubtedly have sent the four of them sprawling to the carpeted floor. The two women were in a highly agitated state, and they clung tightly to each other as if fearing at any moment, strong hands might try to tear them apart. One of them appealed to Lord Bainbridge so desperately, her eyes filled up with tears.

"Oh, sir, can you help us please!" she begged. "We couldn't find any life belts in our cabin!"

"None at all!" the second woman echoed in dismay.

Casting his eye at Alfred, Lord Bainbridge could tell by the frown on his companion's face and the way his eyes were narrowing that he was reacting in his usual manner to these young women as he did to all women.

"Please, sir, we don't want to drown!" the first woman wailed.

Surprisingly, it was Alfred who acted to calm them. Taking Lord Bainbridge's life belt from him, he handed it along with his own to the two young women.

Eagerly grasping the life belts, the two young women thanked them profoundly over and over, and then clutching the life belts and each other, they scurried off in haste as if the ship were at that moment sinking beneath their feet.

"The belts won't do them much good if they don't put them on," Alfred observed as they watched the women scamper away.

In answer to Lord Bainbridge's silent inquiry as to why he had given away their life belts, Alfred shrugged. "Those two women were so annoying, I'd have done anything to get rid of them. Besides," he reasoned, "we're both good swimmers if it comes to that."

Lord Bainbridge nodded thoughtfully, having come to the conclusion himself that if they did have to go into the water, which at this point he seriously doubted, the cumbersome life belts would certainly hinder their movements. They would be able to move much freer and faster without them. Of that he was sure.

They followed the crowd of passengers up the grand staircase to the A deck foyer. Here is where most of the people were gathering, few if any caring to venture out into the cold night air on the boat deck above despite Captain Smith's orders. And why should they? There certainly seemed to be no eminent danger; the ship had stopped, but she appeared as solid, as unsinkable as ever. Besides the atmosphere in the foyer had become quite festive. Passengers sat in the white wicker chairs scattered about the room or stood about in groups, chatting and laughing while waiters actually passed among them with drinks from a makeshift bar that had been set up near the staircase.

"Anything for you, gentlemen?" a waiter asked them.

Lord Bainbridge would have declined, but Alfred spoke up first, "Two whiskeys." And a few moments later when the first of the whiskey passed down his throat, Lord Bainbridge was thankful for Alfred's quick decision.

Some members of the ship's orchestra had gathered around a small piano in one corner of the foyer, and to the delight of many of the passengers, they now broke into a spirited rendition of "Great Big Beautiful Doll." A number of young couples even began to dance to the gay music.

"It's like a bloomin' party," Alfred observed.

"Yes," Lord Bainbridge agreed but without much enthusiasm. He craned his neck trying to spot a familiar face, but he saw none of his friends.

Alfred, however, had caught sight of someone. He nudged Lord Bainbridge. "Look there," he pointed.

Coming up the staircase from the deck below was the American woman who occupied the luxury suite nearest his own stateroom. Draped in a fur coat and carrying her ever present little dog, she walked slowly, regally, well aware that most eyes had turned to observe her entrance. Following behind her was the handsome bodyguard, wearing a long black overcoat and a bowler hat and carrying a medium sized case, which obviously held the lady's jewelry.

They paraded right past Lord Bainbridge and Alfred, so close in fact that Lord Bainbridge got a good look at the woman's face behind the tight veil drawn down from her hat. Her eyes shifted toward him for just a brief second. And with a slight tilt of her head and a fleeting quiver of her lips as if they had started and then relinquished a smile, she acknowledged his presence before she moved on. Alfred received no such glimmer of recognition from the bodyguard, who passed him with his nose in the air and his eyes averted.

"That's typical, ain't it?" Alfred muttered to Lord Bainbridge. "You have sex with 'em, and then the next time they see you, they pretend they don't know you."

Lord Bainbridge smiled to himself, having to admit that Alfred's remark was not far off. He was about to suggest they go up to the boat deck and see what, if anything, was going on when he saw Maude coming across the foyer toward them. She, for one, had put on her life belt, and given her own ample endowment in the chest area, the addition of the life belt gave her a decidedly prominent prow and helped her easily navigate her way through the crowd in the foyer. She was carrying what looked to be a rather large pocketbook, which appeared to be crammed full of papers. "My notes for my Egyptian novel," she told Lord Bainbridge when she reached them. "There was no way I was going to leave those behind no matter what. I hope you brought your own notes along as well?" she inquired.

Lord Bainbridge patted the bulge in his jacket pocket. "Right here," he assured her.

Maude nodded her approval. "Good."

"And on your head?" Lord Bainbridge asked with a quizzical smile.

Maude was wearing the pith helmet that she had taken to Egypt. She explained her chose of headgear. "Well, it seemed rather out of place to put on some silly fancy thing all decked out with feathers and lace. Besides if we have to bail, this will do quite nicely," she added, meaning it as a joke. She also revealed a matter more delicate in a whisper to Lord Bainbridge. "I dressed in such a hurry I forgot to put on my knickers. I shall be in a terrible muddle if I get tossed head over heels into a lifeboat."

Lord Bainbridge couldn't hold back his laughter, and he made such a display of it that heads turned in their direction.

"What's wrong with you, you gone daft?" Alfred grumbled.

"Maude, you're priceless," Lord Bainbridge said, struggling to put his arms around her and her life belt to give her a warm hug.

Meeting his gaze, Maude immediately became serious. "What's all this ruckus about, Ducks?" she asked him.

Lord Bainbridge shrugged. "Damned if I know. Apparently, we struck some ice, and then everybody was ordered up on deck. And here we all stand, waiting. No one seems to know what's going on."

"Well then," Maude concluded, "we'll just have to find out for ourselves. Come along." And with that, she marched across the foyer to the grand staircase.

Looking back to see that the two young men had not quickly followed after her, she prodded them impatiently, "Well, come along now!"

Sharing a confused glance, Lord Bainbridge and Alfred shrugged and obeyed her command, neither sure of what she had in mind. They trailed her up the grand staircase and then through a door and out onto the open boat deck. The cold night air instantly hit them in the face and explained why everyone else had chosen to remain below in the warm and cozy foyer from which the gay twinkle of ragtime could still be heard. As they followed Maude along the deck toward the bow, Lord Bainbridge noted that the few passengers who had ventured up on deck, those who he assumed were more hearty or perhaps more uneasy than their fellows, were gathered in little groups back against the deckhouses, away from the rail. Most of them, he also noticed, were watching the knots of seamen who were swarming over the lifeboats, quite obviously preparing them to be launched. This Lord Bainbridge found hardly comforting.

They had almost reached the forward end of the boat deck when Lord Bainbridge asked Maude where they were headed. He had to yell out his question to be heard above the ship's funnels, which were still blowing off steam.

"To see EJ and find out what's really going on," Maude called back to him, neatly stepping over a chain, which had been strung up to cordon off deck space meant for use by the ship's officers.

As they took an iron stairway, which led up to the bridge, Alfred expressed his misgivings. "I don't think we're supposed to be going up here."

As if in agreement, an officer appeared at the top of the stairs, blocking their way. "I'm sorry, madam, you can't come up here. This is the bridge," he informed Maude.

Maude had no trouble brushing him aside. "Nonsense, I'm going to see EJ," she told the startled officer as she left him in her wake.

"She's quite determined," Lord Bainbridge offered in way of an apology to the officer who, having recovered himself, took off in pursuit of this rather rash intruder.

But a row was prevented, for just then, Captain Smith stepped out of the wheelhouse and spotted Maude charging toward him. The captain waved off the pursuing officer, and taking Maude's arm, he guided her to a quiet corner of the bridge, sheltered from both the noise and cold air. Lord Bainbridge followed after them while Alfred remained at a respectful distance.

Lord Bainbridge was shocked by the captain's appearance. This robust hearty man, who only hours ago had sat across the table from him in the restaurant, now seemed to have shrunk to a man half his size. His carriage, which had been ramrod stiff like a military man, was now stooped and bent. He looked to have aged considerably since dinner. Deflated, Lord Bainbridge thought, like all the air, all the life, had gone out of him.

"EJ, what is it? Is it serious?" Maude asked, clutching his arm that still grasped hers.

For a long moment, Captain Smith didn't answer as if he had suddenly gone mute. Then he shook his head vigorously as if to rid himself of some terrible thoughts, and he looked her in the face. "Maude, the ship has an hour perhaps two at most before she sinks," he finally answered.

"God Almighty!" Maude whispered. "But how . . . I thought this ship was unsinkable," she stammered.

"No ship is unsinkable," Captain Smith said. "The *Titanic* is too badly damaged, her demise is inevitable." He took a deep breath and glanced first at Maude and then over to Lord Bainbridge. "And there's more," he told them. "There are only places in the lifeboats for about half the total number of people on board." As he said these last words, he looked away from them, unable to meet their glances as he revealed such terrible news.

"But surely, it won't come to that," Maude protested. "There must be other ships nearby."

The captain nodded. "Hopefully. We're sending out distress calls by wireless. We can only pray that someone hears us and reaches us in time."

From the interior of the bridge, someone called out to him, and he responded that he would be right with them.

Then Captain Smith took Maude's hands in his, and leaning forward, he kissed her on the cheek the way one would kiss a dear friend who was setting out on a long journey.

To Lord Bainbridge, the captain offered instructions and advice. "Make sure that Maude gets into a lifeboat immediately. There is no time for dawdling. And look to your own safety as well."

"I will," Lord Bainbridge promised.

Captain Smith gave them both a final look and said, his voice breaking with emotion, "I'm so sorry about this, so terribly sorry." Then he turned away, squared his shoulders, and retreated back into the depths of the bridge.

Stunned by the news, Lord Bainbridge and Maude left the bridge and took the stairs down to the boat deck. Alfred trailed behind them. Reaching the bottom of the stairs, Maude had to reach out for Lord Bainbridge's arm for support. "I can't believe it," she said. "This beautiful ship will soon be gone forever." She glanced back up at the bridge where Captain Smith's figure could still be seen but shadowy and hazy as if it were now a figure seen in a dream. "And that poor dear man will never again see his wife and child," Maude lamented.

Looking into her face, Lord Bainbridge could see, even in the starlight, the tears that watered her eyes. "It's going to be all right," he said.

Maude shook her head. "No it isn't, Ducks. People are going to die tonight."

"You heard Captain Smith," Lord Bainbridge reminded her, "they're sending out distress calls. Ships are probably racing to us at this very moment."

Maude glanced past him out at the dark water, so still, so undisturbed. "The water will be freezing," she said.

"Maude, don't be ridiculous, it's not going to come to that," Lord Bainbridge protested as much for his own comfort as hers.

Maude looked into his face, the tears still filling her eyes. "I didn't tell you this before because I was afraid you'd think it was just some silly old woman's superstition," she began. "The night before I boarded the ship at Cherbourg, I had a dream. In the first part of the dream, everyone was all dressed up, and they were dancing and laughing and drinking champagne. You and I were both there, along with all our friends. And then the next thing I remember, we were all climbing up these nets on the side of a ship, but we were all still laughing and sipping champagne. Then everything became hazy as if a great fog had rolled in, and I couldn't see anything. But I heard screams, hundreds of screams over and over, like fans cheering at a football game. And although I still couldn't see anything, I knew what those screams were."

"What were they?" Lord Bainbridge asked.

"They were the screams of people drowning," Maude answered, "hundreds and hundreds of people." She grabbed Lord Bainbridge's arm. "Come on, Ducks, we're not going to drown!" she told him resolutely as she headed them down the boat deck toward one of the lifeboats.

Alfred was left once again to follow after them. It was typical of the relationship between them that Maude mostly ignored him, treating him as if he wasn't there. Even now in a time of crisis, she chose to overlook his presence. There had always been a certain amount of animosity between them, each one seeking to influence Lord Bainbridge in their own way and each fearing the other was trying to influence him against them. And now even with the *Titanic* sinking beneath their feet, the bad blood between them could still not be set aside.

They joined a small knot of passengers gathered around one of the lifeboats, watching as the crewmen, having pulled off the boat's canvas covering, cranked the davits and lowered the wooden boat to lie flush with the floor of the boat deck. The crew's efforts while diligent appeared, to Lord Bainbridge at least, to lack a certain amount of organization as if, though they knew what to do, they had not had much practice in doing it. As they fed out lines and pulled on ropes, they often got in one another's way or stumbled over each other, which often resulted in good-natured jabs and banter. The crew, like most of the passengers, seemed unaware of the gravity of the situation. Only the officer directing their efforts remained solemn, and he took no part in their merriment.

A sailor lent a knife to one of his mates to help him cut a piece of rope, and the lender wanted to make sure he got it back. "Remember me when we get back to Southampton and be sure and return it to me," he called out, obviously thinking the ship must have suffered some mechanical failure and would need to be returned to Southampton for repairs.

Lord Bainbridge, however, now knew better. And at that moment, a distress rocket shot up from the bridge. Startled faces watched its ascent up to what seemed the very tip of heaven where, with a gentle crack like a shot heard across a woodland field, it burst, and a shower of white stars drifted slowly down toward the sea.

"A rocket," someone close to Lord Bainbridge said in a voice that was almost a whisper as if the speaker feared that to divulge such information out loud would once and for all attest to the seriousness of their situation.

Lord Bainbridge, who hardly considered himself a seaman, nonetheless realized that when a ship sends up distress rockets, white flares, she is calling for help, calling on any other ship near or far to come to her rescue.

As the shower of stars drew closer toward them, falling from the sky like shattered remnants of real celestial bodies, they lighted up the faces of those standing on the boat deck in a blue white flash of light and, for an instant, revealed their thoughts to their companions.

It was Alfred's face that Lord Bainbridge noticed, and he could see in its grim set that although Alfred had not heard Captain Smith's troubling prophecy, he understood completely the grave situation they were in.

The rocket likewise apparently motivated the officer in charge of the lifeboat in front of them into action. For now, he stood with one foot in the boat the other on the deck and held out his hand. "Come along now, ladies. Who'll be first for the boat?" he asked.

The response was hardly overwhelming. For in spite of the rocket, in spite of the sense among many now that everything was not all right, the idea of giving up the apparent security of the ship to be placed in a frail-looking craft and lowered seventy feet to the dark water below was not a popular choice.

One well-fed gentleman in evening dress even said as much. "We'd be a hell of a lot safer here on this ship than being put out to sea in that little boat," he mocked.

"I would never allow anyone to put me into such an unseaworthy looking vessel," a woman stated to the officer, her mind apparently quite made up.

"I've never been in an open boat in all my life," another woman told those around her.

Lord Bainbridge opened his mouth, ready to tell them what he had heard from Captain Smith. But he quickly closed it, realizing that probably most of them wouldn't believe him, and if they did, such knowledge could start a panic.

The officer, clearly frustrated by the lack of cooperation, tried again. "Ladies, please, we're wasting valuable time. Now come along."

"Is it to be ladies only?" a male voice called out.

"I have no intention of going without my husband," one woman stated firmly, clutching the arm of her male companion.

"Then shouldn't you go and find him, dear?" another woman shot back at her.

This little exchange prompted a chorus of titters that rippled like a shiver through the crowd gathered around the lifeboat.

The officer, sensing the mood of the crowd, modified his request. "Ladies, gentlemen, whomever," he now called for.

A number of couples stepped forward and got into the boat, followed by a group of single men. The officer looked around for more converts.

Maude grasped Lord Bainbridge's arm, "Let's go, Ducks."

But Lord Bainbridge held back. "You go ahead," he told her. "I'm going to stick to the ship for a bit."

Maude was appalled at this suggestion. "What are you thinking?" she implored. "Remember what Captain Smith told us," she added in a whisper.

"I have to look for Madame Renoir and Sebastian and make sure they too get safely away," Lord Bainbridge said.

"Then we'll look for them together," Maude told him.

Lord Bainbridge shook his head and took her hands in his. "No, dearest, I must know that you're safe. I have enough to worry about, don't make me worry about you as well."

"But I don't want us to be separated," Maude protested, biting her lip to hold back the tears.

"I'm sure it won't be for long," Lord Bainbridge assured her. He fumbled in the pocket of his jacket, and pulling out the pages of his novel along with the picture of his father, he handed them to her. "Will you keep these safe for me?" he asked.

"Of course," Maude answered, taking them from him and placing them in her large pocketbook.

Then Lord Bainbridge gave her a gentle push toward the officer holding out his hand. "Now get quickly into the boat," he told her. "You're keeping the others waiting."

Maude hesitated a moment longer. Placing a hand on his cheek, she looked into his eyes. "Don't deprive the world of all the wonderful things you've yet to write just to be a hero," she declared.

Lord Bainbridge smiled at her and shook his head. "Don't worry, I was never meant to be a hero," he said.

As the officer helped Maude into the lifeboat, hoisting her over the gunwale with the assistance of two other crewmen, he tugged at her pocketbook. "Sorry, madam, no baggage allowed," he stated.

Maude pulled her pocketbook from his grasp. "Don't be absurd," she reproached him. "This isn't baggage, it's my life. Take that away from me and you might as well throw me overboard."

The officer shrugged in defeat and made no more fuss about her pocketbook, probably content enough to have at least secured one more passenger for the boat.

Before she took her seat in the boat, Maude spoke to Alfred who stood beside Lord Bainbridge on the deck. "Look out for him," she instructed the servant.

Alfred seemed momentarily startled that she had actually addressed him, and even Lord Bainbridge was surprised by her action, sensing quite rightly that Maude was so concerned about his welfare, she was willing to enlist the aid of a man whom she frankly disliked to look out for him.

Even though the officer had been able to entice only twenty people into a boat that should have carried sixty-five, he apparently felt he could delay its launching no longer. He added four seamen to do the rowing, and with the davits creaking and sailors straining on the ropes, the lifeboat began its decent. Its downward motion was jerky rather than smooth as first one side then the other was lowered. There was a tense moment when one of the lines became snarled, and it looked as if the lifeboat's unfortunate passengers were about to be dumped into the sea. But the officer stepped in, and with a swift hand, he untangled the line. A few minutes later, lifeboat No. 7, the first boat to leave the stricken *Titanic*, reached the water.

Lord Bainbridge leaned on the rail. He casually lit a cigarette and waved to Maude although he wasn't sure she could see him from the distance and in the dark. He watched the lifeboat until he saw it safely row away from the side of the ship. Then he turned to Alfred. "We've got to find the others," he told him.

"You won't find him up here on the boat deck," Alfred said. "Access to the lifeboats is one of the many privileges you get only with a first-class ticket."

Lord Bainbridge stared back at him. Although he had maintained to Maude that it was Madame Renoir and her son he was concerned about as he also was about Count Fraboli and his wife, Alfred had been smart enough to realize it was Tom who was paramount in his thoughts.

"But they can't possibly keep the steerage passengers down below when this ship is in danger of sinking," Lord Bainbridge insisted.

"Is this ship going to sink?" Alfred asked him, eyeing him carefully.

"Yes," Lord Bainbridge answered. "And Alfred."

"What?" he asked, his gray eyes narrowing with suspicion.

"There are only enough places in the boats for about half of those on board the ship," he answered.

Alfred took a long moment to digest this news. "Well, let's hope we're in the right half," he finally said, smiling weakly.

They were left for a moment standing completely alone as all the other passengers, all the activity, had quickly moved onto the next lifeboat that was to be launched.

Then as had happened before, the young junior officer suddenly appeared. But unlike earlier when Lord Bainbridge had encountered him, his step was no longer jaunty, and there was no friendly beaming smile spread across his face. In fact, this time he was walking along the deck with his head bowed, his hands shoved deep into the pockets of his greatcoat, and he appeared to be in deep thought. He would have walked right by them had Lord Bainbridge not called out to him.

Stopping, the young man looked up at them, the lines of his face pinched and tightened. "It's bad," he whispered to them, "very bad. The berg practically gutted the ship below the waterline."

"We know," Lord Bainbridge said.

"There must be no panic," the officer said to them, "no panic at all."

"What about the steerage passengers?" Lord Bainbridge asked him.

The young officer gave him a queer look as if Lord Bainbridge had spoken to him in a foreign tongue. But he quickly recovered. "Oh, you don't have to worry about them, sir. I imagine they're being kept under control."

"What do you mean under control?" Lord Bainbridge wanted to know.

The officer hastened to explain, "I suppose they're being kept below deck so they don't cause any problems."

"What kind of problems?" Alfred asked.

"Well, you know, riots or fights or the likes of that," the officer answered. "Most of them carry knives, you know."

"But if the ship is going to sink," Lord Bainbridge protested, hardly able to hold back his anger, "shouldn't they be given the same chance to escape as the rest of us?"

The young officer took a moment to think this one over. "Well, they are steerage passengers," he reminded Lord Bainbridge. "They'll probably let them up when the rest of the passengers have been taken off," he suggested.

"By that time, there probably won't be any boats left," Lord Bainbridge stated grimly.

The officer nodded in agreement. "Perhaps not, sir." He appeared to think about this for a second, and then he came quickly back to the moment. "I've got to get to work," he said. He gave Lord Bainbridge a final word of advice. "Don't stay aboard too long, sir." Then he started off along the deck again but stopped and turned back to them as if he had just remembered something. "I'm assigned to boat No. 1," he told them, pointing down the deck toward the bow. "We won't be loading for a bit until they've finished with some of the other boats. "I'll save you gentlemen a couple of seats," he suggested.

"Thank you." Lord Bainbridge nodded, watching as the young officer took off along the deck, and this time his steps were hurried as if he were terribly late for some pressing engagement.

For a few moments, neither Lord Bainbridge nor Alfred said anything as they watched the crewmen begin loading the next lifeboat. Finally, Alfred made an observation having to do with the conduct of the passengers who were standing around them on the deck. "Look at them as clam and pious as if they were in church on Sunday. The fools!" he added with contempt.

"Most of them are unaware, I'm sure, of the real danger we are in," Lord Bainbridge said.

The members of the ship's orchestra, who had left the A deck foyer and followed the steady stream of passenger traffic up to the boat deck, had reassembled themselves just a few feet from them in front of the entrance to the grand staircase. Immediately, they began pumping out another ragtime tune as if this was just another tea dance. And their vibrant music floated out over the water like the chorale of some strange new species of seabird.

"Oh great," Alfred groaned, "music to drown by! Only the English could come up with such an idea."

"Indeed," Lord Bainbridge agreed. Then he turned serious. "You know what I must do?"

Alfred sighed and grimaced. "Unfortunately I do," he answered.

"I've got to go and find him. I won't leave him down there to drown," Lord Bainbridge stated.

"I don't much fancy drowning myself," Alfred said. "And going down there seems the quickest way to bring that about," he added.

"I need you to show me the way," Lord Bainbridge proposed to him. "I'll never find him without you." He paused a moment. "I know it's a lot to ask."

Alfred looked away from him a moment, and for a second, his dark face was caught in the light of another rocket going off above them. Then his face twisted into almost a smile, and he looked back at Lord Bainbridge. "Where you go, I go," he said. "Haven't you figured that out by now?"

"Thanks," Lord Bainbridge acknowledged, gripping his arm.

"Fool that I am," Alfred muttered to himself.

"First, I want to see if we can find Madame Renoir and Sebastian," Lord Bainbridge told him. He was concerned too about the Frabolis. But he felt confident the count and his wife were well prepared to take care of themselves. And too, their very age, made it probable that others would look out for them as well.

After having searched the entire starboard side of the boat deck, Lord Bainbridge caught no sight of any of his friends. "Let's try the other side of the ship," he suggested.

Alfred shrugged his shoulders and followed after him.

Chapter X

On the port side of the boat deck, they found the same scenes being reacted as those they had just left behind on the starboard side. Passengers were calmly, patiently, waiting to board the lifeboats as officers and crew moved from one boat to the next. It was like a mirror scene of what was going on on the other side of the ship. But there was one major difference, which they would soon learn.

"There!" Alfred called out, pointing to a crowd of people gathered around the next lifeboat that was being prepared to be loaded. In the forefront of the crowd stood Madame Renoir clutching tightly to the arm of her son.

"Thank God, I've found you!" Lord Bainbridge exclaimed as he reached their side. He ushered them a little away from the others. "The ship is going to sink," he told them bluntly. "You both need to get into this boat as soon as it's ready."

For a moment, Madame Renoir stared uncomprehendingly back at him, her face a blank. As was to be expected, she had obviously dressed carefully and meticulously as if she had been preparing herself for a day's enjoyable outing. In fact, she looked to have stepped right out of the latest Paris fashion magazine in a stylish black velvet two-piece suit. Over this, she wore a fur wrap and on her head a large-brimmed hat with a tiny flowered veil. Long gloves and high-button shoes completed her exquisite look, which was marred only by the bulky life belt she also, probably quite unwillingly, sported.

It was Sebastian however who first acknowledged Lord Bainbridge's news. "Jeremy, are we really going to sink?" he asked with childish, if misplaced, enthusiasm. For his own attire, the boy wore a wool three-piece suit topped off with a wool overcoat and a leather cap with a snap-down brim. Lord Bainbridge was a little surprised to see him in long trousers. For except when he wore formal evening clothes where long pants were required, Sebastian had been waging a battle with his mother to get himself out of his usual knee breeches and into long pants. It was a battle that Madame Renoir won on most occasions, but tonight, Lord Bainbridge assumed, she had more important things on her mind than the length of her son's trousers.

Lord Bainbridge told them what he had heard from Captain Smith. He ended with an understatement, "It's very serious."

"But surely a ship this size couldn't possibly sink," Madame Renoir protested.

"It will," Lord Bainbridge said.

"There must be other ships coming to help us then," she insisted.

"Yes, there are," Lord Bainbridge acknowledged. "We can only hope they reach us in time."

"What a sight it would be to see this great ship go under!" Sebastian said, again with childish bravado and excitement.

Lord Bainbridge's head jerked up, and he gripped the boy by the shoulder, not gently. "That was a stupid thing to say, Sebastian!" he scolded.

Instantly ashamed, Sebastian hung his head, acutely aware of the terrible error of his words. "I'm sorry," he murmured.

Quite prepared to further chastise the boy for such a cruel and thoughtless remark, Lord Bainbridge was distracted by a glimpse of two people standing apart from the rest of the crowd. Their posture was almost of indifference as if they somehow considered what was going on as having little to do with themselves. Excusing himself for a moment from the Renoirs, Lord Bainbridge made his way over to them.

"What's all this nonsense about?" Ronnie Standish asked of Lord Bainbridge as he approached them.

"I'm afraid it's far from nonsense," Lord Bainbridge answered. At that moment, he had a great desire to punch Ronnie full in the face for what he had done to Sebastian, but he realized this was hardly the time; a much bigger drama was unfolding.

"I was most rudely awakened from a most delicious dream," Ronnie went on, giving Lord Bainbridge a lascivious grin. "And I was forced to dress in such haste I'm sure I must look a fright," he added, one gloved hand, the one that didn't hold his ebony walking stick, flicking an imaginary speck of dust from his black wool overcoat with its fur collar.

Like Madame Renoir, Lord Bainbridge was quite sure Ronnie Standish didn't go anywhere, including onto the deck of a sinking ocean liner, until he was properly coiffured and costumed.

"I see you brought your man along," Ronnie said, pointing toward Alfred, who stood watching them a short distance away with a scowl on his face. "I'm sure he'll be handy to have around should we get in a pinch," Ronnie added. He smiled at Lord Bainbridge. "Although I must say, Jeremy, given the way he's dressed, it's hard to tell who's the master and who's the servant." He shook a gloved finger at Lord Bainbridge. "Really, you do insist on blurring the lines of proper social conduct," he admonished him.

Choosing to ignore him, Lord Bainbridge turned to his wife. "You must get into a lifeboat at once," he told her.

A startled shadow passed across Elaine Standish's beautiful face. She was wearing a hooded cape of dark blue velvet, and even in the poor light, he noticed the way the color of the hood that framed her face had turned her eyes from deep violet to blue. Neither she nor her husband had seen fit to encumber themselves with a life belt. Elaine reached out and took his hand. "Jeremy, are things really that bad?"

Lord Bainbridge nodded. "They are." He glanced at Ronnie. "The captain told me there aren't enough boats for all the people on board," he said.

Ronnie hardly seemed distressed by the news. He shrugged. "There will certainly be enough boats for the first-class passengers," he concluded.

"People very well may die here tonight," Lord Bainbridge whispered in an angry undertone to Ronnie.

"And what will your choice be at that moment of decision?" Ronnie asked him. "Will you step back onto the deck so that a lesser man might live?" The corners of his full lips crinkled into a mocking smile. "Oh, yes of course, I almost forgot about your little steerage friend." He chuckled. "One sleeps with them, Jeremy, but one hardly gives up his life for them."

At that moment with preparations complete, the officer in charge, standing as the other had with one foot on the deck and the other in the readied boat, called out for passengers. "If you will please, ladies."

And though the crowd of passengers surged toward the boat like on the starboard side, few of them accepted his kind invitation. Many more were just curious to see what was going on. Like theatergoers, they eagerly pressed forward to watch the show, but few had any desire or intention of taking part in the drama themselves. And to some, it was even a joke.

"You'll need a pass to get back on in the morning," one woman called to another who had just stepped into the lifeboat.

Lord Bainbridge took a moment to appraise the appearance of the officer struggling to fill the lifeboat much as another man of a different persuasion might make a casual observation of an attractive woman he had suddenly come upon with nothing more in mind than an appreciative glance. The officer, whom he judged to be in his mid-thirties, was tall, tanned, and handsome. He had a commanding presence, leaving no doubt as to whom was in charge, and his voice as he urged the women to come forward was deep but not unpleasant. All in all, Lord Bainbridge concluded, he looked to be the ideal specimen of a ship's officer. Indeed, if Maude had needed a model of a ship's officer for one of her novels, the perfect example stood right before them.

Eager to help the officer with his, at the moment, thankless task and just as eager to see Madame Renoir and Sebastian safely away, Lord Bainbridge pushed them toward the boat. He went even further, taking Madame Renoir's hand and placing it in the officer's.

The officer nodded. "Yes, madam, come along please," he encouraged.

Madame Renoir held back a moment. "You're coming with us, aren't you?" she asked Lord Bainbridge, searching his face.

eaving the two seamen still laughing uproariously at the rail, Alfred led Lord
ridge back along the boat deck toward the stern of the ship. They took a
outside stairs down to A deck, and there they entered a door that brought
onto the landing of the aft first-class staircase. Although not as grand as the
class staircase in the forward section of the ship, it was nevertheless elegant
gh, decorated in similar style with oak carvings and elaborate wrought-iron
trades. They hurried down the stairs, taking them two at a time, until they
ed C deck. Here they paused a moment to get their bearings as well as catch
breath, for they had come down the stairs at practically full tilt, neither one
ng a reminder that their time was precious.

hey had encountered a few others on their mad dash down the stairs: a
e of passengers here and there, undoubtedly the last to be roused from
slumber, and an occasional crewman, either terribly late in reporting to his
n or perhaps sent off on some urgent errand. But for the most part, this
cular area of the ship seemed strangely deserted and very quiet. With the
now no longer underway, all the usual shipboard noises had ceased, and all
came to their ears was a faint faraway sound of creaking timbers as if some
of this great ship was undergoing structural torment. As if, to put it bluntly,
thing vital was breaking apart. It was not a comforting sound. And for a
ent, it unnerved Alfred.

Everyone else," he noted sarcastically, "is headed in the opposite direction in
you hadn't noticed. We're the only fools going down deeper into the ship!"
urned and stomped away, and for a moment, Lord Bainbridge thought he
deserting him. But following after him, he found they were out on the open
again though a number of decks below the boat deck. They slipped over
in stretched across the deck and found themselves in an area reserved for
-class passengers. Alfred led the way through a door, and once inside, they
a broad stairway that led down to the lower decks.

I don't know where his cabin is," Alfred said. "That first night, I had him meet
the smoking room over there," he added, pointing across the corridor.
ord Bainbridge headed for the door to the smoking room. But before he
ed it, a man came through the door and practically stumbled into his path.
Bainbridge recoiled quickly as if he feared the man was about to set upon
in some unpleasant manner. However, it was only the man's breath that
lted him. The man was obviously quite drunk, and he had blown a blast of
ur breath right into Lord Bainbridge's face.

t was Alfred who pushed the man away and sent him reeling across the
dor toward the stairway, hiccupping and belching at the same time. The
k came close to tumbling head first down the stairway. But he managed to
himself at the last moment, and pulling himself back from the edge, he
bled off down a corridor and disappeared from their sight.

"Women and children only," the officer said, eyeing him suspiciously for a moment.

Lord Bainbridge agreed, "Quite rightly. I'll get a seat in another boat," he told Madame Renoir.

Reluctantly, she let Lord Bainbridge and the officer help her over the side and into the lifeboat where she took a seat.

Next, Lord Bainbridge turned to Sebastian. "You go along with your mother," he said to the boy.

"I'd rather stay here with you," Sebastian protested.

"Your mother will need you to look out for her," Lord Bainbridge said. He patted him on the shoulder. "She'll manage better with you at her side."

"All right," Sebastian surrendered, another far-from-willing convert.

Lord Bainbridge led him up to the boat. But the officer shook his head. "He can't go. It's women and children only."

"He's only a boy," Lord Bainbridge insisted. "He's only fourteen."

"Too old!" the officer snapped.

Lord Bainbridge was incredulous. "What do you mean too old? He's a boy!" He stared hard into the officer's face, and he saw, in the equally hard look that stared back at him, that the man was neither mean or cruel. He was worse—he was inflexible. He was the type of man who had lived his whole life by a rigid set of rules and morals that could not be broken and would not until the day he died.

In the lifeboat, Madame Renoir, seeing the disturbance, stood up and frantically called out her son's name. "Sebastian!"

Lord Bainbridge tried one last appeal to the officer. "Look," he said, "the boy needs to go with his mother." He lowered his voice. "We both know what's going to happen here, don't have his death on your conscience."

The officer continued to stare at him for a half second longer, and in that brief flicker of time, Lord Bainbridge was quite certain the man had somehow uncovered his accurate nature, and true to the rigid code he lived by, he of course found it unacceptable. "No boys allowed!" the officer stated, and Lord Bainbridge took his words to apply to much more then the simple confines of a lifeboat.

Now it was the turn of Sebastian himself to enter into the fray. Embarrassed by the struggle that had ensued over him and convinced that it had put him in a bad light, certainly not a manly one, he rebelled against Lord Bainbridge's efforts on his behalf. "I'm not a child anymore," he told him. "I don't want to go with the babies. Jeremy, I want to stay here with you and the rest of the men."

At the same time, Madame Renoir, seeing that her son was not going to join her, struggled to get out of the lifeboat. And when two of the boat's crewmen tried to restrain her, laying their hands on her to pull her back into the boat, the officer hollered out to them in a tone of extreme exasperation.

"Don't waste time with her if she won't go! Let her get out if she wants!"

Reunited with her son, Madame Renoir clutched his arm tightly while Lord Bainbridge burned with righteous indignation. "This is absurd!" he said to those gathered around him. "On the other side of the ship, they're letting anyone who wants to get into the boats."

"Men as well?" someone asked.

"Anyone," Lord Bainbridge confirmed.

Meanwhile, the officer had gone back to loading the lifeboat, and when he had gotten it about half full, having turned away a number of women unwilling to leave their husbands behind, he ordered it to be lowered.

Watching the lifeboat creak slowly downward, Lord Bainbridge shook his head. "Barely half full," he muttered. He glanced toward the officer, intending to give him a severe glance if nothing else, but the officer had already moved onto the next boat, taking most of the crowd with him.

Lord Bainbridge took Madame Renoir's hands in his. "Marguerite, you and Sebastian go over to the other side of the ship. You'll both be able to get a seat in one of those boats." He kissed her on the cheek. "Hurry now!" Then he turned to Sebastian. "Promise me you'll go with your mother in one of the boats."

"But . . ." Sebastian protested, biting his lip.

Lord Bainbridge gripped his shoulder. "Sebastian, your mother needs you. If anything happened to you, I'm quite certain she wouldn't want to go on living. You must go with her," he insisted.

Sebastian thought about this for a second. "All right, I will," he agreed. "You'll come soon?"

Lord Bainbridge nodded. "Yes, soon." He smiled at this boy, whom he had such deep affection for, affection made all the more sweet because it was so pure. He glanced down at Sebastian's trousers. "Long pants, I see," he acknowledged.

"Yes." Sebastian smiled. "I think mother was perhaps too preoccupied to notice I was wearing them. I don't ever intend to take them off," he added.

"A questionable resolution at best," Lord Bainbridge laughed. Then he hurried them on their way, watching as mother and son, arm in arm, made their way through the crowd and to what he hoped would be safety. He felt guilty about not going with them and making sure they got into a boat. But it seemed like there was so little time left, and he had to find Tom.

Ronnie too took his wife's arm. "Come along, my dear, I have an urgent desire to see the view from the other side of the ship." He caught Lord Bainbridge's eye. "Really, Jeremy, what else did you expect me to do?" he asked with a satisfied grin on his dark face.

Lord Bainbridge had just a glimpse of Elaine's own face twisted into a frown before Ronnie rushed her away.

"You can't save them all, you know. You're not that big a hero."

Lord Bainbridge turned to find Alfred at his elbow. "I'm not tryin[g] hero," he answered rather shortly. He looked into Alfred's face. "We'd and find Tom," he said.

He watched a moment as Alfred glanced longingly at the lifeboa[t] of them that was being prepared for lowering. "On the other side, they the men into the boats," Alfred murmured wistfully.

"Go ahead if you want to. I'll manage without you. I release y[ou,] Bainbridge told him.

Alfred's face twisted into a smile, a smirk really. "You release m[e?] me from what?"

"I just meant you're free to go."

"Haven't I always been?"

"Yes, of course," Lord Bainbridge returned, knowing in reality tha[t] bound together forever.

"Oh, let's get on with it," Alfred grunted impatiently. "Let's go a[nd] damn boyfriend from drowning. Though we'd better hurry," he add[ed] short, the water's probably already up to his chin." He laughed at h[im,] his gray eyes crinkling with amusement.

Just before they started their descent, they came upon two crew[men] casually on the rail, watching the loading of the boats. They were ta[lking] loudly, obviously not caring who overheard them, and though the na[ture of] conversation was most distressing, their mood was easygoing, almo[st]

"I tell you, she's gonna go. She's already down at the head," one o[f them] was saying. "And there ain't half enough boats for this great lot," he a[dded.] a lot of us are gonna find ourselves paddling about in the drink befo[re] jerked his thumb toward the crowd gathered around the nearest li[feboat,] not just us, but some of those rich and titled gents as well."

"I ain't never learned to swim," his companion lamented quietl[y.]

"Jesus, man!" the first sailor exclaimed. "You took to sea with[out] how to swim?"

"Well, I was planning on being on a boat, you know, not in th[e water,]" other explained rather sheepishly.

His friend, obviously thinking this was the funniest thing he h[ad heard in a] long while, laughed heartily and slapped the other man good-nat[uredly on the] back a couple of times. "You ain't got a chance," he told him.

The other nodded. "Yah, I know." He shook his head. "Nev[er thought I'd] end my days being drowned," he mused.

"Oh, you won't drown," his mate made haste to assure him. "[It's too] damn cold. You'll freeze to death before you've had a chance to d[rown]"

His friend smiled weakly. "Well, at least that's some comfor[t."] then they both burst into fresh laughter as if this was the funnies[t]

"Women and children only," the officer said, eyeing him suspiciously for a moment.

Lord Bainbridge agreed, "Quite rightly. I'll get a seat in another boat," he told Madame Renoir.

Reluctantly, she let Lord Bainbridge and the officer help her over the side and into the lifeboat where she took a seat.

Next, Lord Bainbridge turned to Sebastian. "You go along with your mother," he said to the boy.

"I'd rather stay here with you," Sebastian protested.

"Your mother will need you to look out for her," Lord Bainbridge said. He patted him on the shoulder. "She'll manage better with you at her side."

"All right," Sebastian surrendered, another far-from-willing convert.

Lord Bainbridge led him up to the boat. But the officer shook his head. "He can't go. It's women and children only."

"He's only a boy," Lord Bainbridge insisted. "He's only fourteen."

"Too old!" the officer snapped.

Lord Bainbridge was incredulous. "What do you mean too old? He's a boy!" He stared hard into the officer's face, and he saw, in the equally hard look that stared back at him, that the man was neither mean or cruel. He was worse—he was inflexible. He was the type of man who had lived his whole life by a rigid set of rules and morals that could not be broken and would not until the day he died.

In the lifeboat, Madame Renoir, seeing the disturbance, stood up and frantically called out her son's name. "Sebastian!"

Lord Bainbridge tried one last appeal to the officer. "Look," he said, "the boy needs to go with his mother." He lowered his voice. "We both know what's going to happen here, don't have his death on your conscience."

The officer continued to stare at him for a half second longer, and in that brief flicker of time, Lord Bainbridge was quite certain the man had somehow uncovered his accurate nature, and true to the rigid code he lived by, he of course found it unacceptable. "No boys allowed!" the officer stated, and Lord Bainbridge took his words to apply to much more then the simple confines of a lifeboat.

Now it was the turn of Sebastian himself to enter into the fray. Embarrassed by the struggle that had ensued over him and convinced that it had put him in a bad light, certainly not a manly one, he rebelled against Lord Bainbridge's efforts on his behalf. "I'm not a child anymore," he told him. "I don't want to go with the babies. Jeremy, I want to stay here with you and the rest of the men."

At the same time, Madame Renoir, seeing that her son was not going to join her, struggled to get out of the lifeboat. And when two of the boat's crewmen tried to restrain her, laying their hands on her to pull her back into the boat, the officer hollered out to them in a tone of extreme exasperation.

"Don't waste time with her if she won't go! Let her get out if she wants!"

Reunited with her son, Madame Renoir clutched his arm tightly while Lord Bainbridge burned with righteous indignation. "This is absurd!" he said to those gathered around him. "On the other side of the ship, they're letting anyone who wants to get into the boats."

"Men as well?" someone asked.

"Anyone," Lord Bainbridge confirmed.

Meanwhile, the officer had gone back to loading the lifeboat, and when he had gotten it about half full, having turned away a number of women unwilling to leave their husbands behind, he ordered it to be lowered.

Watching the lifeboat creak slowly downward, Lord Bainbridge shook his head. "Barely half full," he muttered. He glanced toward the officer, intending to give him a severe glance if nothing else, but the officer had already moved onto the next boat, taking most of the crowd with him.

Lord Bainbridge took Madame Renoir's hands in his. "Marguerite, you and Sebastian go over to the other side of the ship. You'll both be able to get a seat in one of those boats." He kissed her on the cheek. "Hurry now!" Then he turned to Sebastian. "Promise me you'll go with your mother in one of the boats."

"But . . ." Sebastian protested, biting his lip.

Lord Bainbridge gripped his shoulder. "Sebastian, your mother needs you. If anything happened to you, I'm quite certain she wouldn't want to go on living. You must go with her," he insisted.

Sebastian thought about this for a second. "All right, I will," he agreed. "You'll come soon?"

Lord Bainbridge nodded. "Yes, soon." He smiled at this boy, whom he had such deep affection for, affection made all the more sweet because it was so pure. He glanced down at Sebastian's trousers. "Long pants, I see," he acknowledged.

"Yes." Sebastian smiled. "I think mother was perhaps too preoccupied to notice I was wearing them. I don't ever intend to take them off," he added.

"A questionable resolution at best," Lord Bainbridge laughed. Then he hurried them on their way, watching as mother and son, arm in arm, made their way through the crowd and to what he hoped would be safety. He felt guilty about not going with them and making sure they got into a boat. But it seemed like there was so little time left, and he had to find Tom.

Ronnie too took his wife's arm. "Come along, my dear, I have an urgent desire to see the view from the other side of the ship." He caught Lord Bainbridge's eye. "Really, Jeremy, what else did you expect me to do?" he asked with a satisfied grin on his dark face.

Lord Bainbridge had just a glimpse of Elaine's own face twisted into a frown before Ronnie rushed her away.

"You can't save them all, you know. You're not that big a hero."

Lord Bainbridge turned to find Alfred at his elbow. "I'm not trying to be a hero," he answered rather shortly. He looked into Alfred's face. "We'd better go and find Tom," he said.

He watched a moment as Alfred glanced longingly at the lifeboat in front of them that was being prepared for lowering. "On the other side, they're letting the men into the boats," Alfred murmured wistfully.

"Go ahead if you want to. I'll manage without you. I release you," Lord Bainbridge told him.

Alfred's face twisted into a smile, a smirk really. "You release me? Release me from what?"

"I just meant you're free to go."

"Haven't I always been?"

"Yes, of course," Lord Bainbridge returned, knowing in reality that they were bound together forever.

"Oh, let's get on with it," Alfred grunted impatiently. "Let's go and save your damn boyfriend from drowning. Though we'd better hurry," he added, "he's so short, the water's probably already up to his chin." He laughed at his own jest, his gray eyes crinkling with amusement.

Just before they started their descent, they came upon two crewmen leaning casually on the rail, watching the loading of the boats. They were talking rather loudly, obviously not caring who overheard them, and though the nature of their conversation was most distressing, their mood was easygoing, almost jovial.

"I tell you, she's gonna go. She's already down at the head," one of the seaman was saying. "And there ain't half enough boats for this great lot," he added. "Quite a lot of us are gonna find ourselves paddling about in the drink before long." He jerked his thumb toward the crowd gathered around the nearest lifeboat. "And not just us, but some of those rich and titled gents as well."

"I ain't never learned to swim," his companion lamented quietly.

"Jesus, man!" the first sailor exclaimed. "You took to sea without knowing how to swim?"

"Well, I was planning on being on a boat, you know, not in the water," the other explained rather sheepishly.

His friend, obviously thinking this was the funniest thing he had heard in a long while, laughed heartily and slapped the other man good-naturedly on the back a couple of times. "You ain't got a chance," he told him.

The other nodded. "Yah, I know." He shook his head. "Never thought I'd end my days being drowned," he mused.

"Oh, you won't drown," his mate made haste to assure him. "The water's too damn cold. You'll freeze to death before you've had a chance to drown."

His friend smiled weakly. "Well, at least that's some comfort," he said, and then they both burst into fresh laughter as if this was the funniest thing of all.

Leaving the two seamen still laughing uproariously at the rail, Alfred led Lord Bainbridge back along the boat deck toward the stern of the ship. They took a set of outside stairs down to A deck, and there they entered a door that brought them onto the landing of the aft first-class staircase. Although not as grand as the first-class staircase in the forward section of the ship, it was nevertheless elegant enough, decorated in similar style with oak carvings and elaborate wrought-iron balustrades. They hurried down the stairs, taking them two at a time, until they reached C deck. Here they paused a moment to get their bearings as well as catch their breath, for they had come down the stairs at practically full tilt, neither one needing a reminder that their time was precious.

They had encountered a few others on their mad dash down the stairs: a couple of passengers here and there, undoubtedly the last to be roused from their slumber, and an occasional crewman, either terribly late in reporting to his station or perhaps sent off on some urgent errand. But for the most part, this particular area of the ship seemed strangely deserted and very quiet. With the ship now no longer underway, all the usual shipboard noises had ceased, and all that came to their ears was a faint faraway sound of creaking timbers as if some part of this great ship was undergoing structural torment. As if, to put it bluntly, something vital was breaking apart. It was not a comforting sound. And for a moment, it unnerved Alfred.

"Everyone else," he noted sarcastically, "is headed in the opposite direction in case you hadn't noticed. We're the only fools going down deeper into the ship!" He turned and stomped away, and for a moment, Lord Bainbridge thought he was deserting him. But following after him, he found they were out on the open deck again though a number of decks below the boat deck. They slipped over a chain stretched across the deck and found themselves in an area reserved for third-class passengers. Alfred led the way through a door, and once inside, they faced a broad stairway that led down to the lower decks.

"I don't know where his cabin is," Alfred said. "That first night, I had him meet me in the smoking room over there," he added, pointing across the corridor.

Lord Bainbridge headed for the door to the smoking room. But before he reached it, a man came through the door and practically stumbled into his path. Lord Bainbridge recoiled quickly as if he feared the man was about to set upon him in some unpleasant manner. However, it was only the man's breath that assaulted him. The man was obviously quite drunk, and he had blown a blast of his sour breath right into Lord Bainbridge's face.

It was Alfred who pushed the man away and sent him reeling across the corridor toward the stairway, hiccupping and belching at the same time. The drunk came close to tumbling head first down the stairway. But he managed to catch himself at the last moment, and pulling himself back from the edge, he stumbled off down a corridor and disappeared from their sight.

"Well, there's one the fish will be feedin' upon before dawn," Alfred predicted with contempt.

"Undoubtedly," Lord Bainbridge agreed grimly.

Alfred led the way across the corridor and into the smoking room. The instant he passed through the door, Lord Bainbridge was reminded of the Crown, the pub in London that had often been his favorite hunting ground. Though the look of the smoking room was similar with its oak paneling, patterned linoleum floor, and its tables and chairs and wooden benches made of teak, it was more the room's atmosphere that triggered his memory. Though they found the room completely empty, there still hung in the air, toward the ceiling, a thin veil of smoke. And Lord Bainbridge was certain he could feel the presence of the working-class men who had filled the room for a smoke and a pint of ale throughout the voyage. It was an eerie sensation that both comforted and saddened him.

"That's it then," Alfred said. "He's not here. We're never going to find him." Lord Bainbridge followed him out of the smoking room.

"The officer told us the steerage passengers we're being kept below so they wouldn't cause any trouble," Lord Bainbridge reminded him. He gestured toward the stairway. "Down there," he said.

"Oh great!" Alfred muttered. "Why don't we just jump over the side of the ship, it'd be quicker!"

But he followed Lord Bainbridge down the stairway to the next deck. On D deck they found a steel gate had been pulled across the entrance to the next level of the stairway. Beyond the gate, down at the foot of the stairs, they could see a crowd of steerage passengers milling restlessly about. Before them, guarding the gate, stood a burly seaman. He was well muscled, and his broad vacant face was squeezed into a scowl. He quickly took in their appearance, eyeing them suspiciously. "Here, what you lot doing down here?" he challenged. "This here's third class. Your accommodations are on the upper decks," he added as if this was just an ordinary situation and these two upper-class dandies had somehow accidentally wandered into the wrong part of the ship.

Lord Bainbridge and Alfred shared a glance. Under the dire circumstances taking place, neither of them had expected to be challenged, and so neither of them had prepared a story if they were. It was Lord Bainbridge who finally spoke up, and sensing that the sailor confronting them most probably despised them and all they stood for, he made a point of lording it over the man rather then try and win him over with kindness, which he surmised would have been fruitless. "I've come to get my man," he told the seaman in a clipped abrupt tone that was meant to convey his annoyance at having to explain his business.

"Your man?" the seaman snapped.

"My servant, my valet," Lord Bainbridge answered. "He's down here somewhere."

The seaman shook his head vigorously. "Ain't no servants down here. They're all bunked up top," he added, gesturing toward the ceiling.

"But I assure you, he's down here," Lord Bainbridge insisted.

"The man's traveling with his family, wife, and kids," Alfred put in quickly. "There was no room for all of 'em in first class. He wanted them to stay together, so they had to bunk in third class."

The seaman shifted his glance from Lord Bainbridge to Alfred. His lips curled around a sneer, "That so?"

"Quite!" Alfred acknowledged sharply.

"So if we could just go below and have a quick look around," Lord Bainbridge suggested. "I'm sure it won't take us long to find him."

"No one goes in or out of this gate until I get the word from those in charge," the seaman told him. "Until then, the gate stays locked."

Alfred took Lord Bainbridge's arm and pulled him aside. "We're wasting time with this idiot. Why don't I just pop him one in the jaw."

Lord Bainbridge was uncertain, "He looks pretty strong."

Alfred shook his head. "I've met his type before," he said. "One shot and he'll go down quicker than a poof on Saturday night."

Lord Bainbridge glanced back to where the seaman stood resolutely before the gate, his thick arms folded across his chest. He was about to agree to Alfred's pugilistic suggestion when there occurred one of those coincidences that he was quite sure happened only in books, the kind of unbelievable contrivance that authors used when they were trapped and there was simply no other way to move the story forward. It was a device, dear Maude had succumbed to more than once in her novels, and now here it was happening to him in real life. For Tom suddenly appeared on the other side of the gate as if he had popped up out of the air.

Lord Bainbridge was so relieved to see him, he made no effort to hide his joy. "Tom, thank God!" he cried out.

The intensity of his words was not missed by the seaman, and glancing at him, Lord Bainbridge saw on his face the same look that he had seen on the face of the officer on the boat deck when he had been trying to get Sebastian safely into the lifeboat. Both men, he suspected, had uncovered his true nature, and both men had reacted to it with contempt. He could tell with just the moment's glance he gave to the burly seaman that if the man despised him for being an upper-class toff, he now hated him even more for being a bugger as well.

Nevertheless, Lord Bainbridge appealed to the man, his voice restrained, his manner almost respectful. "That's him, please open the gate."

"Not a chance," the seaman said, smiling at him and showing a row of discolored and broken teeth. "Not a chance in hell!"

Lord Bainbridge drew closer to the man and lowered his voice. "You know, don't you, that this ship is going to sink?" he asked.

The seaman shrugged in indifference. "Maybe she will, maybe she won't," he answered. "Either way, the gate stays shut until I get the word."

Once again, Alfred stepped into the situation. But instead of offering the man his fist, which he was quite prepared to do, he took a couple of bills from his wallet and held them out to the man. "Here take these and open the damn gate."

The seaman stared down at the money in Alfred's outstretched hand. His tongue darted out of his mouth and wetted his lips. Then his hand reached out and snatched the money as if he feared it was an offer about to be withdrawn. He shoved the money into the pocket of his trousers, and making a big display of selecting the right key from the belt he wore around his waist, he fitted the key into the lock and swung the gate open. As soon as Tom had stepped through the gate, he slammed it shut again.

Lord Bainbridge gripped Tom's shoulder, "Thank God, we found you."

"I was at the bottom of the stairs, just waiting around like everyone else, and I heard your voice," Tom explained. He grinned at him. "At first, I thought it was my imagination or that I was hearing a voice from heaven."

"We're not in heaven yet," Alfred muttered. "Though if we linger down here much longer, we just might be."

"We had no idea where to look for you," Lord Bainbridge said to Tom.

"My cabin's way down at the other end, toward the front of the ship," Tom said. "Apparently the White Star Line wants to make sure that single men and women don't have easy access to each other. The men are bunked down at the other end, the women up here."

"A perfectly acceptable arrangement as far as I'm concerned," Alfred pointed out.

"When I left, there was water coming into my cabin," Tom said in a whisper to Lord Bainbridge. Tom wore a heavy coat and a wool cap. But he had no life belt on. "We couldn't find a single one in our cabin," he revealed.

"It's very serious, Tom," Lord Bainbridge informed him. "This ship is going to sink."

Tom looked up at him, conflicting emotions passing like shadows across his broad young face. "And still you came to search for me?"

Lord Bainbridge tightened the pressure that still gripped Tom's arm. "You fool, do you think I'd leave you down here to drown?"

"There are lots of others down there, Jeremy," Tom said. "Women and children, babies too. What about them?" he asked.

"I imagine they'll let them up when the time comes," Lord Bainbridge answered quickly.

Tom's face hardened. "What time will that be, when the ship is going down?"

Before Lord Bainbridge could respond, the seaman chirped in with a question of his own. "What about his wife and kiddies?" he asked sarcastically, pointing a finger at Tom.

At almost the same moment, fed up with all the chatter and convinced the water was rapidly rising and would soon be covering their shoes, Alfred took charge. "Come on, we've wasted enough time already," he scolded. And he actually physically propelled Lord Bainbridge and Tom toward the stairway that led to the upper decks.

But they had only taken a few steps when a voice called out to them. It was a woman's voice, and when Lord Bainbridge looked back over his shoulder, he saw a woman behind the gate trying to attract his attention. She had one of her hands thrust through the bars of the gate and she called out to him again. "Mister, please, mister!"

"Ah here's the missus now," the seaman laughed, highly amused by the whole situation.

Lord Bainbridge paused before the stairway. "She's no concern of ours," Alfred hissed, trying to hurry him up the stairs.

"She's got children with her," Tom observed.

As if to confirm this, the woman called out once more to Lord Bainbridge. "Please, mister, I've got four little ones with me!"

Glancing at Tom, Lord Bainbridge noticed the look of concern and sympathy on his face. And Lord Bainbridge realized at that moment what a better person Tom was than he himself was. If it had not been for Tom and the look he saw on his face, he would have walked away. For Alfred was right, what concern was this woman of his? But instead he sighed, turned, and walked back to the gate. Equally mindful of Alfred's muttered curse as he did so.

"What do you want?" he asked the woman, peering intently through the gate at her.

Though the woman appeared to be only in her early thirties, Lord Bainbridge noted that her face was care-lined, and her hair was already starting to turn to gray. She wore a long wool coat and on her head, a straw hat decorated with a cluster of artificial cherries. Gathered around her were four children, two boys and two girls, the oldest probably no more than nine or ten. They were neatly dressed and appeared to be well looked after. Being one not overly fond of children, Lord Bainbridge noticed one other thing about these four. Most of the other children he had come in contact with, regardless of their class, always seemed to have faces smeared with dirt or the remains of their last meal. While the four little ones behind the gate, all had faces pink and scrubbed clean as a whistle. He surmised that before they left their cabin, their mother had taken a wet facecloth to each one of them, determined that they should not appear in public in a shameful manner. All of them, mother and children, wore life belts which some kindly steward must have secured for them.

The woman began to explain her situation. She spoke in a soft gentle manner, which in no way revealed the life of hardship she surely must have had to endure. Her words too, indicated she was a woman of some education. "You see, sir, we're from Bristol, and we're going to America to join my husband. Two years it's been now since he left us to get a new start. And now he's settled and got himself a shop, a tobacconist's shop, and a small house for us to live in. He sent us the money for our passage. I have letters here, sir, from my husband that will vouch for everything I've told you," she added, beginning to pull the letters out of the pocket of her coat.

"Yes, yes." Lord Bainbridge nodded, slightly impatient. "But what do you want from me?"

The woman lowered her voice and beckoned him even closer. "Please, sir, I beg of you. Let us go with you, up to the boats. I know something is terribly wrong with this ship. We wouldn't have stopped if there wasn't. And some of the men told us there was water in their cabins. No one in charge down here will tell us anything. They just say to be quiet and wait. Please, sir, if not for me, then for my children." She stroked the head of her nearest child. "They're good children, and they'll be as quiet as church mice, I promise you." And when she saw what she perceived as uncertainty on Lord Bainbridge's face, she added one more fact, which perhaps to her was the most important of all. "We're hardworking folk, sir, not layabouts."

Lord Bainbridge stared back at the woman for a moment longer, and then he glanced at the seaman standing before the gate. The seaman was smiling broadly at him and holding out his hand to him, rubbing two fingers together.

"Pay him!" Lord Bainbridge told Alfred sharply.

Alfred groaned again but complied, eager to do whatever it took to get them out of there. He handed the eager seaman a handful of bills, and the gate was immediately unlocked.

The woman and her children stepped free and quickly surrounded Lord Bainbridge who brushed off their thanks with embarrassment. After all, Tom's smile was all the thanks he needed.

"Come on then, let's get on with it!" Alfred grumbled, already bounding up the stairway to the next deck.

"Now remember, children, do exactly as the kind gentleman says. And I'll not have a peep out of one of you," the woman cautioned her brood as they followed after the others.

"That was a fine thing you did," Tom said to Lord Bainbridge as they reached the next deck.

"I wouldn't have done it if it hadn't been for you," Lord Bainbridge admitted.

"Then I'm a good influence on you?" Tom asked.

Lord Bainbridge shrugged and smiled. "Yes," he answered, "I guess so."

As they began to climb toward the boat deck, they noticed their way became more difficult as the floor was definitely slanting, dipping beneath their feet. "The bow is sinking," Alfred whispered to Lord Bainbridge and Tom. "We probably got out just in time."

The children started to slip and slide on the slanting floor beneath their feet, so Lord Bainbridge and Tom both took one up in their arms. The mother carried her third child, and the fourth, the oldest, attached himself to Alfred, hanging onto his coattails despite Alfred's obvious displeasure.

Alfred took them by a different route this time, and they ended up in the forward A deck foyer in a short time. As they passed through the foyer, they found a group of the ship's boys larking about, smoking cigarettes and playing hide-and-seek among the columns. Among them was the liftboy who had so offended Lord Bainbridge earlier in the day by openly flirting with him in the lift. The boy spotted him now, and with a cigarette dangling from the corner of his mouth, he called out to him.

"Bit of a jam we got ourselves into, ain't it, sir?"

Lord Bainbridge stared back at him, once again amazed at the boy's cockiness.

As they climbed up the grand staircase, they joined a crowd of other passengers also making their way topside. When they reached the top of the stairs, some of the passengers went to the right, others to the left. Reaching the final landing, Lord Bainbridge and his group paused for a moment under the great ornamental clock.

"Which way do we go?" Tom asked. "To the right or the left?"

To Lord Bainbridge that was a question that needed no debate, especially if you were a man or even a boy. A male's chance of survival on this night apparently depended on which side of the boat deck he stepped out onto. On the port side, the officer in charge was allowing only women and children into the boats, excluding all men and those boys whom were above a certain age. While on the starboard side, anyone was allowed into the boats as long as there was room. How amazing and perverse it was that one's survival should depend on such an arbitrary manner of selection and rejection, Lord Bainbridge thought. He quickly led his little group out onto the starboard side of the boat deck.

Though hardly thirty minutes had passed since they had left the boat deck, they found that conditions had changed considerably. Passengers were no longer having to be coaxed into the boats, and it was obvious from the crowds that now lined the deck that at least all those who could and were being allowed to find their way to the boat deck were doing so. On the faces they passed, Lord Bainbridge now saw a sense of urgency, an acknowledgement that most people knew time was running out. It was no longer an amusing game, a mid-ocean nighttime diversion. Most people, he could sense, realized the truth of their situation and with it the inevitable tragic conclusion. There was no panic yet, but hysteria bubbled just beneath the surface. Here at least on this side of the ship, where everyone who wished to get into a boat could, there was still order. Lord Bainbridge imagined that on the other side, where admittance to the boats was cruelly restricted, there surely must be chaos.

He kept looking around to see if he could spot Madame Renoir and Sebastian in the crowd. But there was no sign of them, and Lord Bainbridge satisfied himself, that they must have got off in one of the earlier boats to leave the ship that now could been seen from the deck as dark shadows moving through the water, the only motion in an otherwise placid ocean.

At last, they arrived at the forward end of the boat deck, and Lord Bainbridge was greeted by the young junior officer who had promised to save him a seat in his boat. That boat, No. 1, was smaller then the other boats with a capacity for only forty people. It now lay swung out in its davits ready for boarding that apparently had not already begun, for there was not a single passenger in the boat.

"There's no one around," the officer explained to Lord Bainbridge. "I can't seem to find any passengers."

Looking around, Lord Bainbridge was surprised to find that this area of the deck was almost completely deserted. Though, he reasoned, there had to be hundreds still left on board the ship, they certainly weren't gathered around lifeboat No. 1.

"It's probably because we're so close to the bow, and she's going down by the head," the young officer said to Lord Bainbridge.

"Well, here's a few," Lord Bainbridge said, indicating the woman and her four children. The three crewmen who had been assigned to man the boat, and who had been standing by idly with nothing to do but blow on their hands to keep their fingers from freezing, lifted the children into the boat.

When it came time for their mother to join them, she first took Lord Bainbridge's hand and pumped it vigorously. "Thank you, sir, you have saved me and my children. We will never forget you," she promised.

Somewhat embarrassed at her words, Lord Bainbridge nodded, and giving the woman his arm, he helped her over the gunwale and into the lifeboat. As soon as she was seated, her children crowded around her for warmth and protection.

"What's that light over there?" Alfred suddenly asked, pointing off the bow toward the horizon.

"It's a ship," the junior officer confirmed. "She's been sitting there for some time. I seen them trying to contact her with the Morse lamp from the bridge."

"But surely she must have seen the rockets," Lord Bainbridge suggested, and as if on cue, another rocket shot up into the night sky, broke apart, and shattered stars fell into the sea, illuminating their anxious faces for a few brief seconds.

"You would think so, wouldn't you?" the young officer asked bitterly.

"She can't be far away," Tom put in.

"No more than eight or ten miles, I'd guess," the officer agreed.

"Then why isn't she steaming toward us?" Lord Bainbridge asked. "She could save everyone on board."

The young officer caught his glance. "Most probably," he agreed, with a sad shake of his head.

"Those bastards!" Alfred cussed.

At that moment, another officer appeared on the scene. He was obviously a senior officer, and from his manner and the tone of his voice, it was very apparent that he was not pleased with what he saw before his eyes. "Why hasn't this boat been lowered?" he demanded of his younger subordinate.

The young officer immediately snapped to attention. "I've been awaiting orders to lower away, sir," he explained.

The older man shook his head with exasperation. "You planning to wait until she goes down?" he asked with scorn.

"Well, no, sir," the younger officer answered, swallowing hard. "But I've hardly any passengers. Should I perhaps go and look for some, sir?"

The officer took a look at the pathetic contents of lifeboat No. 1 and grunted his annoyance. "You stay at your post," he instructed the young officer. "I'll try and dig up some passengers and send them to you."

"He'd find plenty below decks," Tom whispered to Lord Bainbridge.

The senior officer drew his fellow officer aside, the movement placing them quite close to where Lord Bainbridge stood. And he could not help but overhear their muted conversation and notice the object that passed between them. Taking a small revolver from the pocket of his greatcoat, the older man pressed it into the hand of his companion. He stared into his young face. "Use it if anyone tries to storm your boat," he told him. "Or you may need it for yourself if things go terribly wrong," he added with a grim look on his face. Then he squared his shoulders, and as if trying to make up for his previous gruffness, he patted the younger man on the back and wished him good luck. He hurried off down the deck, his steps carrying a weight few could imagine.

"That was Mr. Murdoch, the first officer," the junior officer told Lord Bainbridge. "He was in charge of the bridge when we hit the berg. I'm sure he feels responsible for driving the ship into it." He stared down at the gun in his gloved hand and then slipped it into the pocket of his coat. He looked into Lord Bainbridge's face. "Poor bloke," he added, "I think he's going to shoot himself."

Lord Bainbridge was startled by this news. "Really?"

The young officer nodded. "It's the honorable thing to do," he concluded.

Lord Bainbridge wasn't so sure that to shoot one's self was such an act of honorability, especially given the fact that he had often heard it stated that the only honorable thing that men like himself could do to right the terrible wrong they had committed by just being themselves was to shoot themselves. He had never had the desire to put the barrel of a gun to his mouth and most certainly not just because society deemed it to be the honorable thing to do.

"You and your friends had better get into the lifeboat," the officer suggested.

"Yes," Lord Bainbridge agreed.

Alfred needed no second invitation. "Right you are," he said, leaping into the boat unaided.

Lord Bainbridge was about to follow after him when he looked back to see Tom standing in hesitation on the deck. He called his name, "Tom?"

But before Tom could answer, Lord Bainbridge was startled to hear another call out his name.

"Jeremy."

He squinted into the darkness, for with no moon above and only the stars and deck lights to see by, there were patches of total darkness on the deck where nothing could be seen and someone might linger unobserved. He watched in amazement as Elaine Standish emerged from one of those pools of darkness where she had been standing back against the wall of a deckhouse. She had been so close to them, she must have heard their every word, and yet she had remained invisible and undetected until now.

Lord Bainbridge immediately went to her and took her hands. They felt cold to his touch, and he began to warm them with his own. "What are you still doing here?" he asked. "I thought you'd be safely away in a boat by now." Before she could respond, he asked another question. "Where's your husband?"

Elaine shook her head as if to rid herself of some unpleasant memory. "Ronnie went in a boat already," she answered.

Lord Bainbridge looked at her in disbelief, "He went and left you behind?"

"Yes," Elaine answered. "We had a terrible row because I wouldn't get in the boat with him. He got very cross with me, which is so unlike him for he never gets cross with anyone." She paused a moment, struggling to find the words to explain her own actions. "I know it was stupid of me," she continued, "but I felt that if I got into that boat with him, then I'd never be free of him. I decided I'd rather take my chances on the ship than go with him in that lifeboat. I'd rather stay behind even if it cost me my life."

"It won't," Lord Bainbridge made haste to assure her.

"I think Ronnie was more concerned about appearances than he was about me," Elaine added. "His last words to me as he climbed into the boat were, 'How do you think it will look in the papers if I am saved and you are not?'"

"That bastard," Lord Bainbridge swore.

"No, he's not really a bastard," Elaine said, inclined to be more charitable. "He's just Ronnie."

"Well, come along now," Lord Bainbridge said, taking her arm. "We'll get you into the boat, and you'll be safe."

As the junior officer took her other arm to help her over the side of the lifeboat, Elaine turned to Lord Bainbridge. "You're coming too, aren't you, Jeremy?"

"Of course," he responded.

"I don't want to go without you," Elaine protested.

"I'll be right behind you," Lord Bainbridge promised. But before he stepped into the boat, he looked back to see Tom still standing resolutely on the deck, making no move toward the lifeboat.

With a sigh, Lord Bainbridge turned away from the boat and crossed the deck to where Tom was standing. He took him by the arm and led him back into one of the patches of darkness, away from the rail where for the moment no one could see them. "What is it, Tom?" he asked anxiously.

Even though there was very little light, he could still see the conflicting emotions that were playing across the young Irishman's face. Tom strained to put his confused thoughts into words. "Jeremy, I can't get into that boat knowing there are women and children down below who don't have a chance."

"We've done all that we could," Lord Bainbridge told him. "We helped that woman and her children. It's time we thought of ourselves now. Tom, I don't want to die. I want to survive."

"I don't want to die either," Tom insisted. "Especially not now," he added with a hint of his infectious grin flashing for an instant across his face like a burst of light from one of the rockets that had shot up from the ship's bridge. He touched Lord Bainbridge's hand that still clutched him. "But I must try and help those poor people," he concluded.

"I'm afraid I'm not that noble, not that brave," Lord Bainbridge said.

"Oh, I think you are," Tom corrected. "Perhaps you just don't know it yet." He stared into Lord Bainbridge's very troubled face, moving even closer to him, so that for a moment their bodies touched. "We have to do this, Jeremy," he whispered. "If we don't, we would never be able to live with ourselves afterward."

"And if we do, we may not live at all," Lord Bainbridge reminded him.

Tom nodded. "I know that. But if we must die, then let us die in a noble cause and together." And then, despite the fact that they were in a public place, though they were hidden in semidarkness, this shy young Irishman, who was still troubled by his own feelings, still reluctant to make any public display, reached out and placed a kiss on Lord Bainbridge, not on his cheek, but boldly on his lips.

Long afterward, Lord Bainbridge when he thought back to this moment, could not help but wonder if Tom had kissed him just because of his feelings for him or also because he wished to bend him to his will. Either way, he was instantly won over to the young man's cause.

Breaking apart, Lord Bainbridge made his way back across the deck to the lifeboat, Tom trailing after him. Alfred, sensing that all was not well, had leaped out of the boat and was standing on the deck gripping his umbrella, an angry scowl on his lips.

Lord Bainbridge spoke to the young officer. "My friend and I are going to go and find some more passengers for the boat," he told him. "Try and hold the boat as long as you can. We will return."

The officer said nothing for a second, and Lord Bainbridge watched his eyes move from his face to Tom's and then back again as if he were trying to figure out the relationship between them and at the same time wondering what had transpired between the two of them back in the shadows. But he was willing to comply. "I'll hold the boat as long as I can, sir," he promised.

Alfred however, who had overheard their exchange, was not so agreeable. "Are you mad?" he asked Lord Bainbridge. "This is not the time to go mucking about for more passengers. We need to go in that boat now! This ship is sinking, or have you forgotten that little minor detail?"

"Tom and I are going below to try and bring up some of the steerage women and children," Lord Bainbridge explained to him.

"You're insane!" Alfred snarled.

"You stay here. Keep an eye on Mrs. Standish, will you?" Lord Bainbridge asked.

"Like hell I will!" Alfred snapped, and he stomped off along the deck, each step echoing his displeasure.

"We'll be back as quickly as possible," Lord Bainbridge called back to Elaine who had risen anxiously from her seat in the lifeboat when she saw that he was not about to join her.

Lord Bainbridge and Tom hurried along the boat deck to catch up with Alfred, who in his anger had already put some distance between them. He led them quickly down a flight of metal stairs onto A deck. And then they followed him down almost the full length of the deck toward the stern of the ship. They went through a door and found themselves once again facing the aft grand staircase. But instead of starting down the stairs, Alfred headed across the foyer and pushed open the door to the adjoining first-class smoking room.

"What are we doing in here, Alfred?" Lord Bainbridge asked as he and Tom followed him into the smoking room.

Alfred glanced at him. "I need a drink," he answered. He shifted his eyes to Tom. "You're Irish, you should understand the need for a nip."

"Alfred, we don't have time for this," Lord Bainbridge protested.

Alfred's full lips curled back into a tight little smile. "If we've time to go back down into stinkin' steerage to rescue people who mean nothing to us, then we've time for a quick drink," he answered.

At that moment as convenience would have it, a steward came scrambling out of the bar, a couple of bottles quite obviously stuffed into the pockets of his coat.

"Any chance of getting a drink?" Alfred asked him.

Still on the run, the steward pointed back toward the bar. "Take whatever you want. It's an open bar now, lad! On the house!" Then he swung through the door to the foyer, letting it slam shut behind him.

Alfred made straight for the bar, leaving Lord Bainbridge and Tom to stand around, impatiently waiting for his return. The room was warm and cozy, giving off no hint of the disaster that was to come. It appeared deserted except for an elderly gentleman with a full gray beard who sat in a leather armchair, calmly turning the pages of a book he seemed quite engrossed in while on a table beside him, a half-finished cigar, still lit, rested on the edge of an ashtray, giving off its definite pungent male aroma.

"I wonder what he's reading," Tom whispered.

"No matter, I doubt he'll find the time to finish it," Lord Bainbridge said in a rather grim attempt at humor.

But despite their situation, the old gentleman did look quite at home in this setting, for the smoking room had the cozy opulence of an exclusive London men's club. With its mahogany paneling, heavy leather furniture, gilt-edged mirrors, and strategically placed spittoons, it certainly did resemble one of those finer establishments where men might retire to for cigars and brandy and to get away, for a little while, from their problems and their women. For these clubs were off limits to all women as were the smoking rooms of the *Titanic*.

Now of course, Lord Bainbridge also preferred to frequent clubs whose memberships were exclusively male. However, these clubs were far less elegant, and their clientele was hardly there for brandy and cigars. So as he stood there for a moment in the *Titanic's* first-class smoking room, Lord Bainbridge felt himself in an alien world, a world that certainly had no welcome for him but too a world into which he sought no entrance. The smoking room before him represented the proper society that had shunned him, shut him out, and closed its door in his face. They had rejected him, but no less than he had rejected them. Even the previous evening when he had brought Tom here on their grand tour of the ship, he had felt uncomfortable, unwanted, and completely out of place. It was a world into which he had been born, but now one into which he felt as if he no longer belonged.

Alfred returned from the bar with a bottle of whiskey and three glasses. And when Lord Bainbridge insisted that this was hardly the time to start drinking, Alfred shook his head with impatience. "Drink up," he urged. "It'll help to keep us warm if we end up in the water."

Unable to argue with logic such as that, Lord Bainbridge accepted a half glass of whiskey.

"We need a toast," Alfred proposed.

"How about to the *Titanic*," Lord Bainbridge suggested, meaning to be sarcastic.

"My brothers helped to build this ship," Tom said to Alfred.

Alfred gave him a rather patronizing stare. "Well," he clarified, "it's we English who sailed her."

"And now we've gone and lost her," Lord Bainbridge added. He raised his glass. "To the *Titanic*," he said, now with no longer any trace of ridicule in his voice.

After Alfred had downed his whiskey, he suddenly became quite mellow and now quite willing to proceed with the task at hand. Giving his umbrella a jaunty wave above his head, he started toward the door to the foyer. "Well, come along," he called back to the other two. "Let's get on with it! It's time to go and rescue the downtrodden and unwashed!"

About to follow after him, Lord Bainbridge paused a moment and stared across the room. Something had caught his eye, a blur of color, an undefined movement, something so slight as to appear to be nothing more than a particle of a dream or a wisp of a memory. And yet he knew there was something real there, something he knew he had to investigate. So he walked across the smoking room, leaving Alfred and Tom behind.

Coming upon a half-secluded alcove, shielded from the rest of the room by a panel of stained glass done up in magnificent colors, Lord Bainbridge was startled to find Count Fraboli and his wife. They were seated at a little table, sipping sherry and as calm and unperturbed as if he had encountered them at some elegant restaurant or smart Continental cafe.

Obviously delighted to see him, Lucianna held out her hand. "Jeremy, how wonderful! Won't you join us for a sherry?"

"Though I'm afraid you'll find the service somewhat lacking," Alonzo put in. "You'll have to get your own drink from the bar."

Stunned, Lord Bainbridge slipped into a chair beside them. "But why are you in here?" he asked. "You should be up on deck. They're filling the lifeboats."

"We were," Lucianna confirmed. "But there was such madness up there, everyone running about and pushing and shoving. People shouting. It was just too much."

"We wanted a quieter place to wait," Alonzo added

"Wait for what?" Lord Bainbridge implored.

"Why the rescue ship of course," Lucianna answered, patting his hand. "They can let us know when it arrives. We're all dressed and ready for boarding when the time comes."

The two of them were indeed attired as if they were about to embark on another journey. Lucianna had selected a slim dress of dark blue wool. Over this, she wore a dark blue wrapper with a fur collar. A matching fur hat, long gloves, and a white fur muff completed her ensemble. Her husband had a camel hair topcoat draped over his shoulders, a smart homburg on his head, and his hands were enclosed in soft leather gloves. Beside them stood two small carrying cases, the count's rolled umbrella, and Lucianna's large handbag. They looked quite ready for an overnight getaway to the country. On a nearby table lay their lifebelts.

"My dears," Lord Bainbridge said to them, "we've no guarantee a ship will reach us in time." He decided against telling them about the light Alfred had spotted on the horizon, which the young officer had assured them was another ship, another ship that sat there motionless while their own was sinking beneath their feet.

Alonzo shook his finger at him good-naturedly, the way a father might to a child who had just misspoken. "Jeremy, this newfangled wireless the ship has is a miracle. It can send messages hundreds of miles across the ocean. There must be any number of ships racing to our rescue at this very moment."

"But just in case, you should go up on deck and get into a lifeboat at once," Lord Bainbridge insisted.

The couple shared a smile, and then Alonzo spoke to Lord Bainbridge once again, "It seems to me that it would be rather selfish of me to take a seat in one of the boats away from another whose life expectancy promised to greatly exceed my own," he said.

"We will wait right here," Lucianna reaffirmed, patting Lord Bainbridge's hand once more. She laughed lightly in that musical way of hers. "I feel quite improper sitting here in a smoking room," she confessed. "I imagine at another time it might have caused quite a scandal."

Her husband laughed with her, "You're right, my dear. They'd probably have thrown you in the ship's brig."

"Oh dear, I shouldn't care for that at all," Lucianna lamented, still amused.

Looking into their calm, smiling faces, Lord Bainbridge at once understood. It came to him like a rush of cold air when someone first opens a door to the outside on a frosty morning. They both knew they were going to die, and they accepted that fact, even preferred it. Count Fraboli was already dying, and Lord Bainbridge had often wondered how Lucianna would manage after her husband's inevitable passing. They had been so much a part of each other's lives for so many years. How could she possibly go on alone? That was it—they had made their decision to die together. They had made up their minds to commit suicide. This had probably been their plan all along, and now this tragedy had arranged it all neatly and effortlessly for them. All they had to do was sit back, sip their sherries, and wait.

Knowing there was nothing further he could say, no final protest he could make, Lord Bainbridge got to his feet. He leaned down and kissed Lucianna warmly on the cheek. For a last moment, he gripped Alonzo's hand tightly. And then he turned and walked quickly away, not looking back.

There were tears in his eyes, and through them, he was startled to see that Alfred and Tom had come back into the room, obviously in search of him. They were standing quietly a few feet away from the table where the Frabolis sat. How much the two young men had overheard Lord Bainbridge could not be sure.

As they walked toward the door, Alfred indicated that he at least had somehow understood what had transpired. "You can't save those who don't want to be saved," he said. And for once, there was no mockery in his tone. His sympathy, this time, was sincere.

"I know," Lord Bainbridge replied, the tears falling from his eyes. And as they pushed their way through the door to the foyer leaving the smoking room behind, he felt Tom's hand, seeking to comfort, reach for his own.

Chapter XI

Lord Bainbridge and the others had no sooner left the smoking room and crossed the foyer in preparation to once again take the aft grand staircase down to the ship's lower regions when they had another encounter. For an individual was coming up the staircase in great haste, his footsteps pounding as if he were being chased by the very devil himself or at least by the very ocean itself, which given their present circumstances, was most assuredly a more immediate threat. This individual was charging with his head down, and either he didn't see them or didn't care if he did, for he ran right into Alfred, hitting him square in the chest.

As to be expected, Alfred was deeply offended by such a rude introduction, and he pushed the intruder off himself with an oath. "Get off me, you idiot!"

Marco Borsalino bobbed his head up to see whom he had assaulted. "Oh, it's you," he said when he recognized Alfred, whom he knew had little love for him and for whom he held similar affection. The Italian lad was much more pleased to see Lord Bainbridge. And apparently having already forgotten his thinly veiled threats and promises to do him mischief, Marco once again turned on the charm with smiles and much fluttering of his absurdly long eyelashes.

"What were you running from?" Lord Bainbridge asked him.

"A couple of crewmen," Marco answered. "They were mad as hell that I escaped."

Lord Bainbridge was confused. "Escaped from what?" he asked.

Marco hastened to explain, "Well, you see, right after the ship hit, whatever it was she hit."

"An iceberg," Lord Bainbridge informed him.

Now it was Marco's turn to be confused. "We hit an iceberg?" he asked in disbelief. "How is it possible that we hit an iceberg?"

"Incredible as it may seem, that's what happened," Lord Bainbridge assured him.

"But surely an iceberg is so big they would have been able to see it in time," Marco reasoned.

"One would have thought so," Lord Bainbridge had to agree. "But why were you being chased?"

Marco continued his explanation. "Right after the ship hit the iceberg, everyone knew something was wrong. And these members of the crew came along and locked all of us who worked in the restaurant, all the waiters and cooks, into our cabins."

"But why did they do that?" Lord Bainbridge asked.

Marco shrugged. "They never told us why they were doing it. But," he went on, "after they had turned the key in the lock to my door, I heard one of the crewmen say to the others, 'This should hold those lowlife troublemakers.'"

"How did you escape?" Lord Bainbridge inquired.

"I picked the lock," Marco answered with obvious pride. "It was easy. There's not a lock in the world that Marco can't pick. I am an expert," he added, throwing out his thin chest. He looked back over his shoulder down the flight of stairs he had just charged up. "I guess they gave up chasing me," he said. "They know Marco is too fast for them." He had one more piece of information to share with them. "I put on my best clothes," he told them, indicating the rather worn three-piece suit of black wool, the scruffy-looking overcoat, which was at least two sizes too big for him, and the wool cap he had pulled down over his black curls. "I figured if I was dressed up in my best, then, once I reached first class, they'd just think I was another passenger. You won't give me away?" he asked anxiously.

Lord Bainbridge assured him they wouldn't, and then glancing at Alfred, he could tell he was dying to make some cutting remark about Marco's wardrobe. But this time, he held his tongue.

Tom, meanwhile, was watching Marco with curiosity, and Lord Bainbridge was quite certain the young Irishman had already figured out the relationship between the two of them. It was a rather uncomfortable moment for Lord Bainbridge, for he had never imagined that the two of them, Tom and Marco, would ever meet. One was his past, all of it really, and the other was to be, he hoped, his future.

"So this ship, she is really going to sink?" Marco asked, looking around at their faces.

"As sure as we're standing here," Alfred said.

Marco nodded thoughtfully. "I knew something bad was gonna happen this morning. I was lying in my bunk, and just before dawn, I heard a rooster crow—crow three times it did. Back in the village where I came from, if a rooster crows three times in a row, it means something terrible is going to happen before the day is done."

"What would a rooster be doing on the *Titanic*?" Alfred asked with a sneer.

Marco had a ready answer. "We've had eggs every morning for breakfast. So if they've got hens on board, then they've probably got roosters as well," he replied. "And we've had milk too, which means they got cows someplace too."

He gave Alfred a disdainful glance. "You don't have to be a genius to figure that one out."

But Alfred was hardly impressed. "We're wasting time, standing here gabbing," he told them. "In case you gentlemen have forgotten, there's a ship sinking beneath our feet."

"We'd better get to the boats," Marco suggested eagerly.

"For once we are in agreement," Alfred said.

"We're going down into steerage and see if we bring some of those people up to the boats," Lord Bainbridge told Marco.

Marco glanced down the staircase as if he were looking down into hell itself. "You're going down there? You're crazy!" he shouted.

Lord Bainbridge would not have disagreed with him, but one look at Tom's earnest face and he knew he was committed to the undertaking no matter how dangerous, how hopeless it seemed.

"There's water down there! I've seen it!" Marco protested. "And the people down there, they're crazy. Most of 'em are just standing around, waiting to be told what to do. They're fools," he added. "Only the ones like me, the ones who try to save themselves, are gonna survive," he concluded.

Lord Bainbridge thought of the Englishwoman with the four children whom they had seen safely into boat No. 1. It was certainly true of her. She had stepped forward and made an effort to save herself and her children.

"And almost none of 'em speak English," Marco put in. "They won't understand a word you're saying to 'em."

"I speak French and a little Italian," Lord Bainbridge said.

"Won't do you any good!" Marco insisted. "None of 'em I heard spoke Italian. Most of 'em speak some crazy gibberish that don't make no sense to anyone except their own kind."

"How do you know all this?" Lord Bainbridge challenged.

Marco gave him a wicked smile. "I told you, I know every part of this ship and everyone on it," he boasted.

"Well there's plenty of Irish on board and they speak English," Tom reminded them.

"Sort of," Alfred added in his usual tart tongue.

"Whatever the case, we're going to try," Lord Bainbridge said, making for the stairway.

Marco stood there and watched the three of start down the stairs, and then he threw up his arms and started after them. "I'll show you a quicker and easier way to get down into steerage," he told them. He took the lead down the stairway, all the while shaking his head and muttering the word *crazy* over and over again.

Beneath his feet, Lord Bainbridge could tell that the slant of the stairs had become much steeper, and a couple of times he even had to grasp the railing to keep from stumbling. He decided not to mention this disturbing fact to the others although he sensed they too were probably aware of it.

When they reached the next deck instead of continuing down the stairway, Marco led them across the foyer and down a corridor, past some first-class staterooms. Next, he led them through a door on which, Lord Bainbridge could tell by a quick glance, the lock appeared to have been jimmied. *Most probably by Marco,* he concluded. Lord Bainbridge was also quite sure they were traveling through a part of the ship that was meant to be used only by the crew, used by them to get quickly from one part of the ship to the other. It was like being in a giant beehive.

At last, Marco brought them out to a long corridor that looked to run almost the entire length of the ship. He pointed them toward the stern of the ship, and off they trooped. The corridor was completely deserted as were most of the cabins they passed, many with their doors flung wide open as if their occupants had left in great haste. They did come upon one cabin that was occupied, and they glanced inside as they hurried by. Inside, were four or five men and women on their knees, with rosary beads in their hands, softly praying.

Marco was contemptuous of their behavior. "Fools!" he spit out. "Moaning for the Madonna to help them instead of helping themselves. They'll still be there on their knees when the water washes over their heads," he predicted.

A little farther along the corridor, they encountered some water of their own. It wasn't much, just a puddle that barely covered the tops of their shoes, and it didn't appear to be flowing from anyplace in particular. To Lord Bainbridge, it looked as if either someone somewhere had forgotten to turn off a faucet, or there was a leak from the deck above them, which didn't seem to make any sense.

A few moments later, they came out into a wide-open space, and looking about, Lord Bainbridge realized they were at the bottom of the same stairway where earlier he had found Tom and the Englishwoman. The gate at the top of the stairs appeared to be still locked although he couldn't tell from where he stood if the burly seaman who had given them such a hard time was still standing guard up there.

There were many passengers gathered in this area, perhaps as many as a hundred. And by the looks of it, many had brought along most of their baggage as well. There were suitcases, trunks, and bundles tied up in rope or string of every size and shape stacked everywhere. The trunks at least were serving as seats for many while others sat on the stairs, and some of the numerous children present sat on the floor, many clutching a favorite toy. There was no great commotion among these people. They stood or sat there quietly waiting, some milling about restlessly, apprehensive perhaps, but certainly not rebellious or hysterical. And at that moment, there seemed no reason for them to be so. For though there was now a definite tilt to the linoleum floor beneath their feet, the lights still burned brightly, and here in the bowels of the ship there was no sign of the disaster that was to come.

The passengers tended to stick together by nationality, obviously feeling comfort in the company of their countrymen. There were a large number of different nationalities represented. England and Ireland had the largest contingents, but all four Scandinavian countries also had a goodly number on board. There were others from Belgium, Austria, Italy, and Switzerland. But the White Star Line's efforts to recruit passengers for the lucrative immigrant trade had not stopped there. They had cast their nets further abroad, and natives from at least three Middle Eastern countries—Syria, Turkey, and Lebanon—were also on board the *Titanic* as well as a sprinkling of Orientals. But no matter from what country these people came, they were hardly the poor, huddled masses as the newspapers of the day liked to refer to the flood of immigrants that were flowing to the shores of America. The goal most of these people sought was a better life, and they brought their skills and their diligence to achieve it. A few were fleeing persecution and intolerance. Some had already been to America and given up on it. They had returned to their homeland only to find it was worse there than what they had left behind in America. So they were setting out a second time for the Promised Land. Others, having found success in the New World, returned to their native country and were now bringing other relatives with them back to America: wives and children, brothers and sisters. Many of the large number of young men on board had good-paying jobs waiting for them in America, and not a few of the young women had fiancés waiting impatiently for them. Many of these passengers had purchased tickets for the first ship available, and as luck would have it, good or ill, that ship had turned out to be the *Titanic*. But for all of them on board the ship, their stories were as varied as their nationalities, and their hopes were as high as the *Titanic's* four funnels.

As the four young men entered the area, all of the conversations that had been going on among the various ethnic groups came to a sudden stop, and heads turned toward the newcomers. Some may have thought they were the ship's representatives come at last to tell them what to do. Others fell silent, impressed by the elegant attire worn by two of the young men.

A harried-looking steward, with thinning hair and nervous hands, approached them rather apprehensively. Alfred and Lord Bainbridge shared a glance, and the word *obvious* passed silently between them.

"This is steerage down here," the steward told them. He, like the others in the room, was eyeing Lord Bainbridge's and Alfred's fancy attire. "You gentleman must have made a wrong turn," the steward added.

"That we did," Alfred muttered in agreement.

"Looks like you've got confusion down here," Lord Bainbridge observed.

The steward's thin hands fluttered as if they were tinkling the keys of an invisible piano. "It's hopeless," he lamented. "I can't even get them to keep their life belts on. As soon as I get them strapped on, they take them off. They just don't understand."

"Do they understand English?" Tom asked.

"Well, of course the English and the Irish ones do," the steward answered. "I had an interpreter down here to help me with the Scandinavians, but now he seems to have gone and disappeared."

"You know, don't you, that they're lowering the lifeboats?" Lord Bainbridge asked.

The steward nodded rather miserably. "Yes, I heard they were."

"Then shouldn't you get these people up to the boat deck, so they might have a chance?" Lord Bainbridge reasoned.

"Unfortunately, we haven't had the word yet," the steward replied.

"The word?" Lord Bainbridge queried.

"The word from those in charge, the officers, to open the gates and let them go up," the steward said. He whispered his next words as if he feared they might be overheard. "The gate up there is still locked."

"Don't you have the key?" Tom asked impatiently.

"No," the steward responded with a sad shake of his head. "Only the master of arms and one or two of the officers carry those keys."

"Well, maybe by the time you get the word, all the boats will be gone," Lord Bainbridge said to him. He tried not to make his voice sound unkind, for he sensed the man was a good man, struggling under terrible conditions to do his job as he had been instructed.

The poor steward's face turned white. "Oh dear, do you really think so?" He shook his head again quite distressed. "Oh, I shall hope not."

"Look," Lord Bainbridge began, "my friends and I have come down here to try and bring some of these people up to the boats, especially the women and the children."

"But the gate is still locked," the steward insisted.

"We've found another way to get up there," Lord Bainbridge said. "Will you help us?"

"Well, it's against the rules," the steward pondered. He thought for a moment longer and then came to a quick decision. "What do you want me to do?" he asked.

"Talk to them, see if you can convince some of them to come with us," Lord Bainbridge responded.

The steward nodded, but then he paused and looked shyly at Lord Bainbridge. "You'd do better to speak to them yourself, sir," he suggested. "You make a much nicer appearance," he added, actually blushing as he said the words.

"Go ahead, Jeremy," Tom prompted.

Lord Bainbridge nervously cleared his throat, knowing he had to be very careful what he said. He knew if he told them the whole truth, he risked starting a panic, but he knew he had to tell them enough to convince at least some of them to come with them. He began in an unsteady voice but picked up confidence as he heard the sound of his own words. "We came down here to take those of you who want to go up to the boat deck where they're loading the lifeboats," he began. "There are other ships coming to our aid, but as a precaution, they are putting the *Titanic's* passengers off into the lifeboats. We would especially like as many women and children as possible to come with us."

His words were greeted with a complete silence. Not a soul stepped forward to join them.

Lord Bainbridge looked to the steward who shrugged his shoulders. "Many of them don't understand English, sir," he suggested.

"Spread out," Lord Bainbridge said to his companions. "Try and get some of them to come with us."

"We don't have much time," Alfred warned.

There were a number of what were obviously large family groups, parents with numerous children, scattered about the room. Lord Bainbridge approached one of these. The husband and wife were seated on a large steamer trunk, and around them were gathered six children, the youngest still a baby in his mother's arms. The parents looked rather stern, especially the man, who had narrow eyes, a large mustache, and slicked-back hair. The whole family was sitting there so quietly, not even the baby squirmed, and so stiffly, to Lord Bainbridge, they looked as if they were posing to have their photograph taken. Thinking they might be French, he started to speak to them in that language.

But he had only gotten a few words out before the woman interrupted him. "We're from London, sir," she told him.

"I'm sorry," Lord Bainbridge apologized with a smile. "I thought because you didn't respond to what I said before you might not understand English. And I'm afraid French is the only other language I know well."

"We understood every word you said," the man informed him coldly.

"Well then," Lord Bainbridge continued, still smiling, "you understand then that's it's very important you come with us up to the boat deck."

The man shook his head. "No, we will wait here until the men in charge tell us what to do," he said. He looked Lord Bainbridge up and down. "You're not in charge of this boat," he added.

"Now look here, my good man—" Lord Bainbridge began, but the man cut him off.

"This once you toffs aren't in charge," he said, his stare hostile as his eyes grew even narrower, and under his droopy mustache, his lips turned down. "I know your type," he added.

Now, what the hell is that supposed to mean? Lord Bainbridge asked himself, wondering if the man was referring to his membership in the society of the privileged class or that other society he belonged to whose membership was much more exclusive.

"Perhaps—" the woman started to venture.

But her husband instantly cut her off. "We stay here," he said adamantly, still frowning with malice at Lord Bainbridge.

Realizing a mountain couldn't move this man, burdened down as he was with all his prejudices and ignorances, Lord Bainbridge gave up and walked away from the family.

He was quickly joined by Marco, who had had a similar unsuccessful venture. He had cornered a young Italian couple, and though he pleaded with them earnestly, and as has already been shown, Marco did have a way with words, he had been unable to persuade them to join them. "Fools!" Marco muttered at them over his shoulder. "They deserve whatever happens to them."

Even Tom was unable to secure any converts despite the large number of his countrymen who were gathered in an area around the stairs. He did learn that his two cabinmates had set off on their own earlier. This gave him some measure of relief. Alfred also returned alone and with the suggestion that since the whole enterprise had obviously turned out to be a complete failure, they should return immediately to the boat deck.

Discouraged by their results, Lord Bainbridge agreed. "At least we tried," Tom said to him with a weak smile.

Then just as they were about to leave, an elderly couple approached them. They were both small in stature, rotund in figure, and with their wrinkled, chubby faces, they looked like cheerful little elves. Each was an exact duplicate of the other even down to the sparse white whiskers on their chins. Lord Bainbridge accurately judged that they were both easily into their seventies. The man, who carried a cane and with his hat respectfully clutched in his hands, addressed Lord Bainbridge.

"Mister, we would be quite willing to go with you if you'll have us," he said. And then perhaps because he feared Lord Bainbridge might reject their bid, the old man pushed on in a rush of words. "My name is Josef Kaminska, and this is my wife, Ida." The old woman shyly bobbed her babushka-covered head. Her husband continued. "We come from Prague where, for many years, we were both schoolteachers. And now we go to America to be free, free to practice our own religion without fear," he added, his eyes fixed directly on Lord Bainbridge in almost, but not quite, a challenge.

Above the old man's head, Lord Bainbridge caught sight of Alfred silently mouthing the word *Jew*.

"Of course you're welcome to come with us," Lord Bainbridge assured them. "You speak English very well," he told the old man.

Josef Kaminska nodded. "Thank you. My wife and I both study hard for over two years in preparation for our trip to America."

"But why were you the only ones to step forward," Lord Bainbridge asked. "Why would no one else agree to come with us?"

The old man shrugged. "Most of them are afraid, afraid to go, afraid to stay here. But there were a few," he went on, "who have already set off on their own to find a way up to the boats. I guess they were more brave or more resourceful than the others. My wife and I would have gone with them except they said we were too old and would only slow them down." His old eyes took on a look close to panic, and he boldly reached out and grasped Lord Bainbridge's arm. "I promise you, mister, we will not slow you down. My wife and I will both keep up. This cane you see in my hand is just an old man's affectation. I have no real need of it. See!" He demonstrated by twirling the cane above his head.

Lord Bainbridge laughed and reassured him. "Do not worry, we will not leave you behind," he promised. Remembering with a pang how he had been unable to save the Frabolis, he resolved then and there that he would save this elderly couple.

Another person caught his attention, and despite Alfred's protests, Lord Bainbridge crossed to one of the far corners of the room. There sitting in the corner, alone and friendless, was a young Asian man. He was smartly dressed and sitting on an upturned suitcase, elegantly smoking a cigarette. He looked up as Lord Bainbridge approached.

Their eyes met and held for a silent moment, and Lord Bainbridge found himself looking into one of the most beautiful faces, male or female, he had ever seen. The young man was wearing a low-brimmed hat that was very fashionable at the time, and it was not until he was right up to him that Lord Bainbridge got the full effect of his appearance. His skin was gold in color, with high aristocratic cheekbones and vivid green eyes that set deep in their sockets like rare precious stones of jade. All his clothes were expensive and stylish, strange attire for one traveling in steerage.

But then right on cue, Alfred appeared beside them and without hesitation expressed his usual bigoted opinion. "Don't waste your time on him," he hissed. "There's others better worth saving than a Chink."

"Actually, I'm Japanese," the Asian said in English that was perfect and educated.

Lord Bainbridge brushed Alfred aside and spoke to the young man. "This ship is going to sink," he said candidly. "Make no mistake about that."

As the other continued to stare back at him while still puffing elegantly on his cigarette, Lord Bainbridge felt there was a sense of disdain in his stare. It was as if, and this he found quite extraordinary, this Asian man was contemptuous of him! As if he were actually looking down his nose at him. And when a moment later he spoke, his full lips were definitely curled into a sneer.

"Why do you want to bother with me?" he asked of Lord Bainbridge. "Down here, I'm the most despised of the despised, and up in your world I'd be detested even more." He paused a moment to take a final puff on his cigarette before he tossed it away with a graceful gesture. "Is it because you, a white man, feel sorry for a poor little yellow man like me?" he asked.

Stung, Lord Bainbridge was quite ready to walk away from him when the Asian suddenly changed his tone although on his face there remained an unmistakable look of contempt. "I'll come with you," he said, "because I think what you say about this ship is true." He slipped a wool overcoat around his shoulders and looked longingly at the suitcase at his feet for a moment, but then leaving it behind, he joined them.

So they started off with their small band of converts: the young Asian man and the elderly Polish couple. Both Lord Bainbridge and Tom were dispirited by their lack of success. While Alfred, as to be expected, grumbled that it had all been a big waste of precious time. As for Marco, he was just glad they were once again headed up to the boat deck, and he eagerly led the way.

As they were leaving the area around the staircase, Lord Bainbridge spoke to the nervous steward who was watching their departure with a look that could only be described as intensely melancholy. "Why don't you come with us?" Lord Bainbridge suggested.

The steward's face lit up immediately. "Really?" he stammered in obvious gratitude. Then almost at the same time, his features fell and he shook his head. "No, my place is here with them," he said, glancing around at the crowd of steerage passengers—some confused, others complacent, and a few even, having already given up, resigned to accept whatever fate had in store for them no matter how horrible it turned out to be. "I can't leave until I'm told," the steward said to Lord Bainbridge.

"I'm sorry," Lord Bainbridge told him sincerely.

"No less than I am, I assure you," the steward said. "Good luck," he added with a faint smile.

Lord Bainbridge nodded and then quickly followed after his little party that had already begun their departure. As he moved out into the corridor, he came abreast of three Middle Eastern women in colorful scarfs and long dresses, each one held a baby wrapped in a blanket. The women, obviously completely unaware of the danger they and their children were in, smiled and nodded in a friendly manner as Lord Bainbridge came upon them. One of them was cooing at her baby and making little clicking sounds with her teeth to which the baby responded to with gurgles of delight.

Suddenly, having a spur of the moment thought, Lord Bainbridge called out to Tom and Alfred, who were just ahead of him. "Grab the babies!" he shouted to them. His companions turned and looked back at him, both quite convinced that he momentarily at least had gone quite out of his head. "If we take the babies, the mothers will follow," Lord Bainbridge explained, already lifting one of the babies from its startled mother's arms.

Tom and Alfred each grabbed a baby as well though Alfred did so with extreme reluctance, having little use for anyone who fell into the broad racial classification that he referred to as Arabs and even less use for babies.

Their actions of course created instant pandemonium as the mothers, screaming and cursing in a language only they themselves could understand, took off in pursuit of their children, who they undoubtedly thought were being stolen to be sold into slavery by these white demons. The whole scene, had it not been for the tragic circumstances that had necessitated it, would have been rather comical as the distraught mothers pursued in vengeance, forcing Lord Bainbridge and the others to pick up their speed, at one point even running through the winding corridors. In some places, they splashed their way through water that had seeped in from some unknown source. The angle of the stairs they were forced to climb had become more acute as the *Titanic's* bow continued to sink. The elderly couple from Prague especially found the stairs difficult to manage, but Lord Bainbridge, true to his word, would not leave them behind.

When at last they had returned to the first-class part of the ship, they had to all stop a moment and catch their breath. The Middle Eastern women, sensing that their children were not being kidnapped, and these white strangers were only trying to help them, calmed down, retrieved their babies and, from then on, followed after them quite willingly.

As they made their way down a corridor lined with expensive first-class cabins, Marco detached himself from the group and began fiddling with the knobs on the cabin doors.

"What are you doing?" Lord Bainbridge demanded.

Marco shrugged. "I told you there wasn't a lock I couldn't pick," he answered, continuing his efforts.

"If they catch you, they'll shoot you," Lord Bainbridge warned him.

Only now did Marco look up at him, his green eyes gleaming eagerly against his olive skin. "I wasn't born with a silver spoon under my pillow," he said. "I have to scratch and dig for everything I get. Besides, they're going to have to catch me first." He winked at Lord Bainbridge and returned to his nefarious endeavors.

Giving up on him, sure that he would either get shot or end up drowning in the ship's brig, Lord Bainbridge hurried to catch up to the others. They finally came into the A deck foyer, and before them was the aft grand staircase that led up to the boat deck. Slumped on the bottom steps of the staircase was a slight figure, his head buried in his arms, weeping uncontrollably. The others passed him by, but Lord Bainbridge paused before the distraught individual.

"Go ahead," Lord Bainbridge said to Tom, who looked anxiously back at him. "I'll catch up."

He turned his attention back to the figure on the stairs, who was still weeping as if his heart was breaking, his shoulders heaving, his sobs coming from somewhere deep inside of him. Lord Bainbridge could tell by the suit of evening clothes he wore that he was obviously a first-class passenger, and without seeing his face but judging by his build, he felt certain he was hardly more than a boy. Lord Bainbridge imagined that, just hours ago, he had perhaps listened to the lively ragtime in the Palm Court and perhaps even danced with some pretty young thing. And perhaps later, he had gone to the smoking room, had his first glass of brandy, sat in on a round of cards, and felt very grown-up. And now, here he was crumbled on the stairs, weeping as if his whole world were coming apart, and in truth, it very much was.

"Stop crying," Lord Bainbridge commanded.

A tear-streaked face looked up at him, and for an instant, Lord Bainbridge was startled. For a moment, he felt as if he was looking into Denham's upturned face—the same blond hair, the same soft features that would harden with maturity as he had noted in Egypt, the same expressive blue eyes, all were there. For just a second, he had turned a page of the photo album in his heart and came upon a treasured picture. But it was only a trick of his imagination. For an instant later, all resemblance to Denham vanished from the boy's upturned face. It had happened before, and Lord Bainbridge was sure that for the rest of his life he would be forever coming upon some youth and, for an instant or two, seeing Denham's face before him.

"Get up," Lord Bainbridge instructed, this time more gently.

The boy, who looked to be about the same age as Denham was when they first met, got obediently to his feet. He had stopped crying, but his nose was running, and he fumbled in his pocket for a handkerchief that wasn't there.

Lord Bainbridge offered him his own. The boy took it, wiped his eyes, and gave his nose a good blow. And when he presented the linen back to its owner, Lord Bainbridge smiled ever so slightly and shook his head. "It's yours," he said.

"Thank you, sir," the boy returned. He swallowed hard and entered his plea. "Please, sir, will you help me?"

That's twice he's called me sir, Lord Bainbridge thought, slightly irritated. *He certainly knows how to charm a fellow.*

"Please, I don't want to die!" the boy pleaded. "I tried three times to get into a lifeboat, and each time, they threw me out. They said I was too old. But I'm only sixteen," he added desperately.

A boy when he wants to get into a lifeboat, a man when he wants a brandy, Lord Bainbridge thought to himself. And though he had no way of knowing this for sure, he felt certain that the officer who had turned away this boy was the same one who had refused to let Sebastian Renoir into the lifeboat.

"Will you help me?" the boy asked once more.

"Why do you want to live?" Lord Bainbridge asked, measuring the lad before him with a steady gaze.

The boy hesitated. Caught off guard, he fumbled for an answer. "Everyone wants to live," he finally replied.

"Yes"—Lord Bainbridge agreed—"but why do you?"

"Well," the boy began, nervously wetting his lips, "I'm so young, and there's so much I haven't done."

"Like what?" Lord Bainbridge prompted. He could almost see the wheels spinning in the boy's head as he struggled to come up with the right answer. It was quite obvious that he was very anxious to please. Watching him, Lord Bainbridge realized this was hardly the time for such a game, but he couldn't help himself.

Then as if to remind both of them of the reality of their situation, to their ears came the sound of creaking timber and a great groaning noise as if something vital in the ship was threatening to come loose. Also, there could be heard above their heads the sound of many feet running madly down the boat deck.

"I've never been up in one of those new aeroplanes," the boy answered hurriedly. "I should like very much to do that."

"What else?" Lord Bainbridge asked.

The boy stared hard into the face of his inquisitor. "I've never loved anyone," he answered boldly, a hint of the flirt, probably not unintentional, in his eyes.

Lord Bainbridge smiled, more to himself than to the boy. "Yes of course," he said. He took the boy's arm, leading him quickly up the stairs and out onto the starboard side of the boat deck.

Here, Lord Bainbridge found things moving at a far more frantic pace than before. The deck was crowded with people, and no one now seemed reluctant to enter a lifeboat. Ushering the boy hurriedly along toward the bow, Lord Bainbridge could see that things were getting more desperate. Now, no one had any doubt about what was going to happen to the *Titanic,* and panic that had been bubbling just below the surface for so long began to appear on the faces and in the voices of the vast throng that crowded along the length of the boat deck.

They heard a number of screams, and when they paused a moment to seek their source, they saw that a woman, in her attempt to enter a lifeboat, had misjudged her step and somehow fallen between the lifeboat and the side of the ship. She was in grave danger of either being crushed between the boat and the ship or falling down into the water still many feet below. Finally, someone managed to grab her by the ankle and pull her back onto the deck. So terrified had she become by her ordeal, she brushed off the hands that were about to help her make another attempt to get into the lifeboat and rushed away dissolved in tears of hysteria.

At his side, Lord Bainbridge saw the young boy shudder and let out a little gasp of horror. Lord Bainbridge quickly moved them on. They passed the ship's orchestra still playing gay ragtime in front of the entrance to the forward grand staircase. Their efforts, while perhaps heroic, seemed a little out of place to Lord Bainbridge who thought that they should have been helping to get more people away in the boats rather than playing lively tunes when no one was certainly in the mood for dancing.

As they neared the location of boat No. 1, the crowds thinned out, and there appeared to be no great commotion around this boat as there were around the other lifeboats. But then when they arrived at the boat, Lord Bainbridge could see that, while there was no commotion, there seemed to be some sort of confrontation going on around it.

Tom was the first to greet him. "Thank God, you're here," he said, gripping his arm. "I was scared you wouldn't make it back in time." He eyed the teenage boy beside Lord Bainbridge for a moment.

"Another life saved," Lord Bainbridge explained in answer to Tom's curiosity. "What's going on?" he asked quickly, looking at those gathered around the lifeboat.

"I'm afraid we have a situation," Tom said.

"What kind of a situation?" Lord Bainbridge asked.

But it was Alfred, not Tom, who answered him. "That idiot in the boat thinks he's in charge," Alfred said, pointing to a man standing up in the lifeboat.

Lord Bainbridge had to take a couple of steps toward the lifeboat before he recognized the man to whom Alfred was referring. It was the bodyguard of the American woman, and he was holding a gun in his hand, which at that moment was pointed directly at Alfred.

"Well, go ahead and shoot me," Alfred taunted him, "though I doubt you've got the balls to do it!"

"What's all this about?" Lord Bainbridge asked, catching a quick glimpse of Elaine's anxious face from the lifeboat. He also noticed the young Asian man standing off to one side, watching the scene with a definite smile on his lips.

"These two," Alfred explained, pointing to the bodyguard and the American woman who sat silently beside him in the lifeboat, "came along and climbed into the boat as if they owned the damn thing. Then the idiot with the gun ordered the boat to be lowered immediately. I told him, in no uncertain terms, that we weren't going anywhere until you returned." He grinned and shrugged. "I'm afraid things got rather ugly after that, and there was some name calling."

"Sodomite!" the bodyguard yelled at Alfred from the lifeboat.

"Takes one to know one, old chap," Alfred shot back but now grinning as if the whole scene was nothing more than an amusing charade.

Glancing at the American lady in the boat clutching her little dog, Lord Bainbridge noted that she was sitting as silent and still as a statue, never uttering a word or even lifting her eyes to acknowledge the presence of another person. Lord Bainbridge recalled that earlier in the evening when they had seen her in the restaurant, Count Fraboli had likened her to the Sphinx. And now as he looked at her sitting so still in the lifeboat like that ancient Egyptian wonder, her face gave not a hint of what she was thinking. But though she remained mute, there was no doubt on who's behalf and at who's command the bodyguard was acting. Lord Bainbridge wondered what had happened to the rest of her servants. Obviously, she must have left them behind to fend for themselves.

He noticed that the young junior officer, who should have taken charge of this potentially explosive situation, was standing motionless, a rather confused look on his face. He apparently lacked either the will or the courage to act, and he seemed to have forgotten his own gun, which Lord Bainbridge had seen him slip into the pocket of his coat.

But then almost immediately, there came upon them someone who definitely was in a mood to take charge. The ship's officer whom the junior officer had identified to Lord Bainbridge as First Officer Murdoch came thrashing along the deck toward them. He seemed in a foul mood, fueled no doubt by the desperation he must have felt over their terrible predicament. When he saw them all standing about in what looked to be confusion, he turned on the junior officer.

"Why is this boat still here?" he yelled into the younger man's face.

The poor junior officer, quite unprepared for this attack, stammered out an incoherent reply of which only the word *waiting* could be understood.

"Waiting for what?" Murdoch barked.

"Waiting for more passengers," the junior officer managed to squeak out. "The boat's not even half full."

"She's full enough," the first officer told him, softening his tone a bit. He gestured to Lord Bainbridge and the others still standing on the deck. "Get these people into the boat and yourself as well and lower away," he commanded.

"Yes, sir," the junior officer responded crisply, snapping to attention.

It was at this rather inopportune moment that Marco came puffing along the deck toward them, puffing both because he was hurrying and because he was carrying what looked to be a traveling valise that, judging by his struggle, must have been heavily loaded.

In spite of the fact that the young Italian had obviously been involved in a bit of looting, Lord Bainbridge found it amusing that Marco had apparently grabbed everything he could lay his hands on, like a kid in a candy shop, with no regard to worth. For all Marco knew, and this was the part Lord Bainbridge found so amusing, he could be struggling with a bag of worthless junk.

But First Officer Murdoch was certainly not amused. He stood sternly beside the lifeboat, his hands on his hips. When Marco approached the boat, he eyed him suspiciously. "Where do you think you're going?" he demanded.

Startled by this brisk inquiry, the answer to which seemed rather obvious to the simple Italian boy he was, Marco shrugged his shoulders and offered Murdoch one of his trademark smiles that, at least in the past, he had used to great advantage.

Watching the scene unfold, Lord Bainbridge knew this was one time when Marco's blatant use of his charms would fail to move the man confronting him.

"What's in the bag?" Murdoch asked.

"Everything I own in the world," Marco responded, avoiding his look.

"Get rid of it!" the first officer told him abruptly. "There's no room in the boats for luggage of any kind."

Out of the corner of his eye, Lord Bainbridge noticed the bodyguard, now sitting quietly in the lifeboat, tighten his hold on the case he held in his own lap. Obviously, Lord Bainbridge concluded quite rightly, the case contained the American woman's much-prized and much-discussed collection of jewelry.

"But there's plenty of room in the boat," Marco protested.

"Not for this, there isn't!" Murdoch snapped, grabbing the valise out of Marco's startled hands and effortlessly tossing it over the side of the ship.

There were audible gasps from a number of those both in the lifeboat and standing on the deck as if this little incident, more than anything else that had happened to them up to this moment, had finally brought home the seriousness of their situation. When the first officer flung that traveling valise over the side of the ship, he tossed with it the hopes of many that things would turn out all right, that the *Titanic* would somehow right itself and remain afloat, at least until help arrived.

As for Marco, a fierce look came into his face, the look of an angry jungle cat who has just had his kill snatched away. And for a moment, it looked as if he might actually attack the first officer. But as it always was with all of Marco's emotions, this one quickly vanished and was replaced by an easy smile. Then he shrugged, and contorting his ridiculously long adolescent limbs into an awkward position, he leaped into the lifeboat.

At that moment from the bridge above them, Captain Smith hollered down through his megaphone. "Mr. Murdoch, get that boat away at once!"

Stung by this obvious reprimand from his superior, the first officer leaped into action, venting his own verbal abuse down the chain of command to the poor junior officer. Orders were shouted, and those passengers who were still standing on the deck were hustled into the lifeboat along with the three crewmen to man the boat and the junior officer to take charge. Then at last, the lines were fed out, and lifeboat No. 1 began its descent toward the dark water below them, which on its own was rising steadily to meet them.

"Stay close to the ship!" Murdoch yelled down to them. Then he called out his final words to the junior officer. "Give my best to all those at home!"

As they dropped toward the sea, Lord Bainbridge looked up at the first officer standing on the boat deck, and he could tell by the expression on the man's face that he wanted desperately to join them in the boat. But Lord Bainbridge knew that Murdoch was too much of an officer and a gentleman to do such a thing. And he was also certain that having been, as the junior officer had said, the man who drove the ship into the iceberg, Murdoch would not survive this night. No matter what happened, one way or another he would die; either the cold waters of the North Atlantic or his own hand would take his life.

Felling a shiver run down his spine, Lord Bainbridge turned to Tom sitting beside him. "We'll make it," he assured him. And in the darkness, their hands met and clasped for a brief moment.

But there were soon new problems for boat No. 1. The seamen on the deck above lowering the boat somehow managed to mishandle the falls, and the lines became tangled, which resulted in first one end of the boat and then the other being dipped with a jerky, uneven motion. This of course was most unnerving to the boat's passengers, many of whom cried out in alarm.

"Holy Mother of God, they're going to drown the lot of us!" the Englishwoman screamed in terror while the Middle Eastern women began to shriek with equal horror.

Only the American woman refused to exhibit any reaction. She remained a stoic statue, undoubtedly subscribing to the code of behavior practiced among many of the well-to-do, which mandated that any excessive show of emotion was an unforgivable breach of etiquette no matter what the circumstances. Marco, however, was far less well-bred, and his screams of fear were among the loudest.

But finally, the crewmen above managed to get the lines straightened out, and when the lifeboat at last hit the water, it touched down with nothing more than a gentle splash. But then a new problem presented itself. The falls had been so twisted that when the boat hit the water there wasn't enough slack for them to release the boat. Lifeboat No. 1 remained tied securely to the *Titanic*.

New pandemonium broke out in the boat as the crewmen struggled to release the lines. Their efforts were hampered by the darkness, and they kept bumping into each other and trampling on the passengers seated among them. The night air echoed with a mix of oaths and apologies.

"The ship will take us down with her if we don't get free!" one of the crewmen predicted ominously.

"We need a knife!" the junior officer called out.

Incredibly, none of the crewmen had a knife on their person. But Tom had, and he quickly handed it over to the junior officer. The officer managed to cut the line in the stern of the boat, and then he passed the knife back to one of the crewmen in the bow who used it with equal success.

Instantly, they were freed, and a cheer went up as their boat rowed away from the side of the ship. In all the excitement at their good fortune, neither Tom nor anyone else noticed that his knife was not returned to him. Following the instructions of the first officer, they rowed out only a short distance from the ship. And there, the crewmen laid on their oars, and they waited.

The junior officer had not been idle while he was waiting for Lord Bainbridge and the others to return from their journey below decks. He had his men stock the boat with water and loafs of bread as well as blankets, which were now handed out to the women and children for it was frightfully cold. He had also secured a box of small distress rockets and a lantern, which he had one of the crewmen light and set in the center of the boat.

The rockets, he explained, they would set off to attract the attention of the rescue ships when they arrived. He also took pains to assure them that a number of ships were already on their way to pick them up.

"Do you think they'll be here soon?" Elaine asked anxiously.

"By dawn I would think, " the officer answered nervously.

"Before the *Titanic* sinks?" another ventured.

The junior officer swallowed hard. "Hopefully," he responded softly.

Then one of the crewmen at the bow spoke up, his tone was contemptuous. "They'll never get here in time!" he said. "She'll go soon." He jerked a thumb back toward the ship. "Look how queer she looks."

And every eye in the lifeboat turned to gaze back at the *Titanic*. She did look queer indeed. She was dramatically down at the bow, and her stern had lifted high enough out of the water to expose her huge propellers. But in spite of this rather unnatural posture, the ship still retained a sense of solidarity and security. Her enormous size and tons of steel led many of those in the lifeboats scattered around her in the water to still believe she was unsinkable. In addition, her decks were still brilliantly lit as was nearly every porthole. She was in fact ablaze with light from bow to stern as if she were hosting some festive party or other gala. There was music too. The gay strains of ragtime from the ship's orchestra, still toiling away despite all that was going on around them, drifted out to the boats across the calm still water like a concert under the stars.

But there were other more ominous signs that indicated that despite her mammoth size and structure, the *Titanic* was doomed. They were so close to the ship that Lord Bainbridge could actually see the water pouring into the big square ports on C deck and sweep around the heavy period furniture. His own stateroom was only one deck higher, and he knew for certain it too would soon be flooded.

While all other eyes were still glued on the ship, Lord Bainbridge glanced around the lifeboat at his fellow passengers. While they were all still transfixed by the sight of the mighty, but ultimately frail, leviathan before them, he took a silent roll call of his companions. In the green light from the lantern, the faces of his compatriots glowed with an eerie, lifeless shine. He was instantly reminded of the faces of the wax figures he had seen on a visit to Madame Tussaud's famous wax museum. Lady Bainbridge had taken him and his older sister there once on a rare family outing when he was still quite young. He could still remember that the visit had frightened him much more than it had entertained him.

Facing him and sitting in the very stern of the lifeboat, where he had control of the boat's steering tiller, was the junior officer. Lord Bainbridge's heart went out to him, for he knew here was a poor young man thrust into a situation far beyond his capabilities. Lord Bainbridge was certain that even if he had been a man with thirty years experience at sea behind him, he still would have been unable to cope with this calamity. And despite the fact he tried to hide it, there was almost a look of terror on his face.

Tom sat beside Lord Bainbridge and, though their hands were no longer clasped as they had been for the brief time the lifeboat was in total darkness, their thighs were pressed intimately together, providing each of them with a small measure of comfort. Though he was sure that Tom also could not help but notice the water pouring into the ship's ports on C deck, Lord Bainbridge knew his young friend was not thinking about his own cabin or even Lord Bainbridge's. Undoubtedly, Tom's thoughts were dwelling on the poor people, especially the women and children, who were still, for whatever reason, below decks. Glancing over his shoulder at those sitting behind him, Lord Bainbridge's eyes first fell on Alfred. He noticed that the Englishman had a scowl on his face as he stared back at the ship as if he were blaming the *Titanic* itself for the disaster that had befallen them. But Lord Bainbridge was sure Alfred's facial expression had more to do with his row with the bodyguard than the coming demise of the ship before them. Whatever had taken place between them earlier in that other lifeboat still rankled between them like hot coals that could not be put out even in the midst of a catastrophe such as the one they all now found themselves facing. Close to Alfred sat the Englishwoman with her four children gathered tightly around her. One of the youngsters, a girl of about five, appeared to have taken quite a fancy to Alfred, and one of her tiny hands tightly clutched his arm despite his numerous attempts to dislodge it. The other mothers in the boat, the three Middle Eastern women, were now much more subdued. Stilled was their incessant chatter as they sat holding their babies, murmuring only the occasional soothing word of comfort. A little further back in the boat were to be found the American lady and her bodyguard. The bodyguard still had the same ugly look on his face that Alfred bore, and it was obvious that it wouldn't take much to set him off again.

His companion continued to maintain her rigid, unbending composure as she, like everyone else, stared back at the ship. The only indication that the lady was feeling any emotion at all could be seen in the way she gripped the little dog tightly in her lap, so tightly in fact that the poor creature squirmed to get free. The dog had also attracted the attention of the four English children, who found it more fascinating than all the drama that was going on around them. That they ached to pet it could be seen on their eager faces as they stared longingly at it. But Lord Bainbridge could tell, by the frozen frown on the American woman's face, that she would have thrown her precious pet overboard into the frigid Atlantic before she would let one of those steerage urchins put their grubby little hands on it.

Shifting his eyes toward the middle of the boat, Lord Bainbridge noticed the old Polish couple. He could tell they were frightened, but they were clinging to each other, and such intimacy, he reasoned, must have offered them great comfort. He envied them their freedom to display their affection, their love for each other. And he wished with all his heart that he and Tom had that same freedom. For at that moment, as the great ship before them let out a mighty groan, the sound of steel being torn and twisted as if the ship were crying out to protest her own coming death, Lord Bainbridge wanted nothing so much as to grab hold of Tom and cling to him. So great was this desire, he had to shove his hands deep into the pockets of his jacket to keep them from acting on the emotions that were surging through him. As he continued to let his glance roam over his fellow passengers, Lord Bainbridge spotted Elaine sitting toward the bow of the lifeboat. Her eyes were also on the *Titanic* but, as if she had felt his eyes on her, she turned and looked at him, offering him a weak smile as if to assure him she was all right. Then her attention returned to the ship. Marco had chosen a seat beside her and was chatting animatedly to her. Apparently, either sex was fair game when the young Italian set out to charm, Lord Bainbridge concluded. But even from a distance, he could tell Elaine was paying little notice to Marco, and he also was certain she was not one to succumb to his flaunted appeal. *Unlike himself,* Lord Bainbridge thought with a rueful smile and shake of his head. Also near the bow was the young Asian man. He sat very still, looking quite elegant, quite regal, smoking a cigarette. But even in the small confines of their lifeboat, he appeared alone, friendless, an outcast. Beside him was the teenage boy Lord Bainbridge had found weeping on the staircase. The boy nodded to him and even flashed a grin, obviously happy to be off the ship, happy to be alive.

At the very bow of the boat were the crewmen. Two of them were having a very intense conversation between them, often gesturing toward the stricken *Titanic.*

Lord Bainbridge wondered what they were discussing. As if he had read his mind, the junior officer spoke up. "They're talking about me," he said to Lord Bainbridge. "They don't think I'm fit to be in charge of this boat."

241

"The officer on deck put you in charge," Lord Bainbridge reminded him.

The young man shrugged. "That don't mean squat to them. We're out on the open sea now, and it's might, not rank that counts."

"Stand your ground," Lord Bainbridge advised him though he could see the uncertainty that filled the young officer's face. It was one thing to be doubted by others, but it was when you doubted yourself that your real troubles began.

It was at that moment that one of the crewmen called out from the bow, "We're much too close to her. She'll take us down with her when she goes!"

"The suction will be terrible!" one of his mates agreed.

The junior officer glanced nervously at Lord Bainbridge. "They could be right, you know. She's liable to drag everything down with her," he said.

"We need to pull away now!" the first sailor called out.

"The officer told us to remain close to the ship," Tom put in.

Lord Bainbridge nodded. "Yes, but perhaps we should pull a short distance away just to be safe."

The officer quickly agreed and gave orders to man the oars. Since they had only three crewmen most of the other men in the boat helped with the rowing while the officer took the tiller. Even Tom gave a hand although he obviously felt it was the wrong thing to do. They rowed out a few yards farther from the ship.

"This isn't far enough!" one of the crewmen protested as they came to a stop.

"It'll do for now," the junior officer said, for once taking a stand.

But the sailor wasn't pleased. He cursed and spit over the side of the boat. "It's our lives now, not there's!" he thundered, pointing back to the ship.

Lord Bainbridge caught the eye of the young officer, and even in the poor light, he could see a shudder pass through his body.

Chapter XII

Later, Lord Bainbridge and the others in his lifeboat would not be able to recall how long after they pulled away from the *Titanic* did she go down. While to some it seemed an eternity, to others it seemed to happen in the blink of an eye. But though they had rowed some yards away from the ship, they were still close enough for all of them to bear witness to all that was happening on board the ship. It was like, one would later remark, having a box seat at some terrifying yet mesmerizing theatrical event. They could see the people getting into the last of the lifeboats. It appeared from their distance to be an orderly evacuation until they heard two sharp cracks, reports that rang out across the water with sharp and biting clarity.

"What was that sound?" Elaine asked, nervously glancing around at the others in the lifeboat.

"Gunshots," one of the crewmen answered.

"What's happening?" the Englishwoman inquired with equal alarm.

"Most probably, I'd wager they're shooting down the foreigners so they don't rush the boats," the crewman told her.

"You don't know that for sure," Tom said, aroused to righteous anger.

The sailor ignored him and continued with his explanation. "Likely as not, it's the Italians causing all the ruckus," he said. "They're the worst of the foreign lot."

Elaine looked over to Marco. "Doesn't it bother you to have him insult you in that way?" she asked.

Marco shrugged. "Being Italian has never done anything special for me. But soon, I'll be an American," he said with a wide grin, "that's all that counts."

"Talk about going from bad to worse," the crewman snorted with contempt.

"Hold your tongue!" the bodyguard snapped, swinging around to glare angrily at the sailor while the American lady at his side stared ahead in stoney silence, not a muscle twitching.

How absurd this all is, Lord Bainbridge thought. *Even here in the dead of night in a lifeboat in the middle of the Atlantic Ocean, we can find time for a petty ethnic quarrel.* He was quite prepared to tell them all to be still when suddenly there came to their ears a series of dull booms not unlike cannon shots.

"Her boilers are exploding!" someone cried out excitedly.

"No, them's her watertight bulkheads giving way," one of the crewmen corrected. "It won't be long know," he predicted.

Tom nudged Lord Bainbridge. "All the lifeboats are gone," he said quietly. Lord Bainbridge let his eyes sweep down the length of the *Titanic's* boat deck. It was true; all the boats were gone, at least on this, the starboard, side of the ship and most probably from the port side as well. "There must be hundreds, maybe even a thousand, people still on board," Tom added. He turned his head so that he was staring into Lord Bainbridge's face. "A thousand people," he repeated in a whisper.

They were so close, Lord Bainbridge could feel Tom's breath on his cheek and he could see the misery on his face and in his eyes. He knew in his heart that Tom wished he was back on the ship, and another, anyone at all, was in his place in the lifeboat. For so deep was his sense of honor that he would have most willingly sacrificed his life for another, but he could not abide the fact that perhaps another had been sacrificed so that he might live.

Among those thousand that Tom spoke about, Lord Bainbridge knew Alonzo and Lucianna Fraboli were surely included. He knew their resolve to die together would not be broken and that they were probably still seated in the smoking room even now as the walls of the room came crashing in. He knew if they were not already dead, they would be soon. He could only hope that Madame Renoir and her son had managed to find their way into one of the remaining lifeboats. And he silently cursed once again the ignorant ship's officer who had stopped Sebastian from entering the boat. He also chastised himself for being so concerned about Tom that he hadn't taken the time to escort the Renoirs over to the other side of the ship and seen them safely into a boat. His one comfort was that dear Maude had got away safely.

Those in the lifeboat remained silent for a few moments, looking back at the *Titanic* over which, now that all the boats were gone, there seemed to settle a curious calm. They could see the people on the upper decks, most seeming to cluster inboard, obviously keeping as far away from the rails as possible.

Then a single voice spoke up, and it had been so quiet among them that it startled them almost as much as the man's words.

"I seen the iceberg coming right for us!"

The speaker was one of the crewmen in the boat. The one who had taken no part in the debate regarding how far away from the ship they should row. In fact, he had up until that moment not uttered a single word. But now he seemed to have discovered a great need to communicate, and the words poured out of him as swiftly as the sea was now pouring into the doomed ocean liner before them.

"We was up in the crow's nest, my mate and me," the crewman began. "It was as cold as blazers with the wind whistling through the rigging. The officer on the bridge had told us to keep a sharp lookout for ice. But we didn't have any binoculars, so I don't know how they expected us to see anything."

To Lord Bainbridge this last fact sounded quite incredulous, and he had to speak up. "You didn't have any binoculars in the crow's nest?" he asked.

The crewman stared back at him down the length of the lifeboat and shook his head. "Nope, none."

"But for heaven's sake, man, why not?" Lord Bainbridge persisted.

"Don't know," the crewman answered. "I spoke to one of the officers before we sailed, told him we didn't have no glasses. He said there were none for us, and perhaps we could pick up a pair when we reached New York."

"Unthinkable!" Lord Bainbridge muttered to Tom.

"There was a haze that came up too," the sailor added, "just before we hit the berg."

This fact, Lord Bainbridge found less believable. He had heard no one else speak of there being any haze, and he himself, having glanced out at the ocean a number of times after he had reached the boat deck, had seen no sign of any.

"I remember my mate saying, 'If we can see through this, we'll be lucky,'" the crewman went on, once again caught up in his story. "The berg came out of the haze without warning and was almost upon us before we saw it. I rang three bells and picked up the phone to the bridge." He paused a moment, wetting his lips anxiously as if he were searching for something, something further to defend the position he had obviously chosen to take. "The bridge seemed to take forever to answer, and when they finally did, the officer on the other end seemed hardly to care as if I had called to give him nothing more urgent than a bloody weather report." He snorted with contempt. "The fool even thanked me for calling. My mate and I held our breath as the ship slowly turned, and the berg glided by on the starboard side. As my mate said, 'It looked like a pretty close shave!'" He looked up to see all those in the lifeboat, even the American lady for once, with their eyes glued on him. He swallowed hard and hung his head under their scrutiny. "We had no glasses," he muttered. "We should have had glasses."

"But surely even without glasses and in a haze, you should have been able to see the berg before it was practically on top of us," Alfred insisted.

The crewman looked up at him for a quick moment. "We had no glasses," he repeated for a final time. And then he turned away and said no more.

One of his fellow sailors, obviously seeking to comfort him, handed him a cigarette. Lord Bainbridge noticed the lookout's hand shake as he took it. Undoubtedly, the man was racked with guilt over his failure to spot the iceberg sooner, and in his guilt, he had tried to blame everything else—the lack of binoculars, the mysterious haze, the slow response, and the seeming, if only momentary, indifference of those on the bridge—for his failure.

All three of the crewmen had lit up cigarettes, and their smoke drifted over the others in the lifeboat. To Lord Bainbridge the smell of cigarette smoke was comforting, reminding him of time spent in other places, places that had been filled with the manly smell of tobacco smoke.

But not everyone in the boat was similarly comforted. After a few whispered words with the American woman, the bodyguard spoke up. "The lady requests that you do not smoke," he said to the sailors. "At a time like this, she feels it is hardly proper conduct."

Apparently, Lord Bainbridge thought to himself, the lady hadn't noticed the Asian man smoking earlier, or more probably, she hadn't noticed him at all.

The three crewmen were not impressed with the bodyguard's announcement. Though they made no formal reply, they muttered a few choice words to each other and laughed among themselves while continuing to enjoy their smokes.

Flushed with anger that he was being ignored and thus embarrassed as well, the bodyguard got to his feet and once again pulled out his gun. "Don't make me shoot those cigarettes out of your mouths!" he threatened.

Various women in the boat cried out, and Marco, being no great hero, cowered and tried to hide under his seat. But the sailors were still defiant, and they made no move to put out their cigarettes.

"I'm warning you!" the bodyguard told them, aiming his gun.

"Do something," Lord Bainbridge said to the young officer in front of him. "You've got a gun, use it! Stop this!"

But the young officer appeared paralyzed with fear, or at least indecision, as he sat there gripping the tiller and staring blankly straight ahead.

It was Alfred who did take action. He stood up in the boat, and with his umbrella handle, he tapped the bodyguard, who was standing with his back to him, on the shoulder. The bodyguard whirled around to face him, almost losing his balance.

"I think we've had just about enough of your theatrics," Alfred told him. And before the bodyguard could react, he whacked him hard on the hand with his umbrella handle, and the gun was sent flying over the side of the lifeboat and into the water.

"You bastard!" the bodyguard fumed. But stripped of his weapon, he was no longer a threat, and he knew it. So after glaring at Alfred a moment longer, he slunk back down in his seat beside the American woman, who gave him a distinct look of contempt and then turned away from him with indifference.

"Well done," Lord Bainbridge said to Alfred as he resumed his own seat.

"I had to do something," Alfred responded. "He was really starting to annoy me."

This little dramatic episode as well as the lookout's tale had, for a few minutes, taken everyone's attention away from the ship, which loomed in the background like a great tragic painting, an epic on canvas that was about to depict Dante's *Inferno* come to life.

It was Elaine's cry that brought their eyes back to the ship. "Dear God, look!" she called out, standing up in the boat and pointing to the ship.

Everyone strained to see what had so alarmed the young woman, many also getting to their feet to obtain a better view. "What did you see? What happened?" someone asked her.

Elaine turned her face back to those beside her in the boat. "I saw someone fall or jump from the deck into the water," she answered.

"There goes another!" one of the crewmen hollered. And suddenly, it seemed as if there were hundreds of people leaping or diving off the ship. The reason for their departure from the ship was easy to uncover, for those in the lifeboat could see that the *Titanic* was beginning her death throes.

"Please, everyone, sit down now and remain calm. If you all stand up at once, you'll surely capsize us," the junior officer warned, having found his voice at last, if not his courage.

They all took their seats in the lifeboat and sat there as quietly as children in school with their eyes riveted on the ship and the tragedy that was taking place right before them.

Amazingly, they could still hear the music from the ship's orchestra. It came to them across the ocean in bits and pieces, fading in and out as if someone was fiddling with a switch on a wireless. But there was enough of it for Lord Bainbridge to recognize a lively ragtime tune. As it often was at times like this, other people heard and saw things differently even though they shared the same vantage point. Behind him, the Englishwoman drew her children closer, and Lord Bainbridge heard her speak to them. "Bow your heads in prayer now, my little darlings, for they're playing a hymn." And she actually sang along with the music, her voice soft and sweet, her words a plea to a gentle God in time of peril.

Then the music stopped abruptly, not as if the piece being played had finished, but rather as if it had been interrupted. Those in the lifeboat could see why because at that moment, the water swept over the bridge and rolled along the boat deck. Incredibly, although the stern of the ship was now rising like an elevator, the ship's lights continued to burn brightly. They could see the passengers and crew left on board clinging like little swarms of bees to anything that would hold them—deckhouses, cargo cranes, and hatch covers. Then as the slant of the deck became steeper, they could be seen sliding down the deck and into the water. They could hear their terrified screams as they watched them fall singularly, in pairs, often holding hands, and in groups.

It occurred to Lord Bainbridge, as he watched the appalling spectacle unfolding before his eyes, that to the poor souls now tumbling down the boat deck and into the frigid water, it no longer mattered who or what they were. All distinctions between passengers and crew, all discriminations between classes and nationalities had vanished. And in these terrible moments, all that would matter, all that would count, would be strength and will. Of all those poor unfortunates, only the strong and the lucky would survive.

Turning to Tom at his side, Lord Bainbridge sought his glance, the comfort of his face. But Tom's attention was glued on the ship, and he did not feel Lord Bainbridge's eyes on him. A single tear glistened on his cheek, caught in the light from the million stars that shone above them. That tear, that single tear, touched Lord Bainbridge's heart, and to him, it represented all the tears that were shed that night and all the nights to come.

As the *Titanic's* stern continued to ascend, those in the boat became aware of an ever increasing roar as everything movable inside the vessel—glassware and dishes, carefully packed trunks, every unattached chair, table, sofa, and bed—came free and began to slide toward the bow, tearing out walls and smashing through partitions. To Lord Bainbridge, it sounded like the roar a steam train makes as it picks up speed and pulls out of the station.

However, this sound was soon dwarfed by another. With a great tearing of metal, the forward funnel of the ship broke free of its restraints, tearing the planking from the deck and, with a terrible groan, toppled over the starboard side of the ship and into the water. When it hit the water, a million sparks shot up into the sky like tiny rockets, while the wash from the funnel's splash pushed lifeboat No. 1 farther away from the *Titanic*.

"Oh, those poor people," the Englishwoman murmured, for it was obvious that when the great funnel struck the water it also fell on many of the swimmers who were thrashing about in desperation.

Once again, Lord Bainbridge turned to look at Tom. But the young Irishman's face was still turned toward the ship. The tear still glistened on his cheek, or perhaps it was a fresh one.

The *Titanic's* lights, which up until now had miraculously continued to burn brightly, illuminating every deck, suddenly went out as if someone had pulled a switch. They came on again for a second and then went out again, this time for good. The ship's final act had begun.

The *Titanic*, "the ship that God himself could not sink," began to break in two. She was now almost perpendicular. "A giant black finger pointing toward the heavens," one survivor would elegantly put it later to an eager newspaper reporter. But the ship was unable to maintain this unnatural position, and shrieking with agony as her hull was subjected to stresses it was never designed to withstand, she tore apart between the third funnel and the place where the fourth funnel had been, her plates separating with a cracking sound like fireworks going off. The bow section almost immediately sank below the surface. While what was left of the ship, the stern section, settled back almost to an even keel. It appeared, unbelievably, that this part of the ship might stay afloat even though her decks were exposed from top to bottom as if the ship had been cut neatly in half with a giant knife.

"Blimey, she's going to stay afloat!" one of the crewman cried out.

But then as if to dispel his words, the stern section pivoted and began to sink. The broken end plunged into the water while the actual stern of the ship rose up in the water until it stood straight up. It remained that way, motionless, for a full minute, some said longer, and then it began to plunge into the water, picking up speed as it went as though it were rushing to catch up with the rest of the ship.

"Pull for your lives or we'll be sucked under!" the lookout cried out, fumbling for an oar.

But no one, not even his mates, rushed to help him, and the lifeboat stayed where it was. The others in the boat were probably too numbed by what they were seeing to react. But they needn't have bothered. For there was no suction, only a small ripple of water as the last of the great ship disappeared beneath the surface, a gulp no more. Not even a single wave disturbed the calm surface of the ocean.

"She's gone, lads," one of the sailors said. "That's the last of her."

Lord Bainbridge could not resist pulling out his pocket watch and checking the time by the light of the lantern. "It's 2:20," he announced quietly to the others.

It was at that moment that the bodyguard chose to make what could only be called one of the most thoughtless remarks perhaps ever spoken. Turning to the American woman sitting beside him, he sought to get back into her good graces. "There's all your beautiful priceless things gone forever," he said.

The American turned her long elegant neck and looked at the young man beside her. She shook her head and spoke the only words the others in the boat heard her speak all that night. "You ignorant bastard," she said to the bodyguard, the level of her contempt so great that the poor fellow fairly cringed in his seat. Then the lady turned her back on him and never once looked at him or spoke to him again. And it was obvious that their relationship had come to an abrupt conclusion there in the middle of the North Atlantic.

The water where the ship went down now became troubled, bubbles of air welled up from below, and debris—wooden doors, deck chairs, sections of paneling, furniture, and large pieces of cork—that the ship had discarded on her way to the bottom popped up and littered the surface. And in the midst of this wreckage, better than a thousand souls were thrashing about in the water and calling for help. Their cries sounded to some like a thousand crickets on a summer's night or to others like a thousand football fans cheering a goal. But they were neither. They were the cries of people dying, freezing to death in the twenty-eight-degree water.

The cries meant one thing to Tom, and he immediately turned to Lord Bainbridge. "We must go back and help those in the water," he said urgently.

Staring back at his anxious face, Lord Bainbridge didn't know how to respond. For at that moment, he was quite sure he must be dreaming. *God Almighty,* he thought, *can this really be happening? Isn't it just some horrible nightmare from which I must certainly awaken any moment? Perhaps if I close my eyes for a second and then open them again, it will all be swept away.*

Tom's suggestion had been overheard, and it spread quickly through the lifeboat to be greeted by an almost unanimous chorus of nays. The only one to immediately speak up in support of his suggestion was Elaine.

"We should go back," she told the others. "If we save but one life, it will have been worth it."

But no one agreed with her. Even the Englishwoman, who had appeared to be a good and compassionate woman, protested the idea of going back. "Think of my poor children, sir," she said.

Tom turned around to look at her. "Your children are safe, madam, we saw to that," he told her. "There are other less fortunate children out there drowning."

"Freezing to death is more like it," one of the sailors put in bluntly.

Tom once again appealed to Lord Bainbridge, who had remained silent. "Jeremy, people are dying just a few yards away. We can't ignore their cries," he pleaded.

At that instant, a single voice was heard to rise above the multitude of cries that seemed to mingle into an awful chorus, a requiem for the doomed. The single voice was a man's, and it kept repeating the same two words over and over, "My God! My God!" The words were repeated at least a dozen times, and then they stopped suddenly and were heard no more.

"What do you think we should do?" Lord Bainbridge asked the officer in the stern.

The young man wet his lips anxiously and then shook his head. "I'm not sure," he answered. "If too many of them tried to climb into the boat at the same time, we might get swamped and capsize, and then we'd all be lost. Perhaps if we wait a bit until they've thinned out," he suggested.

"Until they're all dead, don't you mean?" Tom asked with scorn.

"That's not fair, Tom," Lord Bainbridge remarked. "The officer's right, there would be a certain amount of risk involved if we did go back."

"That's a risk we have to take, Jeremy," Tom insisted. "Like the lady said if we save even one life, it will have been worth it."

"And if we lose all of ours in the effort, will it still have been worth it?" Lord Bainbridge asked.

"At least we would have tried," Tom answered. They stared back at each other for a long moment, the green light from the lantern casting an unflattering pallor over their faces while above their heads, a dome of a million stars winked and blinked and waited.

Finally, Lord Bainbridge heaved a great sigh and surrendered to Tom's will even though in his own heart and soul, despite the fact that he was a good man, he did so with much reluctance. It wasn't that he didn't want to try and save some of those struggling for their lives, it was merely that he wasn't prepared to give up his own life in the effort. But if they didn't go back and at least try, then he knew he and Tom would definitely have no future together. He knew that it was Tom's moral compass that was pointing them back to where the *Titanic* had gone down, but he also sensed that this was a test Tom was putting him to. And if he failed this test, he would lose him.

"We have to go back," Lord Bainbridge said quietly to the junior officer.

"They will never agree," the officer said, nodding toward the three crewmen in the bow of the boat who were muttering among themselves.

"Use your gun then, to persuade them," Lord Bainbridge urged.

The young officer shook his head. "I can't use my gun against my own crew," he responded. And he cast his eyes down toward the bottom of the boat, refusing to continue to meet Lord Bainbridge's gaze.

So it's up to me then, Lord Bainbridge thought, hardly pleased with that unfortunate reality. He stood up, and though he intended his words to be heard by everyone in the boat, it was to the three crewmen that he directed them.

"It is up to us to go back and help those in the water," he announced.

For a long moment, silence was the only response he received. Finally, one of the sailors spoke up, challenging his suggestion in a tone of thinly veiled sarcasm. "How do you figure that, Your Lordship?"

"We're the closest boat to them," Lord Bainbridge answered. Though in the darkness, it was hard to tell for sure. They could only make out two or three of the other lifeboats, and these were some distance from them and the site where the ship had gone down.

"We've no room to take on anymore!" the same crewman shot back.

"Nonsense!" Lord Bainbridge returned. "We've room for a dozen or so. It will be cramped, but we'll manage."

The three crewmen spent the next few minutes once again talking among themselves. Then one of them, not the one who had spoken up before but another, expressed his opinion. "By the time we get back there, they'll be nothing left but a bunch of stiffs," he said bluntly.

His words enraged Lord Bainbridge who knew quite well that as they sat there and bickered, more and more of those struggling in the water were dying. Men, women, and children were surrendering their lives while only a few yards away, those who could save them were debating whether or not to do so.

"We'll do it without you then!" Lord Bainbridge snapped at the sailors. "We've enough men in this boat to do the rowing," he added, glancing down at Tom who nodded vigorously in agreement.

"The women can row too. We're not helpless," Elaine insisted with that New World spirit that Lord Bainbridge found so infectious.

Surprisingly, Alfred too jumped right in. Standing up in the boat, he called for action. "Now, gentlemen and ladies, shall we all take hold of an oar and do as His Lordship has suggested?"

But the crewman who had first raised objection to going back was not quite done. He got to his feet and pulled the teenage boy up with him, wrapping his arm around the boy's throat in a tight grip. In his free hand, he flashed Tom's knife, which he had purposely not returned to its owner.

"If one finger is laid on an oar, then this lad here ain't gonna see the sun come up," the sailor threatened, inching the blade closer to the frightened boy's throat.

"But people are dying out there," Elaine protested.

"That ain't my concern, miss," the sailor with the knife said.

"If we go back, they'll swamp the boat, and we'll all drown." This observation was from the lookout. But as soon as he had spoken his words, he appeared to be ashamed of them, for he hung his head and took no further part in the debate.

For the second time that night, the teenage boy looked to Lord Bainbridge and pleaded for his life. "Please, sir, I don't want to die!"

"You're not going to die," Lord Bainbridge assured him. Then he turned to the young officer behind him. "Give me your gun," he whispered.

The officer shook his head. "I can't," he responded. He seemed on the verge of a complete breakdown. So unnerved by the events of the night, he was cowering in the stern of the boat as if he felt that if he made himself small enough and kept quiet, no one would notice him.

"Give me the gun!" Lord Bainbridge demanded, his voice still a whisper but his tone on the verge of anger.

Meekly, the officer withdrew the gun from the pocket of his coat and passed it to Lord Bainbridge.

With the gun in his hand, Lord Bainbridge swung back around and aimed it at the crewman holding the boy. "Release him immediately," he ordered.

The sailor was hardly fazed. Shifting his hold on the boy, he put the knife to his throat. "I'll cut his throat from side to side before you can fire that gun!" he boasted.

"Probably you will," Lord Bainbridge agreed. "But in the next instant, I'll put a bullet into your brain. I'm an expert marksman," he added, which was a lie for in truth, he had never held a gun in his hand before. And he was quite certain that if he was required to pull the trigger, he would most probably miss the crewman and very likely kill someone else in the boat instead.

"What the hell are you doing?" Alfred hissed at him in alarm, well aware of Lord Bainbridge's lack of firearm's expertise.

"You haven't the nerve," the crewman challenged, nervously shifting his position.

"Perhaps not the nerve, but I've got the will," Lord Bainbridge returned. He cocked back the hammer of the pistol, hoping no one was noticing the way his hand was shaking.

The sailor held his ground a moment longer, and then he gave in. He put down the knife and shoved the boy roughly away from him, causing the lad to fall into the bottom of the boat. "But we ain't lifting a finger to help you!" the sailor shouted back at Lord Bainbridge.

"Just don't get in our way," was Lord Bainbridge's curt response.

"Well done, Jeremy," Tom said, smiling approvingly at him.

"You knew it was all a bluff," Lord Bainbridge reminded him.

Tom nodded. "I knew."

"All right then, time to man the oars!" Alfred called out. He immediately took charge though Lord Bainbridge was quite certain that the only other time Alfred had ever been in an open boat before was one Sunday afternoon when, with a couple of young renters at their sides, they had gone rowing on Regent's Park Lake. This was a far different outing. But somehow Alfred got it all sorted out, pairing up the willing rowers two and three to an oar. Almost everyone pitched in save the three crewmen who, still grumbling their displeasure, slumped down in the bow of the boat and refused to have anything to do with their desperate recovery effort. The American lady also declined to be of service, an icy disdainful stare her response to Alfred's suggestion that she might like to have a go at pulling an oar. But the bodyguard, now greatly reduced in status with the loss of his gun and obviously the loss of his position as well willingly joined the effort. The Englishwoman too gave a hand, and she proved to be a hearty rower, matching the others stroke for stroke. Even the elderly Polish couple, determined not to be excluded, struggled with one of the heavy oars, and although their efforts were minimal, at least they tried. The young Asian man rowed beside the teenage boy, who once again owed his life to Lord Bainbridge. The three Middle Eastern women, though they probably had no idea what was going on, seeing the others take hold of the oars did likewise after laying their babies warmly wrapped in blankets gently in the bottom of the boat.

Lord Bainbridge watched as Marco, in an exaggerated display of Continental machismo, struggled to show Elaine how to properly handle an oar. But it was clear that he had no idea what he was doing, and it was Elaine who instructed him that the oar must first be secured in the oarlock.

Satisfied that his crew was prepared as much as possible for the ordeal ahead, Alfred slipped down beside Tom and took up an oar. And with the officer at the tiller steering and Lord Bainbridge still standing in the boat to act as lookout and also with the gun still in his hand, keeping his eye on the disgruntled sailors, lest they spring any last-minute trickery, they started off.

Slowly they made their way in spits and starts, oars bumping, jamming, and splashing in the glass-smooth water. It was a painful going, not only due to the inexperience of their oarsmen, but because it was so dark. With only the stars to guide them, their sense of direction quickly became confused, and they could not even determine the exact location where the *Titanic* had gone down. And there was something else that greatly hampered their efforts. Although it had been less than half an hour since the sinking, the hundreds of desperate voices crying out for help had, for the most part, become silent. The twenty-eight-degree water temperature had quickly taken its toll, first numbing hands and feet and then, after consciousness was lost, sapping the warmth from bodies and forcing hearts to give up their struggle. Now, all that could be heard was an occasional cry or moan like the call of some lonely seabird searching for its mate. The minutes that those in the lifeboat had spent debating over whether to return for those in the water had been precious moments, precious moments that had taken many lives.

Then suddenly without warning, they were in the middle of the wreckage and the bodies. Corpses bumped up against the sides of the boat and, in some places were so thick that those in the boat had to use their oars to gently push them away so that they could move on. Tom and a couple of others turned over several bodies, but they found no signs of life.

"It's too late, they're all dead," someone in the boat muttered.

Just then, a weak cry was heard calling out for help. "Over there!" Lord Bainbridge yelled, pointing in the direction the sound had come from. But though they rowed furiously, when they got there, they found nothing but more lifeless bodies. It went on like that for a while, a cry, a furious row toward the sound, but they never seemed to reach those crying out for help in time. It was like chasing a will-o-the-wisp or playing blindman's bluff in the middle of the ocean.

Suddenly, Tom cried out, "There's one here still alive!" He was leaning half over the side of the boat, gripping one of the bodies in the water. "I need help!" he added desperately. "He's heavy!"

Both Lord Bainbridge and Alfred rushed to lend a hand. But even the efforts of the three of them could not pull the man into the boat. It was only after the bodyguard came to their assistance that the four strong young men, using every ounce of their combined strength, managed to haul the man into the lifeboat.

The need for their strenuous effort was immediately obvious, for before them in the lifeboat, sat a man who must have easily weighed three hundred pounds, and this was when he was bone dry. In addition, he wore a heavy fur coat, which was completely waterlogged, over his life belt. This rather ingenuous mode of attire had not only kept him afloat but had also apparently helped him retain some of his body warmth. He sat there now before them looking like some giant water-soaked dog.

With a little start, Lord Bainbridge recognized the man as Benjamin Chamberlin, the American multimillionaire, and the same man he and Ronnie Standish had encountered at the swimming pool. Although he was wearing considerably more clothing than at their previous encounter. And as he sat there, trembling from the cold, blood dripping from his nose, he hardly looked to be the captain of industry that all the newspapers proclaimed him to be.

As Elaine help him out of his soggy fur coat and wrapped some dry blankets around him, her fellow American thanked his rescuers for their timely arrival. "I thought I was a goner for sure," he told them, his voice shaking. Then he proceeded to relate the details of his miraculous escape. "When the ship went down, I went down with it," he said. "Suddenly a blast of air or something blew me to the surface as if I'd been shot out of a cannon. I paddled around in the water for what seemed like hours. I guess it was all my fat that kept me insulated from the cold," he added. He chuckled at his own joke but then immediately grimaced in pain. "Must have broken a rib or two," he surmised. He looked around at the anxious faces peering intently at him. "I don't suppose any of you gents would have something to drink on you?" he asked. "I could sure use a little nip."

"Here, mate, try this," Alfred said, offering him his flask.

Chamberlin eagerly accepted it and took a long swallow. "Ah, that hit the spot! Warmed me to my very toes," he added, handing the flask back to Alfred. "Thank you, my good fellow."

"There's someone swimming in the water!" the Englishwoman called out from her side of the boat.

The others looked to see a swimmer making his way toward their boat. He was only a few yards away. "Come on, fellow! Come on, you can make it!" they encouraged him.

But the swimmer appeared to need no encouragement. His movements were smooth and effortless as if he were merely taking morning laps in a heated pool. When he reached the lifeboat, he held out a hand, and those on board easily pulled him into the boat, for this one was a lightweight.

He was also of Asian nationality, and he began to thank them profusely in his native tongue, his words pouring out of him like rain.

Alfred however was not impressed. "Just what we need in this boat, another Jap," he snarled.

The young Asian man, whom Lord Bainbridge had brought up from steerage, now spoke up for the first time. "He is Chinese," he said, pointing to the man they had pulled out of the water. "I am Japanese," he reminded Alfred, giving him a withering look of contempt.

"Like that makes a difference," Alfred muttered.

With a blanket thrown over his shoulders, their new arrival continued to chatter away while he eagerly took hold of an oar and lent them a hand.

They had rowed into an area especially dense with bodies, and Lord Bainbridge was leaning over the side to check a couple for signs of life when suddenly a pair of hands gripped the boat right under his nose. They were small hands like a woman's or a child's. A moment later, a head broke the surface, and he found himself staring into the face of a young boy. And in spite of the fact that the youngster's hair was plastered to his skull and he was spitting up sea water, Lord Bainbridge recognized him at once.

It was none other than the liftboy, the one with the impish smile who had so openly flirted with him not once but twice. Blinking the water out of his eyes and looking up at him, the boy actually smiled at him again as if he recognized him. But most likely he didn't, he was probably just glad that he was about to be rescued.

"I've got you, boy," Lord Bainbridge said, reaching out to grasp his hands. Their hands clasped for a second, and then before Lord Bainbridge could strengthen his grip, the boy slipped out of his hold as if he were too tired to hold on any longer. Lord Bainbridge leaned further over the side of the boat and tried frantically to grab onto him again, but the boy slipped beneath the surface, and the last sight of him Lord Bainbridge had was of his face still smiling up at him as he disappeared down into the depths of the ocean.

Lord Bainbridge slumped back into the boat, knowing the last glimpse of the boy's face as he slid beneath the water's surface would be an image that would haunt him all the rest of his days.

"You all right?" Tom asked him, noting the distressed look on his face.

"I've just seen a ghost," Lord Bainbridge answered.

"It's a time for ghosts," Tom agreed quietly.

They managed to pluck two more people from the frigid waters. Both of them were crewmen: one a steward they found clinging to a deck chair and the other, a stoker with badly burned hands.

Then just as those in the lifeboat had concluded sadly that there was no one else they could rescue, Tom appeared to have found another. He was leaning far over the side of the boat, struggling it seemed to reach someone in the water. Suddenly, he disappeared over the side of the boat. It happened so fast that no one actually saw it take place. One minute he was there, the next he was gone. It was as if some giant denizen from the deep had leaped up and snatched him.

"Tom!" Lord Bainbridge's scream was so passionate, so heartfelt, that if it had been any other time, anyone who heard it would have had no doubt how deep his feelings went for this young Irishman. But this was hardly the time for feelings to be analyzed or motives to be scrutinized. In the next instance, Lord Bainbridge himself leaped overboard.

"Oh my God, help them!" Elaine cried out.

The icy water pierced Lord Bainbridge's body like a thousand tiny blades, and it sucked the very life out of him, leaving him dazed and unresponsive as if he had received a blow on the head. He remained that way for some moments, numb almost to the point of unconsciousness and yet dimly aware of where he was and why he was there. His act, he knew, had been one of those spur-of-the-moment things, done without a thought beyond desperation. Tom was about to drown, for he had told him he couldn't swim, boasting that he "couldn't swim a stroke," as if that inadequacy was something to be proud of. The memory of why he had taken that plunge revived Lord Bainbridge and brought him back to himself as if he had been given an electric shock. Looking around, he spotted Tom only a few feet away, struggling desperately in the water, flaying his arms about and taking in mouths of water. With his strong swimming ability, Lord Bainbridge was able to quickly reach him. It was doubtful that Tom at first recognized him, seeing him only as another human being, a lifesaver. He grabbed onto him so tightly it hurt, and at the same time, he continued to thrash wildly about in the water.

"Stop struggling, I've got you!" Lord Bainbridge told him, afraid he would drag them both under.

But like most everyone when they find themselves thrown into an unknown and hostile environment, Tom was panicking, aware only that he was in great danger of dying.

"Tom, it's me, Jeremy!" Lord Bainbridge shouted into his ear. "It's all right now, I've got hold of you!"

For an instant, Tom looked into his eyes, and then he nodded, for he could not speak, and he stopped struggling and let himself relax against Lord Bainbridge's body.

Lord Bainbridge, meanwhile, had come to the startling realization that all his energy was gone. He had used it all up in his effort to reach Tom, and now he didn't have the strength to get them back to the boat. He felt a curious warmth come over his body and with it a sense of unperturbed detachment as if he was watching everything from very far away. He reasoned that he was probably starting to freeze to death, and he wrapped his arms tighter around Tom. *If this is to be it,* he thought to himself, *then so be it. I couldn't have asked for a sweeter death.* He buried his face in Tom's hair and prepared himself to die effortlessly and without a struggle and without shame.

Back in the lifeboat, there was chaos. Everybody was shouting orders, and the crewmen, who at last had been aroused from their indifference, were struggling with the oars as they tried to turn the boat around toward the two men in the water. But the three of them, one was a waiter, another a pantryman and, of course, the third was the lookout, had no more expertise rowing than did their civilian companions. So the boat lurched forward and then stopped suddenly as the oars got tangled up. There was much cursing and shouting. And at this rate, it appeared they would never reach those in the water, certainly not before they froze to death.

It certainly seemed that way to Alfred, who frantically began pulling off his overcoat, preparing to jump into the water himself. But before he could, there was a splash that happened so fast, those left behind in the lifeboat had to look to each other to see whom among had gone into the water.

Lord Bainbridge felt someone take hold of him and begin to propel him toward the boat. He kept a tight grip on Tom, and in a matter of moments, they had made it back to the boat where hands reached down and pulled them on board.

It wasn't until he was once again sitting in the boat that Lord Bainbridge looked up to see who it was who had rescued both he and Tom. His gaze met the eyes of the young Japanese man who, though he was dripping wet and shivering, didn't seem to have suffered much from his ordeal.

"Thank you," Lord Bainbridge said to him.

The young Japanese merely nodded, and then he moved away, back to the place in the boat where he had been sitting before. He graciously accepted a blanket from Elaine, and reaching into the pocket of his coat, which along with his elegant fedora he had left in the boat, he slipped out a cigarette. Then he draped the blanket over his shoulders, popped the fedora on his head and sat down. Lighting up his cigarette, he sat there smoking in silence.

Alfred threw a couple of blankets around Lord Bainbridge's own shoulders and handed him his flask. "That was a right stupid thing to do," he admonished.

But Benjamin Chamberlin had a far different take on his action. "That was a very brave thing you did, sir," he told Lord Bainbridge. And he also took pains to praise the efforts of the Japanese man as well.

I'm sure it would seem far less heroic to you if you knew the reason I did it, Lord Bainbridge thought to himself.

He looked over to where poor Tom, with his head over the side of the lifeboat, was spitting up the seawater he had ingested. The Englishwoman, her motherly instincts fully roused, was seeing to him.

The water all around them was still now—the desperate churning, the furious struggle for life had ceased. "There's no one else," someone in the boat remarked, and they all knew it was true. They had rescued only four out of the hundreds fighting for their lives in the water. Only four, but at least they had gone back.

Under the direction of Benjamin Chamberlin, who appeared to have taken charge of the boat, they picked up the oars and rowed away from the area where the great ship had gone down, an area choked with debris and bodies. They tried to go gently and hit as few of the dead as possible.

Finally, removed from the dreadful haunted site, they lay on their oars and rested, drifting on a calm sea so idyllic it was no more troubled than a mill pond.

They were one of twenty little boats scattered over five miles. Eighteen of the boats had been launched successfully. But the last two collapsibles had not got away in time, and they had floated off the boat deck. One landed in the water upside down, and the other was swamped. But both boats had people clinging desperately to them. Lord Bainbridge's boat was the only boat that seemed to have a light, so the other boats that they could see were visible to them as vague dark shapes outlined under a star-filled sky. Occasionally, a voice called out from one boat to another, usually a distraught passenger seeking a dear one left behind.

It was cold too, deathly cold, especially for those who had been in the water. The stoker with the badly burned hands lay in the bottom of the boat, floating in and out of consciousness, muttering disjointed words and phrases every time he came to. Only Chamberlin seemed entirely unaffected by either the cold or his immersion in the water. Perhaps it was his excess poundage that kept him insulated, but whatever it was, he seemed to have reserves of boundless energy and fortitude. He lent a vigorous hand to the rowing, and when that was done, he organized those in the lifeboat in a forthright manner that kept the weight in the boat, including his own, evenly distributed. His presence was a calming influence that comforted and forestalled any bickering or complaining that, given their circumstances, might have broken out. His whole take-charge and organizational manner impressed Lord Bainbridge, and reminded him once again of the way Americans seemed to know what to do or say and wasted no time in doing or saying it.

For himself, Lord Bainbridge was sure he had never been so cold, and he was unable to stop his teeth from chattering. Beside him, Tom, having rid himself of the last of his ingested seawater, was feeling somewhat better. Their bodies were pressed close together, both for warmth and comfort, and occasionally their hands would even clasp and hold. It was too dark for anyone else to notice their intimacy except for the officer who sat facing them.

But that poor young man was most probably too distraught to even notice their familiarity, and even if he did, he perhaps didn't understand it, or if he did, then he could only envy it, for at a time like this, he certainly could have used a little comfort of his own. Certainly, he must have felt himself a coward for his inaction, his failure to take charge of the boat as was his duty. He had been tested, and he had failed. Now, all he could do was hang his head and keep his eyes averted from any of the others in the boat who by chance might glance his way.

Tom nudged Lord Bainbridge and pointed up to the sky. "Look, a shooting star!" he said.

"There's another," Lord Bainbridge indicated, nodding toward a different part of the heavens.

As they watched the sky, there seemed to be at least a half dozen shooting stars streaking across the great black dome above them. "There's an old Irish legend that every time there's a shooting star, it means someone has died," Tom told him.

"Then," Lord Bainbridge said in a voice that was barely more than a whisper, "this night should be as light as day." Inside he felt numb. It was all just too much to grasp, too much to comprehend. Later, when everything had finally settled into place, then he knew he would weep for the friends he had lost and for the hundreds of others, known and unknown to him, who had perished. And until the day he died, he knew he would be forever haunted by the face of the little liftboy as he sank beneath the surface. It was an image he knew would return and return in his dreams. And it would be the image he would retain years later when other memories of the night *Titanic* went down had dimmed and some had even vanished altogether.

"I owe you my life, not once but twice," Tom said to him quietly.

Lord Bainbridge's eyes were still on the heavens, and despite the closeness of the one he loved, he never in his life felt so much alone as he did at that moment. Perhaps that was why he spoke his next words almost in an angry tone as if he wished to place distance between them, although, in truth, that was the last thing he wished to do. "Please don't feel that puts you under any obligation to me," he told Tom. He actually laughed. "You know, we're not one of those societies that believe if you save a man's life, then that life is yours to do with as you please."

"The only obligation I feel toward you is here in my heart," Tom returned.

Lord Bainbridge swung his eyes around to look at him. "My God," he marveled, looking into Tom's young face, "you've the soul and words of a poet. I should just put aside my pen and never write another word," he added.

Tom smiled and patted his pocket. "I have your book right here in my pocket. In all the confusion, it was the only thing I could think to grab," he confessed. "It was the only thing that seemed important at the moment." He shrugged. "I'm afraid it might be slightly waterlogged."

His words reminded Lord Bainbridge of the notes for his next novel. He was glad he had given them to Maude for safekeeping. *If we get out of this,* he promised himself, *I'm damn well going to write that book.*

The next few minutes passed in complete silence except for the soft sweet voice of one of the Middle Eastern women as she sung her baby a gentle lullaby. They all were lost in their own thoughts, some praying for their survival, others, like Lord Bainbridge, still too numb to truly comprehend what they had been through and thus letting their minds dwell on more trivial things, and others still wrestling with their own private demons over what they had done or had not done.

Into this silence broke the voice of one of the crewmen suddenly raised in near hysteria. "We're lost! We've no charts or compass, and we're hundreds of miles from land! Nobody will ever find us. We'll drift for days until we're all dead!"

At first, no one had an answer to his outburst, and they all sat in stunned silence, many believing his words had at least a ring of truth to them. It was Elaine who finally responded. First, she chastised the crewman and labeled him a coward in no uncertain terms. Then she pointed to the sky. "That's the North Star, isn't it," she told him. "We can follow it if we have to. So stop your bellyaching and act like a man!"

Benjamin Chamberlin immediately applauded her words. "You tell him, lass!" he barked. "Why, come daylight, we'll row all the way to New York if we have to."

"We may not have to do that," Lord Bainbridge said quietly. "I just saw a flash of light on the horizon."

"It's just another damn falling star," the same crewman grumbled.

Lord Bainbridge shook his head. "I don't think so."

"Lightning then," the crewman suggested, apparently determined to play the pessimist's role to the end.

Every eye in the boat scanned the horizon toward the southeast where Lord Bainbridge indicated he had seen the light. Their efforts were soon rewarded with another flash, followed by a far-off boom.

The unconscious stoker suddenly sat up in the bottom of the boat "That was a cannon!" he shouted.

But it was no cannon, and as the eastern horizon began to brighten with the first light of the new day, those in the lifeboat were able to make out first one masthead light, then another and, soon after that, a green running light.

"My God, it is a ship!" Chamberlin called out. "It's a ship coming hard for us and firing rockets! Quick," he said to the young officer send up those rockets you've got there!"

With trembling hands, the officer launched three of his green rockets up into the heavens. They burst above their heads like fireworks at some gala celebration and almost everyone in the boat let out a cheer as if they had just witnessed a most wonderful display.

Once again, Chamberlin took charge. "Come on now, we'll go to meet her!" he shouted. "Everyone grab an oar and put your backs into it. Row like the wind!"

And almost everyone did. Caught up in his exuberance and excitement and relieved that rescue was at hand, they all eagerly pitched in. Even the American lady for once let her icy composure slip away and took hold of an oar though, hardly surprising, her efforts were not remarkable.

A swell had come up, and the boat rose and fell with a gentle motion that somehow reminded Lord Bainbridge of a ride on a carousel he had once taken as a child. The faint glow of dawn began to steal across the sky, and the stars slowly dimmed and then went out one by one as if they were being blown out like candles.

Tom had slipped down to the bottom of the boat to try and revive the stoker, who had once again slipped into unconsciousness. He slapped his face a number of times. "Come on, brace up!" he urged the man. "There's a ship coming for us. We're saved!"

The stoker opened his eyes and tried to push Tom's hands away. "Who are you?" he asked. "What do you want of me?" Then he closed his eyes again, and Tom knew that this time, he was gone for good. He gently laid him back down on the floor of the boat.

The rescue ship must have spotted the green flares that the young officer had set off, for she made straight for them, pounding through the sea with remarkable speed until she reached them. Then she gradually reduced her speed, finally coasting up to them. As the ship approached, the wind picked up, and the sea became choppy.

"Are you all right?" an anonymous voice called down from the deck high above them.

The junior officer glanced quickly at Lord Bainbridge, and then he turned his attention to the ship. "Yes, we're fine," he called back. "Will you take us on board please?"

"Hang on!"

It was at that moment that the Englishwoman, obviously overcome by their ordeal, screamed out to those on the ship. "The *Titanic* has gone down with everyone on board!"

Lord Bainbridge instantly reprimanded her. "Be still!" he snapped.

The Englishwoman quickly recovered herself and immediately apologized for her lapse.

A few feet above their heads, a gangway door opened in the side of the ship, and lines were thrown down to them, which the crewmen in the lifeboat made fast. Then a rope ladder was swung down and also secured.

"Women and children first!" someone from above instructed.

"Can you manage it?" Lord Bainbridge asked as Elaine stepped onto the ladder.

"Like walking up a flight of stairs," she assured him with a smile.

"Steady the ladder, she's a lightweight," one of the crewmen from the ship warned as Elaine began her climb. Lord Bainbridge watched her journey until she tumbled safely into the arms of one of the ship's crew.

The Englishwoman was also keen to have a go at the ladder, but there was a problem. "What about my poor little ones? They can't possibly make that climb," she said to Lord Bainbridge.

"We've got small children down here!" he hollered up to the ship.

A moment later, a canvas mailbag was lowered down on a rope. "Put the little tykes in this," a sailor from the ship called down. "Special delivery!" he added with a laugh, which broke the tension for a moment.

The children were hauled up much to their delight. While their mother managed a hearty scramble up the rope ladder that was quite remarkable for a woman of her age. Most of the rest of the passengers also used the rope ladder except for the three Middle Eastern women with their babies and the elderly Polish couple. For these few, a chair sling was lowered down, and they were securely tied in before they made the trip up to the open gangway.

Lord Bainbridge was the last passenger to leave the lifeboat, and as he stepped through the gangway and onto the ship, he felt a great relief to once again find a solid deck beneath his feet.

Chapter XIII

The minute he stepped on board the rescue ship, Lord Bainbridge was surrounded by attentive ship's personnel, warm blankets were thrown over him and a steward passed him a cup of hot tea. There was an officer taking down everyone's name as they climbed aboard, and then they were directed to one of the ship's three dining saloons, depending on class, where the ship's doctors had set up first-aid stations. Lord Bainbridge decided against going immediately below though Alfred protested he had better get out of his still wet clothes, or he was sure to catch pneumonia. Leaving the others behind however, Lord Bainbridge climbed up to the promenade deck where he leaned on the rail and stared out at the new day just beginning to unfold before him.

Above his head, the eastern sky was fast turning gold and blue as the sun edged over the horizon, giving promise of a beautiful day to come. After a while when he felt the first rays of the sun on his face, the warmth seemed to invade his whole body. In the west, the shadows of the night and its horrors still lingered as if reluctant to give way to day. Near the horizon, a pale crescent moon appeared at last, having slept unobserved and unobserving throughout the whole night. The sea, now choppy in the morning breeze, was a vivid dark blue as rich as velvet. As far as Lord Bainbridge eyes could see, from the north to the west, there stretched an enormous field of ice braced here and there by towering bergs, some he estimated to be at least seventy feet tall. Smaller bergs dotted the open water between the ice floe and the ship. The icebergs had a magnificent majestic beauty of their own as they dazzled in the early sun's rays. They were a rainbow of colors—white, pink, mauve, and deep blue—their hue depending on how the sun hit them and how the shadows fell upon them.

It was one of those, Lord Bainbridge thought to himself, staring at the bergs. It was one of those dazzling creatures of ice that had first crippled and then sank the *Titanic,* leaving such terrible death and destruction behind. One berg in particular caught his attention. It thrust itself boldly out of the water, perhaps a little higher than the deck on which he stood. The side that faced him was jagged and torn as if a part of it had been ripped away or perhaps shaved off. And he was quite certain he could determine a smear of what might be red paint across its base. *Could this be the one?* he wondered. *Could this be the one that sank the*

Titanic? It seemed to be sitting there in smug triumphant, the undisputed victor in a war between two titans.

It was then that Lord Bainbridge first noticed the little convoy of lifeboats coming toward the rescue ship as if they were emerging out of the night and into the day. A sad little fleet of boats, all that was left of the world's biggest and most luxurious ocean liner. From some of the boats, he distinctly heard cheers as their occupants realized rescue was at hand, and their oars splashed vigorously in the water as they surged toward the ship. But from other boats, there was only silence, and some made no effort at all to reach them but sat drifting aimlessly in the sea as if those on board had lost all hope, all will.

The ship on which Lord Bainbridge stood was named *Carpathia*. She was of the Cunard Line, a small unremarkable vessel of 13,600 tons with a single smokestack. Despite his gratitude to be standing on her deck, Lord Bainbridge could not help but compare the *Carpathia* to the grand and lavish *Titanic* with her four smokestacks and seemingly endless gleaming decks. But the reality of it was the *Titanic* now rested at the bottom of the ocean, and it was the poky little *Carpathia* that had come to the relief of her survivors. On the same day the *Titanic* had left Southampton, the *Carpathia* had sailed eastward from New York bound for the Mediterranean. Her 750 passengers were mostly elderly, tourists in first and second class and, in third class, Italians who had immigrated to America and were now returning to their homeland for a visit. As fate would conveniently have it, the *Carpathia's* passenger accommodations were hardly half full. So she had the room to take on the *Titanic's* survivors.

The *Carpathia's* captain was forty-three-year old Arthur Rostron, a twenty-seven-year veteran of the sea. Rostron was an experienced mariner known for his decisiveness and boundless energy. He was also noted for his piety; he neither smoked nor drank nor uttered a word of profanity. And he was not a man ashamed to turn to prayer when he needed guidance.

It was 12:30 AM, almost an hour after the *Titanic* had struck the iceberg when the *Carpathia's* wireless operator burst unannounced into Rostron's cabin. The captain had retired for the night, and he was at first incensed at such undisciplined behavior. But his reprimand died on his lips when his wireless man told him the *Titanic* had struck a berg and needed immediate assistance. Rostron ordered his ship turned and plotted on a course toward the *Titanic* fifty-eight miles away. The *Carpathia's* top speed was fourteen knots, but that night, she managed an incredible seventeen knots as she knifed through the water on her desperate mission, dodging icebergs on all sides but never slacking her speed. Yet in spite of that valiant effort when at 4:00 AM they arrived at the *Titanic's* last reported position, they knew they were too late. She was gone, and all they could do was pick up her survivors.

"I'm Captain Rostron."

Startled, Lord Bainbridge turned to see the tall figure of the *Carpathia's* captain standing beside him at the rail.

"The *Titanic* has gone down?" Rostron asked.

Lord Bainbridge nodded. "Yes, at 2:20."

The captain stared into the young Englishman's face. "Were there many people still on board when she sank?"

Lord Bainbridge nodded again. "Hundreds, probably as many as a thousand. We managed to get a few into our boat. The rest . . ." his voice broke, and he looked away. " . . . the rest didn't have a chance in the freezing water."

"God help them!" Captain Rostron murmured. "You should go below," he suggested.

"I will in a bit," Lord Bainbridge told him. "Thank you for coming to our rescue," he added, knowing how trite that must sound.

Captain Rostron's hands gripped the rail. "If only we had arrived in time," he mused, obviously distraught that they had not.

"If only the *Titanic* had had enough lifeboats for all," Lord Bainbridge put in. "And if only the ones she did have had been completely filled."

The captain looked quite startled. "What do you mean?" he asked.

"I know for a fact that a number of the boats were lowered half full, a few even less than that," Lord Bainbridge answered. "People were turned away from the boats even when there was plenty of room because of their sex. No matter what their age," he added, feeling a rekindling of the righteous anger he had felt ever since Sebastian Renoir had been turned away from the lifeboat he had tried to enter.

Captain Rostron made no immediate comment, but Lord Bainbridge could tell by the expression on the older man's face that his revelation had, at the very least, surprised him. "Have the surviving senior officer come to the bridge as soon as he's on board," the captain said to his subordinate who had been standing at his side. Then he nodded to Lord Bainbridge and made his way back to the bridge.

Lord Bainbridge watched the man walk away from him until he turned down a companionway and disappeared from his sight. Then he turned his attention back down to the sea and the lifeboats. One of them had reached the side of the ship, and lines were being tossed down to it. Lord Bainbridge noticed how the life belts most everyone in the boat were wearing made them all look like they were dressed in white. He strained his eyes to see if he could recognize any of these sitting calmly in the boat, waiting to disembark. At first, he couldn't distinguish their faces, but as each person stood and turned to start their ascent up the side of the ship, he had a quick but good glimpse of them. Sadly, he didn't recognize anyone from that second lifeboat to reach the *Carpathia*, not even so much as a casual acquaintance. He knew that of all his friends only Maude had got away safely for sure. As for the others, he had already accepted the fact that the elderly Frabolis were lost, having determined their own fate. He could only hope that Madame Renoir and her son had managed to get into a boat before it was too late. When he thought of them, he could not help but also remember the officer who had prevented Sebastian from getting into his boat and, in doing so, had turned both the boy and his mother away. Lord Bainbridge wondered if this same officer, this same man with such a marked sense of misplaced propriety, had also turned away the little liftboy and left him to drown deep in the dark water. Though he wished for no man's death on this horrible night, if there was one face Lord Bainbridge didn't care to see step out of a lifeboat and onto the deck of the *Carpathia*, it was that same officer. Better for him would be the same fate he had sentenced others to.

A third lifeboat had just pulled up to the side of the ship when Lord Bainbridge became aware of someone standing beside him at the rail. He looked over to see a gentleman of perhaps sixty, or even seventy, beaming at him. He had a kindly face with a little twirly mustache and deep blue eyes that despite his very obvious years, seemed to twinkle with the vitality of youth. Lord Bainbridge suspected at once that he was a "fellow traveler."

One of the old man's hands, its slim fingers bejeweled, reached out to Lord Bainbridge. "Do you mind?" he asked. "You've got some ice in your hair." His hand gently brushed the ice away.

"Thank you," Lord Bainbridge said to him, aware that the gentleman was peering at him with great intensity.

"You're from the *Titanic*?" he asked.

"Yes," Lord Bainbridge answered.

"And she sank, did she?"

"Yes," Lord Bainbridge replied.

"How horrible! What a dreadful calamity!" the old gentleman murmured. Though his words were delivered in a high-pitched voice that was made even more comical by the trace of a lisp, there was no doubt that his distress was sincere. He leaned closer to Lord Bainbridge and stared intimately into his face. "Young man, you look positively undone by your ordeal," he told him. "Why don't you come down to my cabin and have a spot of brandy? And I'm sure I can find you some dry clothes as well."

Lord Bainbridge wasn't sure if he was being propositioned or if the old man was just being kind. If it was the former, it was hardly the time or place for such a suggestion, but he knew from his own experiences that in the world they lived in, one had to grasp opportunities when they came around no matter how awkward or untimely the circumstances.

He thanked the gentleman for his perceived kindness, adding, "I'd better stay here a while and look for my friends."

The old gentleman nodded sympathetically. "Of course, of course. Later perhaps," he suggested. "I'm in cabin B32," he announced just before he moved off, fluttering away like a gaily colored butterfly.

As he watched the old man fly away, Lord Bainbridge felt a shiver run down his spine as he wondered if he had just seen a vision of himself in another forty years. Being young, he had not yet begun to think of what lay ahead of him, what his life would be like in his declining years. But now, suddenly he had been reminded of what his future might be, and he was both shocked and resolved to not let it happen. He would not let himself become an old queen, chasing after youths young enough to be his grandsons. Never! And yet, at the same moment, a small voice inside of him reminded him that the choice very well might not end up being his.

Then there was no more time for such thoughts as the drama of that April morning intensified. More and more people were joining him at the rail. Some of them were *Titanic* survivors from the second lifeboat, who like himself had wandered up to the boat deck to search for familiar faces among those in the boats to come. Others were the *Carpathia's* own passengers, stirred from their slumbers by all the commotion. Some of these, like many of the *Titanic's* passengers had done so only hours earlier, emerged on deck hastily dressed, a few with only wraps thrown over their nightclothes.

One woman, a passenger of the *Carpathia*, came close to where Lord Bainbridge was standing. She was on the verge of tears. "What is it?" she demanded. "What's happening? Are we abandoning ship?"

A man next to her calmed her and pointed to the lifeboats in the water below them. "They're from the *Titanic*," he said. "She's gone to the bottom."

Passengers from a third lifeboat were beginning their ascent up to the *Carpathia's* open gangway. Keeping an eye peeled for his friends, Lord Bainbridge noted how quiet those in the lifeboat were—the wail of a baby was the only sound he heard. Those around him on the deck, for the most part, were quiet too. *Perhaps everyone is just in shock,* he thought. Or perhaps they were all just in the presence of something that was too big, too terrible, to grasp. The tears, the lamentations, the screams would come later.

Then quite suddenly, all the silence was broken, and a woman's voice, loud and distinct, came from the lifeboat being unloaded. "You want me to do what!"

Recognizing the voice at once, Lord Bainbridge leaned over the rail and instantly caught sight of Maude standing in the center of the lifeboat, her pith helmet firmly in place on her head, and clutching her large pocketbook that contained her precious work as well as his own notes for his next book. Again, Maude's voice came clearly up to those on the boat deck. "There's no way on God's sweet earth I'm going to climb up that puny little thing!"

The seaman who was trying to persuade her to make the climb up the rope ladder had one hand on the ladder, and with the other, he was gesturing adamantly. His words could not be heard by those above, but Maude's response certainly was.

"Then, they can damn well tie a rope around me and haul me up like a piece of cargo!"

Seeing Maude, Lord Bainbridge would have gladly waved and called out to her, but looking around at the shattered faces of other *Titanic* survivors who were desperately searching for loved ones they didn't see, it seemed a mean thing to do. So he kept silent. But he was unable to hide his amusement as he watched the crewmen struggle to strap the large Englishwoman into what surely must have been an oversized sling chair. One of them grabbed her pocketbook from her arms and tossed it up to the gangway where happily for the sake of his neck, it was caught by one of the *Carpathia's* crew. Then with much to-do from Maude herself and those above struggling to achieve her ascent, she was finally hoisted on board the *Carpathia*. A sigh of relief seemed to pass audibly among those at the ship's rail as this herculean task was satisfactorily completed.

Thinking he might go below to greet Maude, Lord Bainbridge was detained at the rail by the sight of more and more lifeboats converging on the ship. They seemed to be coming from all directions now, gleaming white in the full light of a beautiful morning while in the water all around them, chunks of ice from the size of a large table to others no bigger than a man's fist bobbed in the water.

Lord Bainbridge needn't have gone in search of Maude, for in no time she found him. She came charging down the deck toward him, waving vigorously. "Ducks! Ducks, there you are at last!" She tried to embrace him but was hampered by the cumbersome life belt she wore. "Oh do help me get rid of this wretched thing," she implored of him, struggling with the life belt's straps.

Lord Bainbridge helped her out of the life belt, which Maude tossed carelessly to the floor of the boat deck, and then they had a proper embrace.

"I spoke with the officer writing down everyone's name as they came on board, and he told me you had arrived in the first boat," she informed him. "Well done, Ducks!" she added as if arriving in the first lifeboat was some praiseworthy accomplishment. "Then that pretty little American girl told me in the dining saloon that you had gone up on deck. I'm so glad she's safe. She's such a dear."

"She was with me in the same boat," Lord Bainbridge explained. "Along with Alfred of course."

Maude nodded, hardly impressed. "From the first day I laid eyes on that one, I knew he was a survivor," she commented, her old animosity toward Alfred rearing its head once again.

"And the young man I care deeply about as well," Lord Bainbridge added quickly as surprised to hear himself speak the words as Maude must have been to hear them. He hadn't meant to say them; such matters had never before been spoken between them. But somehow they just popped out, and after they were said, he realized he was glad they had been spoken. If the awful tragedy they were now in the midst of had taught him one thing, it was that the time had passed for keeping secrets, for keeping one's life under a bushel. Life was too precious and its duration too short to keep what you treasured the most hidden away in some dark corner.

Maude's eyes met his, and for just a second, he thought he saw a glimmer of reproof in her glance. But he should have known better, for almost instantly her lips broke into a broad smile. She patted his hand, kissed him on the cheek, and murmured her approval. "I'm so glad, Ducks, so damn glad for you." That was all she said on the matter, but it was enough to let him know she was still and would be forever his staunch ally, his literary mentor, his beloved friend.

"Have any of the others arrived yet?" Maude asked.

Lord Bainbridge shook his head regretfully. "No," he answered, and he quickly told her about the situations with both the Frabolis and the Renoirs—how the Frabolis had, he sensed, willed themselves to die together and how Sebastian Renoir had been refused admittance to a lifeboat.

But Maude didn't appear to take the news as ominously as he had. "I shouldn't fret," she told him. "I'm sure they'll all be along soon. Just look at how many boats there are out there!"

"Maude, there weren't enough lifeboats on the *Titanic* for even half those on board," Lord Bainbridge reminded her. "Many people, hundreds, have died," he added.

Maude was silent for a long moment, staring out to sea. Then she turned to look at Lord Bainbridge. "We heard their cries for help in our boat," she said. "The crewmen refused to row back and not one of the other passengers spoke up. They sat there like cowardly sheep. I was the only one who wanted to go back, and finally, one of the crewmen told me if I didn't shut up about it, they'd throw me overboard." She shook her head in distress. "Jeremy, our boat wasn't even half full, and the crewmen picked up their oars and actually rowed away from those poor people in the water."

"I know." Lord Bainbridge nodded. "On the day of reckoning, a lot of people will have a lot to answer for," he said.

They watched in silence as the rest of the boats pulled up alongside the *Carpathia* and began to unload their precious cargo. Though he was certain he scanned almost every upturned face, Lord Bainbridge didn't catch sight of any of his other friends. In fact, he recognized very few that he knew, even by as little as a casual acquaintanceship. He did, however, spot Ronnie Standish as he climbed on board. Actually, Ronnie would have been hard for anyone to miss. One of the few in the lifeboats to disdain to wear a life belt, he climbed the rope ladder with his ebony cane in hand, looking very elegant as if he were bound for a smart party or an exclusive club rather than the deck of a rescue ship in the middle of the Atlantic.

In a short time, too short for many, word spread to those on the *Carpathia's* deck that all the *Titanic's* lifeboats but one had been picked up. And all eyes at the rail strained toward this final boat, this final hope. The lifeboat was still several hundred yards from the ship, and it was barely moving. Those on the boat deck felt the vibrations underneath their feet as the *Carpathia* started up her engines and slowly maneuvered toward the lifeboat, finally drawing within a few yards of her. From the deck, those on the ship could see why the lifeboat was struggling so—her gunwales were almost down to the water, for she was so overcrowded with passengers. In addition, the morning breeze had become stiffer, and the sea had grown rougher with waves breaking over the lifeboat's sides. Any moment it looked as if the boat would be swamped, and everyone on board tossed into the sea. There was an officer in the stern and sailors at the oars and the officer, an obviously experienced hand, was struggling to get into the *Carpathia's* lee and thus be sheltered from the waves. Another wave hit them, but this one fortunately brought them into the *Carpathia's* side and safety. A cheer went up from those on the deck when the lifeboat was secure, and more than one passenger praised the admirable efforts of the officer who had guided her to safety.

This last lifeboat was quickly unloaded, and though she had been crammed full with over seventy-five passengers, very few of the now considerable crowd of Titanic survivors lining the *Carpathia's* rails found among those seventy-five the face of a loved one they so desperately sought. Their hearts crushed, most of them turned away from the rail and went below in shock and disbelief.

Lord Bainbridge had scanned the face of every passenger in that final lifeboat, and he knew for certain that none of his friends were among them. He knew at that moment that they were dead, all four of them were gone, two by choice, two by cruel circumstances. After all the other passengers and most of the crew had left the boat deck, he continued to stare down at the single figure still left in the lifeboat. This was the stalwart officer who had so expertly guided her to the *Carpathia's* side. And now, like the good officer he was, he was tidying up his boat, making sure everything was shipshape before he too disembarked. Then a curious thing happened, the officer, with one foot already on the rope ladder, turned his glance upward, not to the gangway, but farther up to the boat deck. And perhaps it was by chance, or perhaps it was not, but his eyes met and held Lord Bainbridge's. But then, not having achieved any degree of recognition, the officer turned his glance away and started up the rope ladder.

Lord Bainbridge, however, had certainly recognized him, and that recognition was like a cold slap in the face. For it was the same officer who had turned Sebastian Renoir away from the lifeboat and was therefore, at least in Lord

Bainbridge's mind, responsible for the boy's death and his mother's as well. But the man, Lord Bainbridge fumed, had managed to save his own skin.

This realization coupled with the reality that his friends were dead caused such an explosion of emotion in his brain that Lord Bainbridge felt his head start to spin. Beside him, Maude was saying something to him, but he couldn't hear her words. And then, because he knew what was about to happen, he grabbed hold of the deck rail just as his world went black.

The next thing Lord Bainbridge was aware of he was waking up in a strange bunk with the covers pulled up to his chin. He sat up, and rubbing his eyes, he tried to figure out where he was. Throwing the covers aside, he swung his legs over the side of the bunk and was startled to see that he was wearing pajamas. *Where the hell had they come from?* He hadn't worn pajamas since that night at Bellington House when he and Denham had first slept together. Denham's revelation that he never wore pajamas and always slept stark naked had put him off pajamas from that day on. It's funny, he thought for a moment, how every once in a while his thoughts would return to Denham. Even though Denham was no longer his great passion, and he had even spurned his advances in Egypt, he still was a part of him and always would be. Denham had been his first love, and as such, his place in his heart and his mind was forever enshrined.

Looking around the small but obviously first-class cabin, Lord Bainbridge saw that he was not alone. Alfred was stretched out in a chair, his legs thrown over one of the chair's arms, his head thrown back, and his mouth half open, emanating a low buzz that Lord Bainbridge knew well. As Lord Bainbridge stepped down from the bunk, Alfred stirred and awoke.

"How long have I been sleeping?" Lord Bainbridge asked.

Alfred yawned and stretched. "All day," he answered. He checked his pocket watch. "It's six-thirty in the evening."

"Where are we?" Lord Bainbridge asked.

Alfred grinned as he lit up a cigarette. "Well," he began, obviously ready to enjoy the story he was about to tell. "Apparently, you fainted up on deck." He shook a finger at him. "Hardly a very manly thing to do." Then he continued. "I went up to look for you and found you flat on your back with a crowd gathered around you. I had just managed to hoist you over my shoulder when this old queen comes tottering up to me, suggesting that I take you down to his cabin." Lord Bainbridge interrupted him to describe the kindly old gentleman who had approached him earlier. Alfred nodded. "Yah, that's the one. You know him?"

"We've met," Lord Bainbridge answered.

"Well I think the old queen wanted to know you a lot better," Alfred added with a snicker. "After we got you down here and laid out on the bunk, he put a cold cloth to your forehead. I think he would have climbed into the bunk with you if I hadn't been here."

"He was just showing kindness," Lord Bainbridge insisted.

Alfred snorted with implied contempt. "I've spent enough time around old queens to know when they're on the prowl," he said, reminding Lord Bainbridge that there were still a few dark corners in Alfred's past that he did not know about. "He would have had his way with you, I'm sure if I hadn't been here," Alfred told him. He chuckled. "You can thank me later for protecting your virtue."

"Did you ever think that could be us in a few years?" Lord Bainbridge asked.

"Not me!" Alfred said, emphatically stamping out his cigarette. "I'll shoot myself first."

Lord Bainbridge looked down at the pajamas he was wearing. "Where did these come from?" he inquired.

"They belong to the old guy," Alfred answered. "You came to for a moment, mumbled something that neither of us could understand, and then promptly fell asleep," Alfred explained. "I told the old queen you never wore pajamas, but he persisted. Perhaps he intends to treasure them afterwards or use them for some sort of secret sexual self-satisfaction."

"Don't be disgusting," Lord Bainbridge snapped.

Alfred shrugged, hardly fazed by the reprimand. "He was quite determined to get you into those pajamas himself."

Lord Bainbridge became alarmed, "You didn't let him?"

Alfred laughed. "Of course not! I shooed him out the door, got you out of your wet clothes, dried you down with some towels, and slipped you neatly into those charming pajamas. I figured you'd rather he see you in those than in nothing at all."

"Thank you," Lord Bainbridge said. He suddenly realized he hadn't eaten anything for over twenty-four hours. "I'm half starved," he remarked.

Then as if a fairy godmother had heard him and was about to fulfill his wish, there was a discrete knock at the cabin door.

"Ah, your ancient admirer returns," Alfred chuckled.

The door to the corridor swung open, and the elderly gent entered the cabin. He was followed by a steward with a tray loaded down with sandwiches and coffee. Over his arm, the old man carried the clothes Lord Bainbridge had left the *Titanic* in. "While you were sleeping, I came back and took your clothes and had them cleaned and pressed," he told Lord Bainbridge. "I hope you don't mind."

"Mind?" Lord Bainbridge laughed. "I'm eternally grateful."

"A gentleman must maintain his appearance even at the worst of times," the old man said. He gestured toward the steward with the tray. "I thought you could probably use some nourishment."

"Thank you," Lord Bainbridge acknowledged. "Thank you for all of this, you've been most kind."

"Oh, it's nothing at all!" the old gent trilled. Then supervising the steward with an eye peeled to every fussy detail, he got everything set out neatly on a table in the center of the room. And when it was all ready, he sat on the edge of the bunk, and like a proud parent or, perhaps better, a delighted hostess, he watched Lord Bainbridge and Alfred tuck into the food, which they both found most welcome.

When they had finished, their benefactor made a not unexpected proposal to Lord Bainbridge. "You must stay here until we reach New York," he suggested. "It's small, but you'll find it comfortable."

"Oh, I couldn't put you out like that," Lord Bainbridge protested.

"I've made other arrangements for myself," the elderly man told him. "Most agreeable ones at that," he added with a coy wink.

After the old man had left a few minutes later for a dinner engagement, Lord Bainbridge slipped out of the pajamas and began pulling on his own clothes.

Alfred had stretched himself out on the cabin's sofa. Through the haze of another cigarette, he watched Lord Bainbridge as he dressed. "I've no need to guess where you're going," he said a bit tersely.

"I have to make sure he's all right, that he's taken care of," Lord Bainbridge said, slipping on his jacket. "Steerage passengers never get the best of it no matter what the circumstances or what ship they're on."

"A fact which never gave you much pause before," Alfred reminded him.

"Things have changed," Lord Bainbridge returned.

"Yes, I know love changes everything," Alfred said, smiling sarcastically.

"Only the things that matter," Lord Bainbridge said just before he opened the door and walked out into the corridor, closing the door behind him with a little more emphasis than was necessary.

Once he was out on the open deck, he turned his steps toward the stern of the ship where he assumed he would find the steerage quarters. Peering out to sea, he noticed a couple of flashes of lightning dancing in the distant horizon.

After all we've gone through, now we may have to put up with a storm as well, Lord Bainbridge thought to himself. He shook his head. It hardly seemed fair.

Quite suddenly, he came upon a figure pacing nervously back and forth along the deck. In the swiftly approaching darkness, they in fact emerged upon one another so quickly that they almost collided. Lord Bainbridge was just able to pull back at the last moment and thus prevent what could have been a disastrous impact. It took him a moment or two before he recognized the other fellow as the young *Titanic* officer who had befriended him, the same man who was supposed to have been in charge of the lifeboat on which they both escaped from the sinking ship.

The junior officer appeared quite agitated, and even after he had acknowledged Lord Bainbridge's presence, he continued pacing the deck, wringing his hands and muttering to himself. Finally, he stopped and looked Lord Bainbridge squarely in the face.

"There was another ship, you know," he said to him.

Lord Bainbridge shook his head. "I'm sorry, I don't understand."

"There was another ship!" the officer practically yelled into Lord Bainbridge's face as if he were speaking to someone whom he felt surely must have gone deaf.

"Calm down and tell me what you're talking about," Lord Bainbridge told him, laying a hand on his arm to try and still his turmoil.

His touch worked, for almost immediately, the young officer returned to his senses. And after apologizing for his inappropriate behavior, he went on to explain, in a much calmer voice, what he had been referring to. "There was another ship out there, one much closer to the *Titanic* than this one. Remember the light we saw off the bow?" Lord Bainbridge nodded. "That was her," the officer added. "She certainly could have reached us in time and taken everyone safely off the *Titanic* before she sank." His voice grew softer, sadder. "No one needed to have died, not a single soul, if she had had only come. After the *Titanic* had gone down," he added, "I looked back in that direction again, and the light was gone. She had snuck off and left all those people to die."

"Extraordinary," Lord Bainbridge said, his own voice barely above a whisper.

The junior officer was leaning on the rail, and after a moment, he turned to look back at Lord Bainbridge, who was standing slightly behind him. "I behaved rather badly," the young man admitted.

This then is what is really eating at him, Lord Bainbridge thought. As appalling as the story of the mystery ship was, and he himself had seen its light, what really was distressing the young officer before him was his own conduct.

"It was a stressful time for everyone," Lord Bainbridge said diplomatically.

The officer shook his head. "No, I should have done better. I just didn't know what to do. It was as if I were frozen, incapable of acting or even thinking." He searched Lord Bainbridge's face. "I was a coward, wasn't I?" he asked in a plaintive voice.

Lord Bainbridge didn't know what to say to him, and so they stood there a moment, staring at each other in uncomfortable silence. Lord Bainbridge jammed his hands into the pockets of his jacket, and the fingers of one of them came upon the officer's gun, which he had forgotten he still had in his possession. He pulled it out and returned it to its owner. "I won't be needing this anymore," he said.

The junior officer looked down at the gun in his hand for a long moment. "A lot of good it did me," he said and then he let it slip out of his hand, over the side of the ship, and into the sea.

At that moment, another person approached them along the deck, and as he drew nearer and in spite of the increasing darkness and the fact that he wore an officer's coat with its collar turned up, which half buried his face, and his officer's cap was pulled down over his brow, Lord Bainbridge was still able to recognize him for just an instant. The officer gave them a nod, and then he quickly moved on.

Watching his retreating back, with hate surging up in his throat like bile, Lord Bainbridge eyes quickly came back to the young officer, startled by his next words.

"Now there goes a real hero!" the junior officer said with admiration in his tone and envy too.

"Who was that?" Lord Bainbridge asked, trying to keep his own voice level.

"Mr. Lightoller, the *Titanic's* second officer," the man beside him answered.

"Why did you call him a hero?" Lord Bainbridge inquired, certainly seeing the man in a far different light.

The young officer explained. "When the *Titanic* was going down, Mr. Lightoller was thrown overboard. He swam to one of the collapsible lifeboats, which had landed upside down in the water. I heard there were at least two dozen men clinging to that collapsible when Mr. Lightoller climbed on board. He immediately took charge, and from what a number of men who were on that unfortunate boat have told me, none of them would have survived that terrible night had it not been for Mr. Lightoller. He saved the life of everyone of them," the officer added.

Yes, Lord Bainbridge thought with fresh bitterness toward the man in spite of the heroics the junior officer had just told him about, *and he also condemned others, young men and boys like Sebastian Renoir and the liftboy, to horrible watery graves.*

The young officer seemed to have a great need to talk to someone. And Lord Bainbridge tried to be charitable and remain a few minutes longer and listen to him though he was most anxious to be off and find Tom. Most of the officer's banter concerned rumors he had heard since coming on board the *Carpathia,* fanciful and far-fetched stories that were beyond common sense. One of the most incredulous tales suggested that some of those thought lost had perhaps been able to climb onto one of the large ice floes that surrounded them and were, at that very moment, still alive and waiting desperately to be rescued. The junior officer, so frantic to believe anything that might lessen his own sense of guilt, had apparently bought the story as gospel. He suggested that Lord Bainbridge go along with him to see the captain of the *Carpathia* and try and convince him to turn the ship around and begin an extensive search of the ice floes.

Lord Bainbridge at first tried to let the young man down gently. "I doubt if anyone managed to reach the ice floes," he told him.

"But we don't know until we check them!" the officer persisted in his desperation.

Deciding it would be better if he were blunt, even a little cruel, rather than let the officer continue in this delusional manner, Lord Bainbridge said what he really was thinking, "It's a stupid suggestion and one that has no basis in reality. There are no people out there clinging to ice floes!" he added with emphasis.

The look on the junior officer's face as he stared back at him in silence told Lord Bainbridge that his frankness had not done the job. It was obvious the young man did not believe him, preferring instead to cling to the absurd rumor he had picked up and now refused to put down.

Lord Bainbridge quickly made his excuses and left the officer. He looked back over his shoulder to see him once again nervously pacing the deck and muttering to himself.

When he reached the stern of the ship, Lord Bainbridge took the stairs down to the lowest of the open decks. As he reached out to open the gate that led onto the third-class deck area, he was stopped by a crewman.

"There's nothing but steerage people down there," the man told him, nodding toward the stern.

Lord Bainbridge held the man's gaze for a second, pleased at the way the man's eyelids flickered nervously under his steady glance. "I'll try not to get my hands dirty," he said to him coldly. Then he passed through the gate and reached the stern of the ship.

Despite the approach of nightfall, he found the steerage deck swarming with passengers. Probably, he reasoned, the crowded conditions below decks, after all the *Titanic's* steerage passengers were sharing accommodations with those on the *Carpathia* traveling third class, made many of them wish to stay up on deck in the open air as long as possible. And there was another reason that occurred to him. There were surely more than a few of the *Titanic's* steerage passengers who, having barely escaped with their lives from the depths of the *Titanic's* holds, now felt a great deal safer keeping themselves out on the open deck, above the waterline.

Lord Bainbridge craned his neck, but there was no sight of Tom although the size of the crowd and the fast approaching darkness could have easily concealed him. But there were others who quickly noticed Lord Bainbridge, and they descended upon him. Led by the Englishwoman with her four children in tow, the group included the elderly Polish couple and the three Middle Eastern women still with their babies cradled in their arms. They all gathered around him.

"We wanted to give you a proper thanks for saving our lives, sir," the Englishwoman said to him. "Truly, sir, none of us would be standing here on this deck if it hadn't been for you."

The others nodded in agreement, even the Middle Eastern women who obviously didn't understand a word of what the Englishwoman had said but did, however, understand the sentiments that were being expressed and agreed wholeheartedly with them.

Feeling slightly uncomfortable at being submitted to their praise, Lord Bainbridge thanked them and then extracted himself from their presence as quickly as he could without giving offense.

There was still no sight of Tom, and Lord Bainbridge was about to go below and search for him when he caught sight of another. The young Japanese man looked up as Lord Bainbridge walked over to him. He was sitting on a hatch cover, elegantly smoking a cigarette and looking as unconcerned and aloof as when Lord Bainbridge had first spotted him down in the *Titanic's* steerage section. And like then, Lord Bainbridge had the distinct impression that the Asian was sitting in judgment of him and that his verdict was hardly favorable.

"I wanted to ask you," Lord Bainbridge began rather haltingly, somewhat unnerved by the other man's penetrating and disapproving stare. "I wanted to ask you why you jumped into the water to save me and my friend." he finally blurted out.

The Asian continued to regard him silently, his look casual, almost lazy, as if he found whom he was staring at, this being Lord Bainbridge, hardly worth the effort it took to maintain eye contact. Finally, he expelled the smoke from his cigarette thru his nostrils in a grand gesture and spoke.

"You saved my life by bringing me up to the lifeboat," he explained. "That put me in your debt. I wish to be in no man's debt, so I had to pay that debt back. So I leaped into the water when I saw you were in trouble." He took another long drag on his cigarette, held the smoke in his mouth for a moment as if savoring it, and then once again expelled it thru his nostrils with great flair. "Now we are even. I am no longer in your debt. It's a matter of honor," he added in a tone that implied honor was something Lord Bainbridge, indeed the whole English speaking race, was incapable of understanding.

Looking into his face, Lord Bainbridge realized the Asian held him in as much contempt as Alfred did all foreigners. They may have saved one another's lives, but that still left them as far apart as if one dwelled on earth and the other on the moon.

Feeling both rebuffed and insulted, Lord Bainbridge hurried away and was greatly relieved to catch a sight of Tom at last. The young Irishman was alone, leaning on the rail at the far end of the stern of the ship. He did not at first look up when Lord Bainbridge reached his side. Instead, his eyes remained fixed on the stretch of water they were quickly leaving behind, seeing something perhaps only he could see. He might have been reliving the horrors of the night before that, at least for him, instead of having ended, remained just beyond the last wave, a haunted part of the ocean that would forever be contaminated.

As he stood at his side, Lord Bainbridge was reminded of that final morning on the *Titanic* when the two of them had lingered at the ship's rail happy and carefree as the dawn broke upon them like a glorious revelation. That moment now seemed like a hundred years ago though it was hardly more than thirty-six hours ago.

Fog was swiftly rolling in now, and as if to announce its arrival, the *Carpathia's* fog horn moaned its lonely call. "I heard a rumor that the reason we hit the iceberg was because the *Titanic* was surrounded by fog," Tom said, finally having found his voice.

"All sorts of rumors are buzzing about this ship, most unfounded, some quite preposterous," Lord Bainbridge remarked, remembering his conversation with the troubled junior officer.

Tom turned to look at him for the first time since Lord Bainbridge had joined him at the rail. Lord Bainbridge could see at once even in the fast fading daylight that he was troubled. It was evident that Tom had changed or been changed. The glow was gone from his face, his eyes, once bright were dull and, around his lips, lines that Lord Bainbridge had never noticed before were drawn tight and severe. And he greatly feared that Tom's marvelous grin might never appear again.

"I can't help wondering what all those people must have been thinking just before they died," Tom said. "I mean, they must have been filled with an awful terror, but they must have also had a great sense of disbelief that this was happening to them." He looked into Lord Bainbridge's face. "What dreams, what plans, do you suppose they had?"

"Plans and dreams like those all of us have," Lord Bainbridge answered softly.

But there was more that was troubling Tom much more. "A woman came up to me below deck and called me a coward for getting into a lifeboat," he revealed, his eyes downcast. "She said it would have been better if I'd drowned with the rest of the men."

"That was a stupid ignorant thing for her to say!" Lord Bainbridge snapped angrily, quite ready to seek out that woman and throttle her severely. He reached out and turned Tom's face up into his own again. "I'm not ashamed to be alive, Tom," he told him. "I'm glad I survived. I'm damn glad to be alive."

Tom shivered, and for a terrible moment, Lord Bainbridge feared it might be from his touch rather than the cold. In fact, Tom did move a little away from him at the rail. "It's different for you," he said.

"How do you mean?" Lord Bainbridge asked.

"Everyone's calling you a hero," Tom answered. "The Englishwoman has told everyone how you saved all our lives. Among the steerage passengers, you're regarded as this heroic, almost mythical figure. This great English lord who reached out to save those of the poor, downtrodden lower class." There was just a hint, nothing more than a whiff really, of ridicule in Tom's tone, and most probably it was not even intended. It was more what he said than how he said it.

"I'm no hero," Lord Bainbridge assured him quickly. "I would never have done anything if you had not been there. I would have got calmly into a lifeboat and let them row away from the wreck without a word of protest. I only did what I did because it meant so much to you," he added honestly.

"You're a hero, Jeremy, whether you want to be or not," Tom told him. "You saved my life twice."

"And I'd save it again and again if I had to," Lord Bainbridge responded. He shook his head. "How ironic it is that they label me a hero, and yet if my true nature were known, then how fast the applause would fade."

Out of the corner of his eye, he saw Tom shiver again, and a coldness clutched at his own heart as he realized without a doubt what it was that lay at the core of what was torturing Tom. He knew he had to proceed with caution. "When we reach New York," he began carefully, "we can talk it all out. I mean about us, and then we can decide what we're going to do."

"I've already decided," Tom said quietly.

At that moment, Lord Bainbridge felt as though he were standing on the edge of a great abyss and knowing without a doubt that he was about to tumble into it, for he knew he was about to lose Tom forever.

He tried desperately to postpone that moment. "We'll wait and talk about it later," he blurted out frantically.

Tom's next words were so unexpected that for a moment, Lord Bainbridge was stunned, stunned like a condemned man who has just been granted a last-minute reprieve. The words were these: "I love you, Jeremy, I know that now for sure. And I fear, I shall always do so." And at least for the brief moment that he spoke these words, Tom kept his eyes trained on Lord Bainbridge.

Except for the word *fear*, which seemed awkward and out of place in a declaration of love, Lord Bainbridge found Tom's statement most encouraging. And the hope that had all but died in his own heart flared up again as if someone had carelessly thrown a toxic combustible onto an all but dying flame.

"And you must be aware that I love you as well," Lord Bainbridge said to him.

For just an instant, Tom's face brightened, and his famous grin threatened to appear if only for a second. "Yes, Jeremy, I am quite aware of that," Tom smiled. Then he quickly grew serious and dark once again. And his grin, which hadn't quite managed to reach the surface, fell back deep into his soul.

"When we reach New York—" Lord Bainbridge started again.

But this time, Tom interrupted him. "When we reach New York, I will be met by my sister and brother-in-law," he said. "And I will go to live with them.

I will go to work in the factory that makes shirtwaists, and I will marry the girl they have picked out for me. I am not brave like you, Jeremy."

"I told you, I'm no hero," Lord Bainbridge protested.

"I'm not talking about that," Tom answered. "You're brave enough to live your life the way you truly want." He shook his head. "I am not. When it comes to that, I am a coward."

"I told you we could live together anyway you want," Lord Bainbridge insisted. "We can live just as friends if you like. That's it!" he cried out as if he had stumbled upon a miraculous solution. "We can be friends, boon companions living together in a completely platonic relationship. No sex! No love!"

"I could never be near you and not want to hold you, to kiss you," Tom said, his words both caressing and hurting Lord Bainbridge at the same time.

"Then what do we do?" Lord Bainbridge asked in a weak voice although he already knew and dreaded the answer.

"We must say good-bye here and now," Tom answered.

A white-hot heat burned through Lord Bainbridge's brain and his heart as he heard his sentence. And that it should be the one he loved who was dooming him to such a purgatory only made the pain that much greater. And in his pain, his despair, a wild idea came into his head. He would reach out, wrap his arms around Tom, and hurl them both over the side of the ship, down into the dark waters below. Without life belts, they would sink swiftly to the bottom of the ocean, and there they would lay together in each other's arms forever. No one would ever separate them, and they would be added to the tragic toll of *Titanic* dead. He actually reached out and took hold of Tom, and Tom, thinking he was merely seeking to embrace him for a final time, did not resist. He let himself be enveloped in Lord Bainbridge's arms. He let their bodies come together intimately one last time.

Whether he would have truly gone through with his desperate act, Lord Bainbridge would never be sure. But as it so often happens in life, he was spared from making that fatal decision. And to add a touch of absurdity to the situation, his rescuer, who came charging down the deck toward them like a freight train, was none other than Marco Borsalino. It was typical of Marco that he always seemed to be running somewhere as if he were trying to outrun life or at least the life fate had dealt him. As benefited one who was always so absorbed in himself, Marco failed to notice that Lord Bainbridge and Tom were in an embrace. He clutched Lord Bainbridge's arm, pulling them apart.

"I have been looking for you all over the ship!" Marco exclaimed.

"Not now, Marco!" Lord Bainbridge told him rather forcibly while at the same time pulling himself free from the Italian's grasp. The only other person he would have hated to see more at this sensitive and inopportune moment would have been Ronnie Standish. Thankfully, he was spared that. But Marco, as was his nature, was to prove to be enough of a trial.

"I need to talk to you!" Marco insisted. "It's urgent!" he added, wedging himself between Lord Bainbridge and a rather startled Tom.

"I told you, not now!" Lord Bainbridge practically yelled into his face. He tried to move around the Italian, but Marco had him pinned to the rail, using his slim body as a weapon and grinding himself against Lord Bainbridge, trying to arouse him sexually.

Tom, having recovered from this rather unexpected assault, began to back away from the scene. His eyes sought Lord Bainbridge's, and there was a half smile on his lips, slightly mocking as if he were saying, "See you won't be alone."

"I have to leave now, Jeremy," he said out loud.

And Lord Bainbridge knew Tom meant he was leaving not just from the moment, but from the rest of his life as well. "Don't go!" he cried out, struggling against Marco's hold.

"I ain't going nowhere, you can count on that," Marco said, thinking Lord Bainbridge had called out to him.

"Damn you, Marco, get off me!" Lord Bainbridge shouted, finally managing to push himself free.

But by then, Tom was already a few paces down the deck. He turned around once and raised his hand in a wave, the way he had done on that first morning when they had parted on the boat deck of the *Titanic*. Then it had only been for a few hours; this time it was forever. Lord Bainbridge had a last glimpse of him and then he was gone, swallowed up into the darkness like a myth.

At last free from his entanglement with Marco, Lord Bainbridge could have run after Tom, but instead he stood there frozen on the deck, knowing any pursuit would have been futile. He could have chased Tom to the ends of the earth, and he still would not have caught up with him. It was over between them, and he had to accept it. He had found and lost the great love of his life. And the only thing he could do was stand there numb with grief and stare at the place where Tom had disappeared into the darkness.

But if he had forgotten about Marco, Marco certainly hadn't forgotten about him. He pushed himself into Lord Bainbridge's face once again. "Jeremy, I need your help!" he pleaded.

If at that moment he had had anything in his hand that he could have used to inflict pain, he would have lifted it and smashed it into Marco's dark smiling face and continued to beat him until his face and whole head had been reduced to a bloody pulp. Fortunately for them both, his hands were empty.

"What is it you want from me?" he asked wearily.

As always, Marco was quick to leap in when an opening was given him. "Jeremy, I'm destitute. I haven't a penny," Marco told him. "I've searched the whole ship looking for Monsieur Gatti. I figured he owed me at least some wages, half the voyage anyway. It's not my fault the ship hit that stupid iceberg. But I couldn't find him anywhere. The bastard must have drowned," he concluded with little sympathy.

"What about the money I gave you the other night?" Lord Bainbridge asked dully, only wanting to be rid of him.

Macro hung his head and actually looked sheepish for a moment. "I lost it all in a round of cards," he confessed. Then he went on to reveal that his loss hadn't come in one of those high-stake card games in the first-class smoking room that he had boasted he would sit in on and come away a big winner, but rather he had lost the money to two of his fellow waiters in a quick game in one of the restaurants back pantries. "You have to give me something," he persisted, "just a little something to get me started."

And Lord Bainbridge would have, just to get rid of him, but with his next words Marco overplayed his hand as he had probably done in the unfortunate card game with his mates. "I could make trouble for you when we reach New York," he hinted to Lord Bainbridge. "The newspapers will pay big money for my story."

Lord Bainbridge fixed him with a steely gaze, and the hand that was about to reach into his coat for his wallet quickly withdrew. "Not a penny!" he said with a finality that even Marco understood.

Ever resourceful, the young Italian tried another tact, moving closer to Lord Bainbridge and batting his absurdly long dark lashes at him. "But, Jeremy, what will become of me?" he asked coquettishly. "I don't know a soul in America."

"I'm sure you'll quickly make friends," Lord Bainbridge returned with all the malice he could muster. Then he quickly walked away, leaving a rather subdued and shocked Marco Borsalino alone at the rail.

One final encounter wrapped up the day for Lord Bainbridge. Finding himself back in the first-class section of the *Carpathia*, he came face to face with the American woman's bodyguard, although, with what he had witnessed passing between them in the lifeboat, he doubted the man was still so gainfully employed. The two men stared at one another for a moment, and then wordlessly, the bodyguard offered his hand. When Lord Bainbridge accepted it, the bodyguard gave it a hardy shake and then moved on.

Back in the cabin lent to him by the kindly old gentleman, Lord Bainbridge told Alfred of the incident. He was hardly impressed. "You'd better count your fingers," Alfred advised him. "That one's as sly and shifty as they come."

"I think he was just trying to make peace," Lord Bainbridge suggested.

Alfred snorted his contempt. "For that one, there is no peace nor will there ever be." And then he said no more.

Lord Bainbridge laid the matter aside, for his mind had room for but one thought, and that thought was Tom.

Chapter XIV

Shortly after 8:00 PM on Thursday night, the *Carpathia* entered New York Harbor. The weather was dismal; a cold April rain was falling in sheets accompanied by flashes of lightning and claps of rolling thunder. This foul weather had come upon the *Carpathia* Tuesday night and, like a vengeful demon, had pursued it all the way to New York. As the ship made her way down the Ambrose Channel, a flotilla of smaller boats, steam launches, tugboats, ferryboats, and private yachts, overtook her. On board these vessels, most charted by the New York newspapers, were hordes of reporters and photographers. Right from the start, Captain Rostron had made it clear that he would allow no one on his ship once they reached New York, no family members, no reporters, not even the mayor of New York himself. So the newspapers, desperate to get the whole story, the exclusive interview, had sent out their packs of hounds to chase down the *Carpathia* and tree their quarry.

The quarry they sought began to appear, first in small numbers, on the open deck of the *Carpathia*. One of the reporters called out a question, "From the *Titanic*?" And when someone called back in the affirmative, those on the ship were startled by the sudden flashes of the photographers' magnesium flares. Questions were shouted to them, many seeking the fate of prominent personages who had been on the *Titanic*. Other reporters promised great rewards for an exclusive story.

Lord Bainbridge and Elaine Standish were among the first to appear on the *Carpathia's* deck. The next morning, a picture of the two of them, looking quite startled, almost frightened, would appear on the front page of the *New York Times*.

Beside them, a young *Titanic* crewman laughed out loud and shook his head when one of the reporters waved a handful of money at him and yelled up at him to jump into the water. "We'll pick you up!" he promised.

The crewman winked at Lord Bainbridge. "That fellow's daft if he thinks I'd go into the water again!" he said, still highly amused. "I've had all the water I want for the rest of my life. I doubt I'll ever take a bath again!"

Lord Bainbridge wrinkled his nose as if he feared the young man might have already begun his boycott. He turned to look at Elaine. Her face was pale, and every time a magnesium flare or a flash of lightning went off, he could see her tremble.

"Are you all right?" he asked, concerned.

"Yes," she answered. "It's like a scene from a nightmare," she mused, "or from hell."

"Oh yes," Lord Bainbridge agreed. "Hell punctuated by the absurd," he added, gesturing toward the reporter on the boat below who was still trying to persuade some hearty soul to jump into the water.

"Speaking of the absurd," Elaine said, turning to face him, her beautiful eyes filled with amusement. "Do you know that as I was getting ready to come up on deck, one of the *Carpathia's* women passengers came up to me and said, 'My dear, you certainly aren't planning to go up on deck with your head uncovered.' I was so startled I almost fell over, and I asked her what she was talking about. The woman informed me that no proper young lady ever went anywhere without wearing a hat. She even offered me one of her own hats to wear, an ugly old thing that I wouldn't have worn under any circumstances." She shook her head in disbelief. "After all we've been through, to be bothered by something which now seems so meaningless is the height of absurdity," Elaine finished.

"I'm sure she was just trying to be kind," Lord Bainbridge suggested.

Elaine shrugged and gave her head a little toss, which caused her long dark hair to tremble as if it had been touched by the wind. "Yes, of course," she conceded.

In fact, the *Carpathia's* passengers could not have been more generous. Opening up their suitcases and trunks, they had given away their own clothing to their unexpected guests, many of whom had arrived from the *Titanic* ill-attired for the chilly North Atlantic weather, which turned even colder on Tuesday morning. Others, like the kindly old gent, had even given up their cabins. But in spite of their generosity, there remained between them and the survivors of the *Titanic* a gulf that could never be completely breached. And it was a gulf that would forever divide those who had survived the *Titanic* wreck and anyone else, the outsiders, those who had not been there. For like or not, the *Titanic* survivors now found themselves members of a very exclusive club, a club whose membership would never increase but would only dwindle year by year until there was no one left.

But nevertheless, from Monday morning when the first lifeboat was picked up until the ship pulled into New York Harbor, the passengers and crew of the *Carpathia* did everything they could to see to the comfort and want of the souls from the *Titanic*.

During those four days, Lord Bainbridge and Elaine had spent much of the time together. Poor Maude, feeling both the effects of the ordeal they had gone through and the unsteady motion of the ship as they encountered rough seas and bad weather spent most of those days laying in a berth below deck with a cold cloth to her forehead and a vial of salts close at hand. Alfred meanwhile, being a creature fond of life's comforts, passed his time grousing about the lack of proper amenities on board the ship and lamenting his lost wardrobe. His mood made him hardly good company.

As for his own state of mind, all Lord Bainbridge felt was a kind of numbness. Both his body and his mind were infected with a sort of lethargic inaction that made even the smallest task seem beyond his endurance and pushed rational and constructive thought far beyond his capability. It was as if all his senses and reflexes had been deadened. He was not alone. A majority of the *Titanic's* survivors felt this way. For some, just the very thought that they had survived when so many others had not was beyond their understanding and even their acceptance. There were some even who cursed the very fact that they were still alive. For most, however, it was the simple fact that they were in the presence of something too big, too horrific, to grasp.

For Lord Bainbridge, there was the added misery of having lost the love he had so recently found. Lost not in the same sense as his dear friends the Frabolis and the Renoirs had been lost but lost just as well, and just as permanently he was sure. Through the past four days he had often chastised himself for his constant mourning over Tom, his grieving over an intense but brief romance, when all around him there were others who had suffered far greater misfortunes. Husbands torn from wives, children orphaned, whole families gone to a watery grave. They had all lost loved ones. Well, he too had lost a loved one! And his pain, he told himself, was no less than there's.

Alfred in his rough no-nonsense manner had tried to bring him around. He had sat him down and given him a spirited lecture on the pitfalls of falling in love with one of 'em, as he referred to Tom. "Look, Jeremy, you ain't ever gonna find your life's companion amongst fellows like him. That is unless you want to share him with a wife and a pack of screaming kiddies or at least a steady stream of ladies. None of 'em are in it for the long haul," he added with an urgent jab of his forefinger. Then he had produced a small book from the inside pocket of his jacket and waved it under Lord Bainbridge's nose. "This'll perk you up," he promised.

The book was a guidebook, a homemade edition put together by an elderly gentleman Alfred had once known. The gentleman had made frequent trips to New York City and had recorded, for others who shared his taste, all the city's bars, street corners, and parks where young men of questionable morals and meager means congregated. Back in London, Lord Bainbridge and Alfred had eagerly poured over the book and mapped out their plans the way regular tourists laid out their itineraries to visit more traditional historic sites and points of interest.

After meeting Tom, Lord Bainbridge had brushed the book aside and told Alfred he was through with all that. But now, he knew that one day he would return to the nightly pub crawls be it in America or back in London. Tom could have saved him from that, but Tom was gone and so was his salvation.

He had not seen Tom since their painful parting Monday night. It was not surprising that he had not run into him in the first-class sections of the ship, for despite the tragedy of the *Titanic* when at the ship's very last moment all divisions of class and those between rich and poor had, at least momentarily, vanished and death showed no distinction between millionaires and liftboys, things had quickly returned to normal. Even on board the overcrowded *Carpathia*, steerage passengers were kept below on their own decks. These decks Lord Bainbridge purposely kept away from, not letting himself even glance casually down at them for fear he might catch sight of Tom. And if he did, he greatly feared he might not be able to control his actions.

Then as if he needed something else to depress him, there was this whole damn hero business. Word of how he had forced those in his lifeboat to row back to the wreck to pick up survivors had spread throughout the *Carpathia* like wildfire. And no one had fanned those flames more than Benjamin Chamberlin, the American multimillionaire.

On Tuesday afternoon, Lord Bainbridge had been taking a late luncheon with Elaine in the *Carpathia's* first-class dining saloon. The timing of their meal was precluded by the fact that given the number of extra people on board, the *Carpathia's* kitchen was forced to serve their daily meals in shifts. But in spite of this, the food they offered was well prepared and plentiful. Lord Bainbridge and Elaine had just finished their desert and had ordered coffee when Benjamin Chamberlin appeared before their table. After a polite exchange, during which he inquired about their health and commented on the foul weather, which crowded everyone inside and made the *Carpathia's* limited space even more cramped, he asked if he might join them for a few minutes. Such an invitation was graciously extended.

Pulling out an empty chair, Chamberlin set his large bulk down and got right to the point, a trait that Lord Bainbridge had come to expect from the few Americans he had so far encountered.

"When we reach New York," Chamberlin began, "I intend to immediately contact the newspapers and tell them all about how you forced those cowardly crewmen to row back to help us poor souls struggling in the water. And at the point of a gun! Well done, lad! We Americans admire someone with that type of raw courage."

"I'd rather you didn't contact the newspapers," Lord Bainbridge protested.

"Nonsense, lad!" Chamberlin huffed, waving his hand about as if he were physically brushing aside Lord Bainbridge's protest. "You're a hero, and the world needs to know it!" He lowered his voice a bit. "There's cowards enough on board this ship," he added. "I heard tell of one man who not only got into a lifeboat, but he brought along his manservant and his damn little doggie as well."

"But really, I—" Lord Bainbridge started.

But Chamberlin waved him off again. "If others had been as brave and forthcoming as you, young sir, many more lives would have been saved." Finished, he pounded the table for emphasis, got to his feet, and said his final piece, "I owe you my life, sir, and that's a debt I don't ever intend to forget."

A moment later, Lord Bainbridge and Elaine were left alone in what could only be called a rather stunned silence. Lord Bainbridge shook his head. "It's all rather ridiculous," he murmured.

"He's right though," Elaine said emphatically. "Right on the money. You are a hero," she told him.

Lord Bainbridge winced and wished that everyone would stop calling him a hero. What he had done he had done because of Tom. He would have done none of it if it hadn't been for him. In his own heart, he was convinced he was no hero, only a man so desperate to hang onto the new love he had found he would do anything not to lose it, even jump into the frigid Atlantic in the middle of the night. And all this business about these stories of his bravery being bandied about, and even worse appearing in the newspapers, he found most irritating. Why couldn't people just forget it all and let him be? Thankfully, he was certain in a few months this whole *Titanic* affair would be forgotten, pushed off the front pages of the newspapers and the front burners of people's minds by new and unfortunate tragedies. The idea of his story showing up in the newspapers gave him something else to worry about. What if reporters started probing into his life, started digging into his past? What might they unearth? And what if others came forth with "different" stories about him? Hadn't Marco already threatened to unmask him to the world?

Back on the deck as the ship continued its journey into the harbor, Lord Bainbridge glanced along the rail to see the devil himself, Marco, smiling back at him. He even raised his hand in a wave. But he was not alone. For at his side, looking smug and quite satisfied with himself stood Ronnie Standish.

"I see he's already found a new playmate," Elaine said, nodding toward her husband.

Lord Bainbridge was hardly surprised that the two of them had finally come together—it was inevitable. *Well, they probably deserve each other,* he thought with some small satisfaction.

Elaine, apparently, had come to the same conclusion. "They make a perfect couple," she said. "They're both in love with the same person—themselves."

Lord Bainbridge smiled at this, remembering the obvious flirtations attentions he had observed Marco paying to Elaine back in the lifeboat.

"A lot of prominent wealthy women have lost their husbands," Elaine observed, gazing at some of the other people now lining the deck, which was now becoming quite crowded as more and more of the *Titanic's* survivors came up from below, anxious for their first glimpse of New York. "I overheard one woman," she went on, "I think she was from Philadelphia, declare, that because her husband had been saved, she was going to divorce him. She said she was ashamed of him because he was still alive, and it would have been better for both of them if he'd drowned. She actually added that it would be more socially acceptable if he had perished." Elaine shook her head with disdain. "What a stupid thing to say!" She let her eyes wander along the deck to where Ronnie and Marco were laughing and joking about something, whispering together like silly schoolgirls. Their behavior, so reproachful at a tragic time like this, was earning them looks of rebuke from many of those around them. "I wouldn't want anyone to think I was leaving Ronnie because he had survived," Elaine continued, now turning her eyes back to Lord Bainbridge. "Later, when all this has died down, I will leave him. My father is a lawyer. He'll know how to get it done quickly and quietly. Then I will find a new life for myself," she added softly.

As he stared back at her, Lord Bainbridge found himself startled by the look in her eyes, those exquisite deep violet eyes that regarded him with such compassion, such understanding. He realized with a little shock that she was probably half in love with him already. She knew all about him, his preferred lifestyle, and yet she still wanted him. Lord Bainbridge could tell Elaine was waiting for him to say something, and for a long moment, the two of them stood there in silence, oblivious to everyone else around them, deaf to the great human drama that was unfolding before them. He had only to open his mouth, and his whole life could change forever. He might suggest he visit her in Boston, or he could even offer to escort her there from New York. After all, it was a time when a gentleman would offer his protection to a woman traveling alone. It would all be quite proper. *Strange,* he thought, *the decisions we make, the choices, the roads we take, the others we don't.* But he knew his choice had been made long ago, and there was, for him, no going back. In spite of the fact that he was attracted to this beautiful woman beside him and saw her as his ideal of what womanhood should be, they had no future together. She had made one mistake, he certainly wasn't going to help her make another. So Lord Bainbridge said nothing, and a moment later, his eyes turned to gaze at the approaching New York skyline. And Elaine, for her part, understood and accepted graciously the meaning of his silence and perhaps had even grown to love him a little more for his honesty, which had been spoken without a word.

As the *Carpathia* continued up New York Harbor, she was buffeted by strong winds and heavy rains while angry stabs of lightning ripped through the night sky. The ship passed the Battery at Manhattan's southern tip where thousands of spectators had gathered to watch her arrival despite the cold and persistent rain. Instead of stopping at her own pier, Cunard Pier 54, the *Carpathia* steamed to the White Star dock, where she took the time to unload the *Titanic's* lifeboats. It was a poignant moment as all that was left of the once mighty liner was returned to her owner.

By this time, Lord Bainbridge and Elaine had been joined on deck by Alfred and Maude. In fact, all of the *Carpathia's* decks were now crowded with her own passengers as well as those from the *Titanic*, all eager for disembarkation.

It was 9:00 PM by the time that the *Carpathia* was made fast to her own pier and the canopied gangways were hauled into place. A stickler for propriety and discipline to the end, Captain Rostron was determined that his ship would be evacuated in an orderly manner. To this aim, he decided that the *Carpathia's* own passengers would disembark first to be followed by the *Titanic's* first—and second-class passengers. Steerage passengers from the *Titanic* and her crew would not go ashore until all others had departed the ship.

Having to wait, even a short while longer, did not sit well with Alfred. He paced the deck nervously, mumbling his irritation. Lord Bainbridge sensed that he had had quite enough with being on board a ship, any ship, even one in dock and was very anxious to once again put his foot on dry land.

But in the next instant, Alfred seemed to have recovered himself. "Cheer up, mate," he said to Lord Bainbridge, slapping him on the shoulder. "We'll soon be in proper digs with some proper clothes."

Maude was quite startled by Alfred's action, which she regarded as most inappropriate. Even Elaine looked perplexed while Lord Bainbridge himself merely shrugged it off.

The proper digs to which Alfred referred was no less than the Waldorf-Astoria Hotel, one of New York's most prestigious addresses. Months ago when Lord Bainbridge and Maude had been planning their trip, they had selected the Waldorf-Astoria to be their place of residence upon their arrival in New York, and they had cabled ahead for reservations. Now, those reservations would certainly come in handy. Given the fact that empty hotel rooms were now a rarity in the city, what with the unexpected arrival of both the *Titanic's* and *Carpathia's* passengers and the influx of anxious relatives and friends who had streamed in from other parts of the country. What few rooms were still available when the *Carpathia* docked were quickly snapped up. Maude had eagerly agreed to share her rooms at the Waldorf-Astoria with Elaine who, at the last moment, had decided to remain in New York for a few days. She certainly had no desire to accompany her husband who had elected to return immediately to Boston with his new companion. Elaine had confided to her English friends that her father, her only living relative, was in poor health and therefore would not, she was sure, be coming to New York to meet her. As soon as they reached their hotel, she planned to send him a cable that she was safe and in good hands.

Finally, all of the *Carpathia's* passengers had departed, and it was time for the *Titanic* survivors, first and second class that is, to make their way down the canopied gangways and onto the pier. As he followed Maude and Elaine down the gangway, with Alfred trailing behind him, Lord Bainbridge let his eyes drift back to the ship for a final look, seeking out one of the lower decks where a group of *Titanic* steerage passengers were quietly waiting for their turn. They were too far away for him to make out their faces. So he had no notion if Tom was among them or not. He had hoped for a last glance of him, a last glance that would have to last him a lifetime. But apparently, not even that was to be granted him, and he turned his eyes away. For an instant, tears welled up in the corners of his eyes, but he quickly and angrily blinked them away.

Another hurriedly brushed by them on the gangway. It was the teenage boy whom Lord Bainbridge had rescued, not once but twice. The boy was one of the few passengers still dressed in evening clothes from that last night on the *Titanic*. He had come across the boy a number of times on board the *Carpathia*, and each time, the boy had taken his hand and thanked him profusely for saving his life. Now, as he watched the boy, filled with joy and obviously happy to be alive, being embraced by an older couple who must have been his parents, Lord Bainbridge found himself wondering what the boy's future had in store for him. Then with a shrug he accepted the fact that that was something he would never know.

As they came down off the gangway and stepped onto the pier, it was like coming from night into day, for the pier was lit up by huge spotlights shining onto the anxious waiting crowd, so survivors could more easily spot their relatives. And what a crowd it was. The police would later estimate that the pier itself had been packed with over thirty thousand people while thousands more waited outside in the rain.

From the deck of the *Carpathia*, Lord Bainbridge had stared down at the crowd that lined the pier, and he had been startled by the sea of anxious faces that were turned up to meet his gaze. *All those thousands of people,* he had thought, *waiting and praying for someone, someone who is not me.* He had felt small and helpless and very much alone.

Now, as his feet actually touched the pier with Elaine at his side tightly clutching his arm and Maude and Alfred following close behind, Lord Bainbridge was struck by the demeanor of the crowd. They were hushed and stilled as they waited in expectation of spotting a familiar face, for in spite of the fact that the *Carpathia's* wireless operator had struggled tirelessly for days to cable to New York as many of the names of the survivors as he could, the names were often misspelled or otherwise misidentified. And some names were omitted altogether. So until this moment when the *Carpathia* docked and the *Titanic's* survivors began to disembark, no one could be absolutely sure who had survived and who had not.

As Lord Bainbridge and the others made their way along the pier, the crowd parted respectfully, almost reverently, for them and then, once they had passed, closed ranks again.

"Everyone's so quiet," Elaine whispered to Lord Bainbridge. "Almost as if they were holding their breath."

Then as if to dispute her observation, a woman's scream of despair shattered the silence. Her piercing wail seemed to echo in the cavernous building for some time, floating up to the ceiling like a cloud of mist. Turning their heads back toward the *Carpathia*, Lord Bainbridge and his companions failed to locate the source of the disturbance. But the unknown woman's cry seemed to act as a signal. The once peaceful crowd broke apart into mass confusion and then almost into panic, for as more and more of the *Titanic's* passengers stepped onto the pier, those who had been waiting, waiting desperately for a glimpse of a dear face, began to realize that their loved ones had not survived. The crowd began to become unruly. There was much pushing and shoving as names were shouted out, some in joyful recognition, but many others in grief and despair.

An elegantly attired young woman, completely distraught and on the verge of madness, ran back and forth across the pier chanting in a high-pitched voice, "There must be more! There must be more!"

There are more, Lord Bainbridge thought bitterly to himself, *they're lying at the bottom of the Atlantic.*

Reporters from the various New York newspapers with their photographers close at hand, were everywhere. Like vultures circling a fresh kill, they prowled through the anxious crowd, ruthlessly searching for a scoop, mercilessly pressing for an exclusive interview. The photographers' cameras flashed like lightning, frightening everyone and capturing for posterity the startled faces that filled the pier. Most of these faces had no desire to see their picture plastered on the pages of some newspaper at anytime. A decent woman, so it was said, only had her picture in the newspaper three times in her lifetime—when she was introduced into society, when she married, and when she died. So most of the reporters' advances were quickly rebuffed, and arms and hands quickly flew up to faces to try and block the camera's unmerciful intrusion. In fact, many of the *Titanic's* survivors were so traumatized by their ordeal, or perhaps embarrassed by their own behavior, that as soon as they were free of the pier, they refused to even speak of the *Titanic*, and many took to even denying they were on the ship. Some even continued with this denial until their dying day.

Lord Bainbridge and his little party found themselves trapped in the middle of the great crowd that filled the pier and were making little progress toward the doors to the street when an eager young reporter managed to push and shove his way up to them.

The young man, who had bright eyes and an easygoing if slightly sinister-looking smile, actually wore a card with the word *Press* printed on it stuck in the band of his bowler hat. He carried a notebook and pencil, and as he approached Lord Bainbridge, he quickly flipped to a clean page to write down the exciting words he was so sure he was about to hear. "How about an exclusive interview, mister?" he asked Lord Bainbridge, smiling at him with insincere sincerity. "My paper will pay you a hundred bucks for your story."

Lord Bainbridge was appalled at the very suggestion of such an exchange. Already upset that Benjamin Chamberlin planned to tell his story to the newspapers and still not utterly convinced that Marco would not also reveal all for a tidy sum, he certainly had no desire to see himself splashed across the pages of a third cheap tabloid. Wordlessly, he waved the reporter away.

But the young man was hardly put off. Maude quickly became his next target. "What about you, madam?" he proposed. "You certainly look like you'd have a tale to tell."

Maude's heavy jowls trembled with what could only be called indignation. She fixed the reporter with a steely gaze and told him exactly how she felt. "My words are reserved for books, not newspapers," she answered with all the disdain she could muster. "Good day to you, sir!" she added. And then taking the lead, she plowed them through the crowd like Moses parting the Red Sea.

Looking back over his shoulder, Lord Bainbridge noticed Alfred having a few quick words with the reporter before he hurried to catch up with them. At the time, Lord Bainbridge thought little of it, guessing only that perhaps Alfred was chatting him up for a future date as the young fellow was not unattractive.

With Maude leading the way, they made rapid progress and had almost reached one of the giant wooden doors that led out into the street when the door suddenly swung open and a liveried chauffeur stepped right into their path. Ignoring them, he began to call out the name of the party he was seeking in a loud booming voice. "Lord Bainbridge! Lord Bainbridge!"

"That's you, Ducks," Maude reminded Lord Bainbridge with a nudge.

Lord Bainbridge had been so startled to hear his name bellowed out by a complete stranger in a foreign land, he had been dumbfounded for a moment. He quickly recovered himself however. "I'm Lord Bainbridge," he announced to the man.

The chauffeur dropped his eyes to look at him, and the quizzical look etched on his face detailed how strongly he doubted Lord Bainbridge's claim.

"I really am," the young Englishman told him. "I've got papers to prove it," he said, starting to reach into his pocket.

"That won't be necessary, sir. Your word is good enough," the chauffeur quickly assured him. "I'm sorry, sir," he apologized. "I thought you'd be, well, an older gentleman."

"He's just a pup," Maude put in good-naturedly.

"I'm from the Waldorf-Astoria," the chauffeur explained to them, pointing to the fancy stitching on the front of his uniform that spelled out the hotel's name along with its logo. "I've a car waiting," he added. He looked from one to the other and then back to Lord Bainbridge. "Any luggage, sir?"

Lord Bainbridge frowned, "Hardly."

"No, of course not," the chauffeur returned quickly. He paused a moment to stare at the large, and now completely out of control, crowd that was surging back and forth across the pier like a restless human tide. "A bad business, sir," he said to Lord Bainbridge.

Lord Bainbridge nodded. "Yes, a very bad business indeed."

The chauffeur opened one of the doors to the street, and they followed him outside. The downpour that had been falling all day had been replaced by a light rain, a gentle almost comforting drizzle as if the heavens themselves were weeping over the city of New York. Outside, they found a crowd of people so large it seemed to go on forever, a vast sea of faces, every eye of which seemed to fix on the four of them as they emerged from the pier.

My God, Lord Bainbridge thought to himself, *I feel like I've stepped out onto the stage of the Royal Albert Hall before a full house.*

The crowd was remarkably well behaved save for a number of youths who had climbed up lampposts for a better view. The rest were standing silently, almost meekly, behind a series of ropes dotted with green lights that the police had set up to confine them to the sidewalks and keep the streets clear for traffic. Perhaps the presence of hundreds of New York City policemen, on foot and horseback, was the reason for their restrained conduct. But in reality, for the most part, the only emotion those on the sidewalks displayed was curiosity. Their eyes eagerly leaped on each new figure to emerge from inside the pier.

"Who are all these people?" Maude exclaimed, gazing at the crowd. "Surely they all didn't have loved ones on the *Titanic.*"

"Not at all, ma'am," the chauffeur answered as he unfurled the large umbrella he had been carrying over his arm to protect the two women from the light rain. Then he went on with his explanation. "They're what we here in America call curiosity seekers. It seems that whenever there's an event of epic proportions, especially if it's one with tragic circumstances, then hundreds, even thousands, of people come from all over to be part of it. I was in San Francisco during the great quake, and I saw the same thing happen there."

"Damn morbid of them if you ask me," Maude muttered.

"Perhaps so, ma'am," the chauffeur conceded. "Though I see it as just ordinary folk wanting desperately to be a part of any newsworthy event. I don't think they mean any harm in it, truly I don't."

Listening to the chauffeur as he guided them along the short distance to where his motorcar was parked, Lord Bainbridge was struck by the man's open friendly manner. It was the same kind of demeanor possessed by Benjamin Chamberlin and also by the young woman who still tightly clutched his arm. Most Americans it appeared, well, at least the small number he had encountered except of course for the American woman who had been in his lifeboat, were quite different from his own countrymen. His fellow Englishmen and women were, more often than not, cold, standoffish, downright rude and, worst of all, boring. Lord Bainbridge decided, right then and there, that he was going to like Americans.

One other thing about the chauffeur impressed Lord Bainbridge. Though the man was obviously a talker, he thankfully had the good sense not to pepper them with questions about the tragedy they had all so recently gone through. His description of the affair as "a bad business," had been his one reference to it. In fact, as he chatted amiably to them, he seemed to be doing his best to take their minds off the *Titanic* and her demise.

"Here we are now," the chauffeur announced, bringing them to a stop.

Before them stood a motorcar that Lord Bainbridge knew at once even his mother would have highly approved of. It was an elegant silver gray luxury vehicle with raised headlights and rich dark blue leather upholstery. Alfred's loud whistle of appreciation indicated that he too was impressed.

The chauffeur held open the door and gave first Maude and then Elaine a hand as they climbed into the backseat. Lord Bainbridge followed after them. Then the chauffeur went around to the other side and climbed into the driver's seat.

Only Alfred hesitated. Instead of slipping in beside the driver, he opened the backdoor and stuck his head in. "I've something to attend to. I'll catch up to you at the hotel," he told Lord Bainbridge.

Irritated and tired, and now quite convinced that Alfred was deserting them for a sexual escapade with the young reporter back at the pier, Lord Bainbridge spoke sharply to him. "Alfred, this is hardly the time for such activity!"

A glint came into Alfred's gray eyes. "And what kind of activity would that be, sir?" he asked, winking at him and well aware that both Maude and Elaine were watching and listening to them.

"Oh, go and do what you have to do!" Lord Bainbridge snapped, waving him away.

"I won't be long," Alfred promised before he shut the motorcar door and took off down the street back toward the pier.

"I don't understand why you put up with that ruffian," Maude said as their motorcar started up.

"It's a long story," Lord Bainbridge acknowledged with a sigh. Beside him, he felt Elaine stir uneasily. And when he turned to look at her, there was a little sympathetic smile on her beautiful face, which he found both comforting and irritating. He put his head back against the soft leather upholstery and closed his eyes.

Lord Bainbridge awoke with a start as if someone was shaking him awake. But he was alone, and more than that, he had no idea where he was. He closed his eyes again and tried to remember. The last thing he recalled was putting his head back and closing his eyes in the motorcar that was taking them to their hotel. Opening his eyes again and glancing around the well-appointed room, he realized he must be in that hotel, but he had no memory of how he got there.

The door to an adjoining room opened, and Alfred came into the room. "Well, you had yourself a nice sleep," he said.

"What time is it?" Lord Bainbridge asked, stretching.

"Half past ten," Alfred answered. "In the morning," he added with emphasis.

"I've no memory of how I got here," Lord Bainbridge commented, still rather confused.

Alfred shrugged. "Well I got back here about midnight. Found you sprawled across the bed in your clothes. So I got them off you, plunked you under the covers, and went off to bed myself," he said, nodding toward the adjoining room.

"The last thing I remember is being in that motorcar," Lord Bainbridge mused.

"Perhaps the chauffeur carried you in," Alfred suggested. "Not a very dignified entrance I must say," he chastised with a smile. "Your lady friends are bedded down across the hall," he added. He propped Lord Bainbridge's pillows up and poured him a cup of hot tea from a silver service that was set up on a table in the center of the room. As he handed him his tea, their eyes met, and Lord Bainbridge wondered why Alfred was being so extremely attentive on this particular morning. It certainly couldn't be that he was feeling remorse for his misbehavior the night before when he had run off for his little sordid tryst with that newspaper reporter. Contrition was not something Alfred practiced on a regular basis. As he sipped his tea, Lord Bainbridge was about to reprimand him for his behavior, especially given the fact that it had occurred in front of Maude and Elaine, but he quickly decided to let it pass. After all, he had to admit to himself that he was hardly one who could throw stones in that direction.

Alfred, meanwhile, continued to play the role of the perfect servant although all the while, a sly smile curled around the corners of his lips. "I got you some new clothes," he said, indicating the pile of clothing draped over the back of a brocade-covered chair standing in front of a tall wardrobe. "I'm afraid the suit is what the Americans call ready-made," he sniffed, with very apparent contempt. "Hardly acceptable, I know, but it will have to do until we can find a proper tailor. I've been to the bank. We're all set on that score. And I brought you the morning papers. I think you'll find them interesting." He placed the newspapers beside Lord Bainbridge on the bed. "And now that you're awake, I'll go and draw your bath," Alfred added.

He was halfway across the room when he remembered one last thing. He took an envelope off the table and brought it to Lord Bainbridge. "This letter came for you, special delivery. The persistent bloke who delivered it wanted me to awaken you immediately. I told him that was out of the question and that I would see to it. I sent him packing without a tip for being so impertinent," Alfred finished with satisfaction.

Frowning, Lord Bainbridge took the letter from him and tore it open. He scanned its contents. "This isn't a letter, it's a subpoena," he announced.

"You mean like in a court?" Alfred inquired.

Lord Bainbridge nodded. "I've been called to testify before a committee of the United States Senate looking into the sinking of the *Titanic*."

"Well, I'll be damned!" Alfred exclaimed. "Ain't that something! When do you have to go?"

"This very afternoon at 3:00 PM," Lord Bainbridge answered. "They're meeting right here in the hotel."

"Damn, I wish I could have gotten you some proper clothes," Alfred lamented. "Well, let me go and get your bath ready. We'll have to fix you up as best we can," he added before hurrying into the bathroom.

Lord Bainbridge put down the subpoena and lay back on his pillows. To say he was stunned by his summons was to put it mildly. What could they possibly want to hear from him? he asked himself.

Alfred appeared in the door to the bathroom for a moment. From behind him came the sound of running water as the bathtub filled. "I heard a bloke in the bank say that the United States Senate was getting into the act because they want to figure out who to blame for the ship going down," he said. "You know, someone's got to be held responsible for all the cargo and the passengers' personal belongs that were lost, someone's going to have to pay damages. I heard all the well-to-do passengers are putting claims in for what they lost. We'd better make our own list so we don't get left out," he advised before going back to the bathroom.

And what about all the lives that were lost, who's going to pay for them? Lord Bainbridge asked himself.

He put down the subpoena and absently picked up one of the newspapers beside him. Its jarring front-page headline so startled him that he sat up so violently, he came close to banging his head on the bed's headboard. His hands trembled as he read the words splashed across the top of the page in bold type: ALL SAVED FROM TITANIC AFTER COLLISION. *My God*, he thought for just an instant, *was everything I experienced just a nightmare, and this the real truth!* But then, he quickly came to his senses and saw, by the date on the newspaper, that it was four days old and obviously filled with erroneous reports that were filed before the truth became known. He tossed the newspaper with its mocking headlines aside and picked up another. This one, at least was current, and its headlines told of the sinking of the *Titanic* and the terrible loss of life. Other columns reported on the survivors' arrival in New York. Lord Bainbridge skimmed through the front page, reading only a few words here and there of a story he knew all too well. It was when he turned to the second page of the paper that he received his second shock of the morning. For there in bold print was the headline he had hoped he would not see: YOUNG ENGLISH LORD LABELED TITANIC HERO. And as he had feared, the accompanying article, that was in the form of an interview with Benjamin Chamberlin went to great lengths to praise him as the man who had rescued the American multimillionaire as well as many others. Chamberlin had kept his word to see that his story was told to the world. But there was even worse to come. Reaching for a third newspaper with much trepidation, Lord Bainbridge feared he was about to be greeted by the lurid headline: INNOCENT ITALIAN YOUTH CLAIMS HE WAS ATTACKED BY DEVIANT ON BOARD TITANIC. But what he actually saw shocked him even more. For right there on the front page was not only his own picture, but beside it, Alfred's as well.

Alfred chose this really bad moment to emerge from the bathroom and announce that his bath was ready.

Enraged, Lord Bainbridge leaped from the bed and waved the offending newspaper at him. "What is this? What is this?" he screamed.

Even Alfred was somewhat startled by the degree of Lord Bainbridge's anger, and he took a couple of steps away from him. "Come on, Jeremy," he said, "you knew, I was going back to the pier to see that reporter when I left you last night. What did you think, I was going to have sex with him?" The look on Lord Bainbridge's face told all. "You did!" Alfred cried out triumphantly. "You actually thought I went back to have sex with him." He shook his head, confident that now he had won the moment and probably the day as well. "You, of all people, should know he's not my type," he added, sounding deeply offended.

"How much did he pay you?" Lord Bainbridge demanded.

"A hundred bucks as he promised," Alfred answered.

"What do you need a hundred bucks for? I've always given you every penny you've ever needed," Lord Bainbridge said.

Alfred shrugged. "When you've come up through life the hard way, a hundred bucks is a hundred bucks. Besides," he added, "it's certainly the first and last time I'm ever going to have my name and picture in the newspaper." He gave Lord Bainbridge a hard defiant look. "Remember, the likes of me never gets mentioned in the papers, not even when we die."

"I still wish you hadn't done it," Lord Bainbridge said, calmer now.

Sensing that the storm had passed, Alfred offered him one of his sly smiles. "I said nothing but good about you, Jeremy," he told him.

Lord Bainbridge glanced again at the newspaper, wincing as he read the headline above their photographs: AN EXCITING EPIC OF A TITANIC HERO—AN

EYEWITNESS ACCOUNT AS TOLD BY HIS MANSERVANT. Then he looked down at their photographs, and although Alfred's was obviously taken the night before, his own was an old picture of him, taken many years ago. *Why, I look like a schoolboy,* he thought.

"Where did you get this photograph of me?" he asked Alfred.

"You gave it to me back when we first met," Alfred reminded him.

"And you've carried it around with you all this time?"

Alfred nodded. "Sure, what of it? Now, you'll have to give me another one," he added.

Shaking his head, Lord Bainbridge glanced once again at the newspaper in his hands, and two other pictures caught his attention. Both were of ship's officers of the *Titanic*. The first one, he at first failed to recognize as the same officer who had turned Sebastian Renoir away from the lifeboat. And it wasn't until a moment later when he read the name, Lightoller, under the picture that he gained recognition. The article accompanying the picture was full of praise for the man's activities, and like Lord Bainbridge himself, the man was generously anointed a hero. It goes without saying that Lord Bainbridge did not think of this man Lightoller as a hero. Quite the contrary, he held him in contempt, held him responsible for the deaths of Sebastian and his mother and most probably countless others. Lord Bainbridge had been on the *Carpathia's* boat deck, and he had seen many of the *Titanic's* lifeboats arrive not even half full. Undoubtedly, many of them had been launched by Lightoller with his strict code of women and children only no boys or men allowed even if the boat was sent away with empty seats. Then it came to Lord Bainbridge that if the members of the United States Senate wanted to hear what he had to say about the *Titanic* disaster, he did have something to tell them. He would tell them the truth about Second Officer Charles Lightoller. He owed it to Sebastian and his mother and all the nameless others who had been kept from entering the lifeboats by this man.

His mind quite made up, Lord Bainbridge was about to toss the paper aside and retire to his waiting bath when he remembered there had been a picture of another *Titanic* officer in the paper. He looked at it again, and this time, he instantly recognized the face that stared back at him. It was the young junior officer, the one who had befriended him and had been put in charge of their lifeboat and whose name he had never learned until now. In the photograph, the young man was smiling broadly with the newborn innocence of the unworldly. It was the same expression he had worn when Lord Bainbridge had first encountered him and continued to wear until his world, as the world of so many others, had shattered like a mirror that is dropped. In the brief column beside the young officer's likeness, Lord Bainbridge was greatly distressed to read the poor man had to be forcibly removed from the *Carpathia* in a state that the paper indelicately described as "complete madness." The paper went on to surmise that the officer's condition was no doubt the result of the terrible ordeal he had gone through and that he was to be committed to a New York State insane asylum for an indefinite period. *The poor kid,* Lord Bainbridge thought, *now he'll probably never get to find out if New York was as lively as he heard it was.*

"Your bathwater is getting cold," Alfred reminded him.

Heading to the bathroom, Lord Bainbridge tossed Alfred the newspaper. "By the way," he said over his shoulder, "they misspelled your name."

"What!" Alfred cried out, grabbing the newspaper and turning to the front page. "Those stupid buggers!" he swore as he saw that they had identified him as Alfred Walkins.

Slipping into his bath, Lord Bainbridge allowed himself a small smile of satisfaction.

On the roof of the Waldorf-Astoria, there was an elegant outdoor dining and dancing area formally known as the Waldorf Roof Garden. In spring and summer, it was filled with flowers and spacious greenery. Its white wrought iron tables and chairs were protected from the sun by colorful striped awnings. Especially popular for dining and dancing under the stars, it also served a well-regarded and well-attended luncheon. And it was here after he had refreshed himself with his bath and slipped into the new clothes that Alfred had provided for him that Lord Bainbridge took lunch with Maude and Elaine.

The two women had also managed to secure new clothing in the short period of time since their arrival at the hotel the previous night. It had been their good fortune to be taken under the wing of a mother and daughter who were visiting New York from Elaine's home city of Boston. And while Elaine was not previously acquainted with the two, they generously opened both their arms and their wardrobes to the two women from the *Titanic.* The two older women matched each other in size and proportion as did the two younger. So there was no problem with fit. Color and style were another matter indeed! At least they were for Maude, and she lamented her distress as they settled into their chairs on the roof garden.

"The dear lady, while generous beyond reproach, has a decidedly demented lack of taste," Maude complained. Looking down at the dress she wore—a rose-colored silk adorned with large pink roses made out of felt and which made it look as she were covered with spots from some exotic, and probably fatal, tropical disease—Maude shook her head. "And would you believe, this was the plainest, simplest, dress in her whole collection?" she asked the others. At least the hat she wore, a relatively unaffected straw trimmed with a few artificial cherries and leaves, was more subdued.

Elaine had had better luck. The light blue linen suit she wore was both stylish and a perfect fit. She too, wore a hat, of blue felt with a small black veil pulled back over the brim. Remembering the promise she had made to Lord Bainbridge that she was never going to be bothered with such petty things as hats anymore, she smiled at him from across the little table between them and made a confession. "I'm afraid I'm not such a rebel after all."

As they began to order their luncheon from the generous menus the attentive waiter had placed before them, Maude was still going on about her unfortunate dress. All her life, she had worn nothing but subdued tones of black, dark blue, and purple, and now, here she was looking as she put it, "Like she belonged on the music hall stage or in a carnival." Then she put down her menu and stared at her two companions. "Dear Lord," she said to them, "will you listen to me. Here I am going on and on about something so trivial as a dress while only days ago, hundreds of poor souls met a terrible and untimely death." She beseeched them with tears welling up in her eyes. "What kind of a terrible person am I?"

Instantly, Elaine reached over and took her hand. "Don't reproach yourself," she told Maude. "You are a kind and dear lady. It's natural after going through such a horrible ordeal for one to cling to the trivial, the small everyday things that make up our lives. It's the way our brain has of dealing with something so shocking. One cannot possibly think about it every moment. We must dwell on other things, everyday things if we are to get on with our lives." She glanced at Lord Bainbridge for a moment. "It's the way we have to keep from going mad," Elaine added.

Lord Bainbridge nodded in agreement. It was very apparent to him that the two women had formed a warm bond of friendship. This pleased him immensely and offered him great comfort.

While they waited for their first course, Maude, who had recovered herself, revealed to Lord Bainbridge that Elaine had invited her to stay with her in Boston at her father's house from where she would start her book tour. "And after my tour is over," Maude went on, "Elaine is going to return with me to London for a visit. I know at least a hundred fine lads of good family who will swoon at your feet," she promised the younger woman.

"One would be plenty," Elaine responded quietly, rather demurely.

Maude was, for the moment, caught up in her own enthusiasm. "I've quite made up my mind to mold the heroine of my Egyptian novel after you, my dear," she told Elaine. "She'll be a gorgeous young creature filled with the spirit and independence that typifies you American girls."

"And will your book have a happy ending?" Elaine asked, darting a glance at Lord Bainbridge.

"But of course," Maude responded quickly. "All my books have happy endings. My readers wouldn't have it any other way." She looked across the table at Lord Bainbridge. "And what about you, Ducks?"

"Me?" Lord Bainbridge asked, slightly startled.

"What are your plans, silly?" Maude chastised good-naturedly. "Will you still go ahead with your vacation, your trip through America?"

Lord Bainbridge hesitated a moment. "I guess . . . I have no other plans. I certainly don't fancy another boat trip anytime soon."

Elaine shivered. "Nor do I. I'm not sure I'll ever be able to get on a ship again." She turned to Maude. "We may have to find another way to get back to London," she suggested.

"Well, there's always those new contraptions called aeroplanes," Maude mused.

"I don't think they could manage the distance," Lord Bainbridge said.

"We'll find a way," Maude replied with supreme confidence.

The waiter arrived with steaming bowls of chicken soup, filled to the brim, and there was a few minutes of silence as the three of them concentrated on the food before them, each one surprised to find that in spite of everything, they were quite hungry.

Then Maude asked Lord Bainbridge a question that quite startled him. "And what about your new friend?"

Lord Bainbridge stirred uneasily in his chair, momentarily disturbed by her rather bold question.

Elaine, seeing his distress, sought to comfort him. "It's all right," she told him, "there are no secrets at this table."

"It's over," Lord Bainbridge answered after a moment.

"For good?" Maude inquired.

"I'm afraid so," he responded.

"And there's no chance at all," Maude persisted.

"None at all," Lord Bainbridge answered, and then immediately asked himself, *And how am I going to bear it?*

"I'm so sorry, Ducks," Maude said with great sympathy. "We'll have to find you someone else," she added as if it were a task so simply accomplished. "Meanwhile, you must get right to work on your new book," she advised. "I have your notes along with the portrait of your father, which you gave me for safekeeping. I shall turn them over to you at once."

"I am determined no matter what to write that book," Lord Bainbridge stated.

"And will your book also have a happy ending?" Elaine asked, putting down her spoon.

"Oh yes," Lord Bainbridge answered. *I promised myself that a long time ago,* he thought to himself.

It was during their main course when Lord Bainbridge realized he had forgotten to tell them about his summons to appear before the Senate committee in now what was less than two hours. He relayed to them the particulars and his own reluctance in doing so.

"You must go and set the record straight," Maude told him. Then a look of sadness came into her face. "Ducks, please don't let them put all the blame on poor Captain Smith. I'm sure he did everything he could," she said of her friend.

But it wasn't Captain Smith that Lord Bainbridge was concerned about, for his sights were set on the second officer, and on him, he would set the record straight.

"Elaine and I shall go with you and lend you support," Maude suggested.

"There's no need of that," Lord Bainbridge insisted.

"Nonsense, Ducks," Maude said to him. "We'll sit very quietly in the gallery and clap discretely when you're finished," she promised as if he were going to appear on stage performing a recitation.

"After all, you are a hero," Elaine reminded him.

"Oh, please don't mention that," Lord Bainbridge groaned, pushing his plate away.

Maude had another piece of advice. "You must send copies of all those flattering newspaper articles about you to your publisher. They'll do wonders for the sales of your next book."

"But I don't want to be a hero," he implored of both of them.

Maude fixed him with a steady gaze. "But you are, Ducks, you are," she affirmed.

Chapter XV

The United States Senate's investigation of the sinking of the *Titanic* was called to order at 10:30 AM on Friday, April 19 in the East Room of the Waldorf-Astoria Hotel in New York City.

Arriving for his subpoenaed appearance at exactly 2:45 PM, Lord Bainbridge found the corridor outside the East Room so crowded, he and his two female companions had to wait until a line of police and security men could clear a path for them. When they finally reached the doors to the East Room and Lord Bainbridge had given his name to the sergeant at arms, who stood guard before the doors, he was told he would not be called for a few minutes as the Senate committee was just finishing up with the previous witness. So there was nothing for them to do but wait. They managed to squeeze into seats on a long wooden bench that was situated across from the doors leading into the East Room.

Lord Bainbridge lit a cigarette and tried to calm his nerves, for he had suddenly gone weak in the knees as he came to the realization that once he walked through those doors, he would be subjected to intense questioning that, while on the surface would pertain to the sinking of the *Titanic*, could not help but reveal his own actions and, worse still, his motivations. He had been made a reluctant and unwilling hero, and now he was about to be put under the microscopic glare of public view.

His face must have gone quite white at this last thought because Elaine touched his arm and expressed her concern. "Are you all right?"

Lord Bainbridge shook his head. "Not really," he answered with a weak smile.

"Don't be nervous, you'll do splendidly," she assured him with a gentle pat.

Maude, meanwhile, having severely chastised a man who had the misfortune to trod over one of her feet, shook her head and grumbled that the whole atmosphere before them was like a circus.

And indeed it was. The corridor was filled with so much human traffic, individual movement had become almost impossible. The policemen and security guards, who had been trying to keep order, were themselves swallowed up by the mob and became part of it. Who all these people were was at first hard to determine. That some of them, those who passed in and out of the East Room with a sense of diligent importance and with no hindrance from the sergeant at arms guarding the doors were somehow officially involved with the proceedings taking place behind those closed doors seemed obvious. Others, and there were many of these, were easily identified as newspaper reporters by their press cards tucked into their hatbands. They, along with their partners in crime, the news photographers, who wielded their cameras like weapons, pointing them at almost anything that moved, seemed to be waiting breathlessly for someone in particular to emerge from the East Room. But besides the reporters and those officially connected to the proceedings, there appeared to be many others gathered in the corridor who were nothing more than sightseers. These were apparently the ordinary folks the chauffeur from the Waldorf-Astoria had spoken about, those who, having no link to a particular event, nonetheless felt compelled to become a part of it. And here in the corridor outside the East Room, they pushed and shoved with the best of them to get a better look at what was going on.

Lord Bainbridge was at least thankful that the reporters and photographers appeared not to recognize him. They in fact ignored him and his companions completely, obviously more intent on bagging bigger game. It must have been the picture that Alfred had given to the newspaper that had spared him, he rationalized. The picture had been taken so many years ago, at first he had hardly recognized himself.

But he was not to be left entirely alone. Two middle-aged women, dressed all in black with heavy black veils drawn tightly down over their faces, suddenly appeared before him. They seemed to have emerged out of nowhere as if they had swooped down out of the sky like two vengeful vultures. They both lifted their veils at the same time. Their faces were ugly and puffy from grief and hours of weeping. Their eyes stared at him accusingly while their lips were twisted into snarls of hate.

"You're Lord Bainbridge, aren't you?" one of the woman asked.

"Yes, madam," Lord Bainbridge answered. Not quite sure what was coming, he rose politely from his seat.

"And you were on the *Titanic*?" the second inquired.

Again, Lord Bainbridge responded in the affirmative. "What can I do for you ladies?" he asked.

The two women spoke almost in unison, the words of one echoing the words of the other. "Our husbands were also on the *Titanic*. They both drowned. We're *Titanic* widows," they added, claiming membership in that exclusive and tragic sisterhood.

"Ladies, I am truly sorry for your loss, and you have my heartfelt sympathy," Lord Bainbridge told them.

But sympathy was not what these two women were seeking. They moved closer to Lord Bainbridge and began to assault him with questions, their words aimed with the accuracy of deadly arrows. "How were you saved?" "How did you manage to get into a lifeboat?" "Did you bribe your way in?"

This last insinuation was too much for Lord Bainbridge, and though he thoroughly understood the intense grief these two must be going through, he could not remain silent. He drew himself up and spoke quietly, but forcefully, to them, "Once again, ladies, I offer my sincerest condolences for you loses, but I see no reason why I must explain or justify my own survival."

Elaine and Maude had also risen to their feet, and Lord Bainbridge could sense the anger and tension that Maude was barely managing to hold back. He knew it was only a matter of moments before she exploded and unleashed her volcanic wrath and indignation on those poor unsuspecting widows.

But they were spared her attack because, at that very moment, the heavy oak doors of the East Room were flung open, and a great crowd came pouring out into the corridor. The two widows were literally swept away as those already in the corridor struggled to reach the newcomers. Everyone's attention was riveted on two men in particular who had just emerged from the East Room. The first man had his face turned away from Lord Bainbridge's line of vision, so he was unable to recognize him. The second man, who was in the midst of giving an animated and very loud speech to the reporters and curious onlookers who crowded around him, was none other than J. Bruce Ismay, managing director of the White Star Line. Obviously, he had just finished with his own testimony before the Senate committee, and now, he was complaining loudly and questioning the legality of the investigation and whether the United States Senate had the right to subpoena British citizens.

"But, Mr. Ismay, with so many prominent Americans among the dead, don't the American people have a right to know exactly why this terrible catastrophe took place?" one of the reporters asked him.

Ismay nodded his head vigorously. "They do, they do," he agreed. "And I assure you, I told the Senate everything I knew. But, gentlemen, you must remember, I was merely a passenger on the *Titanic*. I had nothing to do with the running of the ship," he added.

That's a lie if there ever was one, Lord Bainbridge thought to himself, remembering the many times he had seen Ismay poking about in all parts of the ship, once even arguing, quite animatedly, with Captain Smith. But all during the time the ship was sinking, he could not remember having seen him, not even once. Even more curious was the fact that though he had stood at the *Carpathia's* rail and watched all the lifeboats being unloaded and scanned the face of almost every survivor searching for his friends, he had never seen Ismay come on board. In fact, Lord Bainbridge had concluded the man must have gone down with his ship until another passenger told him Ismay was indeed on board the *Carpathia* and had secluded himself in the ship's surgeon's cabin, refusing to see or speak to anyone. This same passenger also related to Lord Bainbridge the manner of Ismay's escape from the doomed *Titanic*. It seems, Ismay was seen helping to load the boats on the starboard side of the ship, and then, at the very last moment as the last boat was being loaded, he slipped quietly into the lifeboat as it made its way down to the waiting water below.

This behavior had earned him the scorn, if not the hatred, of the American public. Desperate for a scapegoat to help them cope with the tragedy, the Americans had turned on J. Bruce Ismay. The American press was particularly virulent. Calling him J. "Brute" Ismay, they printed the most vilest and odious of rumors about him as facts. In one of the same newspapers that he had found himself hailed as a hero, Lord Bainbridge had read a quote from another survivor who said he had seen Ismay sneak his way into a lifeboat decked out in women's clothing. Though he certainly was no fan of the man, thinking him smug and arrogant with that irritating half smile of his that seemed to register amusement and contempt at the same time, Lord Bainbridge thought the reaction to Ismay's survival was somewhat blown out of proportion. True, he was the managing director of the White Star Line and therefore indirectly the owner of the *Titanic*. And he had lived while hundreds of others, his passengers, his customers if you will, had not. But as another sympathetic survivor had put it to Lord Bainbridge, "What purpose would Ismay's death have served? His name would have just been added to a tragic weary roll that was already far too long."

Watching him now as he wound up his oratory to the reporters gathered around him, Lord Bainbridge knew Ismay was doing what he would have to do for the rest of his life—justifying his existence. Even though they were some distance apart, Lord Bainbridge noticed the beads of sweat on the man's forehead. And when a photographer's magnesium flash went off close to his face, Ismay jumped as if he had been shot. In spite of his dislike for the man, Lord Bainbridge felt a small degree of sympathy for him and the life that lay ahead of him.

It was at this moment that the sergeant at arms came out of the East Room and called for the next witness.

"Lord Jeremy Bainbridge! Lord Bainbridge, if you would!"

And the crowd, like a child on Christmas morning who has already tired of the first toy they unwrapped and turns with eager enthusiasm to the next brightly wrapped package, swung their attention away from Ismay and onto a rather startled Lord Bainbridge.

The sergeant at arms cleared a way for him through the crowd, and with Maude and Elaine trailing in his wake, Lord Bainbridge moved toward the doors to the East Room. Before he reached them however, it was inevitable, if not predestined, that he and Ismay should come face to face. As they did, Ismay, who had never before offered him little more than a smile and a nod, tipped his hat and held out his hand. He greeted Lord Bainbridge as if they were old friends, meeting by chance on an afternoon stroll through Regent's Park. "Ah, Lord Bainbridge, how nice to see you," he said. "I trust you are well?"

Somewhat taken back, Lord Bainbridge returned his greeting and reluctantly took his hand. Not surprisingly, he found Ismay's handshake cold and clammy and insincere.

"Next for the hot seat, are you?" Ismay asked him with a conspirator's wink as if they were lifelong chums. "Steel yourself, they're tough in there," were his words of advice.

The man who had been standing by Ismay's side, now revealed himself to be none other than Charles Lightoller, the *Titanic's* second officer. The next few moments proved rather awkward as Lord Bainbridge and Lightoller stared silently, uncomfortably, at each other. Ismay, who had been distracted by a reporter's question, apparently saw no reason to introduce the two men. Around the heads of the three of them, photographers' flashes went off like little bombs.

I wonder if he remembers me? Lord Bainbridge asked himself, thinking back on the confrontation they had on the boat deck over Sebastian Renoir. Lightoller's blank face gave away no secrets, and he looked almost bored as he returned Lord Bainbridge's gaze.

Strange, Lord Bainbridge thought, *one of these men has been labeled a hero, the other a coward, but I find it is the hero I despise, not the coward.* Looking into Lightoller's face, Lord Bainbridge saw Sebastian's face and the face of the poor little liftboy and the faces of so many others whom he had turned away from the lifeboats just because they were of the male sex. He had half made up his mind to confront the officer about his actions right there in front of all the reporters and onlookers when the sergeant at arms spoke to him in a respectful but rather urgent manner.

"The Senate awaits, Lord Bainbridge."

Lord Bainbridge nodded, realizing his words would be better served before the Senate than outside in a crowded hallway. But before he could move toward the doors to the East Room, a reporter came up with an idea that sent a shiver down Lord Bainbridge's spine.

"Let's have a photograph of the two heroes shaking hands," the man suggested.

His idea met with instant approval, and Lord Bainbridge found himself being pushed, none too gently, closer to Lightoller while Ismay was, with equal force, shoved aside.

"Big smiles, please, gentlemen," the photographer who had been selected to take the shot, prompted as he lined up his camera.

Lord Bainbridge looked down at Lightoller's hand that was extended to him. He stared at that hand for a long moment. A hush fell over the crowd around them as everyone waited for him to take Lightoller's hand. Then Lord Bainbridge shot a glance up at the second officer's face, which was smiling back at him. "Not likely," Lord Bainbridge said, turning and walking away.

A murmur of shock ran through the crowd, and just before he entered the East Room, Lord Bainbridge distinctly heard a woman tell her companion, in a tone of voice that was meant to be overheard, that in her experience she had always found the British to be a cold and unfriendly people.

The first thing Lord Bainbridge noticed as he walked into the East Room was that despite its grand size, the Waldorf-Astoria's ballroom, with its crystal chandeliers, gleaming white woodwork, and brocade drapes, was as packed with people as was the corridor outside. A long conference table had been set up in the center of the room while most of the rest of the room was taken up by rows of straight-backed chairs. Every chair was filled, and all that was left for latecomers was standing room in the back of the hall. A casual glance at those filling up the chairs gave one the quick impression that though there appeared to be a scattering of individuals who might actually have business before the committee and a few others, given the sad and haggard looks on their faces, who very well might have lost relatives or friends in the disaster, the majority of seats were taken up by members of New York society. And they, especially the women, had done themselves up in the latest finery as if they were attending the opening of a new opera or ballet.

As the sergeant at arms led Lord Bainbridge to the conference table, Elaine and Maude were left, for a moment, standing uncertainly in the middle of the room. But this was still the age of gallantry, and two gentlemen immediately relinquished their chairs to the two ladies and went and stood in the back of the room.

Lord Bainbridge took the witness chair at the conference table, and when he was seated, he looked up and saw that almost every face in the room was turned expectantly on him. He could not help but feel intimidated. In addition, standing around the table like scavengers, ready to take down his every word, were rows of newspaper reporters, their pads and pencils at the ready. *Well, now I know how those poor souls felt who appeared before the Inquisition,* Lord Bainbridge thought, smiling grimly to himself.

Seated across from him was a row of distinguished-looking gentlemen. One in particular caught his immediate attention. At the moment, the man was rapidly shuffling through a large stack of papers before him as if he had misplaced a valuable document. He seemed a bit put out by his own inability to find what he was looking for as he muttered to himself and shook his head. It was obvious this was the man who was in charge of these proceedings as the other gentlemen at the table were quietly waiting on him as indeed was everyone else in the room. So Lord Bainbridge was obliged to sit there in uneasy silence until the man at last, and with a triumphant clearing of his throat as if he had finally succeeded in dislodging a rather pesky morsel, finally came upon the document he had been so diligently seeking. He placed it before him, smoothing out its edges, and then taking off his spectacles, he looked across the table and offered Lord Bainbridge the kindest of smiles. Then he proceeded to introduce himself.

To many of the Americans in the room, William Alden Smith, the junior senator from the state of Michigan, needed no introduction. That "Brash bumpkin from the wilds of Michigan," as he was often affectionately referred to, was a figure straight out of American mythology. Having risen out of wretched poverty in true Horatio Alger fashion, he had worked his way up the ladder of success and respect until he stood at the top as a member of the United States Senate. Though a Republican, he often sided with liberal Democrats, especially when it came to matters of personal liberty and the rights of minorities. Though he was short, only five feet six inches tall, he had a rich powerful speaking voice, and like many short men, he bore himself with a mixture of arrogance and self-confidence. He was idolized, some would even say lionized, by his constituents. Known for his political shrewdness, he also had what one newspaper reporter called "an aggressive honesty and devotion to principle."

As soon as Senator Smith heard about the *Titanic* disaster and its appalling loss of life, he sprung into action. On the floor of the Senate, he proposed a special investigation under the auspices of the Senate Commerce Committee, of which, by coincidence, he was a member. His resolution passed unanimously, and he was made chairman of the committee and charged to investigate the causes leading up to the wreck of the White Star Liner *Titanic* and to study whether new laws or an international treaty was needed to prevent a repetition. But above all else, it was the human aspect of the tragedy that touched Senator Smith the most. He had been to the Cunard Pier the night the *Carpathia* arrived with her meager cargo of *Titanic* survivors. The Senator had gone there to serve J. Bruce Ismay with a subpoena to appear before his committee the following day. He had witnessed the terrible scene on the pier and he later recalled the spectacle as one of, "joy and sorrow so intermingled that it was impossible to discern light from shadow." He had been recognized and then besieged by weeping relations and friends of those *Titanic* passengers who had not returned home. And these distraught ones, in their anguish and despair, had peppered him with outlandish suggestions that their unaccounted for loved ones might still be alive, somewhere out there on the vast North Atlantic. Perhaps they were floating atop icebergs? Or perhaps hostile foreign ships had picked them up and were holding them for ransom? Or perhaps, and this was the most horrible of all to imagine, they were trapped below in the *Titanic's* watertight compartments, still alive but slowly suffocating at the bottom of the sea? Moved by their grief, and in spite of the fact that he knew their suggestions were beyond probability, the Senator promised them he would do all that he could. Senator William Alden Smith would do all that he could to find out why 1,500 people had been left on the decks of the *Titanic* when she went down.

Lord Bainbridge took a moment to take in the kindly face that stared across the table at him. Senator Smith was fifty-three years old and, though he was now regarding Lord Bainbridge with warm affection, almost as if they were long-standing acquaintances, his face was curiously expressive and able to change from mild affability to fierce rage in seconds. Clean-shaven in an era when beards and mustaches dominated the faces of most men, especially after they had moved into middle age, the senator had a broad often called mid-Western nose. He had a rather large full-lipped mouth, which he certainly needed to contain the excess of teeth that he seemed to possess, especially when he smiled, which he did often. About the whole man, there was an air of feverish energy and undaunted determination.

Senator Smith began his examination of the witness before him with an apology. "Lord Bainbridge, forgive us for calling you on such short notice after your ordeal. But since you were staying right here at the Waldorf-Astoria and I know you are probably most anxious to return home, I took the liberty. In addition, certain articles in this morning's newspapers mention you most prominently."

Instantly, Lord Bainbridge felt a chill run down his spine. This is what he had hoped to avoid—talk of his own actions, his own heroics as they had been labeled. He had hoped that the committee would be concerned only with matters pertaining to the activities of the ship's crew and what they did or did not do that contributed to the loss of the *Titanic* and the great loss of life as well. He tried to minimize his own contributions. "I'm afraid, Senator, those newspaper articles greatly exaggerated my part in the tragic event."

But Senator Smith would have none of his attempted humility. "On the contrary, sir," he told him, his voice rising as it did when he felt himself to be in the right while the other fellow was most certainly in the wrong. "I have a number of affidavits here," he said, patting the stack of papers in front of him, "that unquestionably state that you acted quite heroically and saved many lives." He picked up the first sheet of paper, the one he had been searching for so frantically, and passed it across the table to Lord Bainbridge. "That is a sworn statement from Benjamin Chamberlin, one of our most prominent American citizens," Senator Smith said. "In it, Mr. Chamberlin says, in no uncertain terms, that you saved his life. That at the point of a gun you forced the reluctant crewmen of your lifeboat to row back to the scene of the wreck and pick up people in the water."

"If I may, Senator," Lord Bainbridge interrupted, which brought a frown to the American's face. "It is true that I did hold a gun on the crew in my lifeboat but only to prevent them from interfering with our attempts to return to the scene of the sinking to look for survivors. I'm afraid it was the other passengers, even the women, who did the rowing back to the scene. Sad to say, the crewmen refused to lend a hand."

Senator Smith was dumbfounded for a moment. "The crew refused to help you?" he asked in disbelief.

Lord Bainbridge nodded. "Yes, Senator."

"Well, I'll be damned!" Senator Smith sputtered. "I've never heard of anything so disgraceful in my life." The color had risen in his cheeks. "Thank you for clarifying that piece of the puzzle, Lord Bainbridge. It shall be looked into further, I assure you."

Meanwhile, the Senator consulted another piece of paper from the pile before him. "This affidavit is from a Mrs. Elizabeth Dowling, formally of 2433 Chapel Road East, Bristol," he announced.

Lord Bainbridge was puzzled, "I'm sure, I don't know anyone by that name, Senator."

Senator Smith raised a quizzical eyebrow, "Really? Well, Mrs. Dowling states that you brought her and her four children up from steerage and saw them safely into a lifeboat."

Yes, of course, Lord Bainbridge thought to himself, *Mrs. Dowling must have been the Englishwoman with the four children.* He realized then that in spite of all they had gone through together, he never did learn her name.

"Furthermore," Senator Smith continued, "Mrs. Dowling states that you returned to the steerage part of the ship a second time and brought up yet another group of steerage passengers, including, what she described, as three Arabic-looking women with infants." Senator Smith put down the piece of paper he had been reading from, took off his spectacles, and fixed Lord Bainbridge with a steady gaze. "I put it to you, Lord Bainbridge, that these actions I have just read to you are indeed the actions of a hero."

At that moment, there was something of a disturbance at the doors leading into the room. The sergeant at arms was heard to announce in a loud voice, "Madam, you can't go in there. The committee is in session."

Senator Smith's feathers instantly became ruffled. "What is going on there?" he demanded.

But the intruder would not be stopped, and she marched straight into the room and up to the conference table, boldly confronting Senator Smith.

"Madam, this is highly irregular," the senator complained.

Lord Bainbridge was so shocked, he almost fell out of his chair. For in spite of the fact that the woman was wrapped in furs and part of her face was hidden by a wide-brimmed hat, he instantly recognized her. It was the American woman who had occupied one of the two most expensive suites on the *Titanic* and, along with her bodyguard, had been in his lifeboat. Today, the bodyguard was nowhere in sight.

The woman spoke directly to Senator Smith. "Senator, I am Theresa Van Arsdale." A shocked murmur ran through the room, for though Theresa Van Arsdale came from one of the leading families in New York City, she was a woman who was almost a recluse. She lived and traveled alone, except for her servants, was hardly ever recognized, and spoke to no one unless it was absolutely necessary. Her only friend appeared to be her little dog, which she took with her wherever she went. Today, however, the little dog, like her bodyguard, was not in attendance.

One of the other senators moved as if to offer her his chair, but she waved him off with an imperious toss of her head.

"Madam, do you have something to say to this committee?" Senator Smith asked, frowning intensely at this disruption of proper protocol.

"I do," Theresa Van Arsdale said. "I was in the same lifeboat as this young Englishman here, and I want it put into the record that he saved more than a dozen lives. He even jumped into the water to rescue a man who had been pulled overboard." Her voice, which had been hardly heard in the lifeboat, not to mention on board the *Titanic*, was surprisingly gentle for a woman of such a stoic and frigid appearance. She turned to look at Lord Bainbridge. "On behalf of everyone in that lifeboat, I want to thank you for bringing us to safety," she said to him. "You, sir, are a true gentleman and a real man."

Then Theresa Van Arsdale turned and walked from the room as quickly as she had entered, her posture and her steps the same as when she had been striding regally through the rooms of the *Titanic*.

The room fell instantly silent as if every last soul in it had lost the power of speech. And then suddenly, without warning, an enthusiastic and prolonged round of applause fairly shook the room with many people getting to their feet. And although he couldn't see her, Lord Bainbridge was quite certain Maude was on her feet leading the ovation.

The display embarrassed Lord Bainbridge, and apparently didn't sit too well with Senator Smith either. Still frowning, he tried to gavel the room into silence. But it was to no avail. The applause went on and on, and only stopped of its own accord when hands began to sting from their exertion.

When at last the room had returned to quiet, Senator Smith gave a display of his own, a display of his quick-changing temperament. "There will be no more such outrageous displays in this chamber!" he snapped angrily, his eyes sweeping through the rows of spectators like an eagle searching for its prey. "If there is another such display, I will have the sergeant at arms clear the room of all but essential personnel," he promised. Then he immediately regained his composure and once again turned a kindly smile on his witness. "As you can see, Lord Bainbridge, your heroic actions have quite won the hearts of the American people." He paused to take a sip of water from the glass before him. Once again, his eyes turned to Lord Bainbridge. "Now, will you please tell this committee of your experience on board the *Titanic*."

Lord Bainbridge took a deep breath and began to recite his story. And as if he were dodging icebergs of his own, he maneuvered his way around the treacherous waters of his days on board the *Titanic*, careful not to mention either Tom or Marco. He finished his story with his arrival on the *Carpathia*, telling the hushed room how he had stood on the deck of the rescue ship in the cold dawn and searched in vain for his friends as the other lifeboats came alongside the ship.

When he finished speaking, there wasn't a sound in the crowded room except for a solitary cough and the scrape of a chair as if someone, perhaps completely overcome by his story, felt a need to flee the room.

Senator Smith was staring down once again at his pile of papers though he hadn't put his spectacles on. It was obvious that everyone in the room was waiting for him to speak. Finally, the senator looked up at Lord Bainbridge. "Did you see the *Titanic* go down?" he asked.

Lord Bainbridge nodded. "Yes, sir, I did."

"How did she go down?" Senator Smith inquired. "We've heard conflicting reports. Did she go down intact or did she break apart?"

"She broke apart," Lord Bainbridge answered. "Her bow went down first. For a moment, her stern looked like it was going to actually stay afloat, then it turned on end and slid into the water."

"You're quite sure of this?" Senator Smith asked.

"Absolutely."

"Both Mister Ismay and Second Officer Lightoller swore before this committee that she went down intact," Senator Smith informed him.

"Then, they're wrong, Senator," Lord Bainbridge said. "I saw her break up with my own eyes as did everyone else in my lifeboat."

But Senator Smith was already off on another track. It was indicative of the man that this was the way his mind worked. His head was crammed full of knowledge, and he was gifted with an almost photographic memory, which enabled him to recall almost any detail on any given subject. During the days of the *Titanic* hearings, he would frequently bounce from one subject to another completely unrelated one. This method of scattered, seemingly disorganized, questioning was applauded by some, derided by others. But criticism didn't matter a hoot to Senator William Alden Smith. Like a dog with a bone, he held fast and dug for the truth.

"Did you observe Mr. Ismay leaving the *Titanic*?" he inquired of his witness.

Lord Bainbridge shook his head. "No, Senator, I did not see Mr. Ismay at all during the approximately two and one half hours the ship was sinking," he answered. "In fact," he went on, "I never even saw him on board the *Carpathia*.

I didn't know he had survived until one of the other *Titanic* passengers told me he was on the *Carpathia* in seclusion."

"Were you shocked?" Senator Smith asked.

"By what, sir?" Lord Bainbridge returned.

"By the fact that Mr. Ismay had survived when so many others had not," Senator Smith said.

Lord Bainbridge took a moment to gather his thoughts before he answered. "I would say I was surprised, Senator, not shocked. Surprised because, as I said, I had not seen him on board the *Titanic* during her final hours or on board the rescue ship."

But Senator Smith was not quite ready to give up on J. Bruce Ismay. He had one more question. "Did you, at any time, see Mr. Ismay helping to load the lifeboats?"

It was obvious to Lord Bainbridge that like the American press, Senator Smith was not prepared to tread lightly when it came to Mr. Ismay. "No, I did not," he answered. "But I recall another passenger telling me that Mr. Ismay had helped with the loading of the boats."

Lord Bainbridge wasn't quite sure why he was halfheartedly defending Ismay, a man he had no great affection for. Perhaps it was because he felt Ismay had been unfairly pilloried in the American newspapers. Or perhaps it was because he had someone else in mind, someone he felt was more deserving of universal contempt, someone he planned to expose himself before this very committee.

Next, Senator Smith asked Lord Bainbridge if he thought the ship had increased her speed on that fateful Sunday night.

"I'm not certain," Lord Bainbridge answered. He knew it was a lie because he remembered the young officer telling him on deck that they were going faster and his own observations had come to the same conclusion. But for Maude's sake, he wanted to protect Captain Smith's reputation. The poor man was dead. Why do him any more harm? Besides, Lord Bainbridge suspected it was Ismay who in reality had ordered the increase in speed. He shook his head. "You see, I've never been on a ship before, so I'm afraid my knowledge of nautical things is nonexistent."

"So I've been told is mine," Senator Smith acknowledged. His remark sent a ripple of amused chuckles around the room.

The senator went on to ask Lord Bainbridge a series of questions on things he had or had not observed during the *Titanic's* days at sea. Then he paused, took off his spectacles, put them back on, and took them off once again. For a moment, he stared at them as if he had never seen them before. Finally, he looked up at Lord Bainbridge, smiling at him again. "If there is anything else you might like to tell this committee, we would be most anxious to hear it," he suggested, still smiling.

Lord Bainbridge took a deep breath. Here it was then. Here was the moment he had been waiting for, the moment he would nail Lightoller and pull him down from his heroic pedestal. He began cautiously, choosing his words carefully. "Senator, I did witness an incident on the *Titanic* which greatly disturbed me," he began. "I saw a boy, a boy only fourteen years old, turned away from one of the lifeboats. And because of this action, both the boy and his mother perished."

His words caught the attention of everyone in the room. There were even a couple of gasps from among the packed rows of spectators. Senator Smith too was startled by this revelation, and for a moment, he appeared to become confused, and he even stammered out his words. "What? What did you say? A woman and her child were not permitted to enter one of the lifeboats?"

"The woman was already in the lifeboat but because her son was not allowed to join her, she climbed back out onto the deck of the ship," Lord Bainbridge clarified.

"Who was it who forbid the boy from entering the boat?" Senator Smith asked, his rising indignation over the matter showing on his face.

"It was the officer in charge of the loading of the lifeboats on that side of the ship," Lord Bainbridge answered. "Because the woman and her son were dear friends of mine," he went on, "I tried to intercede on their behalf. I explained to the officer that in spite of the boy's height which perhaps made him look older, he was only fourteen and needed to go with his mother."

"And what was the officer's response?" Senator Smith asked.

"He said the boy was too old," Lord Bainbridge replied.

"Too old! Too old at fourteen!" Senator Smith's voice shook with incredibility.

"There were a number of other women who also refused to leave their male family members behind who were likewise denied admission into the boat," Lord Bainbridge continued. "When the boat was finally loaded, it was barely half full. In fact, since the boat I was in was the first lifeboat to reach the *Carpathia*, I was witness to the reality that many of the *Titanic's* lifeboats were hardly more than half full, one or two even less than that."

"We have had testimony from Second Officer Lightoller that the *Titanic's* crew feared that if the lifeboats were loaded to their full capacity, which I believe was sixty people, they would buckle and upend as they were being lowered to the water," Senator Smith said.

"And yet," Lord Bainbridge returned, "I have it on the best authority that the last lifeboat to leave the *Titanic* had over seventy people on board and suffered no such mishap."

Senator Smith nodded in thought, and then he peered intently across the table at Lord Bainbridge. "Lord Bainbridge, do you happen to know the name of the officer who denied a place in the lifeboat to a fourteen-year-old boy?"

I do indeed, Lord Bainbridge thought to himself. But just as he was about to speak Lightoller's name, he paused, realizing that in spite of his personal animosity toward the man for what had happened to his friends, he had heard that the second officer had acted bravely after he had been thrown into the water and had saved many other lives. What purpose would it serve for him to now try and tear the man down? Madame Renoir and Sebastian were gone—nothing could bring them back. And though he still and always would hold Lightoller responsible for their deaths, perhaps if he attempted to shine an unfavorable light on him, that same light might be turned on his own actions, revealing things he wished to keep hidden. So in spite of the fact that he felt himself the coward, he answered Senator Smith's question with a shake of his head. "No, Senator, I'm afraid I don't know his name. But I believe, in my humble opinion, that if there hadn't been this ridiculous discrimination against members of the male sex when it came to the loading of the *Titanic's* lifeboats, many more lives would have been saved, men, women, and children."

There was a moment of silence following his words followed by a brief round of polite applause from the spectators. Then Senator Smith spoke up again.

"We will take all you have told us under careful and serious consideration," he told Lord Bainbridge. "Now, I believe we should detain you no longer. This committee thanks you for your attendance, and I would personally like to offer you my thanks and the thanks of the American people for your heroic efforts which resulted in the salvation of a number of souls on board the *Titanic.*"

"Thank you, Senator," Lord Bainbridge acknowledged, pushing back his chair and starting to rise. He felt a great sense of relief flood over him as he realized his ordeal was over, and he had escaped unscathed.

"I have a question for His Lordship if he would be so kind."

The whole room came to startled attention, for this was a new voice that had not been heard before. Everyone in the room knew that Senator Smith was the driving force behind these proceedings and that he intended to run them virtually as a one-man show. He would ask the questions, he alone would determine which direction the committee took. And now, here was another member of the committee actually speaking up. It was, to say the least, quite unexpected.

Senator Smith offered his colleague a rather tight-lipped smile and nodded in his direction. "Of course, Senator, by all means."

Settling back into his chair, from which he had nearly escaped, Lord Bainbridge regarded his new inquisitor. The man, who was past middle age, had a broad, open face with the tiniest of ears that looked as if they had been pasted on his head as an afterthought. His eyes were small too, and he seemed to be continuously narrowing them as if in mistrust or suspicion. Looking into his face, Lord Bainbridge thought to himself, *Here indeed is the enemy.*

The senator, smiling at Lord Bainbridge with a look that was just shy of contempt, proceeded with his question. "Pardon me, Your Lordship, but do I take it to understand that you do not approve of the law of the sea that mandates women and children first in the time of a disaster?" He spoke with a broad western accent.

"You misunderstand me, Senator," Lord Bainbridge answered. "Of course I believe it should be women and children first in times of peril. My point is that after there were no more woman and children to be found and there were still places available in a particular lifeboat, why were they not filled with boys and men? If this had been done, many more lives would have been saved."

The senator's smile, such as it was, vanished quickly, and his face turned quite purple as if he were about to go into a rage. "Are you aware, Your Lordship, that over one hundred and fifty women and children perished in the *Titanic* disaster?" he demanded, his voice barely under control.

"I am aware of that, Senator. I was there," Lord Bainbridge returned coldly. He went on, struggling to keep his own voice in check. "I would remind the senator that the *Titanic* was as long as four city blocks. When a particular boat was being lowered and there were no woman and children in the immediate vicinity available to board her, I could only conclude that those still on board must have moved on to another boat or some other part of the ship. I would also respectfully remind the senator that there were some women who refused to be parted from their husbands and stayed to die with them. I personally know of one such instance," he added, remembering his last sight of Alonso and Lucianna Fraboli sitting together in the smoking room, awaiting their terrible fate.

The senator immediately had another question, this one even more insinuating. "Tell me, Your Lordship, how do you account for the fact that so many men survived when women and children died?"

Why, he's practically calling me a coward, Lord Bainbridge thought to himself. He felt his cheeks go red, and he strived to keep his temper as he sought a proper response.

But he needn't have bothered, for Senator Smith came quickly to his rescue. He spoke directly to his fellow senator in a tone of mild chastisement, "I don't think we need to go any further with this line of questioning. Lord Bainbridge has no need to defend himself. His actions on board the *Titanic* speak for themselves."

The second senator was instantly apologetic. "Yes, yes, of course. I meant to insinuate nothing less." He offered Lord Bainbridge a gracious, if insincere, smile. "Forgive me if I gave offense, Your Lordship."

Lord Bainbridge nodded but said nothing more. He only wanted it to be over. He only wanted to escape from the glaring spotlight he had been thrust under against his will.

But his nemesis had one last question to put to him and begged the indulgence of the committee, which Senator Smith gave with some impatience. "I understand that you made two trips down into steerage and brought people up to the boats," the senator stated, once again smiling at Lord Bainbridge. "Your Lordship, what prompted you to go down into steerage in the first place?"

Lord Bainbridge felt a chill run down his spine as if a cold hand had suddenly clamped the back of his neck. *He knows,* he thought, staring at the smiling face sitting across the table from him. *He knows I sleep with men!*

The whole room had suddenly gone deathly silent. Everyone in the room seemed to be holding their breath, waiting for his reply. The reporters' pencils were poised above their pads, eager to take down his answer. Even Senator Smith, who appeared to have had quite enough of his colleague's questions, turned a quizzical thoughtful eye on Lord Bainbridge.

Struggling to find a way out of the trap that had been sprung for him, Lord Bainbridge took a long sip from the glass of water in front of him. Then he cleared his throat and began to speak slowly, carefully. "My man, my servant that is, had a friend who was traveling third class. We went down to make sure he was able to get up on deck. We had heard reports that the steerage passengers were being kept below and not being allowed up on the boat deck."

This last bit of information instantly piqued Senator Smith's interest and, in doing so, neatly pulled Lord Bainbridge back from the edge of the precipice where he had been tottering for the past few moments. "And did you find that the steerage passengers were being kept below?" Senator Smith asked.

"Yes," Lord Bainbridge returned. "At least at that time they were. The ones we came across were being kept behind a locked gate."

"They were being denied access to the boats?" Senator Smith asked.

"Yes," Lord Bainbridge answered. "The seaman in charge said they would remain there until he got the word to release them."

"The word from whom?" Senator Smith inquired.

"The officers or the captain, I would imagine," Lord Bainbridge replied.

"How did you manage to get some of them free?" Senator Smith wanted to know.

"I bribed the seaman with money," Lord Bainbridge answered.

"How extraordinary," Senator Smith concluded, stroking his chin thoughtfully. Then he offered Lord Bainbridge a final kindly smile and dismissed him. "I think, Lord Bainbridge, we should detain you no longer. Once again, sir, this committee thanks you for your assistance."

And with that, it was over. Lord Bainbridge rose and left the East Room to a round of applause as if he were leaving the stage after having given a well-received performance.

Maude and Elaine caught up with him in the corridor outside the East Room. Not surprisingly, Maude launched into a spirited attack upon Senator Smith's far-from-diplomatic colleague. "Why, the man practically labeled you a coward!" she fumed to Lord Bainbridge. "I've a good mind to file a formal protest with the British Embassy," she went on. "I most certainly will write a spirited letter to the *Times* when I return home!"

"I'm just glad it's behind me," Lord Bainbridge told them.

He escorted the two women back to their suite, and then he returned to his own rooms where he found Alfred awaiting his return, rather anxiously. "How did it go?" he inquired.

Lord Bainbridge threw himself into a chair and shrugged. "It could have been worse," he answered.

"Did they find out anything?" Alfred asked.

"Like what, Alfred?" Lord Bainbridge asked, turning on him, not forgetting that it was Alfred's words to the newspaper reporter that most probably was at least partially responsible for his invitation to appear before the committee.

"Well, you know," Alfred ventured, "anything about our sexual preferences?"

Lord Bainbridge shot him a dark look. "You can rest assured, Alfred, your reputation remains unsoiled," he answered. "Of course," he added, with a glint of perverse satisfaction, "you were hardly mentioned. No one, it seems, was interested in the heroic efforts of a valet."

Alfred ignored the slap as he paused to light a cigarette. "What are we going to do now?" he asked.

Letting out a great sigh, Lord Bainbridge shook his head. "I don't have the damndest idea," he muttered. Then he suddenly leaped out of the chair as if it had been set on fire. "Good Lord, I've completely forgotten about my mother!"

"I took care of it," Alfred told him. "This morning when I went to the bank, I sent her a wireless. I told her you were safe and planned to continue with your American tour. That is what we're going to do, isn't it?" he asked, eyeing him closely.

Lord Bainbridge took a moment to light his own cigarette, took one drag from it, and then stared at it intently for a long moment. "I truly don't know what to do next," he said finally. "Nothing seems worth the effort anymore."

"Well, we certainly don't want to get back on another ship anytime soon," Alfred said with a half smile.

Even Lord Bainbridge managed a slight smile at that suggestion, "God forbid!"

Then Alfred came to him and put his arms around his shoulders, something he had not done for a very long time. "Look, mate, I'm not truly the coldhearted bastard everyone thinks I am. I know you're grieving over your friends that didn't make it. And I'm sorry about that, I really am." He gave Lord Bainbridge's jaw a little mock punch with his fist. "But we both know what's bothering you the most, don't we? You've lost your boyfriend, that's what's really eatin' at you, ain't it?"

"I love him, Alfred," Lord Bainbridge said unashamedly, feeling a wetness come into his eyes.

"Well then, go and get him!" Alfred urged. Although the look on his face acknowledged he still considered any chance of such a relationship becoming permanent was nil to zero.

"I can't," Lord Bainbridge lamented. "He made it perfectly clear it was over."

Alfred gave him a hearty slap on the back. "Then, let's get on with our lives!" He produced a scrap of paper from his pocket. "While you were at the hearing, I had a conversation with a most charming young bellhop. He gave me directions to a club where he and some of his mates retire to after hours to supplement their incomes."

"That's the last thing I need," Lord Bainbridge protested, brushing him off.

"It's exactly what you need!" Alfred corrected. "We'll go tonight."

"I don't think so," Lord Bainbridge responded, shaking his head.

But go they did, for Lord Bainbridge, having neither the will to go nor the will to resist, passively let Alfred drag him along to a rendezvous for which he had no desire. He went willingly, having no will of his own. The directions Alfred had received took them down a series of dark alleys in what surely must have been one of New York City's seamiest districts. Lord Bainbridge was quite convinced that at any moment they would be set upon by a band of street thugs and robbed of everything they had, or even worse. In his current state of mind, he found such a fate far from unwelcome.

However, they arrived at their destination unmolested. When they were seated at a table and had ordered their first round of drinks, Lord Bainbridge took a look around. For a moment, he thought he was back at the Crown in London. It was all too familiar—the smoke filled room, the smell of beer and ale, the constant chatter and excited laughter. And of course there were the smiling, laughing young men with flashing teeth and intentions just as sharp. He had come all this way to find he had come no distance at all. He was back to where he had started from. Alfred kept having round after round of drinks sent to their table, and before long, they were joined by two young men. One of them boldly placed Lord Bainbridge's hand on his crotch and whispered to him, "Bet you've never felt a bundle like that before, eh?"

Shocked more by his own body's reaction, than the young man's impudence, Lord Bainbridge quickly removed his hand and staggered to his feet. The last thing he remembered was seeing the table before him rising up off the floor to meet him and the sound of Alfred's voice crying out, "Look out, he's going to pass out!"

The next thing Lord Bainbridge knew, he found himself back in his bed at the Waldorf-Astoria, and it was morning. He remembered few details from the night before, only that he had gone to some club with Alfred, drank heavily, and most obviously returned to the hotel with some unknown and unremembered young man. This last fact was made evident by the condition of the bed he now lay in. The bed's covers were twisted and tossed about as if a wrestling match had taken place. The pillows except for the one under his aching head had been thrown to the floor. Whatever had happened between them must have been conducted in a robust manner, to say the least. But he couldn't remember a single moment, not even his brief companion's face or name. He might just as well have tussled with the Devil himself for all the memory he had of the encounter.

It was at that moment that he realized he was not alone in the room. A young man, sitting across from him, was gulping down coffee and scarfing down muffins as if he hadn't eaten for days.

"Who the blazes are you?" Lord Bainbridge inquired.

"I'm Adam," the young man answered through a mouthful.

Alfred strolled in from the other room. He ruffled the young man's hair. "What'd you think?" he asked. "Interested?"

Lord Bainbridge threw the bedcovers over his head. "I told you, I'm through with all that."

"Well, you certainly weren't through with it last night," Alfred reminded him. "You and your young man had a right ambitious go at it in spite of your rather inebriated condition."

"I can't even remember his face," Lord Bainbridge said. He pulled away the bedcovers. "He's not still here, is he?" he asked.

Alfred shook his head. "You fell dead asleep, snoring like a sailor, so I sent him on his way." He turned to the young man beside him. "And now, I think it's time for you to leave as well."

"Okay," Adam said, getting to his feet and stuffing a couple of extra muffins into his pockets. "Shall we come around again tonight?" he asked.

"We'll see," Alfred told him as he let him out the door. "I'll send you word."

"Sure thing," Adam responded, taking off down the hotel corridor, whistling a merry tune.

Alfred closed the door and threw himself down into an armchair. "You know, I think I'm going to like America," he smiled. "I already feel quite at home here." He paused to light a cigarette. "I plan to plow as many American lads as possible," he boasted, rather crudely.

"Alfred, I don't remember a thing from last night. I don't even recall how I got back here to the hotel," Lord Bainbridge complained.

"You passed out at the club, and we had to practically carry you back here," Alfred informed him. "All that fainting you've been doing lately is quite unmanly," he added with the mildest of reprimands. "Oh, by the way, I found a tailor in the hotel. We have an appointment at two." Dressing properly, and to Alfred that meant expensively, was as important to him as breathing. He would sooner have walked out into the street stark naked than walked out wearing the wrong clothes.

A knock on the door of their suite interrupted them. "It's probably those two hoodlums from last night, back for more money," Lord Bainbridge suggested. "Give them whatever they want and get rid of them."

Alfred went to answer the door, and a moment later, he returned with Lord Bainbridge's breakfast tray, which he set down on a table beside his bed. "I thought you might want something to eat," he suggested.

"The thought of food makes me quite ready to pass out again," Lord Bainbridge muttered.

"There's hot black coffee as well," Alfred told him.

Lord Bainbridge instantly perked up. "That I need," he said, struggling to a sitting position on the edge of the bed. Alfred poured him a cup of coffee and then helped him steady it as his hands were shaking. "I could use a cigarette too," Lord Bainbridge said.

Alfred lit him one, passed it to him, and then taking a chair beside the bed, he regarded him. "You're a pretty pathetic sight," he said to him. "I guess that's what loves does to you," he concluded.

"How would you know?" Lord Bainbridge returned, a distinct edge to his voice.

"Oh, I was in love once, a long time ago," Alfred acknowledged, still regarding him.

Lord Bainbridge was startled at this revelation that he had never heard before. He put down his coffee cup. "Really?" he asked, obviously eager for more information.

But Alfred, having opened the door a crack, immediately slammed it shut and took up one of the morning papers that had came up with Lord Bainbridge's breakfast tray. He scanned the headlines and then announced to Lord Bainbridge that he was on the front page again, along with that annoying picture of him when he was so much younger and made him look as if like James Barrie's famous *Peter Pan*, he had failed to grow up. "It's about your testimony before the Senate committee," Alfred informed him. "Apparently you made quite a hit," he added. "The paper calls you the ultimate example of manhood."

If they only knew the truth, Lord Bainbridge thought to himself.

Alfred was still absorbed in the newspaper. "Here's something interesting," he reported. "Apparently, the White Star Line sent out a ship on the seventeenth to pick up bodies of the *Titanic's* victims." He shivered. "There's a gruesome job I wouldn't take for all the tea in China."

Lord Bainbridge got quickly to his feet and crossed to him. "Let me see that," he said. Alfred passed him the paper, and Lord Bainbridge read the small column tucked into the lower corner of the front page. He read it through once and then a second time to make sure he hadn't missed anything. It told him that the White Star Line had charted a cable ship named the *Mackay-Bennett* to search for bodies. A number of ships had reported seeing a large number of bodies floating near the sight of the disaster, apparently being kept afloat by their life belts. The *Mackay-Bennett* was to bring the bodies back to Halifax, Nova Scotia, where family members could come and identify them and take their loved ones home for a proper burial. The last line in the article mentioned that it would be at least a week before the *Mackay-Bennett* was expected to return with its grim cargo.

Letting the newspaper slip from his fingers, Lord Bainbridge stood there in deep thought. Ever since the sinking, he had been tortured by terrible visions of his friends' bodies floating desolately in the middle of the Atlantic, floating there forever, until the elements and the sea creatures had reduced them to nothing. Now here was a chance that they might be recovered and given a decent Christian burial. As far as he knew, neither the Renoirs nor the Frabolis had any living relatives. He knew it was up to him. He knew he owed them at least that.

"I'm going to Halifax," he announced, hurriedly beginning to dress as if his departure was eminent.

"What are you talking about?" Alfred asked in confusion. Then he glanced down at the newspaper on the floor, and he understood. "Jeremy, don't be a fool!" he said. "Forgive me for being so crude about it, but even if they do find your friends, they'll be nothing but corpses."

Lord Bainbridge nodded. "I know. And I'm going to see to it that they are properly attended to."

Looking at the hard set of determination on his face, Alfred knew he couldn't argue him out of it. He shrugged. "So we're going to Halifax." He had a sudden thought. "Where the hell is Halifax anyway?"

"It's in Canada," Lord Bainbridge answered, struggling into his pants.

"Canada!" Alfred retorted sharply. "I read they have polar bears in Canada," he added with little pleasure.

"I'll make sure you're not eaten by one," Lord Bainbridge promised him as he slipped on his collar and tie.

"That's encouraging," Alfred muttered gloomily.

Chapter XVI

By rail, the trip from Boston to Halifax took them approximately twenty-four hours. And even though they had delayed their departure from New York by more than a week, they arrived at their destination before the *Mackay-Bennett* had put into port. When they checked into their hotel, the desk clerk informed them that the word in the town was that the *Mackay-Bennett* would arrive in port the next day.

Their hotel was a small but elegant three-story building that catered exclusively to the upper class. It was tucked in among the gracious Georgian mansions and manicured lawns of Halifax's wealthy South End. Even the exacting Alfred found its amenities more than acceptable. He had not been anywhere near so complimentary about the accommodations on board the train however. In fact, in spite of the fact that the train had included both a dining and a sleeping car, it had seemed to Lord Bainbridge that his companion had groused about his discomfort every second of their twenty-four-hour journey.

Maude and Elaine had accompanied them from New York to Boston. And as they had to change trains in Boston and there was a delay of several hours before the train for Halifax was ready for departure, there had been plenty of time for Lord Bainbridge to see the two women to the home of Elaine's father while Alfred was left to cool his heels at the railroad station and find his amusement wherever he could.

Elaine's father lived alone in a dignified mansion on Boston's famed and tony Commonwealth Avenue, a treelined two-way boulevard bisected by a sweeping pedestrian mall. They had arrived just in time for afternoon tea that was served in a glass-enclosed summerhouse that stood on a half acre of land between the mansion and the one next door to it. The summerhouse doors were open to let in the warm spring breezes, and beyond it and the iron gated garden that fronted it, there was a lovely view of the Commonwealth Mall and its seemingly endless parade of foot traffic.

As Lord Bainbridge and Maude settled into their chairs, Elaine shared a few quick half-whispered words with her father. Lord Bainbridge surmised that she was telling him of her decision to separate from her husband. The old man's head nodded gravely as she spoke, but he showed neither surprise or disapproval. And Lord Bainbridge concluded that it was probably not news that greatly displeased him.

Soon after, tea arrived, and once it was all sorted out, Elaine's father tried at first to steer the rather strained conversation to everyday matters such as the fine weather they were enjoying and the latest Sarah Bernhardt play that had opened in Boston the previous night. But the tragedy that his daughter and her two friends had so recently gone through hung over them like a forbidding shadow, and its ominous presence was impossible to ignore.

"Was it as terrible as the newspapers reported?" he finally asked, his hand shaking a bit as he put down his tea cup.

Maude shared an uneasy glance with Lord Bainbridge, and then she nodded her head briskly. "Yes," she answered, "it was indeed quite terrible."

The old man shook his head. "So many, many lives lost, women and children too."

Elaine patted her father's arm, for he seemed on the verge of tears. Watching them as they sat closely side by side, Lord Bainbridge could tell there was much love between them. Elaine had told him her father was not well, and this was certainly borne out by his frail appearance. He moved about with the aid of two canes, and even making allowances for his ill health, he looked to be at least in his sixties. Elaine had never spoken of her mother. But back on board the *Titanic*, where it seemed that gossipy tales about this or that passenger broke out as frequently as each new wave broke against the ship's bow, Lord Bainbridge had heard a whispered tale about this mysterious woman. The story was that Elaine's father, once a prominent Boston lawyer, had been ensnarled in the clutches of a beautiful young actress still in her teens. When this rather tawdry and torrid affair was finally over, the then middle-aged lawyer had been relieved of most of his prestige, his good health, and a decent portion of his family fortune. Abandoned by the heartless teenage Jezebel, he had survived only because of the baby daughter that had also been left behind. Lord Bainbridge didn't know how much, if any, of this story was true, but sitting across from them, he could see that the bond between daughter and father was deeply forged and enduring.

When it came time for Lord Bainbridge to return to the railroad station to catch his train, Maude gave him a hearty hug and planted a kiss on his forehead, which left him with a thick smear of vivid red lipstick. She was quite distressed that he was going to Halifax and had already warned him, a number of times, to be alert and stay on his guard every moment he was there. When he asked her why he should do so, she reminded him, "You'll be in Canada, Ducks!" Apparently, not unlike Alfred, she likened Canada to the darkest and most dangerous interior of Africa.

Elaine saw him to the door, and as they stood there for a moment, she took his hands in hers. "My thoughts and prayers will be with you throughout your grim journey," she told him. For a second, she lowered her beautiful violet eyes, but not being one to play the coquette, she quickly raised them again and looked into his face. "If on your return trip, you need someone to talk to, someone to listen, I'll be here," she said.

"Thank you," Lord Bainbridge said. "Thank you for all your kindness and your friendship," he added. And as he stood there in the fading light, as afternoon turned gently into evening, he realized that once again she had opened a door for him, a different door that lead into a different room than the one he had chosen for himself. He remembered someone once saying to him, long ago when he first found company among others of his kind, "We go into the secret rooms, the rooms that most of the rest of the world don't even know exist."

So Lord Bainbridge bid Elaine Standish good-bye and left her standing there on her doorstep, both of them knowing he would not come again to see her. For once he was done with the grim business that lay ahead of him in Halifax, he would rush as quickly as possible back to New York. He would rush back and go in search of Tom. He had made up his mind that that would be his course of action. He would find Tom and somehow persuade him that they were destined to spend the rest of their lives together. He was determined that, like the new novel he was about to begin, his own life would have an equally happy ending.

The night before the *Mackay-Bennett* was due to dock, Lord Bainbridge took dinner alone in the hotel's dining room. Though the room was crowded, most every table being taken, there was about the room an unusual subdued and somber air. There was none of the animated gay chatter and laughter one would expect when people gather together to enjoy good food and drink. The reason for this lack of merriment was easy to understand. Like Lord Bainbridge, almost everyone else who had booked rooms at the hotel had come to Halifax to await the sorrowful arrival of the *Mackay-Bennett*. They too had come to this place in the hope of recovering the remains of someone who was dear to them. So the atmosphere in the dining room that evening was one of hushed, almost whispered, conversations and guarded looks. It was as if each person feared that should they look directly into another face, they would surely see the same look of grief and despair staring back at them that they knew showed on their own face.

Although he found the meal placed before him to be of expert quality, Lord Bainbridge, like most of the others in the room, found he had little appetite, and so he pushed the food around his plate more than he digested it.

The waiter serving him seemed genuinely concerned over his lack of enthusiasm for the food, which he had made great haste to bring to him piping hot from the kitchen, and he kept making suggestions for alternate menu items, which Lord Bainbridge politely declined. The man had a glib tongue as well, and with each new course he brought, he whispered a rumor that he had heard concerning the *Mackay-Bennett* and her unfortunate cargo. The one that Lord Bainbridge found the most disturbing and the one that concluded his feeble attempt to partake of his meal altogether suggested that the crew of the *Mackay-Bennett* had found so many bodies they had to throw over two hundred back into the water because they did not have enough embalming materials or coffins to take care of them.

Abandoning the dining room, Lord Bainbridge took refuge in the hotel's lounge where he downed a hot whiskey to calm both his stomach and his nerves. He picked up the local newspaper. Not surprisingly, its lead story on the front page concerned the *Mackay-Bennett*. Its information was limited, revealing only that the ship was due in port in the morning and that she was bringing back with her 190 bodies. Thankfully, there was no mention of any bodies being tossed back into the sea. Searching the paper for other news to take his mind off the *Titanic* disaster, Lord Bainbridge became aware that he was being observed. He lowered his newspaper and found himself staring into the smiling faces of a young couple, sitting opposite him. He nodded and smiled briefly at them.

Encouraged, the young woman leaned toward him in her chair. "It's all rather exciting, isn't it," she said.

"I beg your pardon?" Lord Bainbridge asked, unsure as to what she was referring.

"The arrival of the *Mackay-Bennett* tomorrow morning," the woman reminded him. "That's why you're here, isn't it?"

"Why yes . . ." Lord Bainbridge nodded, thinking, however, that he would hardly call it exciting.

"My brother and I have come all the way up from Philadelphia," the woman went on, clutching the arm of the young man beside her, who was smiling as broadly as she was and seemed as equally enthusiastic.

Studying them for a moment, Lord Bainbridge concluded they were both probably a few years older than he was. They both were good-looking in a quiet nonthreatening way: she, light with fair hair, he, darker skinned with a tiny mustache and dark wavy hair. They both wore eyeglasses that made them look like intellectuals.

The young man proceeded to pick up the conversation that his sister had started. "We received a cablegram from the White Star Line in New York informing us that the *Mackay-Bennett* had picked up our parents."

"They were on their way home from an European tour that we had given them as a present for their thirtieth wedding anniversary," the woman interjected.

"We were distraught when we first heard about the sinking of the *Titanic*, and we thought our parents were lost," the young man continued. He flashed a smile at his sister. "But now, after more than two weeks, to find out that they are alive and we are soon to be reunited is beyond belief!"

"It makes you believe in God," the woman said solemnly.

Lord Bainbridge sat there stunned, letting the newspaper fall to his feet. "But . . ." he stammered and then he covered his mouth with his finger tips to prevent himself from saying anything further. "Don't you read the newspapers?" he finally asked them in a weak voice.

The young woman brushed away his suggestion with a wave of her hand. "Oh, we never read the newspapers," she answered. "They're always filled with such horrible lies and untruths."

Lord Bainbridge sat there dumbfounded, not knowing what to say or do. How could this young couple sitting across from him truly believe that the *Mackay-Bennett* was returning their parents to them alive and well? Surely the cablegram sent them by the White Star Line must have told them it was their parents' bodies that had been found. *Should I try and set them straight?* he pondered. And then, staring into their smiling faces, he suddenly understood. Beneath their smiles and exuberant manner, he could see it all. They were in denial. Deep down inside both of them knew the truth, but they were concealing it under a cover of false excitement and gaiety that bordered on the verge of hysteria.

Lord Bainbridge got quickly up from his chair and made his excuses. As he hurriedly left the lounge, the young woman's merry laughter, triggered by some amusing remark from her brother trailed ominously after him and haunted him throughout the sleepless night that followed.

At 9:30 AM on the morning of Tuesday, April 30, the *Mackay-Bennett* steamed slowly into Halifax Harbor, her flags fluttering mournfully at half-mast. Halifax was a seafaring town, and like all seafaring towns, it boasted a rough exterior. But on this heartbreaking day, it was as if the whole town was grieving. People gathered in small numbers on street corners, many dressed all in black and conversed in reverent and hushed tones. And when the news came of the *Mackay-Bennett's* arrival, they drifted toward the dockyards, not hurrying, but in a dignified and solemn procession. They passed shops and other businesses draped in black bunting, many with pictures of the doomed liner in their windows. When the ship finally came into dock, bells from the town's churches began to toll while overhead, gulls and other seabirds circled and added their own cries of lamentation.

The dock area where the *Mackay-Bennett* was making herself fast was surrounded by a high concrete wall with an iron gate. Admission to this now sacred area was restricted to only those who had official business aboard the newly arrived ship. Twenty sailors, from a cruise ship also in port, stood guard around the perimeter.

There was a little rise of ground that overlooked the dockyards, and in a few brief minutes, it was filled with people straining to get a look at what was taking place beyond the concrete wall. Lord Bainbridge, with Alfred at his side, stood in the middle of the crowd.

"Can't see much from here," Alfred grumbled.

"That's probably just they way the authorities want it," Lord Bainbridge said as they watched a couple of burly policemen hustle away a photographer who had approached the iron gate with his camera and flash raised.

In truth, the Halifax authorities had done whatever they could to limit the view of both the public and the press as the *Mackay-Bennett* unloaded her sad cargo. A canvas-covered gangway was put in place to conceal the coffins being removed from the ship and canvas curtains shielded the embalmers' tents on the pier.

It wasn't long before the first horse-drawn hearse passed through the iron gate of the dockyard and began its slow mournful march down the town's main street. It was soon followed by another and then another. Many of those who had been standing on the knoll across from the dockyards, including Lord Bainbridge and Alfred, turned and followed after the hearses. They were a quiet subdued crowd with only a muffled sob here, a tear wiped away there. Watching them along the sidewalks as they passed, the townspeople of Halifax took off their hats and bowed their heads in respect while from the clock on the tower on Citadel Hill, a promontory that overlooked the busy harbor, the hour of ten was chimed out in measured tones.

The hearses destination was the Mayflower Curling Rink, located only a few blocks from the dockyards, which because of its capacity and closeness to the docks, had been turned into a temporary morgue.

As Lord Bainbridge prepared to enter the rink, he noticed that Alfred was holding back. "What's wrong?" he asked.

"I can't go in there," Alfred stammered, his face having suddenly gone deathly pale.

"Why not?" Lord Bainbridge inquired.

"I can't stand the sight of dead people, never could," Alfred answered. He was sweating, and his knees appeared to have gone quite weak. For a moment, he had to grab onto a lamppost to keep himself from falling.

"Are you going to be sick?" Lord Bainbridge asked, walking toward him.

"I'm all right," Alfred told him, waving him off. After a moment or two, he seemed to recover himself. "When my mother was dying, I couldn't even bring myself to go into the hospital to see her," he confessed.

Why, that's the first time in all the years we've been together that he's ever spoken to me about a member of his family, Lord Bainbridge thought to himself, somewhat startled. The few times he had attempted to solicit information from Alfred regarding his family, his past, he had been firmly rebuffed. So he had always assumed that it was a door Alfred intended to keep forever locked. And now here suddenly and in the most bizarre of moments, that door had been flung open, if only for an instant.

"You go back to the hotel," he told Alfred. "I can manage this alone."

"No," Alfred responded quickly, falling in step beside him. "We'll do this together."

"You sure?"

"Yes," Alfred replied grimly.

"Good man," Lord Bainbridge said. But he was likewise filled with trepidations of his own as they entered the curling rink. Part of him desperately hoped he would find the bodies of his dear friends, but at the same time, he dreaded seeing them dead. He preferred to remember them as they had been, vibrant and alive, not cold and lifeless. But there was something else that tortured him even more. So close had they been in life, mother and son, husband and wife, that he was terrified he might find one, but not the other. To find Marguerite Renoir, but not her beloved son, Sebastian, or to find the body of Alonzo Fraboli, but find no sign of his dear wife, Lucianna, would be the cruelest fate of all. United in life surely, not even God, could have the heart to separate them in death. And there was one further thing that haunted him still. He would never understand what had happened to the Renoirs. How was it that they were not able to find their way into a lifeboat on the starboard of the ship where men and boys were allowed in the boats when there was still room?

They were ushered into the rink's observation room, which in happier times served as a viewing box for watching the spirited curling contests, which for some reason was one of Canada's favorite sports. The first thing that Lord Bainbridge noticed was the smell. It wafted through the air toward them almost like a cloud. And though he couldn't specifically identify it, he assumed it must be some chemical that was used in embalming. He shivered and cast an anxious glance at Alfred. But his companion, though still deathly pale, seemed to be holding his own. The room was crowded, and searching the anxious faces around him, Lord Bainbridge caught no sight of the young couple from Philadelphia whom he had encountered in the hotel's lounge the evening before. He wondered if reality had finally caught up with them.

Everyone's attention was centered on the main curling rink where the coffins from the *Mackay-Bennett* were being unloaded. The rink had been partitioned into canvas-enclosed cubicles to offer a degree of privacy, and as soon as a coffin was deposited in one of these cubicles, a bevy of official-looking men, some in shirtsleeves, would descend upon it, examining its contents and taking notes. It was a slow process, and those in the viewing room were told it would be a number of hours before all the bodies were unloaded and examined. And only then would they be allowed into the rink to search for their loved ones. A number of those waiting in the viewing room had received wireless messages from the White Star

Line, telling them that the bodies of their relatives or friends had been found. But many others in the room had received no such notification, and like Lord Bainbridge, they had come to Halifax because they heard the *Titanic's* dead were being brought there, and perhaps there was a chance they might find the ones they had lost. Understandably, the tension in the room increased as time slowly dragged on. Its laborious passing was emphasized by the tall grandfather clock that stood in one corner of the room, loudly ticking off each passing minute. Men talked in low voices or paced nervously across the parquet floor. The women, for the most part, sat stiffly in straight-backed chairs. Some wept quietly, others remained stoic and, more than one dainty gloved hand, clutched a small bottle of restorative. In deference to the women, when any of the men felt the need for a cigarette, he would step outside into the bright Halifax sunshine.

It was during one of these cigarette breaks when Alfred pressed Lord Bainbridge to take action. They had been waiting for over two hours, and the young Englishman's nerves, like those of most everyone else in the room, were becoming quite frayed.

"Show them one of your cards," Alfred suggested. "That'll make 'em sit up and take notice."

The cards to which he referred Lord Bainbridge carried in a little silver case in his pocket. They read simply: Lord Jeremy Bainbridge, Bellington House, London. The cards had been Alfred's idea actually, and he had seen to their printing. Nothing impressed Alfred so much as being able to impress. He saw to it that the little white cards with Lord Bainbridge's name on them, and more importantly, his title were discreetly presented to get them a better table at a restaurant or front row seats at the theatre. Likewise, more than one attractive young renter, upon receiving one of the cards, had been duly impressed as well and had abandoned whomever else they were with to quickly join them.

For his part, Lord Bainbridge had never give much thought to the fact that there was a title before his name. To him, it was of no more importance than the color of his eyes or his hair. True, it was something he had acquired without effort as was his wealth and position in society, but it was something he neither rejoiced in or lamented over. He was hardly a man filled with self-importance, and yet if his title opened doors for him that were closed to other men, then so be it. And it amused him to watch Alfred scurry about, waving his little white cards like magic wands. In most cases, he gave him free reign to distribute the cards wherever and whenever he so desired. But this one time, he drew the line.

"I hardly think that would be appropriate under these circumstances," he told him.

Alfred frowned and flicked away the butt of his cigarette. "It'd be a hell of a lot better than standing in a bloody queue all day long," he muttered.

After they had gone back inside and stood around for another hour, Lord Bainbridge gave in and slipped one of his cards to Alfred who took it and marched off in triumph.

As expected, Lord Bainbridge didn't have long to wait. A little bald man with spectacles came up to him, bowing and scrapping in a ridiculous and absurd manner that could have been easily mistaken for a mocking parody. He then led the way up a rickety staircase to a second floor office. There, he held the door open and bowed once again, this time so low his nose fairly grazed the floor.

The man who came from behind a desk to greet them was one of the tallest men Lord Bainbridge had ever seen. He was as well exceedingly thin with a long scrawny neck and a protruding Adam's apple that thrust itself out with a vengeance. He introduced himself as the owner and proprietor of Halifax's leading funeral parlor. Dressed all in black, as befitting his profession, he nevertheless had an amiable, almost jovial, manner about him. He appeared to be a man who enjoyed his work, as macabre as it might be, and who took great satisfaction in a job well done.

He politely showed Lord Bainbridge to a chair and then settled himself behind a large mahogany desk that took up much of the space in the room. The little man with the spectacles had ceremoniously bowed himself out of the room, closing the door behind him. Alfred remained standing by the door, his arms folded, his features frozen in a frown.

The undertaker laced his fingers in front of his lips. "Now, Lord Bainbridge, how may I be of service to you?" he asked. He spoke in a soothing solicitous manner, which he had obviously cultivated and polished during the many years spent in his trade.

As Lord Bainbridge laid out his story, the undertaker made notes with quick exact strokes of his pen. He interrupted the young Englishman a number of times to ask questions concerning the deceased. One lengthy inquiry concerning how the departed were dressed the last time he had seen them, necessitated Lord Bainbridge racking his brain to remember the clothes his friends had been wearing that last night on the *Titanic*. He had always prided himself on having a good memory as well as a keen eye for observation, traits, Maude had informed him when they had first met, that were essential for a writer. So he was able to recall exact details such as the large-brimmed hat with a veil that Madame Renoir had been wearing or that fact that Lucianna Fraboli's wrap had been of dark blue with a fur collar. When it came to another question pertaining to distinguishable scars or birthmarks, Lord Bainbridge at first shook his head. And then, he remembered the tiny scar that Sebastian Renoir had just above his left eyebrow, the result of a childhood tumble. After he was done and the undertaker seemed satisfied with the amount of information he had provided,

Lord Bainbridge sat back in his chair and waited for the man behind the desk to respond.

The undertaker remained for some moments in deep thought, nodding to himself as he digested all that Lord Bainbridge had told him. Finally, he leaned toward him, opening his hands that had been clasped almost as if in prayer and offering him a sincere smile. "First of all, Lord Bainbridge, let me say to you that the bodies that were recovered were handled with the most reverence and care both on board the *Mackay-Bennett* and here on land."

Alfred, who could be counted on never to remain silent when he had an opinion to express, spoke up. "We heard they tossed some of 'em back into the sea"

The undertaker's eyebrows shot up like arrows, and for a brief moment, he looked terribly offended. "None of them were the bodies of first-class passengers, I can assure you," he answered.

"But some were thrown back into the water?" Lord Bainbridge persisted.

The undertaker sighed and acknowledged as much. "I'm afraid the crew of the *Mackay-Bennett* were completely overwhelmed with the number of bodies they encountered. They had neither the supplies or space on their ship to deal with so many. So out of necessity, a small number of those who were recovered were regrettably returned to the ocean from which they had been plucked. But not without a proper burial service," he made haste to add.

"Still it's unfortunate that all the bodies could not have been brought back," Lord Bainbridge mused.

The mortician agreed most vigorously, "Indeed! But I have been told that all those left behind were members of the crew, none with any identification whatsoever and many so battered and bruised, they probably would never have been identified." The man leaned forward in his chair as he continued to speak. "Sad to say, Your Lordship, but many of the bodies we received here this morning are likewise in poor condition. Obviously the length of time they were in the water and exposure to various sea creatures is certainly to blame. But in addition, many of the bodies are horribly mutilated—limbs are broken, faces contorted with pain, some are even burned and covered with soot as if they were involved in a terrible explosion. Of course, those with proper identification on them have been readily identified. But many others have not, and the condition of their bodies has made the process that much more difficult. In some cases, we have had problems even deciding which class the individual belonged to."

"In death, all men look alike," Lord Bainbridge said.

The mortician nodded, glad that he understood. "Exactly!"

"But what about the clothes they were wearing, certainly they should give you some clues?" Lord Bainbridge suggested.

"Yes, yes." The mortician nodded again, obviously pleased to be speaking with someone who understood the intricacies of his profession. "But," he went on, "in many cases the outer garments have been so damaged by the elements, seawater in particular, that their proper color, style, and quality have been completely obliterated. In cases like that, we are obliged to turn to the undergarments the body is wearing."

"You check out their knickers?" Alfred asked in a voice that was caught halfway between an expression of amazement and a snicker.

The mortician hardly seemed offended by this rude interruption. "We do," he admitted. "A person's linen is often a truer measure of their station in life than all the fine words that pour from their mouth or the coins that tumble from their pockets. Now to the particulars of your case, Lord Bainbridge," he said, starting to go through a stack of papers on his desk.

There followed a long moment of silence in the room, broken only by the drum beating of Lord Bainbridge's heart, which had moved up into his throat.

The mortician looked up at him and shook his head. "I'm sorry to say the pickings are very slim," he told him. "As to the elderly gentleman you described, there are only two bodies that might possibly have proven a match, and both of them have already been positively identified." He started again leafing through the papers before him. "Now the boy, how old did you say he was?"

"Fourteen," Lord Bainbridge answered, "but tall for his age."

The mortician paused, a piece of paper in his hand. "Color of hair and eyes?" he asked.

Lord Bainbridge swallowed hard, attempting to dislodge his heart from his throat while inside his head, a great roar of wind rushed, and spinning back through time for second, he heard Sebastian Renoir's voice loud and clear, "I'm not a child anymore. I want to stay here with you and the rest of the men."

"Brown hair and eyes," Lord Bainbridge answered quickly.

"No, I'm afraid not," the mortician said, putting the piece of paper he had been studying aside and picking up another. "As far as the women are concerned," he began, "we have only three bodies. Two of them are most certainly third-class passengers. One was easily identified by a bottle of prescription pills with her name on it which we found in her pocket."

"Spot of luck there, eh, gov'nor?" Alfred put in, in his best wise guy manner, which the other two men in the room chose to ignore completely.

"The third woman," the mortician continued, "is certainly not third class. She was probably a second-class passenger although, there's an outside chance she may have been first class. She had no identification on her, and as far as her clothes, well, I'm afraid she was found completely naked."

"Good Lord!" Lord Bainbridge exclaimed, quite shocked.

"I have heard that a number of passengers left the *Titanic* in nothing but their nightclothes," the mortician said. "Perhaps she was one of those and lost what little clothing she had in her struggle in the water. I also heard even worse tales of people fighting each other in the water to stay afloat and in doing so ripping the clothes off one another. Whatever fate befell this poor woman, it is too awful to dwell on," he added with a sad and sympathetic shake of his head.

"How old do you estimate she is?" Lord Bainbridge inquired.

The mortician consulted the piece of paper in his hand. "In her midsixties," he answered.

"Color of hair?" Lord Bainbridge asked, now leaning forward in his chair.

"Gray hair, long," the mortician replied.

"Lucianna Fraboli was in her midsixties with long silver gray hair," Lord Bainbridge told him.

The mortician nodded thoughtfully for a moment, and then he got to his feet. "There's a chance," he said, "a slim chance. Shall we go down and have a look at her?"

Lord Bainbridge nodded. He and Alfred followed the mortician down the rickety staircase and through a door that led directly into the mammoth curling room. Walking into the room, Lord Bainbridge felt a sudden chill dance down his spine as if he had entered a cold storage locker and someone had suddenly slammed the door shut behind him. At the far end of the room, some of those who had also been waiting in the viewing room were now being escorted to the various canvas cubicles that stretched along the four sides of the rink, like tents set up for some morbid street fair.

"It's number thirty-two," the mortician told them, consulting the sheaf of papers he had brought with him. They followed him across the floor and up to the proper cubicle. "Are you sure you're up to this?" the mortician gently asked of Lord Bainbridge.

"No," Lord Bainbridge responded, "I'm not sure at all. But it's something I know I must do."

The mortician nodded and stepped aside. And while Lord Bainbridge went into the cubicle, Alfred remained standing outside nervously shifting from one foot to the other and glancing everywhere but in the direction of the cubicle.

At first, Lord Bainbridge kept his own eyes looking everywhere except at the face of the body laid out before him. He prayed in his heart that he wasn't about to look into the face of Lucianna Fraboli. He didn't want to see her dead and bruised. He didn't want to think of how terrible the last moments of her life must have been. And most of all, he didn't want to see her alone, without her beloved husband.

From the cubicle next door, he heard a woman's soft moan of anguished recognition, followed by gentle measured sobs of despair. The noise prompted him to jerk his head up and stare into the face that lay so still before him. He saw at once that it wasn't Lucianna Fraboli. Even though the face was somewhat discolored and swollen, he knew it was not his dear friend. The woman before him looked like someone's granny, a kindly soul who baked cookies and smelled of lilac toilet water. He quickly left the tiny cubicle.

"That's not her," he told the mortician.

"I'm terribly sorry," the mortician said sympathetically. "I fear that was our only possibility. He paused for a moment, turning something over in his head. He checked through his papers once more, and then he asked a question. "Lord Bainbridge, might I ask of you a favor?"

"Yes, of course," Lord Bainbridge responded quickly, quite willing to assist this man who had been so kind and considerate to him.

"There is another body we have been unable to identify, a young man about your own age, obviously first class," the mortician related to him. "He had no identification on him at all," he added. "And," he said, lowering his voice, "no money or jewelry either. It's quite apparent, he'd been cleaned out."

"Cleaned out?"

"Robbed," the mortician clarified.

"Why that's horrible, to rob a dead person!" Lord Bainbridge protested.

"Unfortunately, it does happen," the mortician said. "We also found a crewman's body whose pockets were stuffed with bank notes of a quantity far beyond the man's earning capacities should he have lived to be a hundred."

"Monstrous!" Lord Bainbridge exclaimed, thinking at once of Marco and his valise, which the officer had thrown over the side of the ship.

"If you could take a look at this young man, perhaps you might recognize him or remembering having seem him on board the *Titanic* in the company of someone else," the mortician suggested.

"Of course," Lord Bainbridge readily agreed.

He followed the other man once more down the long lines of cubicles until they reached the desired one, and then the mortician stepped aside and let him enter. This time, Lord Bainbridge wasted no time and turned his eyes quickly on the face of the body before him. The sight he saw so startled him that he thought, for a moment, he was about to pass out.

The mortician had followed him into the cubicle and, noticing Lord Bainbridge's reaction, he asked a hopeful question. "Do you recognize him, Your Lordship?"

Lord Bainbridge needed a moment to pull himself together, and then he shook his head. "No," he answered, still staring down at the face that had so startled him because it bore an uncanny resemblance to Denham. Unlike the weeping teenage boy he had come upon on the staircase of the *Titanic* and who for an instant bore a passing resemblance to his former schoolmate, this one really did look like Denham. The young man laid out before him had his same blond handsomeness, his same blue eyes. And what shocked Lord Bainbridge even more was that he could not remember having once seen this young man on board the *Titanic*. Surely with his good looks and marked likeness to Denham, he would have caught his attention if only momentarily.

"I'm sorry, I've never seen him before in my life," Lord Bainbridge told the mortician.

"How very unfortunate," the man said, staring down at the body. "I thought this one would be so easy. There's not a mark on him, and his features are not distorted in the least. He looks as if he's done nothing more than drift off to a pleasant sleep." He shook his head and sighed. "It's a mystery all right. There is no name on the passenger list that matches up to him, and although we've had hundreds of inquires, not one of them has been about a young man such as this one. Well, hopefully someone will come along and claim him. I would hate to see him go into an unmarked grave."

"So would I," Lord Bainbridge agreed. He cast one more lingering glance at the young man lying there so alone and seemingly forgotten before he followed the mortician out of the cubicle.

It had turned to evening while they were occupied, and the new electric lights, which had been recently installed inside the rink, had come on, casting a warm glow on an otherwise cold and chilling scene.

"I'm sorry I could not have been more helpful to you, Lord Bainbridge," the mortician told him, offering his hand.

Lord Bainbridge took the man's hand and shook it warmly. "You have done all you could. Thank you for your kindness," he said.

"The *Mackay-Bennett* will be going out again in a few days to try and find more bodies. And there are a couple of other ships out there now, looking as well," the mortician informed him.

"Do you think they'll find anymore bodies?" Lord Bainbridge asked.

"A few perhaps," the mortician answered. "The captain from the *Mackay-Bennett* told me they feared that most of the bodies of the *Titanic* dead had got caught up in the Gulf Stream and dispersed hundreds of miles away, where they, in all probability, will never be found."

"We'll be returning to New York tomorrow," Lord Bainbridge told the mortician. "We'll be at the Waldorf-Astoria at least for a few days, and then I imagine we'll return to England," he added. "You have my card if there are any developments."

"Yes"—the mortician nodded—"I'll wire you immediately."

Lord Bainbridge had a final thought. "What will happen to that young man back there if no one claims his body? I'd be more than willing to see he gets a decent burial."

"You needn't worry about that," the mortician assured him. "The people of Halifax will look after him. He and any other poor unfortunates who are not claimed will be buried here on a hillside overlooking the harbor. Plans are already under way. The people of Halifax will take care of them, they're good people."

"Yes, I've come to realize that," Lord Bainbridge said warmly, feeling a surge of affection for this kindly man, who was so obviously a good man himself and who took such pride in the work he did no matter how macabre it might seem to others.

On their trip back to New York, their stopover in Boston was brief, only a half hour. While Lord Bainbridge stayed on the train, Alfred got off to stretch his legs. But he was back in almost an instant, waving a newspaper.

"You're gonna want to see this!" he said excitedly.

"Not more dreadful stories in the newspaper," Lord Bainbridge protested.

But Alfred ignored him and thrust the paper right under his nose. Its main headline jumped right out at Lord Bainbridge: PROMINENT BOSTON SOCIALITE BRUTALLY MURDERED IN SHOCKING CRIME! As he scanned the article, Lord Bainbridge's mind was assaulted by each seemingly unbelievable detail. The victim was Ronnie Standish, and he had been stabbed to death in the bedroom of his mansion on Boston's Beacon Hill. Stabbed over seventeen times, the paper made haste to emphasis. The alleged culprit was one of his own servants, who had fled the mansion after committing the crime but was quickly picked up by the police. Like in a bad mystery book where the reader is able to unmask the wrongdoer in the first few pages of the book, Lord Bainbridge knew at once, before he had even reached the part of the article that mentioned the suspect's name, who it was who had done the deed. And sure enough, when a few lines farther along he came to the name of Marco Borsalino, he was not surprised. The paper went on to mention that robbery was apparently the motive as the suspect had been found with a great deal of money and some jewelry on his person. But Lord Bainbridge knew there was much more to the story, so much more. At the end of the article, it mentioned that both men were survivors of the *Titanic* disaster.

With great satisfaction, Alfred jabbed the newspaper with his thumb. "I told you that one would come to no good!" he boasted in triumph. Lord Bainbridge knew that Alfred had despised Marco from the first moment he met him. He had despised him because he was an Italian, an inferior as Alfred saw it. His next words confirmed this. "You can't trust those Italians. All of 'em carry knives!" He gave Lord Bainbridge a sharp look. "You were lucky!" he added.

Lord Bainbridge tossed the newspaper aside, leaned back in his seat, and closed his eyes for a moment while thoughts and emotions whirled with hurricane-force winds through his mind. He remembered Marco once telling him he had killed a man, the English photographer who had tried to take liberties with him when he was just a boy. Then as with so many of Marco's stories, he wasn't sure if it was true or not. This time, there seemed to be little doubt. As for motive, Lord Bainbridge knew it wasn't robbery—that was merely an afterthought, a temptation too great to resist. The real motive was uglier, for Lord Bainbridge was sure that undoubtedly it had to do with sex. He had known Ronnie Standish well enough to know the young man always insisted on getting what he wanted. He would push until he achieved his goal, and with those young men like Marco, you could only push them so far before they would push back. "Not on the lips," Marco had said to him when it came to kissing. These young men were like wild animals, able to be tamed for a short while but still remaining the jungle creatures they had always been. He himself had always been careful, knowing how far he could go and never stepping over that boundary. But Ronnie he knew to be reckless, never willing to settle for less than what he wanted, what he demanded. Apparently, Ronnie had wanted something Marco was not willing to give up, certainly more than a kiss on the lips, and when Ronnie had insisted, Marco must have resisted. And in the end, it cost Ronnie his life. And perhaps Marco, his life as well although Lord Bainbridge was not so sure of that. Given the sordidness of the matter, and in spite of the fact that Ronnie Standish's reputation was not unknown even outside of his own circle, it all might be hushed up. A trial could prove to be very messy. Certainly Marco would not hesitate to reveal every sordid little detail. Perhaps, in the end, Marco would only suffer deportation. If that proved to be the case, Lord Bainbridge wondered how long it would be before he was on another boat bound for America.

As far as Ronnie's death was concerned, Lord Bainbridge felt very little. Ronnie had amused him at times, irritated him at other times. And after that incident with Sebastian in the Palm Court of the *Titanic*, if Ronnie had lived, he perhaps would not have punched him in the nose as he wished to do, but Lord Bainbridge certainly would never have spoken to him or associated with him again. Still, he did not wish upon anyone a death such as the one Ronnie Standish had suffered. But he would not mourn his passing.

He actually felt more pity for Marco, for in spite of the horrible deed he had apparently committed, the young Italian, who was still so much a boy, had most probably acted out of the heat of the moment, out of fear. Marco, despite his bravado and big plans, was scared to death of life, scared he would end up an anonymous nothing. Lord Bainbridge recalled thinking to himself that one night in a dark alley, years from now, Marco would meet his end. And if he somehow escaped this incident, Lord Bainbridge still saw that prophecy coming true. Marco Borsalino was a doomed character—it was only a matter of time.

Lord Bainbridge opened his eyes with a start. *I should go and see Elaine,* he thought, beginning to get to his feet. But just then, the train started up, and he was thrown back into his seat. *But what good would that do?* he asked himself.

What comfort could he offer her? She had once told him she had loved Ronnie, but certainly that love must have faded by now. He knew she would be saddened by his death, horrified by its brutality. But she had her father to comfort her, and Maude was there too to lean on. They would see to her, and as each clicking mile of the train took him farther and farther away from Boston, he knew she would be better off not seeing him. For no matter how much she cared for him, his presence would be a reminder of Ronnie and his way of life, and that could only hurt her.

Once they were back in their rooms at the Waldorf-Astoria, Alfred asked the question that had obviously been on his mind for some time and the one to which he was sure he already knew the answer. "You're going after him, aren't you?"

"Yes," Lord Bainbridge answered.

"How will you find him?" Alfred wanted to know. "There's probably at least a thousand Tom Kennedys in New York," he added with a trace of contempt in his voice for that very fact.

"I'll check with the White Star Line first to see if the have an address for him," Lord Bainbridge answered. "If not, then I'll go to the Immigration Bureau. Surely, they keep a record on all those coming into the country."

"Leave it to me," Alfred sighed. He grabbed the hat and coat he had just moments ago discarded and went out, slamming the door behind him. He returned in less than an hour and handed Lord Bainbridge a piece of paper with an address written on it.

"That was quick," Lord Bainbridge noted.

Alfred shrugged. "I can be very persuasive when I want to," he said with a sly wink. He watched Lord Bainbridge head for the door. "What? You're going right now?"

"Yes."

"But I just got back," Alfred protested. "Give me a chance to catch my breath."

"You wait here," Lord Bainbridge told him. "I can do it alone."

"Oh no," Alfred said, slipping his coat on once again. "I was told that address is in a very bad area, an area where no gentleman goes, at least not by himself."

They got into a taxi outside the hotel, and when Alfred gave the driver the address of their destination, he grimaced and likewise pronounced it a very unsavory area. But sensing that there would most probably be a decent tip coming his way, the driver shrugged and started up his engine.

The first part of their journey took them along Fifth Avenue, past elegant hotels and mansions as well as treelined promenades. The street around them was busy with motorcars and, here and there, a few horse-drawn carriages, last symbols of the past century, which were quickly fading away. As they progressed,

Lord Bainbridge was quick to note how the scene changed. He felt as if he were traveling backward through time. On each new street they took, the buildings became less fine, and eventually, they looked to have fallen into ruin and disrepair. The motorcars and carriages began to disappear, replaced by horse-drawn carts, and then, these too vanished, and the streets around them were filled with men and boys pushing or pulling barrows and hand-drawn carts. The final street was so narrow and so congested with foot traffic, their taxi driver had to constantly sound his horn to make any progress. And it appeared, quite obviously to Lord Bainbridge that most of the people who were obliged to move out of the way of their taxi did so with looks of sullen resentment on their faces. There were people everywhere, hundreds of them walking the street, yelling at one another, cursing, laughing. Many of them seemed to have no particular destination in mind but were merely milling about to add to the clamor and the confusion. At one point when they were obliged to come to a complete halt, Lord Bainbridge caught a glimpse of a woman sitting in the window of a worn-down tenement with a child in her arms. The child was giggling and laughing with delight, but the mother was staring straight ahead at nothing, her eyes, like her whole face, dead beyond the point of showing any emotion whatsoever.

At last, they reached their destination, and the moment they came to a stop, a crowd of curious men, women, and children, who had never before seen such a vehicle let alone ridden in one, crowded excitedly around them.

"Wait here," Lord Bainbridge instructed the driver as he and Alfred exited the taxi.

The driver leaned out his window, a clear look of panic on his face. "I ain't staying here by myself, sir!" he called out. "This lot will strip me and my taxi clean the minute you two are out of sight."

"Don't be absurd," Lord Bainbridge chastised him. "They mean you no harm. They're merely curious."

The driver was far from convinced. "Take pity on me, sir," he cried out. "I've a wife and five little ones waiting at home."

"Very well," Lord Bainbridge sighed. "You stay with him," he told Alfred.

Alfred would have protested, but seeing it was useless, he quickly gave in. He pushed his way through the crowd none too gently and climbed back into the taxi.

Lord Bainbridge, meanwhile, climbed the stone steps of the building they had pulled up in front of and opened the door. Stepping inside, he found himself in a darkened hallway that, at first glance, seemed to lead nowhere. The first thing he quickly became aware of was the smell. It wasn't a foul odor, but rather just the opposite, an aroma of disinfectant almost as strong as the smell had been in the curling rink in Halifax. As soon as his eyes became accustomed to the dimness, Lord Bainbridge saw that the hallway curved around to the left, and he followed it. Almost immediately, he literally stumbled on the source of the strong smell that permeated the hallway. At his feet, a rather large woman was on her hands and knees vigorously scrubbing the floor with soap and water from a large bucket beside her. Their encounter was so sudden that Lord Bainbridge had to execute a nifty two-step to keep from falling on top of her while the poor woman, probably thinking she was about to be set upon by a gang of ruffians, flayed her arms about in defense and let out a cry of alarm.

"Forgive me, madam," Lord Bainbridge quickly apologized. "I didn't mean to startle you."

The woman, having recovered both her emotions and her equilibrium, sat back on her haunches and studied him. "What do you want?" she asked suspiciously.

"I'm looking for number twenty-seven," Lord Bainbridge explained.

"What do you want with them? They're good people, ain't done nothing wrong as far as I can see," the woman said to him.

"I'm a friend," Lord Bainbridge answered.

The woman raised an eyebrow, "Really?" It was obvious that his manners and attire made her as mistrustful of him as if he were dressed in dirty rags and was brandishing a sharp knife. "Number twenty-seven's on the second floor, head of the stairs," she finally told him.

Lord Bainbridge thanked her, stepped around her and her bucket, and hurried up the stairs to the second floor, knowing full well the woman was watching his every move. He quickly knocked on the door of number twenty-seven, and as he waited for an answer, he felt his heart leap in his chest as he anticipated that when the door opened, Tom would be standing there.

The door was opened by a young woman holding a baby in one arm while two other children, not more than toddlers, clung to her skirt. Like the other woman, she eyed Lord Bainbridge with suspicion. "Yes?" she asked.

"Would Tom Kennedy be at home?" Lord Bainbridge inquired politely.

"Who'd be wanting to know?" the young woman asked, still eyeing him apprehensively.

"A friend," Lord Bainbridge responded.

"And would this friend have a name?" she asked, shifting the baby, who was beginning to become restless, from one arm to the other.

"Yes of course," Lord Bainbridge answered. "I'm Jeremy Bainbridge."

The look that immediately swept across the young woman's face told him instantly that Tom had told her about him. And too, Lord Bainbridge knew at the same instance that she was Tom's sister. There was a strong resemblance between them. But though she could only have been a couple of years older than Tom, the hard life that she had obviously led had already worn her down, sucked the exuberance out of her, and left her faded and drained, a ghost of her former girlish self.

"Come in, sir. Please come in," Tom's sister insisted, stepping aside. "I'm sorry, I should have known it was you." As she closed the door to the hallway behind them, she wrinkled her nose. "I'm sorry for the smell, sir. But Mrs. Mulligan insists on washing down the hallways and the stairs every blessed day."

"Well at least they're clean," Lord Bainbridge said, trying to be kind but realizing at once that his words were almost insulting.

Tom's sister met his gaze. "We're always clean, sir," she said with a trace of reproach.

"Of course," Lord Bainbridge agreed. "Then Tom told you about me?" he asked quickly.

"He did," the young woman acknowledged as she placed the baby down on a daybed in the room that appeared to function as a kitchen, dining room, and living room all in one. "Let me show you something," she said, leading the way into an adjoining room while the two toddlers tumbled after her.

"This is Tom's room," she told Lord Bainbridge. The room was small but neat with a bed, a chair and a small table, and a bureau. There were newspaper clippings pinned to the wall, and at first, Lord Bainbridge thought they were about the sinking of the *Titanic*. But on closer examination, he saw they were exclusively about him, his heroic deeds, and his testimony before the Senate committee. And in the center of the clippings, his own face stared back at him, carefully clipped from the newspaper as well.

"He told me you saved his life," Tom's sister related. "He said he'd undoubtedly be lying at the bottom of the ocean with all those other poor unfortunates, if it hadn't been for you. For that, sir, you have my gratitude," she added.

But something else in the room had already caught Lord Bainbridge's attention. On the small table, there was an open box of paints, some brushes, and a recently finished painting of the ocean.

"Tom's?" he asked, picking up the painting to examine it closer.

"Yes," the young woman confirmed.

Lord Bainbridge's hands trembled as he held the painting. Not only because he was holding something that Tom had created, but because the painting in itself was powerful and instantly brought back to him memories of the disaster the two of them had endured. There was no trace of the *Titanic* or her demise in the picture. All that was presented was a view of the ocean and the sky and, in the background, an endless field of ice that seemed to stretch to the very edge of the earth. But there was also about the painting an awesome sense of doom and tragedy either yet to come or already passed. It was a picture meant for those who had survived the sinking, those would could tap into their own memories and add what was not there.

"He has a gift," Lord Bainbridge murmured to himself.

"He told me you offered to help him, support him while he painted," Tom's sister said quietly. Lord Bainbridge raised his eyes from the painting to look at the young woman. "Tom's a very proud young man, sir," she went on. "He's honest and noble. When we were children, his older brothers used to tease him for being too good, too kind."

She knows about us, Lord Bainbridge thought, staring into the young woman's upturned face. Tom must have confided in her.

And as if to acknowledge this, Tom's sister said, "Tom and I have always been very close. We tell each other everything. We keep no secrets from one another."

As Lord Bainbridge replaced the painting on the table, the young woman had one more piece of information that, at least to Lord Bainbridge's way of thinking, she seemed most eager to share. "Tom's getting married next week."

Lord Bainbridge's eyes narrowed as he stared at the young woman who stood before him, now with her hands on her hips in an almost defiant poise. In spite of the fact that she was grateful to him for having saved Tom's life, he could see that she regarded him as the enemy, the enemy who would take her brother from her side and lead him down a path of depravity. And at that moment, they very well might have had angry words, angry words that could never have been taken back had not a voice called out from the other room.

"Ah good, they're home at last," the young woman said, leading the way out of Tom's room.

But it was not Tom whom Lord Bainbridge set eyes upon as he emerged from the bedroom, but a tall strapping young man, who would have easily made two, if not three, Tom Kennedys.

"This is my husband," the woman announced, taking his arm and reaching up to plant a rather intimate kiss on the young man's lips. It was a gesture obviously meant to embarrass Lord Bainbridge. But it was her own husband who was startled by her gesture, and he pushed her away as if she had lost her senses or at least the one that pertained to propriety.

"You must be Lord Bainbridge," the young man said, coming forward, grasping his hand, and giving it a firm hardy shake. "It was a fine thing you did, sir, a fine thing indeed, saving young Tom and all those other people," he told him.

"Where's Tom at then?" the woman asked anxiously. She stooped to pick up the baby who was beginning to fuss.

"He went to get some milk for the baby," her husband answered. "He'll be right along." Then realizing he still clutched Lord Bainbridge's hand, he shyly released it. But not before bestowing a final benediction on him. "God bless you, sir."

Somewhat embarrassed by the young man's words, Lord Bainbridge could only smile weakly and nod his thanks.

Then they heard footsteps on the stairs, and before Lord Bainbridge could catch his breath, Tom suddenly walked in through the open door. He was obviously so startled to see Lord Bainbridge standing there, he would have dropped the bottle of milk he carried had not his brother-in-law rescued it from him and placed it on the table, out of harm's way.

"You have a visitor," Tom's sister said, still holding the baby. She, none too gently, rubbed away some specks of dirt from Tom's face. "You're hardly fit to receive company," she scolded.

Tom stepped forward, and taking Lord Bainbridge's hand, he gave it a manly if reserved handshake. "It's good to see you," he said in a tone that was as reserved as the grip of his hand.

For his part, Lord Bainbridge could say nothing. Too overcome for words at the sight of the one he so desired and thought he would never see again, his brain and tongue failed him completely as if for a brief moment they had shut down. All he could do was stare wordlessly at Tom, trying to take in every morsel of his appearance even down to the smudge of dirt across his nose.

The uncomfortable moment of silence that followed between the four of them might have easily gone on for an eternity had not Tom's brother-in-law made a quick suggestion. "Why don't you two young gentleman nip into Tom's room where you can have a nice proper visit."

And before either of them could react, they found themselves ushered into Tom's room with the door closed discretely behind them. But before the door was pulled shut, Lord Bainbridge caught a glimpse of the look of displeasure that filled Tom's sister's face.

Alone, neither of them could find the words to begin their conversation. So they spent a long moment smiling uneasily at one another, like strangers or like two people brought together on a blind date by meddling if well-meaning friends.

Lord Bainbridge wanted nothing more than to take Tom into his arms, press him to his chest, and hold onto him for the rest of his life. But he knew here in this place, even behind a closed door, they could not touch each other.

"Where are you staying?" Tom finally asked.

"At the Waldorf-Astoria," Lord Bainbridge answered.

"That must be some fancy digs," Tom remarked.

"It's nothing special," Lord Bainbridge said.

Tom managed a laugh, "Sure it isn't!"

Lord Bainbridge pointed to the newspaper clippings Tom had pinned to the wall. "Good Lord, it looks like you've set up a shrine to me. All you need are some candles."

"I didn't have any money for candles," Tom said quietly.

"Still it's a little embarrassing," Lord Bainbridge suggested.

"You saved my life," Tom reminded him. Then he struggled to articulate what was going through his mind. "Jeremy, what we had back there on the ship, before everything went wrong that is, was something wonderful, something I'll never forget. But my life now is different. It's as it should be."

"I heard you're going to get married," Lord Bainbridge said numbly.

Tom shrugged. "I don't know, perhaps. I haven't made up my mind yet. My sister wants me to."

"Do you have to do everything your sister wants?" Lord Bainbridge asked.

Tom became defensive, "I owe her everything, Jeremy. She made it possible for me to come here."

"You don't owe her the rest of your life," Lord Bainbridge snapped, harsher than he intended to. "And what about this?" he inquired, snatching Tom's painting from off the table. "This is incredible, Tom. You have real talent! You should be painting, not working in a factory!"

"I have to earn a living," Tom said quietly. "I can't make any money painting."

"But you will in time," Lord Bainbridge insisted. "You're that good!"

Tom was silent for a long moment, and as his eyes drifted slowly about his little room, they took in everything except the young man standing so anxiously before him. "I haven't told a soul outside my family that I was on the *Titanic*," Tom said. "I found out that there's a certain stigma attached to being a male who survived the sinking when so many woman and children died."

"That's rubbish," Lord Bainbridge scolded. "You have nothing to be ashamed about, neither of us do. So we survived, now we should make the most of that survival. Come with me, please."

Even as he stared into his face, Lord Bainbridge knew what Tom's answer would be. "I can't," Tom said. And as tears came into his eyes, he added, "I must stay here with my family."

"You're crying," Lord Bainbridge noted as he watched the tears now falling freely down Tom's cheeks.

"Yes," Tom acknowledged, making no attempt to wipe his tears away, "I know."

"Tom . . ." Lord Bainbridge started, his own tears now filling his eyes.

"Please go now," Tom said, turning away so he wouldn't have to look at him. "I can't!"

"You must," Tom insisted.

And then somehow although he would never be able to remember exactly how it happened, Lord Bainbridge found himself once again down in the street. He would never be able to remember whether he and Tom had said anything further to each other or even if he had bid good-bye to Tom's sister and brother-in-law. It was as if those few moments had been erased from his memory forever. Perhaps God, in his mercy, had deemed them too painful to ever be recalled.

The next thing Lord Bainbridge was aware of was Alfred, who popped out of the waiting taxi. Giving him the once-over and shaking his head, Alfred pronounced his unflattering assessment. "You look like hell!"

Back at the Waldorf-Astoria, the bitter taste of his tears still in his throat, Lord Bainbridge sprung into action. "Start packing," he told Alfred, "we're going back to England on the next boat. No, first go to the shipping office and get us tickets on the next ship sailing home."

Alfred was obviously disappointed. "Are you sure about this?" he asked. He dismissed Tom with a curt wave of his hand. "There are a thousand more like him right here in this city. We can sample them all if you like."

Lord Bainbridge eyed him with an unfriendly glare. "There are none like him anywhere in the universe," he said in a quiet voice that was nonetheless filled with a kind of rage. "And I've no desire to sample a single one of them."

Alfred shrugged and grabbed his hat and coat. "We'll, more than likely have another ship go down beneath our feet on the way home," he groused.

"All the better than," Lord Bainbridge muttered.

Startled, Alfred turned to look back at him. "Do you really mean that?" he asked.

Lord Bainbridge shook his head, "No, of course I don't. It was a horrible thing to say. It's only that I'm hurting, Alfred."

"You'll get over it," Alfred suggested.

No, Lord Bainbridge thought to himself, *I never shall.*

Before Alfred had reached the door to the hall, a gentle knock was heard on it. Still irritated that he was going to have to leave all those delicious American youths behind, Alfred flung open the door, expecting to be confronted by some annoying hotel employee. What he saw, startled even him.

For there standing before him was Tom, a forlorn figure, clutching a worn suitcase and looking almost swallowed up in the vast glittering hallway. And like he had done before, on a night that now seemed at least a thousand nights ago, he paused, hesitating as if he were afraid to enter the room.

And Alfred, a crooked smile lighting up his face, uttered almost the exact same words he had uttered on that night so long ago. "Well, come in, he ain't gonna bite you."

"You're here!" Lord Bainbridge exclaimed so dumbfounded he could only state the obvious.

Tom put down his suitcase. "The minute I saw you walk out that door, I knew I had to be with you," he explained. "I threw my things into my suitcase like a madman. I'm not even sure what I grabbed except my paints and brushes." He paused for a moment. "My sister told me that if I went with you, I could never return. She said she wouldn't want me under the same roof as her children." His eyes welled up, and it was clear that this break with his sister had hurt him deeply. But there was more to his story, and Tom went on. "But then a strange thing happened. My brother-in-law caught up with me on the stairs as I was leaving, and he told me that in spite of my sister's words, he would see that the door was always open to me if I should ever want to come back. He also gave me money for the taxi. I'm not sure if he quite understands the relationship between us, but if he does, it doesn't seem to bother him the way it does my sister." He shrugged. "It's funny how people surprise you."

"Indeed it is," Lord Bainbridge agreed.

Alfred cleared his throat, determined not to be forgotten. "Well then, it's three tickets I'm going for, is it?" he asked.

"Yes," Lord Bainbridge agreed, "three tickets." His eyes quickly returned to Tom. "We're going back to England. But we can go anywhere you like. Italy perhaps?" he proposed. "I've heard the light there is perfect for painters."

"It doesn't matter to me where we go as long as we're together," Tom responded.

"I'll be off then," Alfred told them, pausing at the door for a moment. Watching them, he shook his head as a thin veil of contempt crossed his face to be replaced a moment later by a quicksilver flash of envy that vanished almost as soon as it appeared. "I'll be back before you've had a chance to miss me," he added just before he closed the door after himself.

But neither Lord Bainbridge nor Tom heard him, for they only had eyes for each other. Lord Bainbridge smiled. "Are you ready?" he asked Tom. "Here it comes."

"What?" Tom asked, equally amused.

"That happy ending," Lord Bainbridge answered as they moved into one another's arms and turned their faces into the light.